Xibalbá Gate

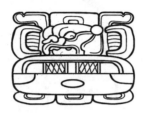

Map of the Maya

Xibalbá Gate

A Novel of the Ancient Maya

ROB SWIGART

WITHDRAWN

ALTAMIRA
PRESS

A Division of
ROWMAN & LITTLEFIELD PUBLISHERS, INC.
Walnut Creek • Lanham • New York • Toronto • Oxford

ALTAMIRA PRESS
A division of Rowman & Littlefield Publishers, Inc.
1630 North Main Street, #367
Walnut Creek, CA 94596
www.altamirapress.com

Rowman & Littlefield Publishers, Inc.
A wholly owned subsidiary of The Rowman & Littlefield Publishing Group, Inc.
4501 Forbes Boulevard, Suite 200
Lanham, MD 20706

PO Box 317, Oxford OX2 9RU, UK

British Library Cataloguing in Publication Information Available

Library of Congress Cataloging-in-Publication Data

Swigart, Rob.
  Xibalbá Gate : a novel of the ancient Maya / Rob Swigart.
    p.   cm.
  Includes bibliographical references.
  ISBN 0-7591-0878-1 (cloth : alk. paper)—ISBN 0-7591-0879-X (pbk. : alk. paper)
  1. Mayas—Fiction. I. Title.
PS3569.W52X53   2005
813'.54—dc22   2004028329

Printed in the United States of America

The paper used in this publication meets the minimum requirements of American
National Standard for Information Sciences—Permanence of Paper for Printed
Library Materials, ANSI/NISO Z39.48-1992.

Contents

CROSSROADS

Preface

Xibalbá Gate is a work of fiction. The unnamed university is an invention, the site of Xultunich is an amalgam of many real Mayan sites in Central America, and the city, characters, and events are all imaginary, as are many of the other cities mentioned in the simulation. Other population centers mentioned are real.

Xultunich is probably located somewhere between Tikal and Uaxactun, west of the border with Belize in the Maya lowlands, though it has a lagoon very similar to that of Lamanai. The Xibalbá Gate simulation does not yet exist, but online gaming has nearly reached the level of technological development depicted here, and one would hope that a complex simulation of the Late Classic might one day prove of use.

Xibalbá is the Mayan underworld, sometimes called the "Otherworld." The kings and other elites who consolidated their power through ritual go there after death. A king, once deified, continues on to dwell in the thirteen circles of the sky. Xibalbá is a frightful place, dark, sharp-edged, stinky, and cold, and its nine lords are unpleasant skeletal, pot-bellied creatures. It is spelled with an X because that was the only letter the Spanish priests had to capture the *sh* sound. The apostrophe in Maya names represents a glottal stop, a tightening of the throat. The letter *h* is soft, as in *house*, and *j* is harder, as in Scottish *loch*. Double vowels are long.

The collapse of complex societies has received a fair amount of attention lately. Some say we shouldn't use the word *collapse*, since often (in the case of the Maya, certainly) it did not mean the people disappeared, although in some places, such as Peten, the population dropped dramatically.

I use the word *collapse* in the sense that Joseph Tainter uses it (see the bibliography): a society's shift to a simpler organizational structure. The Maya went from a hierarchical state society with "kings," monumental architecture, and public inscriptions to village farming life. Monumental architecture continued for some time in the Yucatán at Chichén Itzá before eventually dying out, and things were written down in books (codices) until the Spanish conquest, when the Spanish burned all but four of them. As far as we know, this writing discussed augury and divination, not the history of dynasties and political events, as the writing on the stelae did during the Classic period.

When I began reading about the Maya in the 1970s, they were considered a peaceful people who built elaborate ceremonial centers where they pursued an interest in astronomy. They lived elsewhere, away from these centers. It wasn't until Eric Thomson's generation had moved on that the writing system was decoded and a new history of the Maya gradually came into focus. Peaceful astronomers they were not, but they had developed a full-blown writing system on their own (with some preliminary help from their predecessors, the Olmec), a rare event in human history. They built beautiful and elaborate architectural centers with extraordinary art, and participated in an elaborate and complex web of trade and warfare. It's been a privilege to visit many of them and see firsthand what the archaeologists are uncovering daily.

There are many people to thank, especially Mary Dell Lucas, who runs Far Horizons, a travel agency specializing in archaeological tourism; without Far Horizons I would never have met the many dedicated archaeologists who so graciously shared their work.

Special thanks to Bill Rathje, who introduced me to Mitch Allen of AltaMira Press; Peter Mathews for an extraordinary, pun-filled raft trip down the Usumacinta River; David Pendergast, godfather of Belize archaeology; Richard Leventhal and Wendy Ashmore at Xunantunich; Susan Gillespie; Arlen and Diane Chase at Caracol; Bill and Barbara Fash and Will Andrews at Copan; Gillett Griffin (who showed pre-Columbian artifacts to a green Princeton undergraduate so long ago); Elizabeth P. Benson (who got me into Dunbarton Oaks for an extraordinary day in the library); D. Trudeau; and the incomparable Merle Greene Robertson of the pre-Columbian Art Research Institute (http://www.mesoweb.com/).

11 Ajaw 18 Keh

Monday, November 28
The Long Count date is 12.19.12.15.0
It has been 1,869,420 days since the Maya Zero Date
The calendar round date is 11 Ajaw 18 Keh
Moon is 27 days old
God 3 rules the night

MEDIA CIRCUS

An hour and a half after the explosion, Paula Reed interviewed Bryson Jones live on the six o'clock news. An intermittent light rain was falling on the chaos of lights, vehicles, firefighters, police officers, and the County Hazardous Materials truck just then arriving off camera. "Professor Weathers is missing," Paula Reed said, brushing her blond bangs from her eyes with the back of the hand holding her notes. "Was he inside the building when the bomb went off?"

Professor Bryson Jones's bluff, open manner projected a comfort in front of the camera unusual for an academic. "I doubt it was a bomb," he said gently. There had been no announcement, no claim of responsibility, and no injuries. There was a lot of smoke, which set off the fire alarms. The fire doors had locked automatically, and classes were canceled. That was all. "Things like this do occasionally happen, Paula," he added, gracing the camera with his famous smile.

"Professor Weathers's son is in a coma at University Hospital," she persisted. "As you saw right here on Channel Four just a few minutes ago, Mrs. Weathers is quite naturally distraught. The boy needs his father's blood, and he needs it now. She's appealed for information on her husband's whereabouts. Think, Professor Jones. Anything might help."

A firefighter shouted something in the background and drowned out his answer. Paula repeated, "What could you tell us about Professor

Weathers, Dr. Jones, about what kind of a man he is, personally, I mean? Why would he disappear? Did he have enemies?"

"I don't know where he is, Miss Reed, really I don't. Perhaps he went to get a haircut, or had a dentist appointment. As for enemies, I don't know of any, not personally, but of course everyone has enemies. Even I have enemies."

"You're both in the Anthropology Department, aren't you?"

"Yes, of course." He looked directly at her for a moment, then looked away. "Well, I did hear that he'd been having trouble sleeping, but you know how people talk."

She leaned forward. "What do they say?"

"There was talk a couple of months ago, at the beginning of the semester, just before he opened the Xibalbá Gate."

"Xibalbá Gate?"

"A simulation of the Classic Maya culture."

"And his problems sleeping?"

Professor Jones let out a sigh. "They say he started having dreams."

THE MIDDLE WORLD

SEPTEMBER

7 Manik 10 Zec

April 14, 837 AD
The Long Count date is 10.0.7.3.7
It has been 1,442,587 days since the Maya Zero Date
The calendar round date is 7 Manik 10 Zec
Moon is 1 day old
God 4 rules the night

DREAMS

Dreams are true. The king knows this, as he knows the paths through his city, as he knows the ancestor spirits that come to him from the gaping serpent mouth in the smoke of sacrifice. And now, with the sacred *balché* setting fire to his blood, he knows that dreams are true, for they show him the future.

In his dream, he leads his warriors on a raid of Dry Place, city of its king, Fire Shell. Beside him, dancing, capering, turning somersaults and leaps, cracked voice and sour breath, his animal *way*, half jaguar, half crocodile, spirit guide and image, grins and chatters.

No one else, not his war leader or the fifty young warriors, can hear or see it. But they have their own spirit guides, like watery shadow-shapes along the *sacbe*, the White Road they travel out of Xultunich in the early hours. The road gleams in the fading starlight as it turns to dawn, and Hunahpu, the Day Sun, appears over the forest canopy.

"You will die, you will die," the king's *way* chatters, leaping over him to land on the other side. The king, who calls himself Knot-Eye, walks on.

The mother-of-pearl reflections of other eyes peer from the jungle, and then the howling starts, for it is dawn and the monkeys are awake. They are the tormented souls of the dead, of suicides and those who died in childbirth, of which there are many. The howling brings the Day Sun into the light. And then it is time to leave the White Road, for they have reached the edges of Knot-Eye's power, and the land between Xultunich and Dry Place is full of lost spirits, full of danger.

There is a deer trail here, and the king and his war leader and his fifty warriors follow it. Their sandals fall lightly on the forest floor, sending up an occasional scuff of a leaf or the soft wet sound of a twig breaking, nothing more than an animal would make.

They reach an open place, sloping down a bit toward the plain, which extends into haze and heat. A day's long walk beyond that is the ocean, the salt water, and beyond that a boat journey takes you to an island sacred to Ixchel, goddess of the moon and childbirth.

Keeping to the trees along the edge of the jungle, they move south, a line of men with short jabbing spears and war clubs set with sharp obsidian chips, flitting like spirits of the already-dead among the trunks.

The *way* capers grotesquely, clacking its teeth, waving its shaggy paws, pointing.

They see in the distance a small band of farmers weeding a field. Dry Place has flat ground and little water, but the farmers must weed just the same.

Once, in grandfather's time, they would have left the farmers alone. Such men were adequate for slaves but not fit for sacrifice. In these days, though, there would be warriors nearby if the farmers were so far from their city, out of sight of Dry Place with its three uneven temple pyramids. They would capture the farmers later, after the battle.

The day grows hot; from the heat Knot-Eye hears a deep hiss. The vision serpent would come at this inconvenient time, but then Knot-Eye knows also that this is a dream and that dreams are true, so he waits as the head, small at first, grows swiftly larger, approaching. A narrow blood-red tongue darts and seeks, testing the air.

When it is close and Knot-Eye can feel the heat from its coils, it lifts its head and lunges toward him, mouth opening so the jaws arch wide and the fangs, dripping poison, curve out and down, toward him.

He does not flinch, does not draw back, for he sees deep into the throat, white, pale, and bloodless; he sees what he wants to see, what is true: the face of One Monkey, first ancestor, a middle-aged man with gaping, empty eyes, leaning out of the open serpent mouth toward him. One Monkey's mouth is moving, but no words form. In the mouth Knot-Eye can see things, small, dark, furtive things. They are insects, or they are words.

Then they come forth, the words. First the words *Were destroyed* come forth. They float like leaves falling, this way and that way, back and forth.

Then the words, *New corn, new moon, new jaguar*, come without any sound at all, only the rustle of the dancing, capering animal spirit companion, which cannot be heard.

The mouth leans down, and in the white flesh of its roof Knot-Eye can see, beyond the waving of the head of One Monkey still trying to talk, the nodding plumage of the war headdress of the king of Dry Place, the great war headdress of Fire Shell, and with him the noble warriors; and the forest is filled then with the clotted smell of fresh blood, the smell of damp earth, the smell of rotted flesh, as if the doorway to Xibalbá had opened and the Lords were capering and dancing, too, pointing at him with their bone fingers, their pus bellies spilling out.

He is squatting, then, knees up, in a small, close place, a stone place, an earth place. It is dark and there is no air.

Something drips on his cheek, on his eyelid, something warm, and it is jaguar blood, dripping from the severed neck, from the point of the kill-stone, the kill-knife, the sacrifice, for he is in the place of sacrifice; he is buried in the place of death under the temples, for the gods need fresh blood to live, and he must give it to them.

He can no longer breathe, and the dream is not really a dream, and the scream that cannot come from his mouth is not a scream, but they both are something more, and they both are true, and he knows that he is truly dead, as the animal-spirit companion had told him.

13 K'an 2 Ch'en

Tuesday, September 13
The Long Count date is 12.19.12.11.4
It has been 1,869,344 days since the Maya Zero Date
The calendar round date is 13 K'an 2 Ch'en
Moon is 2 days old
God 8 rules the night

FATHER AND SON

Pulling himself from sleep was a tormented thrashing through turbulent dark water into the air. Van sat up with a gasp. He put his hand to his forehead; it came away wet with sweat. It was the heat. It shouldn't be this hot in September.

"Dream again?" Glenna murmured beside him.

"Yes. Go back to sleep."

But she already had, her soft breathing steady and serene.

He got up for a glass of water and stared at himself in the bathroom mirror. His narrow skull, the first sprinkles of gray in his hair, the dark stains underneath his brown eyes, were completely ordinary and familiar. He was solid and alive. He drank greedily, put the glass down and, leaning over the sink, closed his eyes cautiously.

And felt the slow, thick dripping of jaguar blood on his lids. You will die, you will die. Well, of course. He opened his eyes and blinked. For just a moment the mouth of the vision serpent gaped in the mirror, and it was his own face leaning out between the curved fangs, which were only the reflection of Glenna's white bathrobe hanging on the door hook.

He went softly through the bedroom and down the corridor, past his son's room, to his study. His old leather chair faced the curtains and the crooked pattern of sycamore branches cast by the streetlight just past the

Cavanaugh's house next door. The curtains seemed to undulate gently, the branches to reach and clutch.

For the past week, the dream had come in fragments, different pieces each time: the vision serpent, the tomb and sacrifice of jaguar blood, the capering animal spirits, the long march through heat, the feeling of impending terror.

He studied these people, the Maya Indians of Central America. He knew their buildings, their writing, their mythology. He had spent years in the jungle digging their story out of the ground. For months he had been building the Xibalbá Gate, the simulation of their world. It was going online later today.

He told himself it was natural to dream about them.

The Maya had ways into the Otherworld, the place of fear, the house of spirits and knives, of sickness and death. It was close, a parallel universe just the other side of waking. Van Weathers had spent his career trying to find a way through that membrane, obsessed, like so many others before him, by the fact that the great Maya civilization had fallen mute, leaving only broken stones and ruin.

In a way, it was exciting, this dreaming, as if he were close to finding a way through himself.

"Dad?" His son was at the door, long T-shirt flapping around his knobby knees.

"Jag? What are you doing up? It's after two."

"You had that dream again, didn't you, Dad?"

"What makes you say that?"

Jag threw himself down in the chair under the window opposite his father. "I can tell. Every time you come in here lately in the middle of the night you have that look."

"What look?"

"The dream look. Haunted, kind of."

Van shook his head. "I'm fine, Jag. What are you doing up?"

Jag tipped his head and looked away. "I was surfing the net. I heard we're going to have a paper due the second week in social science. I like to get a little bit ahead. So, research, you know."

"Sure, I know." Van looked at the window, a dark rectangle that reflected the back of his son's head, his own face half-obscured by the curtain.

"Great," Jag said with a grin. "Then we can have one of those father-son things."

"What father-son things are those?"

"You know, Dad. Talks. How I'm about to become a man, that sort of thing."

"About to become a man? You're fifteen. You mean sex?"

Jag smiled. "No, I think we pretty much covered that in sex ed. I was thinking more about career, what to do in life, what it means, why I'm here. That sort of stuff."

"It's two in the morning, Jag. Even if you don't start school until Tuesday, today's the first day of classes for me. You want to talk about the meaning of life. . . ." Van stopped with a sudden burst of laughter. "Of course you do. We all stayed up half the night talking about it when I was your age."

"So. What's the answer?"

"I don't know."

Jag shrugged. "All right, then. Tell me about the Maya."

"Can't sleep, huh?"

"Shoot, Dad, you see right through me, don't you?"

"I've known you all your life, Jag. That must count for something. How about this: we do our work, we treat each other kindly, we find something we're passionate about, and we do our best."

"That's it? Philosophy 101 from Professor Weathers?"

"Go to bed, son. Get some sleep. And stay off the Internet for a couple of hours, all right?"

"OK, Dad." He paused at the door for a moment, his hand on the jamb.

The doorway was a black opening beyond which Van could see the capering *way* beckoning to his son.

You will die, you will die.

He shook his head as Jag turned back to him.

"It's just a dream, dad."

"Why do you say that?"

"You used to tell me that," Jag said. "I've known you all my life, too, dad."

"I'm fine, Jag," Van said, but his son was gone.

CLASS STRUGGLE

The dream had dissipated by afternoon. Van leaned over the lectern in his first seminar of the semester and blinked rapidly three times. It was a code, an initial S. His arms, crossed on the sloping wood, ended in long hands dangling over the edges, fingers like tallow flowing down the scarred sides. His narrow shoulders hunched against his red plaid shirt collar and his eyes drooped shut slowly, once, twice, three times, a drawn out Morse O. He cleared his throat. "I am Professor Sylvanus Weathers. In case you were wondering, I was named after the great Mayan archaeologist who excavated at Chichén Itzá, Sylvanus Griswold Morley." He blinked three times again.

SOS. Save Our Souls.

Very likely they were not wondering about his name. Wonder, Van thought, had been washed out of them by years of television, movies, celebrity religion, endless hissing electronic sleet.

He released a slow breath. The first day was always difficult. His words bounced off their youth like the fall sunlight off the plastic surfaces of the tables. His sly Morse code went unnoticed, but two of the nine hand-picked graduate students slowly nodded.

He pushed away from the lectern and placed the back of his plaid shirt against the blackboard. In this way, he could half sit, half lean on the chalk ledge and cross his arms, tucking long fingers into his armpits. In Van's syllabus, Communication and Texts was a graduate seminar in critical thinking and an introduction to Mayan Indian cultures, especially the hieroglyphic writing system only recently deciphered.

The plump blond girl behind the second row of tables clutched her facsimile copy of *The Dresden Codex*. Her chin doubled with her nod. Van smiled in approval, and an answering smile seemed to illuminate her face. She would do, Van thought. She already had his book, *Graphic Communication and the Structure of History*, and the photocopied handouts, ready for explication. His book was not required reading for this class, but many of the graduate students carried it around.

The other nodder, a boy seated at an angle as if his legs were too long and awkward to fit under the cream Formica, had the front table to himself. He slouched, the heels of his jungle boots resting on a chair, toes pointed toward the door. Van stifled a groan. The ponytail, camouflage shirt, and piercing, earnest blue eyes all deepened his dread. In his experience, the ones in front were the enthusiasts, eager to share their opinions about the astrological savvy of the ancient Maya. They were conspiracy theorists, ancient astro-nuts. This one would wannabe a back-to-nature-in-touch-with-the-spiritual-side-of-the-primitive-culture-stargazing-peaceful-blood-sacrifice Mayan Indian. Van allowed the ponytail a nod and released his eyes to roam the room.

He continued. "Morley was a small, nearsighted, energetic, charming man. Everybody loved him. Originally, he was interested in Egyptology; everyone was, back then, in 1908. But he was steered toward the New World, and became a partisan." Van emphasized the first syllable, *parti*san. "His *National Geographic* articles often depicted Maya priests sacrificing scantily clad virgins by throwing them into the sacred well at Chichén Itzá."

This produced, as usual, a quick round of truncated laughter, quickly stifled by the women in the room. Scantily clad virgins were passé, not PC.

"Morley died the year I was born." He paused, but the eighteen eyes were empty of questions of their own. "My mother was an avid reader of *National Geographic*, and an almost fanatical fan of the flamboyant Dr. Morley, so this event was profoundly moving for her—Morley's death, I mean—so she combined it with my birth and gave me his name."

Footsteps battered the floor outside, rising and falling in Doppler effect as, he decided, two athletic scholarships ran past the door, going east, toward the elevators, eager no doubt to collect their first scholarship checks, class or no class. The footsteps at their peak smothered whatever appreciative chuckles these nine might have offered him.

"There may appear to be little reason for you to care about my personal name," he continued. "But you will be learning about the Maya in this seminar, and I've always felt it appropriate to begin with the naming of things." He pointed at the young woman with the codex. "Let's begin with you."

She looked around, but the slouching man with the ponytail chewed nervously on his thumbnail and the thin boy in a white shirt to her left stared solemnly at the surface of the table. Dr. Weathers looked directly at her, so she coughed once and began, "I. . . ."

Van interrupted. "Ego aside, what is the origin of your name? Quickly, we don't have that much time."

"Anne. My grandmother, I was named after her." The girl had a ring in her left nostril.

"I see." He was leaning over the lectern once more, and stole a surreptitious glance at the computer printout between his forearms. He found the first name Anne. "Then you must be Ms. Opple, Anne. I see you already have your master's degree, good. And her name, Ms. Opple, whence her name Anne?"

"My grandmother was named after the queen." Anne looked around again, but the others were interested in something else. "England. 1665–1714."

Van reared back. "Wonderful!" He clapped his hands, once. "You've specialized until now in classical archaeology: Greece, Rome, that sort of thing. Yes, Anne was a queen. Like Lady Xook!" He pronounced it "Shook."

The girl shook her head.

"Also a queen," Van assured her. "Yaxchilan, temple 23, her building. Lady Xook—the 'x' is the way the Spanish wrote an 'sh' sound—pierced her tongue, pulled a cord lined with thorns through the hole for blood sacrifice. Scene lit by her husband Shield-Jaguar holding a torch. Body piercing is not so new, you see." He touched his nose. "You'll hear more about it." Van turned to the boy with the ponytail. "You!" he said.

The boy jumped and spit a fragment of nail. "Charles. Father." His eyes turned guileless, looking back at Van like a coconspirator.

Van nodded with another glance down. "Very good, Mr. McGuirk. Very good."

They all had names. They had origins, birth dates. They had hopes and fears.

"Maya Glyphs," he said softly, lowering his shoulders. "We are learning every day more about these people, their complex and rich history. We are learning it because *they wrote it down*." He emphasized the last words, speaking them slowly, a revelation.

Anne of the *Dresden Codex* shrugged her shoulders and smiled at him in a cozy way.

Footsteps in the hall ran the other way. Coeds, late leaving the bathroom, late for class. Probably smoking dope in there, giggling. Van closed his eyes.

"You will be participating," he went on, "in a very robust simulation of Maya culture. It is a new thing, called the Xibalbá Gate. Xibalbá," he pronounced it she-balb-A, "is the Maya underworld, or more properly, Otherworld. The Gate is a way to enter. This simulation will be open tonight. I expect everyone to be familiar with it by our next meeting. You will enter the simulation and adopt an identity. You will explore and interact. You will learn."

He lowered the screen and turned down the lights. The screen lit up with strange signs: they would also learn, he said, the signs and numbers, day glyphs, emblem glyphs for the ruined cities, name glyphs for the kings and queens, kinship and succession, gods and goddesses. They would learn to read dates, long count and calendar round; they would identify the sites from which the passages they studied came, the important ceremonies performed there, the significance of the site itself in the context of the Mayan polity. And they would live part of the time in the Maya world.

By the time he finished his recitation of requirements, Van could tell that the two sleepy men in the last row would probably drop the course by next week, as if the word "polity" could frighten even graduate students.

"They had large cities, temples, intensive agriculture, broad white highways between the cities, trade across most of Central America. Their mathematics was more advanced than that of Europe. They had invented the zero. They could predict with incredible accuracy the appearances of Venus, the phases of the moon, eclipses, and other celestial events. Their art and literature were complex. Their calendar, like ours, recorded and predicted a number of different cycles. We track weekdays Monday, Saturday; months, like this one, September; day numbers, like today, the fourteenth. The Maya used two calendars, both based on a base-twenty vegisimal system, clearly the total number of fingers and toes." There was a ripple of appreciative laughter.

"One calendar had twenty named days and thirteen numbers, making a 260-day sacred calendar, the *Tzolk'in*; the other 'vague year' or *haab* calendar had eighteen months of twenty days, making a 360-day year with a short five-day month at the end to add up to 365. The two calendars combined made up the calendar round.

"Mostly during the Classic period (250–909 AD), they also wrote down a so-called long count, written in our alphabet as a series of five numbers separated by periods. A typical date looked like this: 10.0.7.3.7. The rightmost number counts seven days, or *k'in*; the next number to the left counts three *winals*, or months, of twenty days, but which somewhat confusingly work to base 18 in order to accommodate the solar year—you see, eighteen times twenty. Thus every eighteen days the *winal* number goes up one. Next to the left is the *tun*, or seven years of 360 days. Every twenty *winals*, the *tun* number goes up one. Next is the *k'atun* number (approximately every forty years—or, in this case, ten times 144,000 days). And finally, the *bak'tun* turns over approximately every 400 years. The long count began at a time far in the past, and in fact long before the Maya began writing dates down (in 3114 BC, the creation date of the present universe). A rollover from the end of the ninth *bak'tun* to the tenth would go from 9.19.19.17.19 to 10.0.0.0.0.

"A calendar round date is thus the five long count numbers plus a numbered month and a numbered day. The simulation is opening on 10.0.7.3.7, 7 Manik 10 Zec, that is, April 14, 837 AD.

"One further complication exists, and that is the problem of the correlation number used to convert the long count into the Christian calendar (not to mention whether one is using the Julian or Gregorian Christian calendar). The most commonly accepted number is the Goodman-Martinez-Thompson number, but in fact most people today use a two-day shift from GMT as standard. Most of the other systems in current use give dates within a couple of days of one another. This is partly because recorded Maya events often took place over several days, and there are very few precise inscriptions to use for comparison (though there is at least one eclipse recorded, which fell three days after the original GMT date and one day after the standard two-day amendment). Hence the Maya dates are still slightly uncertain. You can find a number of resources on the Web to convert from Christian to Maya and back. There is one at pauahtun.org for instance.

"They also kept tabs on the age of each moon, which of the nine gods ruled the night, how long it had been since the original zero date, just as we keep track of years and centuries and millennia. These cycles meshed together, repeating in differing sequences. And they kept track of which of the four direction gods, the *k'awiils*, ruled which part of the sky, for they watched the sky very carefully. Almost as carefully as we do, but with a different lens for understanding it.

"Then suddenly, at their peak, their society collapsed. The cities fell into ruin, their temples reverted to jungle."

Before he let them go, he told them the overriding goal of the course was understanding. "Can we draw any lessons from their disappearance?" he asked, knowing the question was rhetorical, and might always be rhetorical.

Electronic sleet buzzed through the room. Drifts of fluorescent noise fell from the ceiling. The girl with the codex and nose ring was nodding. The ponytail was biting anxiously at a thumbnail. The vision serpent uncoiled above the lectern and floated away like smoke in the late afternoon air.

"Can we understand why?" Van asked the class. "Why did it happen?"

JAG

Jonathan Weathers was talking to his mother about causes. "Dad claims everything has a cause," he said.

"Yes," Glenna agreed. "I'd say everything has a cause, at least one, if not more. Perhaps many more."

"So," Jag persisted, "if everything has a cause or, for the sake of argument, several causes, doesn't it follow that if we can recognize the causes, see them as they are happening, then we can predict, with confidence, the consequences? We could say what will happen in the future?"

"Perhaps, yes, but doubtful." Glenna put her finger on the page of a catalog of Asian textiles she was studying. Her finger traced an image, abstract birds hidden in blue and gold chevrons. Without looking up, she added, "It's a big *if*. There are often unexpected events, surprises, emergent properties, unforeseen consequences."

Jag was tuned to talk radio, stock quotes, the economic forecast. Glenna could hear his headset twitter, rolling through the world's statistics. "Well, there are signs." He was drinking thoughtfully from a bottle of raspberry-flavored tea and watching dust motes dance in the late-afternoon sunlight slanting through the kitchen window.

"Are there?" She closed the book on her finger and looked at him closely. "I suppose there are, at that." Her son often talked like this. "But signs of what?"

"Things. Changes."

"Anything we should know about?" Glenna asked, but he put down his tea and set off abruptly down the hall, one finger running along the bottoms of the picture frames. The photographs swung back and forth.

"Hey!" she called after him. "Don't do that! You'll knock them down again."

"Down twelve point six points," the radio was saying. "London's Footsie up three. In Paris. . . ."

Jag left the door of his room open. Its full-sized, red stop sign, a relic of his childhood, was now a meaningless pattern.

Glenna sighed and followed him. From the doorway, she watched him wake up his computer, watched the brief rush and whir as phosphor dots came to light with the insatiable buzz of information.

He typed rapidly: -12.6; $+3$; $+120$; -17.9. He began entering other numbers, and she recognized the exchange rates for major world currencies. The yen, she saw, was stronger against the dollar. The dollar was weaker against the euro.

"What are you doing?" she asked.

Jag looked up at her and smiled. "I'm writing a program to analyze for hidden patterns. I collect data, the billions of dollars, euros, yen, that sort of thing." He grew very earnest, even passionate. "Every day new currencies appear. We see them for a while, then they disappear along with the countries that issue them. Buried in the world's financial computers are automatic buy programs, sell programs, trade programs. They all swap bits and change the numbers. I track them, looking for patterns. You see? It's a little like the textiles in your book, the patterns in them." He went back to work.

Glenna watched him hunched over his keyboard. She, too, looked for signs. Did he feel distress, anxiety, fear? Bars of color rose and fell on the screen, throbbing like the heartbeat in the thin white skin of his neck. His eyes followed the pulses of rainbow light.

Her hand rested over her heart. Jag her inward son, the pulse beating in his neck. She could find no evidence of unhappiness, so she asked, "Are you ready?"

He held up a hand, just a minute, something important. There was a burst of color and he turned. "I'm always ready." He gestured at the screen.

"Oh, I meant tenth grade, Jag. Sophomore year."

"Oh, that." He dipped his side, ear close to his bony shoulder. Jag had shoulders like his father, lifting hard points and edges out of thin flesh. "Yeah, I'm ready. It doesn't much matter, though, whether I'm ready or not. Time takes you there, wherever."

"You are your father's son," she said with a smile. He was wearing that shirt again, the huge white T-shirt that flapped over his backside, his thin arm lost in the sleeve. He slept in it sometimes.

He looked up at that. "What I mean is, there's chaos, you know. Random events. I could be run over by my best friend's father driving down our street. It's the sort of thing that happens, not always to other people."

"Is this what the signs are telling you?"

He laughed. "Of course not. I'm working on economics this week. Random events could happen in the markets, you see. Sudden up or down. We should study them, don't you think?"

"Oh, of course we should. But you're only fifteen. Shouldn't you be a teenager for a while?"

"The whole idea of a teenager is a recent marketing category, Mom. I'm doing fine."

It was ever thus, her disordered retreat down the hall followed by those wide brown eyes and his irrefutable logic. She wondered if Jag had a best friend. She had to confess she didn't know who he or she might be.

She paused to look at the photographs in the hall, now hanging motionless. They were fragments of frozen time: she and her sister Mary, Van with the boy in a pouch on his chest when Jag was, oh, a year at most, a small, tousled blond, wide eyes looking into the camera.

She pulled her laptop out of a drawer in the kitchen and sat once more at the table. She was trying to write an article for the art museum publication on traditional patterns in the museum's collection of Muong weaving. The Muong had a written language once; now it was lost, only the shapes of forgotten words threaded into woven material. She wrote a couple of sentences and then looked out the window, deep in thought. She realized she didn't know much about Jag's friends. In spite of his historical analysis of the recent appearance of the teenager, adolescence had silenced him somehow. It was as if his language, like the Muong weaving, was also lost.

It was a phase, no doubt.

Soon her son floated back through the bright afternoon kitchen. The shirt ballooned behind him, a sail of purity but for the two plain black initials on the front and back: D. A.

Glenna wondered if they were the initials of some musical group (District Attorney? Deaf Anteaters? Deadly Anthrax?). She didn't remember a group called D. A. on the car radio, but Jag's culture was as tribal as that of the highlands of Southeast Asia.

She watched as he rummaged in the cupboards, found a jar, a bowl, some crackers. He stood, so like his father, by the sink, staring through the window, chewing, his spoon moving smoothly in continuous motion.

"Hey," he said. The spoon fell into the bowl with a soft click.

"You'll spoil your dinner." Glenna crossed her ankle over her knee and pressed down, stretching the thigh, working against a phantom pain. He was watching her, head cocked to one side, lank hair across his eyes. Those eyes seemed tired suddenly, and she hoped it was a trick of the light that filled the room and blurred all edges.

"Don't worry, I'll be hungry again."

"I know you will," she said. "But go to bed early tonight. You need sleep. Tomorrow, you know. First day."

"OK," he said at last, putting his bowl in the sink. "First day."

"Were you going to ask something?" she pressed.

"Ask? Naw, never mind. I gotta go, meet some friends. Don't worry. I'll go to bed early."

He was gone. The last thing she saw were the two letters on the back of his T-shirt, flapping through the door and out.

HER WORK

Glenna worked on her article for another hour, then closed the computer. She stood at the window for a time, chewing at a nail.

The things that fretted her—a restlessness, a nameless desire, a sudden moment of intense need—were the very sources of her inspiration, proddings of the muse. Often, after a bout of aimless wandering, she found herself a little short of breath. These waves were her passion passing through her, moments of the sacred reaching through the veil of illusion to scare her into inspiration. For that, she sought them out in solitude.

And when they came, as now, she would suddenly find herself back upstairs in the studio, studying her canvas intently. Time ceased to exist. She shook her head and with a glance at the skylight picked up her brush. The light was now perfect.

The canvas was an immense stretch of indefinite blue light concealing small hints of dark lines like some kind of primitive writing struggling for birth into meaning. She thought of calling it *Message*. Or perhaps *Messages*. If she squinted, it looked a little like a Muong tapestry slightly out of focus.

The phone rang once. She stared absently at it, waiting to see if it would ring again. It did not. This happened more and more frequently these days, misdialed numbers, failed communications. She pulled the flesh of her lower lip between her teeth, holding the unused brush upright beside her cheek. The electric crackling blue of her painting stained the cloth she held in her other hand. She noticed at last, put it down, and stuck the brush, bristles up, in the cracked coffee mug that held the other brushes.

The room had good light. She had planned for this northern exposure. "Ganzfeld" her technique was called, a kind of clear infinite wash of even illumination. Her ganzfeld painting, the "whole field," was a pulsating blue, depth beyond depth. She could lean forward, fall in like Alice, down and down. She would force meaning from that emptiness, hence the little flickers of texture like condensations of hope.

With her family gone, the faculty housing development seemed to echo with solitude. North light, even and fine-grained, seeped through the skylight and made no shadows.

She could see the patterns hidden in the even blue, the faintest hints of lines. She put her brush to it, hiding the lines in the strokes themselves, so they caught light and threw traces of shadow. The painting was close, very close. She could feel it, the end, the final vision.

At last, she stopped and wandered silently from room to room. She passed their bedroom, absent Van's study, Jag's room; downstairs, she went by the living room and dining area. From the kitchen, she could look in one direction onto her garden, gone to seed, in the other the street curving away.

She realized she was wandering and forced herself back upstairs to draw a bath as hot as she could stand. She watched the white tub fill. Perhaps, she thought with a laugh, her desires were physical after all; it had been too long.

Water flowed along the sides, boiled under the tap. The patterns it made were chaotic, at the edge of meaning: ganzfeld, white-tinted blue, ripples and swirls on the surface.

Finally, she removed her clothes and slid her long pale body into the water. Vapors rose from the surface, twined around her head, wreathing her. The delicate hair on her upper lip gathered moisture. Her hands folded over her belly and she sighed. The vapor twisted visibly away before her mouth.

Fantasy was afloat in the mist, artful studies in vulnerability and urgent flesh; body parts pressed together, moving to slow rhythms, a montage of genders and ages. Her loneliness slid beside her into the tub and displaced no water. Her fingers drifted unnoticed between her long thighs, brushed gently upward, distant childhood comfort.

Already the air was suffused with a painful blue, its message almost known, almost knowable. She could see the last few brush strokes the painting needed.

It was easy to sink down. She breathed out slowly and closed her eyes against the glare.

ELLIOT

Evening was coming on. Elliot Blackman turned down the lights to balance the glare inside Crowley Hall, then climbed slowly round and round the inside stairwell, holding to the railing.

He was smiling. He was humming. He couldn't help it.

It's a trivial matter, he thought, to fool others. I'm just a small element in the great global sweep of money and ideas. Small, but vitally important, and it's mine, this secret life.

Elliot was fairly new in Crowley Hall, home of Liberal Arts and Sciences. Everyone thought he was the night maintenance foreman. It made him laugh.

He performed his job with the focused attention of a professional. He wasn't a janitor, really, more a kind of a consultant, if you will. The university thought it owned him. So did his other employer. They both thought they were first in line, but Elliot worked for himself first, and others second.

The maintenance job was cover and it was important to maintain his cover well.

So when he began his shift, he lowered the lights and climbed the stairs. As he climbed, he held the railing because he liked the feel of its solidity, its certainty. He liked the solidity because so much of the rest of his life was vague and intangible, little deceptions, tiny secret invasions, subtle perversions of other peoples' destinies. And of course there was the impression of weakness this clutching to the railing gave to others.

He made a ritual survey of his domain. Each floor of the building opened to his inspection. He could hear the elevators humming in the walls as he rounded the last landing.

On the sixth floor, he pushed the heavy fire door halfway open and surveyed the corridor. Only three of the frosted glass windows in the classroom doors were still aglow: two, side by side on the left and one near the far end on the right.

The murmur of late classes rose and fell behind those lighted panels. He nodded in satisfaction and glanced at his watch. Almost six o'clock. Almost time. He stood in the doorway, one hand maintaining the opening, watching the classrooms.

The world was in precarious balance.

One of the left-hand doors opened, and a rush of students poured through, almost instantly joined by the crash of the neighboring door flying open and another strong, swift current. Shouts, laughter, footsteps echoed against blank walls. Elevator doors opened, swallowed a lump of the crowd, closed. A few students brushed past, others disappeared around the far bend, and slowly, as in some cinematic dissolve, the corridor was empty again.

Still Elliot held the door ajar, watching.

After a lengthy pause, the classroom near the far end opened and released a new knot of students. He counted them, one, two, three, then five more, another pause, and finally a plump girl. With her was Elliot's reason for being here on the sixth floor of Crowley Hall at six in the evening on September 13, the reason Elliot had manipulated the university Human Resources computers into accepting him as Crowley Hall maintenance foreman: Sylvanus M. Weathers.

Elliot had required access, and now he had it. He almost laughed out loud it had been so easy. His other employer would be happy at the way things were going.

The girl nodded and scurried around the far corner of the hallway. Doctor Weathers gazed after her for a moment.

When the professor started in his direction, Elliot released the door and retreated down the stairs. He still had a job to do, staving off disorder, the best kind of cover imaginable.

Even though it was the first day of classes, Elliot knew his quarry. Professor Weathers would descend to his office on four, where he would file his papers, put his books back in his metal bookshelves, and leave the room shipshape and squared away. Elliot checked his watch and then descended as he had ascended, slowly, with great deliberation, an imponderable presence returning to his vast basement, humming with inexplicable energies, the gurgle of pipes, the resonance of the day's hurry.

To reach his maintenance offices and the four narrow storerooms with high ceilings invisible behind a complex doodling of pipes, Elliot had to pass the computer lab. The door stood ajar. A few students sat at long tables with terminals aglow in the semidarkness and tapped the keyboards. He walked by with only a brief glance.

It was time to mix. He whistled as he unlocked the storage room and flicked on the light to reveal shelves, stacks of toilet paper, boxes of paper towels, racks of mops and brooms, trolleys fitted out with wood polish, rags, cleanser.

Elliot unlocked a metal cabinet and removed an opaque black gallon bottle from the top shelf. He examined the label, traced a practiced finger over the skull and crossbones, read the brand name out loud: "Saniclor™." He shook the bottle, listened carefully to the slow surge inside.

He smiled and unscrewed the cap. With a sharp hiss, a small cloud of purple-brown vapor escaped from the neck, and an acrid odor bit the inside of his nose. He turned his head and waited for the cloud to drift away.

Then he leaned over the first bucket and poured an exact quantity of the thick brown liquid into it with a muted hiss. He recapped the bottle and set it on the edge of the sink. Next, he picked up the rubber hose attached to the faucet, turned on the water, and tested it from time to time against the inside of his wrist until it was the correct temperature. When he was satisfied, he pinched the hose to shut off the flow of water and laid the mouth against the inside of the bucket. Slowly he released the fold, and warm water swirled down. A wraith of brown vapor rose off the surface as the bucket filled. So potent and volatile was this fluid that Elliot was the only one allowed to do the mixing. He was accustomed to the acrid fumes.

The seven members of the night maintenance crew drifted in from their previous cleanup in the Humanities Building and lined up by the shelving. They waited in silence, mops in hand, for Elliot to release them to their duties. All wore coveralls with the university logo over the breast pocket and laminated identity cards clipped to the flap. Each card had the photograph of its owner under an embedded hologram. Control, Elliot knew, was the most important factor in combating decay. He ignored them as he filled the other six buckets with the same absolute attention to detail.

Finally, he straightened and nodded. One by one, his crew stepped forward, took the handle of a bucket, and pulled it out of the room. The soft sound of their wheels faded away.

It was a satisfaction that the cleaner needed mixing when the university day was over. Elliot came out at night with his crew to do this job; but when the crew was gone he could begin his real work, the work toward which all his training, his history, and his demons drove him. He checked his watch again, grinned, and took a cardboard box labeled "Primus" from the steel cabinet. Almost time.

GORDON

Gordon Flentsch, a short, round, and very blond ethnologist, was seen with Van Weathers so often some junior faculty called them Salt and Pepper. So it was not unusual that on this evening they found themselves entering the basement coffee shop side by side.

"Yo, Mrs. Y," Gordon said to the sturdy woman dozing behind the counter.

"Hi, Dr. Flentsch. First day of school, huh?"

"You said it."

She straightened up a little. "Hello, Dr. Weathers. Always a pleasure to see you down here."

"Hello, Mrs. Yablonsky," Van answered politely. "I'll be down a lot this year at the computer lab."

"Oh, yes, I heard that. Your Indian thing. The usual?" She turned to the coffee machine without waiting for an answer.

They made their way to a table near the back and sat down. "Do you suppose we'll ever see Bryce Jones this year?" Gordon asked with mock seriousness.

Van glanced sideways with a smile. "Did we see him last year?"

"Nope. He was in India making that PBS special."

"I know you don't like him, but I wouldn't judge him too harshly," Van suggested gently. "He helped get funding for the Xibalbá Gate. The Central American Preservation Organization came through because they know who he is. He has his place."

"Yeah, media star. But what about your dig, the real work? You're a dirt archaeologist, not a computer geek."

Van sighed. "I know, Gord. I put in six years at Xultunich, but in the end the foundation felt it just wasn't productive."

"Is that true?"

"It's true we didn't find any hoards of ceramics or fancy burials, and you know how funders like to find treasure that gets into *National Geographic*. But it's a hell of a big site, Gord. It extends way out to the west of where we were digging."

"So? Maybe there's treasure there."

"Private land." Van chewed thoughtfully on his lip. "It's not treasure we're after, Gord, you know that. We want to understand, and sometimes you have to dig a long time for the truth. Oh, there's something there, all right. I have a feeling about it, but we couldn't get the permits."

"But what do you think is there?" Gordon persisted. "On the private land?"

Van looked away. "I don't have anything definitive."

"Did you try to find the owners?"

"Of course. I came up blank. We couldn't track them down, and neither the foundation nor the local government seemed able to help. I'd never seen anything like it before; it was like a blank wall everywhere I went. No reasons given, just permit denied. It wasn't really the local bureaucracy—they seemed to be very helpful, always suggesting alternatives, other people to call or write. It went nowhere. I got stopped whichever way I went. In the end, I had to give up."

"Don't you think that's strange?"

Van looked at him at last. "Yes, Gord, I do think it's strange. But without money and permits I can't dig. So I have to find another way to get at it. Thanks to Bryce, I've got the simulation. It's powerful, flexible, and very convincing. The students will get a lot from it."

"The students!" Gordon exclaimed. "What about you?"

Van stared into a distance and drummed his fingers lightly. A shifty darkness flowed up and down the far corner of the room, stretched toward him, retreated. He shook his head but said nothing.

Mrs. Yablonsky called and Gordon went back to the counter. The cavernous coffee shop was nearly deserted, and he could hear his footsteps echo back from its distant angles. When he got back, he turned his chair around with a screech and sat with his arms crossed on the back, cappuccino held in one hand very close to his mouth. He ducked his head and sipped, leaving a pencil mustache of foam. "I think she's in love with you, Van."

Van looked over at Mrs. Yablonsky, who smiled warmly and gave him a little wave. Van smiled back and stared at his coffee.

"OK," Gordon continued. "The simulation. You said it was like a shared world." Gordon shook his fingers as if shaking off invisible dirt. "So who am I going to meet in this world?"

"Oh," Van answered. "The usual suspects, but you won't know them since they'll have Maya identities. Alberto Bofonchio, you remember him, from the University of Bologna? And Leon, of course."

"Leon? Blatskoi's got a computer at last? They have electricity in St. Petersburg these days?"

"Don't be funny, Gordon, of course they have electricity. And Alberto's visiting him as we speak."

"Mm. So, describe it, the simulated Maya world."

"Eight-thirty-seven AD. April. Hot, damp, loamy. The lost city of Xultunich. I've re-created it as completely as possible, the way it was . . . including the Place of Crocodiles to the west, called Te-Ayiin."

Gordon lifted an eyebrow at that. "Really? OK. It's near the end of a civilization. The Maya Collapse is coming. No one knows why."

"It'll be a kind of open seminar with students and colleagues, mainly a student project."

"But there were lots of reasons why they disappeared." Gordon sipped thoughtfully.

"Lots. No 'maybe' about it," Van agreed.

"Too many people?"

Van nodded. "Population, yes. Pollution. Deforestation."

"Omens in the sky. Disaster. Venus rising, bringing war." Gordon, expert in the world's cultures and mythologies, ducked his mouth to the cardboard cup.

"Unreasonable expectations," Van added. "Disappointment. Increases in fear and anxiety."

"Disease?" Gordon grinned. "Plague?"

Van nodded. "Social problems. Shortage of resources."

"War? Famine? The Four Horsemen?"

"All of them, plus drought, earthquakes, volcanic eruptions. Invasion, foreign influences, cultural imperialism. And so on."

Gordon "I thought the new word was that drought brought them down. *Science* magazine back in 2003 said measurements of annual titanium levels in northern Venezuela sediments showed three periods of severe drought between 810 and 910."

"Well, drought does seem to recur in cycles of roughly 208 years," Van replied. "And 208 years earlier they did not collapse. Drought is certainly one of the theories, and it seems to have been particularly severe in the Yucatán, but my area is the lowlands, where it wasn't so severe. In fact, in many places there were rivers or lakes. They had plenty of water. Besides, David Freidel and a number of others blame endemic warfare, yet as best we can tell warfare was confined mostly to the lowlands. Others say it was environmental degradation, and that certainly happened, but not everywhere. And in the highlands, the Itzá still had a fairly complex organizational system at the Conquest hundreds of years later. So you see the problem? I think it was something else."

"Collapse?"

"Collapse, certainly. Nothing left of a great civilization but peasants, scratching a living out of the ground."

"Always that way, peasants, the ones left." Gordon set down his empty cup and tapped Van's forearm. "Come on," he said. "You haven't touched your coffee."

"They had science, Gordon. Religion, complex trade."

"They had, um, universities," Gordon said. "Professors, students.

Poetry and song, painting and sculpture. Art, theology, history. Leaders, warriors, doctors."

"Gone. All gone."

"Astronomy, cosmology, grand raising of the House of the World."

"Finished."

"Cycles of time within other cycles, wheels grinding finer and finer, gears of time turning each other, the rise and fall of civilizations. . . ."

"Life itself is temporary, a momentary flash of light across the blank face of the cosmos."

"This is a big project, Van. Nothing less than the total meaning of everything."

"That's not fair, Gordon. You're being sarcastic."

"Sorry. It's just that society is complex. Seeing the whole picture seems a little . . . ambitious? You're at the top of your career, Van. Be careful you don't overreach."

"Of course it's ambitious, Gord. Every archaeologist worth his salt wants to know the answer; most of them think they already do—they'll tell you it's whatever destroyed their site, where they dig. Of course I want to know what happened at Xultunich, but I also want to know why the whole material world fell apart for the Maya civilization, a vast interactive network of city-states. I want to know why the spirits took away everything they built."

"Spirits are everywhere, Van. Evil leaks out of the earth, and into it. It takes tremendous effort and vigilance to maintain the balance. Entropy stalks us constantly."

Van shook his head. "No, no, no, that's not what I mean." He paused a moment. "The last week or so I've been having these dreams, Gordon, the vision serpent, ancestors leaning out. Just dreams, though, not evil leaking out of the earth. I'm a scientist, after all, and this is only a simulation on the Internet. Leon's interested in settlement patterns and elite management styles, Alberto studies shamanism and class relations. It's a little fancier form of electronic mail, that's all. No spirits spoiling the milk. Dreams are just dreams." He took a sip of his coffee, put the cardboard cup on the table, and stood. "Let's go."

Gordon also stood, and looked into Van's eyes. His own were a pale green. "The Internet can be addictive," he said with unusual intensity.

"Some people spend hours in there every day. They get trapped and can't tell it from reality. They have support groups."

Van laughed. "I know. They meet in chat rooms on the Internet to discuss their addiction to chat rooms on the Internet."

"I wonder why you couldn't get a permit to dig to the west, Van," Gordon said softly. "Be careful."

Van jerked his head sideways. "Careful? Oh, sure, I'll be careful. You too, you be careful."

EARLY SNOW

It was dark in St. Petersburg and bitterly cold. Two men were walking carefully along the English Embankment, heads tilted toward each other, breath flowing back in ragged plumes. Leon Blatskoi, the taller of the two, moved his gloved hand sideways in an uncertain gesture toward the snow. "I can't live like this!" he said in Russian-accented but rapid English. The words, muffled in his fur collar, were ripped away by dry hard gusts off the river.

"Leon, Leon," the other man said soothingly. "It's been bitter for you, I know. But you will be vindicated, you'll see." His English was more liquid and practiced than Leon's. "We will all be vindicated," he added softly in Italian.

Leon stopped and looked gloomily across the river at the university. "You do not understand, Alberto. I do not mean my career, such as it has been. I mean living here; it is like the end of the Maya, isn't it: great loss of faith, diminishing resources, bad air?"

Alberto touched his friend's arm. "You have a choice," he said quietly.

The street lights were already on, bright halos of dancing particles sleeting through their glow. Leon shook his head. "Look around, Alberto. You are a man of intelligence and, what is the word? discernment. What is it you see?"

Alberto Bofonchio, a plump, dark man with a muffler around his neck, nodded. The river to his right was black, set off by the light dusting on the granite embankment. "I see snow," he said with affection. "We don't get so much snow in Bologna. It's nice."

"Nice? Hah!" Leon barked, throwing his head back. His cigarette, tilted toward the low clouds, hissed when a snowflake landed on the tip. His snort of derision released a cloud of acrid smoke through both nostrils, instantly ripped away. "The snow is early. September. Hah! And they say we have global warming!"

They continued in glum silence past the bronze statue of Peter the Great, horse rearing atop a granite outcropping, trampling a snake some said represented the serfs. A bus rumbled along the edge of the park and turned west away from them, down the embankment, spewing diesel fumes and dark particulate.

Leon stopped as they were crossing the Leytenanta Shmidta Bridge. The dark water below them flowed away to the sea. "You say I have a choice," he said. "Yes, I suppose I do have a choice. But sometimes I stop here and I think that Raskolnikov crossed this bridge on his way to the university." He patted the balustrade with his palm. "He was contemplating the murder of the vicious old pawnbroker, thinking certainly he had a choice."

"He was driven by other demons, Leon. You are a scientist, driven by curiosity, and by passion. You know that what you do is important, even if others do not acknowledge it. You want to find out what Van Weathers also wants to find out, what caused the Maya to disappear as they did. We will find out together. I believe this. You are not Raskolnikov. You are not going to murder an old woman, Leon."

"Of course not." Leon's mood swerved suddenly. He laughed heartily and clapped Alberto on the back. "Of course not, Alberto. But now, you see, I cross this bridge every day, too. We are brothers, Raskolnikov and I, crossing over."

"*Certo!*" Alfredo answered. "We are all brothers in sin, wouldn't you say?"

"No, I would *not* say," Leon declared stoutly. "I am good citizen of former Soviet Union. Or good former citizen of Soviet Union. We are atheist, and do not believe in sin, only in the people."

There was little traffic along the University Embankment. Even the scattered fall of snow seemed meager and withholding.

"How *can* we believe in sin?" Leon asked, pausing to watch a Mercedes sedan glide past a large billboard advertising an American soft drink. The car moved in near silence over the light dusting of snow, windows smoked over and darkness within. "We live in a time when only the gangsters have functioning cars."

"That's the very best time to believe in sin," Bofonchio replied. "I know. Italy has experience."

"Yes, yes, we thank you for Catholic Church and Mafia. Very nice, gifts to world."

"No sense being sarcastic. We are all in this together, Leon. I will tell you something I tell almost no one: my older brother, he is a priest, and that is because our father worked for the Mafia, as you call it. I think this is why I am interested in the social institutions, in class and religion and rule. It is why I study the Maya."

"Because we too are headed for collapse? We see CNN. CNN caused the collapse of Soviet Union. Now maybe the rest of the world will follow us, hah?"

"You and I, Leon, we are not so interested in the Soviet Union. Forget the Soviet Union."

"Ah," Leon said, tossing the tiny stub of his cigarette into a rill of plowed snow beside the road, "you are right, of course. I will forget, soon enough. If only. . . ."

Alberto reached up to punch Leon's upper arm, a comradely gesture. "Old socialists, Leon. We're just old socialists caught in history's backwater. Van Weathers's project is opening. We'll go through his Gate, you and I. We will go back in time, forget all this, forget socialism, forget capitalism. Van will succeed, and we will be with him. He is going to collect data on social exchange, a huge database of information flowing through a social system. His students, and ours if we want, will all participate. It will be a grand social experiment. Gramsci would have loved it. I'm sure it would prove his point about the hegemony of the elites. . . ."

"Not that again, Alberto, please. Enough of your socialism, your class revolt, your beloved Antonio Gramsci and his *ordine nuovo*! Have I not lived through all that?" Leon made a sweeping gesture. "Just look around you."

Alberto laughed. "All right, all right. But in the simulation we're going to see decision points, Leon, moments of small, insignificant decisions that lead to enormous consequences."

"You think so?" Leon seemed surprised, as if the thought were new to him. "You think he will succeed with this? That we will participate? I'm not so sure, you know. Perhaps he should have stayed with his dig, that vast empty city of Xultunich. He would have found evidence of elite mismanagement, I'm sure. I've seen enough of it myself, here in the old soviet, the new republic. It may be he will look a fool, a man who is, what is the word? Quixotical. This simulation might just be a windmill after all."

Alberto was not interested in Leon's doubts. "You must not think this way, Leon. It's exciting, this experiment. Isn't it true of experiments that most of them fail? Even if he fails, we will have learned a lot." He bounced up and down on his toes in sudden excitement. "I know who I will be, Leon, and what I will try to do. Do you? Do you know who you will be?"

"Do I know who I will be? Oh, yes, I believe I do know. I have read his prospectus carefully. I know the characters. I am interested in settlement patterns, in migration, as you know. But I will not tell you precisely who I will be, Alberto." The Russian stopped to shake his finger at the Italian. "Not even you. We must be anonymous in this place. I know at least it will be interesting. Even, perhaps, as you say, useful. My American friends have given me an old computer. It is in this building here, in my office. Academy of Sciences, you see, they give me office. No job, but office anyway. In building designed by Giacomo Quarenghi, in 1783."

"Italian?"

"Sure, why not? Nice building. Needs repair, but nice building. Better to have job, but office in a nice building is good anyway." Leon's voice trailed off with his grammar. They pushed through the doors.

His office, down a series of halls, was narrow and tall. Leon turned on the lights and grunted with surprise when they actually worked. "There, see. Computer, and tonight, electricity. Perhaps phone lines also work, we can enter into Internet, what do you think? Sure, why not?"

Soon a message appeared to inform him that the Xibalbá Gate was almost open. Leon leaned back and lit a cigarette with a sigh. "I am sending Van Weathers another electronic mail. I'm asking when Gate will be open for you and I. I want to get in, Alberto, as much as you do. Of course I have doubts, but this is my only chance, you see. I want to find out what happened, and also, perhaps, to leave for a time this desolate world in which we live."

GREEN ROOM

The programmer was waiting for Van and Gordon outside Van's office, popping the tips of his fingers together with a snap of his wrist. The silver-capped toes of his cowboy boots winked brilliant highlights. "Ready for prime time," he said. His T-shirt advertised a rock group with a graphic of baroque intertwinings, vaguely organic and suggestive of illicit sexuality. "Oh, ho, Professor Weathers."

"Yes, Wendell, prime time. How're the sims?" Van frowned at his office door, half turned away from his programming assistant. "That's funny," he muttered.

"The sims? The sims are good," Wendell replied. "Real good, if I do say so. What's funny?"

"Nothing," Van shrugged, wondering as always at the younger man's carefully maintained physical resemblance to the lead singer of his T-shirt's popular rock group. He was twenty-five years old and spoke in the rushed baritone of a television evangelist. "The lock looks different, that's all."

"Oh, OK, but the sims? Well, you know, we call them 'bots,' like in robots, see? We spent a lot of time working on personality tables, question responses, social roles and behaviors, you know. They hang around, waiting for a real person to do something. It looks like they're doing things, ordinary things. Real things."

"Who's 'we'?" Van asked.

"Oh, I mean me, of course." Wendell shook his head, and shoulder-length hair flew in dark spirals. "God, I'm good." He wiggled his fingers in front of Van's face, typing air code. His enormous self-confidence may have been combined with an astounding lack of social grace, but he didn't lie. Every day the simulated population of Van's Maya world had grown more real, more fully fleshed, more passionate about their lives. "Come on." Wendell jiggled now from foot to foot, impatient to get in. "I want to show you the final Gate."

"The Gate? First I have to get into the office. Looks like they've changed the lock again. Maintenance is always doing that and not telling me." Van touched bright brass with a spatulate forefinger, spelled out the brand: Primus.

Wendell bobbed his head. "Yeah, looks new."

Van turned the handle and pushed the door open. "At least I won't have to call maintenance this time to let me in."

The office: shelves to the ceiling along the left wall, filled with books, many of them old, including Van's pride, an original 1841 first edition of

John Lloyd Stephens's two-volume *Incidents of Travel in Central America, Chiapas and Yucatan*, with hand-tinted illustrations by Frederick Catherwood, the book that had introduced the mystery of the Maya to the world. His edition had been personally inscribed by Stephens to Charles Darwin. A wide case for maps. A cabinet holding carousels of old-fashioned slides. A metal desk. On the right a long trestle table, covered with paper, maps, ceramic sherds, drawings of carvings, a reproduction of a figurine of a woman seated cross-legged, giving birth, inverted child emerging. Already Wendell was at the computer, bringing the large flat screen to life. The Xibalbá Gate, doorway into the Maya underworld, appeared, the shape of a mountain mouth, a *witz* cave opening framed by monstrous skeletal serpent jaws, bones bleached by the office light.

Gordon clapped the younger man on the back. "Congratulations, Wendell. This is the big day, what you two have worked for. Why isn't our esteemed chairman here?"

"Come on, Gord," Van said, taking Wendell's place at the computer. "This is my project. There's really no need for our colleagues to attend. Anyway, the chairman's in Tulsa—'Gender Identity among the Plains Indians.' The associate chair is home with a cold."

"And Dr. Jones, of course, is away."

"He sent a note." Van gave a brief laugh. "This is it, Wendell, the big day."

"Yes, sir." Wendell leaned over Van's chair, watching the professor's fingers stroke the keys. "Try it out."

Van clicked on the jaws and entered the Green Room. Here the final refinements of transition allowed guests to create a persona: gender, age, social class, height and weight, and personal adornment. He could be a peasant farmer or an artisan, a merchant, or a ruler—with the proper password for elite rank. "I'll just be a junior member of the elite this time," he said, making selections from a menu.

It was a little like suiting up for a deepwater dive, this donning of identity and form to pass through the Xibalbá Gate into the Maya underworld, land of the Nine Lords of Death and all the dark forces, shadow image of the thirteen nested spheres of the Upper World, the one above this one.

Once he had approved his appearance, he was ready. One click and the Green Room disappeared, darkness swirled across the screen and dissolved to a place of his choosing in the Middle World. To any others, sitting like himself at computer terminals somewhere on earth (minds now spun together through the tangled mesh of fiber-optic cable, copper phone wire, satellites, and microwaves), he would simply walk into the scene from around a bend in the trail or the corner of a building.

"Look," he said, and Gordon leaned over his shoulder. They could see fields and mountains lost in distant haze and smoke, for this was burning season and the farmers were clearing the hillsides. There was a sense of life and activity, of *reality*, even though the mountains were still sketched in crude polygons at the edges.

"You can't see yourself?" Gordon asked.

"Not unless you look in a mirror. It's a first-person experience for everyone who enters."

"Must use a lot of storage space."

"Yes, I suppose. Not my department." Van used the mouse to look around. On his left, a river surged and swirled in a brown, hard pull. Wendell's long finger tapped on an enormous stone outcropping. "There," he said. "The caves are under that outcropping."

"You put in the burials?"

"Sure. Two hundred skeletons, all ages, women, children. They've been calcifying in the damp for hundreds of years, some of them. People come here to worship their ancestors. If you watch the cave long enough, someone will show up."

"You're good, Wendell. Really good." Van walked along the river, and there was a farmer.

The man on the screen rolled his eyes up and away. "It's hard to believe this's just a graphic construct," Van muttered. "I mean, the detail is weak but the movement looks real, not like a cartoon at all. Looks almost like video."

"Yeah!" He could hear Wendell preen. "The detail's getting better all the time. The trick's creating eye algorithms, see." Wendell snapped his fingers as if it was easy.

The peasant dipped the gourd into a large clay pot and offered it to Van, who typed the necessary instructions to take the drink. "You are of the city of Xultunich, of Last Stone?" The man spoke humbly, eyes cast down.

"English?" Gordon asked.

"Yes. It would be nice if we were all fluent in Maya, but we have to make some compromises. Most participants will understand English."

Gordon was entranced. "This is amazing. How'd you do the voices? Text to speech?"

Wendell laughed. "Cool, huh? Getting a hint of Maya accent was a good trick, but I really like the effect."

Van couldn't see himself, but he knew the farmer had recognized he was a man of royal blood.

"Watch," Van said. "He's observed I'm from Xultunich. So I'll answer 'Yes.'" Van typed and his voice said the word. He drank and handed the gourd cup back. Smoke filled the sky. Van's sense of presence in the Real World was fading. He was only dimly aware that he was typing his answers to the sim's comments and hearing them spoken.

"You are far from the city," the man said.

"Yes. And you," Van replied. "What of the crop this year?"

Van could feel Wendell, bent over his back, breathing into his creation. The man on screen looked up at the burning hills. Flame glowed fitfully through the blowing smoke. "Not good," he said at last. "The ancestor-gods do not bring enough water. There could be hungry people in the towns. Again," he added.

"Hungry people," Van repeated. He looked up at Wendell. "He blames the king."

The programmer grinned and tossed his hair back. "Too many people, eh?" he said. "King has to take the heat."

An old woman approached them along the narrow path, bent almost double under a load of wood for the tamale fires and copal-incense burners of Xultunich. She passed the two men without glancing their way and disappeared into the trees, her passage marked by a sudden uneasy chatter of monkeys among the leaves.

The farmer hooked his gourd onto his rope belt, picked up his hoe stick and clay water jug with a nod, and walked away toward the hillside, leaving Van alone beside the swirling brown water.

For a time, nothing further happened. Van sat with his fingers poised over the keyboard, waiting. There was smoke-smell, river noise, an increasingly oppressive humidity.

"Check out the town," Wendell said, breaking into Van's seductive reverie.

"OK." He lowered his fingers and walked. The path was marked by bare footprints in the mud of yesterday's meager shower. The old woman's, Van thought. Her feet were small, splayed from years of endless walking, bent low under the weight of wood. And every year she had farther to go for it.

But she, too, was a simulacrum, a scrap of code.

The town sprawled, an incoherent jumble of buildings and paths, houses and storerooms. Only the central plaza and the seven pyramids beyond it were laid out in anything that looked like order.

Peasants, those not engaged in burning and so freed from the fields, were at work plastering the lower steps of the Pyramid of the Ancestors, glowing white in the afternoon sun. Nearer the top of the central temple, they were painting the building the dark brick color called Maya red. On the thirty-foot roof comb above the temple, the seated Lord, shaped in high stucco relief, looked over the city. The Lord's face vaguely suggested Van Weathers's.

"Nice touch," he said. "Making the Ancestor look a little like me but not be me." He tapped the EXIT key and the program winked out, leaving a dull, gray screen.

Wendell's fingers were popping, as they always did when he was excited. "The artist used your picture, flattened and distorted it. Anyways, the world's fully functional. You see how fuckin'-A good the 'bots are, though? You see that?"

"Yes, Wendell, the sims are amazingly real."

"Yeah. See, when others, real people, I mean, are in there, they'll have bodies, too. You won't be able to tell the real people from the sims, I bet, not easily, anyhow. By the way, reminds me, you got another message from that St. Petersburg guy, Blatskoi. He's real anxious to get in, wants to know when it's gonna be open for business."

So Wendell was reading Van's mail. "Leon's a leader in his field, Wendell. Even though he's never left Russia, he knows more about settlement patterns than anyone else on the planet."

"Yeah, I'm sorry, I guess I prolly shouldn't'a read your emails, but the icon was blinking like it was important, you know?"

"We can tell our comrade by the Neva he can log on any time he wants. We're officially open."

"By the way," Wendell added, "you're gonna need a new password. Just a friendly word of advice. Not your wife's name, that's real obvious."

"I'll keep that in mind, Wendell," Van said dryly. He switched off the computer and pulled a pad of Post-its across the desk. He wrote: NEW PASSWORD and stuck the scrap of paper to the side of the monitor.

"Thanks, Wendell. It's looking really good. The culture's under stress, crops failing, population up. They're susceptible, so maybe we'll find out what did them in after all. Make sure all the students in my Communications and Texts seminar get log-in instructions." It was a dismissal, but Wendell kept popping his fingers. Van stared at him. "Thanks, Wendell," he repeated.

"Oh. Yeah. I was just going." Wendell shuffled sideways to the door, leaving rubber streaks on the vinyl. He fingered the inside of Van's new lock a moment, popping the set button in and out a couple of times. Then he gave a little wave, pulled the door open, and walked into Elliot Blackman's fist in the midst of knocking. It hit Wendell's nose, and the programmer fell back, reaching for his face.

"Sorry," Elliot said. "Are you all right?"

"Right," Wendell said, his voice a bit muffled. "Doe Probleb." He hurried away. Van and Gordon looked at each other for a long moment, holding their faces very carefully together.

"Sorry to interrupt, Dr. Weathers. I just wondered if you had noticed the new lock on your door."

"Yes, I did."

"Well, you'll have to come by for a new key. Meanwhile I left it unlocked. So you could get in, you see."

"Yes, I see. I'll come down in a few minutes."

Elliot nodded. "Right. Sure. My office is in the basement. Near the computer lab. I'll be waiting." He backed from the room.

Van and Gordon stared at one another. Finally, a brief snort from Van settled the matter. "Doe probleb," he said.

THE KEY

Elliot walked along the polished basement corridor, the crepe of his shoe soles squeaking a stuttering code from an insect land. Scree-scree, scree-

scree. Someone is coming, someone is going. Under your hand, under your foot. Scree-scree.

Van Weathers, alone, preoccupied, hurried, perplexed, emerged from the elevator. Elliot waited by his office door.

"Your first name's Elliot, isn't it?" Van asked.

"That's right. Nice of you to remember. Maintenance foreman for Crowley Hall. You need anything, you let me know."

"That's nice, Elliot, I'll keep that in mind." Van hesitated. "Right now it's about the lock, Elliot."

"Yes, Dr. Weathers, the lock. The locks are new, you see. Primus. Highest security. Side-bit milling, special code, only good in this building."

"You told me to see you about a key, Elliot. I can't lock my door. If I do, I can't get back in my office."

"That's correct," Elliot agreed. "You can't lock it. You should have a key."

Professor Weathers stood patiently.

"Come with me," Elliot said. He unlocked his own office door (security level two, not the highest, but pretty good) and snapped on the light. Van watched from the doorway as the maintenance man opened a cabinet on the left and removed a key. There was something about the man. Van couldn't quite put his finger on it. Something unreliable? Or something familiar? He looked ordinary enough, medium build, bit of a pot belly, short-cropped gray hair. Was he too friendly, too eager to please?

He relocked the cabinet and sat at his desk to fill out a series of forms, which he presented to Van for signature, social security number, and mother's maiden name. He made Van show his faculty card, with picture. "You lose the key, you got to sign for a new lock, new key, new code. With proper ID. And forfeit the deposit charged to your faculty account. Sorry about that, Dr. Weathers."

"I'll keep that in mind," Van said, wondering if he heard a special emphasis on the word *doctor*.

He shrugged, pocketed the key, and set off down the hall past the door to the computer room. To Elliot Blackman standing in the light cast from his office, clear as the sharp and pungent tang of Saniclor, the pinkish flesh tone of Van's hand vanishing into his pocket left an afterimage smear as he walked toward the stairway door.

PASSWORD

The lean bones of the serpent jaw seemed to flow like water over a small
dam as a slow, wet line crawled up the screen in syncopation with the
fluorescent lights. Van's fingertips supported him on the edge of the desk.
When he leaned forward, he saw the yellow Post-it where it had fallen
beside the monitor: NEW PASSWORD.

It was getting late and Glenna was having her sister for dinner, but this
was an essential piece of housekeeping. If he didn't do it now, he'd probably forget for another month or something, and if someone got in under
his password they could screw things up, undo what he had done. They
could make deals he didn't know about, maybe kill someone important,
all the time pretending to be him or, rather, Knot-Eye, ruler of Xultunich.
He sat down again and stared at the screen, where the flow of electrons
usually seemed so orderly until he got close and the pixels dissolved. He
hunched his shoulders, tensing the muscles at the nape of his neck, and
quickly typed: Password.

Do you wish to change your password?

Yes.

Are you sure?

Yes.

Please type your old password.

Glenna.

Please type your new password.

The cursor blinked, waiting. Behind this tidy dialog, the mouth of the
earth was open. Fangs curled inward, toward the darkness. Once in, he
might never get out again.

He typed: KAAHHUB. It meant "the fall of the town." It was the closest
he could come to "social collapse" in his halting Yucatec Maya.

Please enter your new password again.

The screen said Thank You when he hit the return key. Use your new
password the next time you enter the Xibalbá Gate.

He wrote his password on a new Post-it and stuck it inside his copy of
the *Dresden Codex*. He entered the Green Room and started to set up his
persona.

He had, of course, already picked his name and role. Knot-Eye was in
part a description of the glyph that made up the name, profile head with

complex winding around the eye, and partly a pun, for when he entered this world he would be not I, but someone else entirely.

Unlike the tall and angular twentieth-century Van Weathers, he would be a squat man with too much starch in his diet, though for his day Knot-Eye was a formidable elite ruler with the best of everything at his command. His adornments, his diet, his command of labor, all would mark him as a pivotal figure, a man of middle years with a strong, curved nose and dark, rather thoughtful eyes. He would wear the elaborately twisted breech cloth of a noble, mostly concealed by a cape of multicolored, woven cotton. His hair would be bound with a netted band of shell and paper, which in honor of the Maize God would extend loosely to the back like the tassels of an ear of corn. Earflares and some tattooed dots on his body to represent the jaguar spots important to his lineage would complete his appearance.

Such a figure would stand out, attract the attention of others, including those real people participating in the world around Xultunich. They would be drawn to him, but at least for the early stages of the simulation Van believed it was important he have legitimate reasons to exercise control inside the world, just in case. When he wasn't online, his sim would be sleeping, or eating, or on a journey. When he was present, he could act. Other participants might suspect he was playing the part, but they could never be certain.

Van finished and leaned back with a sigh. Time to go home. He stared for a long moment at the dark pulse of the crawling line going slowly up the screen, over and over. It seemed to be trying to pull him in.

Well, just for a few minutes, he thought.

younger man are high-relief sculptures. One is a seated figure of Lord Itzamná, ruler of the sky, patron god of the lineage and of the sacred hieroglyphic writing that binds the people together; the other is One Monkey, fathermother of them all, first ancestor, falling face down from the skybird beak. The carved front of the sleeping bench is barely visible in the dim light inside, but Knot-Eye can read the carved glyphs that tell of the setting of this house, its date and place in the round of years.

Reed Altar has grown powerful of late. Van can see, in the way he stands with his arms crossed, clasping his biceps, and in the set of his legs, one a little in front of the other, that the twenty men standing around him will jump at his word. In the background, smoke rises from the fires where slaves are preparing the evening meal. Reed Altar is saying, in his posture and motionlessness, that he can now command the labor of many able men.

Such power in one so young and distant from the city is dangerous, but there is little Knot-Eye can do. Distant rumors of unrest and war come closer, and as lineage head he needs all the allies he can find.

It has happened before, of course. There are times when the gods demand more. There are always times when royal blood must fall onto bark paper, rise as smoke, transform into the vision serpent, when the ruler must perform the most potent rituals and dance before the people in order to call the ancestors and gods to the Middle World and enlist their aid.

Knot-Eye planned such a ceremony, something to restore the people's trust. His first wife, Lady Fin, has produced no heir to carry on the lineage, and a marriage with Evening Star of Green Mountain could be the salvation of the city. With enough ceremony, an impressive enough public display, enough sacrifice and bloodletting, this wedding could bind Green Mountain closer to Xultunich, bringing as well the corn and rich hunting of the Green Mountain vicinity. An alliance with Green Mountain could place one more city between Xultunich and the warriors of distant Waterbird River, the city near the sea.

"What do you say?" Reed Altar asks in the traditional greeting.

"Only this. I have walked far to speak with you."

"You have walked far," Reed Altar agrees. "You, my father's brother, have walked far. Knot-Eye wants me to help him find a new wife."

"Not any new wife, Reed Altar. Evening Star, daughter of Quetzal Tree, ruler of Green Mountain. I, Knot-Eye, have need of a new wife."

"Ahh." Reed Altar draws his breath in through his teeth. "This I know, but Knot-Eye must understand it won't be easy. Things have not been well between my mother's city of Green Mountain and the great polity Xultunich. There is bad blood. It will take much."

"*Saa*. It is known that it will take much."

Reed Altar dips his head, but his eyes neither blink nor look away. "The rulers of Waterbird River have been to Green Mountain," he says carefully. "They have spoken to Green Mountain's king."

Knot-Eye has heard this, and Reed Altar clearly knows that he has, and so he has revealed nothing. He is playing a game of nerves, nothing more, but this is a bad sign. Knot-Eye lowers his chin, thoughtful. "How much will it take?" he asks at last.

Reed Altar looks at the sky, where he can see the answer. "Twenty highborn captives. A blood ceremony. A hundred sacks of cacao." He shrugs. "Much."

Knot-Eye tugs his lower lip. "For captives, we must go to war. This will take some time. A month?"

Reed Altar looks at the declining sun, an indefinite blob in the smoke. Finally, he nods. "All right. One *winal*. If her father, my mother's brother, agrees, I will bring Evening Star in twenty days. In one *winal* there will be a great ceremony. Evening Star will bring the stingray spines and green obsidian. This is very important. She will bring them. So I, Reed Altar, declare."

"That is generous. The father-ancestor will be pleased. One Monkey will come, will show his gratitude. One Monkey will be there, at the wedding."

Reed Altar lowers his head. "It is the least we could do to help midwife such a great alliance. My messenger will run; he will be in Green Mountain by nightfall."

Knot-Eye lowers his head in assent and turns back. He walks for some time among the small plots of maize, past the simple stone and thatch houses of the farmers, and soon is passing through the elite residential district on the outskirts of Xultunich. He admires the low houses built around the open family courtyards, the kitchens and storage buildings. Soon he enters the ceremonial center of the city, where the king performs rituals on the top platforms of the highest pyramids to harmonize the universe, where the king gives of his blood to honor the ancestors and to call up the vision serpent, to call up the ancestors themselves, where the king raises the tree stones honoring his lineage and all he has done for the city. After a time, he stops to watch the plasterers at work on the great plaza. They bow their heads deferentially and continue working, their wooden trowels making a scraping sound. One of the plasterers looks up at him, his eyes squinted against the sun.

At that moment Flint Howler, scribe and shaman of Xultunich, approaches and greets his king. Knot-Eye requests new feathered headdresses and backracks, and tells him the date.

"It will be 10 Ak'bal 6 Xul," Knot-Eye says, reckoning on his fingers. "10 Ak'bal 6 Xul is not an auspicious date for a wedding. I will set the date to 4 Ajaw 8 Kumk'u, the beginning date of this cycle of the world."

Flint Howler pulls in his lower lip. "4 Ajaw 8 Kumk'u came around last winter, only five *winals* ago. For you to set the wedding date to a past time, and such a recent one, could be dangerous. Time began on the first 4 Ajaw 8 Kumk'u of them all."

Knot-Eye interrupts. "Tell the Council I have decided." He softens his tone. "It is a risk we must take, Flint Howler. This could be a most important event for our city, for all the Middle World."

Flint Howler nods his agreement and backs away from his king.

This wedding should keep the Council of nobles loyal to his family; they will feel safer with Green Mountain blocking the path of Waterbird River's ambitions. He will show his power, and they will wait. Perhaps they are curious; perhaps they believe. Knot-Eye hopes they believe.

Yet he can feel the end coming; he can smell the burning timbers, taste the dust, see the scattered bone. In another realm called the Real World, he has created this one to be poised on the very edge of extinction. He would like to stop the end, to change this history, but he clearly sees: only a few squatters will huddle in the decaying temples and aristocratic homes, the only people left in the city. They will sit around their tiny fires and remember the days of glory. Then, slowly, they will forget.

He does not want this to happen, and so he will set the calendar back to the sacred day of 4 Ajaw 8 Kumk'u, which comes only once every fifty-two years.

In the shadows beyond the reach of their fires' light the animal spirits will watch in silence, waiting.

Knot-Eye, seventeenth descendant of One Monkey, fathermother of them all, first ancestor and founder of the lineage, turns and climbs the grand stairway of the central pyramid of the holy city of Xultunich, called Last Stone, where he is king.

13 K'an 2 Ch'en

Tuesday, September 13
The Long Count date is 12.19.12.11.4
It has been 1,869,344 days since the Maya Zero Date
The calendar round date is 13 K'an 2 Ch'en
Moon is 2 days old
God 8 rules the night

VAN AT HOME

Later that night, Van, alone in the bathroom amid the gilt and mirrors, tugged on the skin beneath his eye. He sniffed and let go; the skin snapped back and he could frown.

Soon enough, he would go downstairs to have dinner with Glenna's sister, Mary. She was Mary of the appraising eye, the appraiser of real estate, arriving with the latest in her series of men, on display for family approval. Van remembered that the new fellow's name was Foster; he was a curator at the museum where Glenna worked.

He could imagine the conversation. They would discuss Glenna's paintings, her upcoming exhibition. They would avoid talking about Mary's ex-husband, Robert. He was the source of alimony, but otherwise taboo. Mary would cling to Foster as they went out the door. No doubt he would experience her firsthand afterward.

Van's watch read 8:40, September 13. The digital seconds pulsed. He leaned down to stare into the whorled marble pattern of the bowl. The drain made a round chrome O that led to darkness, a portal into the Otherworld. Hot water made a vortex, clockwise around the opening.

He turned it off, stopping the white noise. The last of it drained away. He imagined pipes, sewers, the treatment plant, the outflow to the sea, a system that connected this house with all others. Flow through the system could grow turbulent, curl on itself, eddy, and tumble, chaotic, unquantifiable, complex.

Smiling, he turned sideways naked and saw belly and shoulders slumped forward. Before him, he knew, untold billions of other men, vexed at time's handiwork, had done the same. He sucked in his stomach, turned his head left and looked again at his infinite reflection to right and left, endless naked Vans in overlapping distortion, moving in rippling sequence as he leaned toward them, watching slyly from the edge of his eye. Glenna needed this nest of mirrors. He found this poignant, her need for reassurance. She often said, "I need to know."

Mentally he answered with his own question: Don't we all? Water evaporated slowly from the surface of the marble sink, little molecules bumping one another in the air. History. Jones was always saying history was made up of countless random events, each one small in itself, but adding up. He dressed, satisfied enough with his reflections.

JAG'S ROOM

Later, after Mary had left clinging to Foster's arm and Glenna was sipping a glass of water in the kitchen, Van stood in Jag's doorway watching his son sleep, thin chest rising and falling slowly. On the boy's computer screen, Mickey Mouse in wizard cap swung a broom back and forth across the dark while Tinkerbell scattered stardust. Did they populate his dreams? Did their latent memories reassure him if he awoke in the night?

Van remembered a younger Jag, slender arms inside his grasp, light bones that flexed as Van lifted him into the air. That was years ago. Now he was fifteen; he had more heft, more mass and muscle, yet he still seemed like a child.

A bar of light splashed across the dark blue pile carpet and rose along the built-in drawers of Jag's bunk bed before falling once more across his chest and chin. His hand lay outside the blanket, slightly curved long fingers rising with his breath and subsiding again.

This was the heir, the sum of all their genes and hopes, the knot of Van and Glenna Weathers tied into flesh. The boy's fingers, curled over the satin edge of a blanket, would hold his own child one day. One day, Van thought. Many days, but *one* day, some indefinite moment in the future. Van felt a pressure in his chest and backed from the room. He closed the door.

The world in which he lived, in which they all lived, was full of uncertainties. For a moment, he was struck that Jag was in some terrible danger, though he could not imagine quite what it could be.

1 Imix 19 Yax

Thursday, October 20
The Long Count date is 12.19.12.13.1
It has been 1,869,381 days since the Maya Zero Date
The calendar round date is 1 Imix 19 Yax
Moon is 16 days old
God 9 rules the night

FROM AO TO VW: CONNECTIONS

Professor Weathers,

I hope you don't mind, but I had to tell you not only how much I enjoy the course—you are one of the most impressive teachers I have ever had here at the university—but that your book *Graphic Communication and the Structure of History* clarifies the deepest nature of human discourse in a way my professors in the Linguistics Department never have.

I feel as if there is some kind of connection between us. What do you think? Do you believe that someone's thoughts, ideas, and words can leave traces in the mind that become a kind of beachhead or outpost, a permanent presence? History leaves its traces, certainly, so why not the more direct person-to-person acts of speech, or text? I carry you, a representative of you, in my mind at all times now so you are with me wherever I go. This may sound metaphysical, but it is very real, I assure you.

Sincerely,
Anne Opple

THE LAND BRIDGE

She was in front as always. She had read the *Popol Vuh* and could talk at length about the Hero Twins and First Father, who died and came back to life.

She was a damn good student, perhaps the best he'd ever had.

Van gave her a little bow as he dropped his papers on the table by the lectern. She smiled, and it was radiant, that smile. He had to look away from the years of orthodontics aglow between her plump lips; he thought of Campion's lines:

> Those cherries fairly do enclose
> Of orient pearl a double row
> Which when her lovely laughter shows
> They look like rosebuds filled with snow.

Even her nose ring was attractive. He took covert peeks at it as he unpacked his lecture notes. He glanced at Charles slouching in his chair, ponytail dangling over the back, tilted against the wall beneath the window. Crowley Hall had very narrow windows. No danger of Charles falling out.

"Xibalbá," he began, leaning over the lectern, "is the place of fear. To get there you must go down the Black Road. The Black Road is easy to travel, lined with flowers. It's so easy to travel down, except that it leads into darkness. You must cross Blood River and Pus River to the place of fear, the Otherworld, which is ruled by the Lords of Xibalbá. Do you know them, their names and attributes? Mr. McGuirk?"

Charles dropped the legs of his chair to the floor with a snap. "One Death," he offered.

Van gave a slow smile. "Go on."

"Uh. Seven Death, I think."

"Very good, Mr. McGuirk. How many Lords are there?"

"Nine? But the *Popol Vuh* mentions twelve."

This boy did his homework. Van nodded. "Good. Why do you think that is, that there are nine Lords of the Underworld, and twelve named in the *Popol Vuh?*"

Van could see Anne squirming in her seat. Her arms were hugged tightly to her breast, to keep the answers in. But Charles had a theory. "The *Popol Vuh* was written down after the Spanish Conquest," he said. "An origin myth, the story of the Hero Twins playing some kind of ball game with the Lords of the underworld and the making of mankind.

Seems a little bit like Genesis, but stranger. Anyway, it was very late. Could be Christian, of course, after the twelve apostles. But the book is from the highlands. Quiché Maya, not lowland. They may have had a slightly different mythology. And the Nine Lords, maybe the Nine Lords of the Night, not necessarily Xibalbá."

Van was impressed. The boy was pretty good, but he knew if he had asked Anne she would have known the answer as well. Thank God, he thought, it was now time for what he called The Disillusionment Lecture.

"You are interested in the Native Americans," he began softly. He saw it every semester, the students' hopeful, green idealism. "I will tell you about them, the ancestors of the Maya and all the other indigenous peoples of the Western Hemisphere."

He dimmed the lights, and images flashed on the screen behind him, almost too fast to follow: maps of the Western Hemisphere, diagrams of migration routes, zones of tribal culture, mammoths and saber-toothed tigers, men squatting around fires, men knapping flint spear points. The images sometimes illustrated what he was saying, and sometimes the relationship was not clear.

"We don't yet know for certain, but perhaps thirteen or fourteen thousand years ago, when the last Ice Age was ending, their ancestors came across the land bridge of the Bering Strait, many small waves of hungry *homo sapiens* following the caribou herds. Though it is controversial, it's possible they came in successive waves of different peoples, Asiatics, Caucasians (judging by Kennewick Man, a 9,200-year-old skull found on the banks of the Columbia River in 1996), and one theory of the origins of Olmec sculpture suggests an African origin, though no one really believes this one. Still, this hemisphere has always been diverse. Some of them took up fishing and settled along the coasts. Others were hunters and gatherers—the men, most likely, doing the hunting and the women gathering as they moved, not with purpose, not with any sense they were on a grand adventure, that they were discovering a new land. They came upon two new continents completely empty of others of their kind but thought they were merely following the food, most of them, which happened to turn right at the land bridge instead of left into the vast emptiness of what we now call Siberia.

"They picked off the sick, the old, the young. They butchered as best they could, ate what they needed, and moved on, leaving behind a trail of rotting carcasses.

"It was a long migration for these small-boned people—long, difficult, and deadly. They were cold. They were often hungry. They fell sick, or prey to the big cats and other predators, to weather and the dangerous footing of the rock and ice, to the unpredictable shaking of the earth itself. And so, as they wandered, many of their bones lay beside the carrion they had left for vultures and crows and the other scavengers who were, in turn, following them.

"Cold summers and colder winters passed. They came to a hard, wide place of stone and riverbeds, granite outcroppings, and frozen tundra, and after that a huge wall of ice. Some turned back, only to find the way now blocked by ice and snow. So they settled down to wait, near starvation and always cold as the generations came and went. The great wall of ice before them seemed smaller each year, and then one spring an opening appeared, and they went on, a thin trickle of human beings walking into a limitless world filled with food. This was the greatest larder human beings had ever encountered in the hundred thousand years or so we had been a species."

Van leaned forward over the lectern. Every year it was the same, this tragic story repeated. Yet every year he felt the same intensity, the same glory and sadness. Every year he could see the endless plains rolling before him, rippling with grasses, dotted thickly with animal life as unafraid and placid as stones. He was, every year, compelled to make them see.

"Families of huge mammoths watched and died without curiosity as these people killed them, ate, and moved on, following their old ways. Beyond the next hill, in the next valley, there were always more mammoths, more giant, slow-moving animals for the people to kill and eat.

"They had children, and they died, and their children had children. And always they moved on.

"At roughly eight miles per year they spread out and moved south, killing the large mammals. There were always more animals just ahead, a week, a month, a season beyond where they were.

"The climate grew warmer as the migration progressed. They passed through desert, moving swiftly. They crossed mountain ranges and reached the sea, where they learned to fish. They encountered jungle. Some remained, and others moved on.

"Within a thousand years or so the people were spread from the Arctic circle to the tip of South America.

"In that thousand years, the first people on this side of the planet found that all the large mammals were gone. There were no more mammoths, no more giant sloths, or giant beavers, or horses or camels anywhere on the two continents, and the land bridge back to Siberia was gone, drowned in rising oceans. The people who had come on the vast migration covered the continents with their children and their children's children, scattered across the tundra and desert and jungle.

"With nowhere more to go, they settled, living with what was left of the land, the smaller animals like the deer and the buffalo. Slowly their numbers grew. They now had to make do with less. The herds that once had stared at them without comprehension as they speared them or frightened them into running off a cliff were no more."

He paused. Ms. Opple was staring at him open-mouthed. He read anxiety in her eyes. She would not care for this little talk. But her disappointment in the Native Americans was not nearly so great as that of Charles beside her. *He* looked angry.

Van went on. "As the people's numbers grew, food was scarcer and more difficult to find. The old ways no longer sufficed.

"Some discovered that if they gathered seeds of the teosinte (an image of a tiny grain appeared on the screen) and put them in the ground, they could gather the small cobs. Selective breeding increased the yields over centuries. Because teosinte can pop like today's popcorn, shares a similar life cycle to maize, and is genetically similar, it is presumed to be the ancestor of corn. So they began to settle in one place, cutting the forest with stone tools and burning the slash, then planting the seeds. When the land would not produce enough food, they moved a short distance away, going, over the years, in circles of burning and planting. And so they lived for thousands of years longer, slowly filling in the empty spaces of the land with human beings. Over the generations, the people grew shorter in life and stature, though they did not notice this; it happened too slowly. At the same time, the cobs of maize grew larger, until these people began to think of themselves as the People of Maize, descended from maize, children of the God of Maize, the Maya.

"They put up shelters, some of them, those in the rain forests. Collections of huts formed into villages which grew along river banks, in the valleys, in the high lands around lakes. The huts grew more permanent, with hard floors and thatch roofs.

"And soon the villages had kings, and the kings had power, and stone cities grew, and on limestone slabs before their ever-growing temples the kings proclaimed their greatness in the carved pictures of their writing so that priests could read of their power to the people. Their civilization became complex, and changed because of that complexity."

Charles had been stirring uneasily, and now he had his hand forced into the air, closed into a fist. Van paused. "Yes, Mr. McGuirk?"

"Professor Weathers, are you saying that the Native Americans, the first people here, ruined their environment? That they killed off the big mammals? That they did not live in harmony with the earth? Is that what you're saying?"

"Why, yes, Mr. McGuirk, that is exactly what I'm saying. They were human beings and behaved as such. It will not do to idealize them."

"Oh." His hand came down and he looked out the window, unable to sustain his outrage. Even Ms. Opple was discomfited by Van's lecture, but she did not look away. She never looked away. Ms. Opple was very much present in Van Weathers's class on Communication and Texts. It was his job to deconstruct their naive fantasies, to force them to face the facts of human behavior. The Maya had collapsed; they were responsible for their own fate. He lowered his eyes to his lecture notes. The beginnings of chiefdoms. Kings rising as the populations grew. Soon there would be state and class warfare, ultimate collapse, disease, and death.

"However," Van continued, "Mr. McGuirk has a point. What I have just laid out for you is the old model for settlement in the Western Hemisphere. While the Native Americans lived no more 'in harmony with nature' than any other members of the human species on this planet, there are several other stories we can now tell about settlement here. For instance, linguistic and DNA evidence suggest there were three waves of migration. One gave rise to the Amerind language group, a second to the Na-Dene, spoken by Navajo and some northwest American tribes, and the third lead to the various Esquimo languages. There is even evidence from places like Pedra Furada in Brazil that suggest the presence of *homo sapiens* as much as thirty thousand years ago. The evidence is provocative but so far inconclusive. There is another site in Chile called Monte Verde that suggests much earlier settlement. How did they get there? Perhaps island hopping across the Pacific by boat, perhaps by boat along the Aleutian Island chain from Asia. The jury is still out.

"And then, the large animals may have died out because the Ice Age ended, and the migrants were merely scavengers. Personally I doubt this, but as I said, the evidence is inconclusive, and there are other stories as well, but this is the story I tell," he concluded his lecture with a wave. "It is, in broad outline, the best one I know. Undoubtedly, the reality was far messier and more complicated than what I have told you. That is the nature of the complexity of the universe. All our knowledge is provisional and subject to amendment. Otherwise there would be no need for science."

Charles had turned back from the window, clearly mollified by the professor's placating words, but he continued to glower. Fine, let him glower.

Van turned up the lights. Behind him was the login screen to the Xibalbá Gate. He said, "We have created at this university a simulation of one moment in the glorious and disastrous journey human beings have made here. It is an attempt to understand better. Most of you have already gone in, but there are a few who have not done so as yet. Time is running out, folks."

Ms. Opple's moist blue eyes were fixed on him.

RANDOM NUMBERS

On his way downstairs, Van tried to shake off the feeling there was some profound mystery he could barely detect in Anne Opple's look.

He met Gordon in front of Crowley Hall, and they strolled away, hands in pockets, shoulders hunched against an October chill. The campus sprawled along the lower flanks of a hill sweeping upward into an autumn haze. Stiff leaves stirred into a faint background murmur.

"You ever get the feeling you're receiving messages that don't quite make sense?" Van asked suddenly. "Something you can't quite grasp?"

Gordon, waving his hand at the buildings dimming to silhouettes, suggested, "Just around the corner of your eye?"

"Something like that. I look at Jag sometimes and wonder where he came from. Who is he? Why is he here, in my house, breathing the same air I do? It's a great mystery, how they grow into other people. It's almost as if he isn't my child."

Gordon stopped. "Could that be?" He squinted at Van.

Van stopped, then shook his head and walked on with a little laugh. "Oh, Christ, no, he looks like me. He's mine, but he's also . . . not."

"I don't follow." They entered the silence of the narrow alley between the administration building and the theater and emerged into the North Quad, where once again they heard the leaves sigh, a faint persistent whimper of white noise.

There were benches near the fountain facing the corner where Music met Law. Once they were seated, Van said, "I think about the Maya. Their culture is so alien to us. Their costumes, all feathers and masks; their sacrifices, seeking visions in blood loss and smoke; their hieroglyphics, filled with terrifying images of bats and jaguars. I picture Jag there, in that time and place. It seems sometimes that he belongs there."

"You're kidding," Gordon said. He leaned back with his hands crossed behind his neck. "Jag loves computers and Disney."

Van shook his head wryly. "I know, I know."

They contemplated the abstract fountain for a few minutes. "There's something else, isn't there?" Gordon said softly.

Van woke from his reverie and laughed. "No, not really. You know, just a student. . . ."

"Oh."

"No, not like that. She's bright, engaged, works hard. A good candidate for. . . ."

"Teacher's pet?"

"She stares at me," he said. "Her eyes are pale blue and strange. She sends me email messages full of innuendo, very suggestive. It's distracting."

"Of course it's distracting," Gordon said. "We never know what to do with students like that, do we?"

"She memorizes the Thompson numbers. She knows prefixes and superfixes. She's learning postfixes. She sits in front where I have to look at her."

"Don't drink so much cappuccino," Gordon suggested. "And for God's sake, give up any fantasy you might have of starting something with her. It's unethical, immoral, abusive, politically incorrect, and dangerous. A bad idea."

"Bah and humbug."

"OK, OK. So she likes your simulation. I wonder if you ever worry someone else may try to create one like it." Gordon's voice made a rising and falling countermurmur to the shuffling leaves. The day was beginning to wane. The sculpture in the fountain was an inexplicable shape of tortured metal.

Van snorted. "Perhaps someone will. Not to be arrogant, but no one can do it as well as I can. Everyone else is too specialized. This needs a broad grasp of the culture and a deep knowledge of its details, not to mention field experience. I'm the best there is for this, Gordon. The very best."

"What about Jones? He urged CAPO to fund you. Maybe he's plotting to steal the idea."

"You can't make me paranoid, Gordon. Bryce Jones has some knowledge of the subject, but he's never published and he doesn't do much research."

"You're right on that." Gordon gestured at the sculpture. "Not to change the subject, but do you have any idea what that thing is?"

"Does anybody?" Van asked, leaning back and closing his eyes. "Speculation has been growing for decades. I think it's a leaping fish. I say this because in wetter times it spits water."

"No, it's not a fish. It can't be a fish. First of all, there's too much of it. And you can see through it."

"All right," Van sat up again. "It's two fish. Intertwined and abstract."

"Intertwined? You mean they're copulating? I didn't know fish 'intertwined.'"

Van laughed. "If you like, they're copulating."

"OK, but if they are, why did the university put it here? Is it a message?"

"You're asking me? I'm not a mind reader, I'm an archaeologist. Maybe it belongs to another stratum, an artifact from the sexual revolution. I dig in the dirt. I try to understand stuff that once had deep personal meaning to long-dead people. I don't understand contemporary bureaucrats. Anyway, you're the cultural anthropologist. You tell me."

"The answer is yes," Gordon said with great satisfaction. "It does create a symbolic link between people, so it is a message. It may be the Spirit of Socialist Labor, say, or the Oneness of Good and Evil."

Someone was coming toward them along the winding path, skirting the far side of the empty fountain, a man with a brisk walk.

"Do you know what Jag does," Van mused. "He collects statistics. He wants to find patterns, he says. Signs, he calls them, messages from the random flow of numbers through the world."

"A chip off the old brick?"

"You saying I look for signs?" Van laughed. "You're right. I look for signs. I'm trying to understand. What happened to the Maya has implications."

"You mean history could repeat."

"I mean exactly that."

"OK, it's possible. Anything is possible, but not very many things actually happen. Tell me, in the simulation, how do you keep people from writing messages to each other? What if I'm in there and I tell somebody I've got a gun and I'll shoot them if they don't do what I want. Stuff like that."

"There's a vocabulary filter built in. You can't enter anything that would be out of context." Van watched the figure move around the fountain and pass in front of them. "You see, on the Net we have complete control." Van thought the figure was familiar.

"It's your world," Gordon agreed. The man gave no sign he knew they were there and had soon vanished around the theater.

Van stood up and clapped Gordon on the shoulder. "Yup, the world is mine; I designed it, I've populated it—well, Wendell did the work, but I gave him the data—so it is my world. I'm going to find out what happened to the Maya, Gord. Who was that guy? He looked familiar."

"Elliot. His name's Elliot." Gordon stood and stretched. "So, you study the past and your son's interested in the present, that's all."

"Sure. Jag is trying to grab hold of the world, too, to understand it. Maybe at fifteen he's on to something. He's written a program to do real-time graphing of global statistics. It's weird, watching them pulse up and down, all those different-colored bars. They throb, as if they're alive. In real time. That's what he claims, anyway. Real time."

"Real time?" Gordon echoed. "Is there any other kind?"

THE MEANING OF WORDS

Elliot Blackman had lined up the two professors in his sights through the open latticework of the sculpture. The Dance of Fire, it was called. Meant to be a place people could sit around and tell stories, watching the frozen metal flames leap through falling water.

They were sitting on the other side. Quiet, away from other people, whispering. Elliot was a watcher; he knew things—the reason the fountain was dry, for instance. The cement in the bottom had cracked and two small flowers had pushed pale green tendrils into the air. The tops grew too heavy for the skinny stalks, and the two flowers, pale blue with white centers, had drooped. These flowers meant the fountain would leak. He'd only been on the campus a few months so far, but he saw things. If he'd been in charge he would have ripped those flowers out a lot sooner than this.

Elliot walked briskly around the fountain. He didn't want to give any sign he was observing Sylvanus Weathers, the expert on Indians. The Indians, Elliot thought, were long gone. It wasn't their country any more. Soon enough, it wouldn't be Van's, either.

Weathers said something as Elliot passed. What Weathers said was, "We have complete control."

Elliot straightened, hardly breaking his stride. The two professors didn't notice, because the other guy, Flentsch, the anthropologist, was saying, "It's your world."

Elliot ducked his head between hunched shoulders, fists knotted in his trouser pockets. He noticed their furtive manner, as if they had secret knowledge Elliot could never share.

Silly people. Elliot Blackman, first-place winner of three of the four high school science fairs he had entered, Merit scholar, shy genius of his college senior class, the one from whom they'd expected Great Things, had taken a class his senior year. He had watched from the back of the room when this kid in the front of Introduction to Archaeology talked about the Buenavista Vase. The vase had portraits of the two young men who defeated the Lords of Death and danced their way out of the underworld.

Van Weathers, the smart-ass kid in the archaeology class, was long forgotten by the time Elliot had graduated with honors and disappeared into graduate school. He found a field in applied abstract mathematics no other graduate student seemed to care about, and became an expert. Then he discovered that *no* one cared. There were no jobs, and Elliot left graduate school without turning in his dissertation.

Elliot had drifted for some years through a series of menial jobs to support himself. He spent most of his waking hours studying whatever interested him—quantum mechanics, neurophysiology, solid state physics, computation theory. He got a brief contract gathering some competitive intelligence about one company for another company. He was good at it, and it led to other such jobs. The work was interesting, varied, never repetitive or boring.

He had put Van out of his mind until his other employer had hired him to "keep an eye on the archaeologist for us," and he had a mission. It was a trivial matter to hack into the university computers, get the maintenance foreman position. Now that he was here, he kept his notebooks. He mixed the Saniclor. He watched. And he collected his two salaries.

He paused in the lobby of Crowley Hall to brush his fingertips along the seams between vinyl tiles on the floor. Signs of erosion and decay, the separation of previously flawless welds, the tiny intrusions of entropy. Elliot visualized the lovely symmetrical equations that described the folds of fractal space around this disorder. He had discovered those equations. They should be called the Blackman Equations, but someone else got the credit, some third-rate mathematician from Pennsylvania.

Elliot didn't really mind. He had no ambition for visible power, for position. Power, he believed, lay in the control of information, and everything he heard, or touched, tasted, saw, or smelled (Saniclor, for instance) was information. When he had gathered enough, he would have the power.

On this mission, power lay inside the Xibalbá Gate.

FROM VW TO AO RE: CONNECTIONS

Dear Ms Opple,

Thank you very much for your kind words about the class. It is always a pleasure for a teacher to have a student interested in his scholarly research. You're doing very well in the class. Keep up the good work!

Sincerely,
Prof. Sylvanus Weathers

DEEP STRUCTURE

Elliot Blackman leaned into rising vapors and watched the swirling brown fractals of Saniclor thread into the clear air over the bucket. He was an artist of disinfectant, a maestro of maintenance. His chest swelled at the hard kick of it at the back of his sinuses. The EPA didn't know what Elliot knew.

When the crew had left, a silence fell over his tiny cube, his basin and metallic shelving, his instruments of sanitation and sterility. Mop heads hung along a series of hooks, ropy coils falling over metal brows. Elliot could take his break.

Mrs. Yablonsky slouched over the shining white counter, looking at a young man perched on one of the red-seated stools, pinched face green in the underground light. Elliot sat beside him. "Coffee, Mrs. Y."

"Sure thing, Elliot. Coffee." She pushed away. The young man looked at Elliot, red-rimmed eyes blinking rapidly over a swollen nose. He wore lizard boots with shining metal toe-tips, a parody of a country-western drugstore cowpoke.

"'Lo," Elliot said with a nod.

The cowboy said, "You're Blagman, right? Maindnanz?" His voice was the nasal scratch of long fingernails in a week-old beard, pumped through clogged pipes.

"Uh-huh. Elliot Blackman. I recognize you. Sorry about the nose."

The cowboy nodded. "Yeah, it's OK. Id was a aggzident. I'b Wendell, freelance programmer.

"Programmer," Elliot said, just to say something.

"Yeah. I'b a graduade studend, too."

"You program computers?" Elliot looked at the student with new interest.

"Sure. Prograb for Professor Weathers."

"Ah."

Wendell looked at the older man. "Say, you dough anythig about UNIX?"

"Guys with no . . . you know, balls?" Protective cover, the dumb janitor.

"Daw. Oberating system."

The feeling of being patronized was one he did not like, so he stopped feeling it. It was a trick he had. "Should I?"

"Dod really, Unix's pretty gnarly, but you can do things, you nough, if you have a innarest."

3 Ak'bal 6 Zec

April 10, 837 AD
The Long Count date is 10.0.7.3.3
It has been 1,442,583 days since the Maya Zero Date
The calendar round date is 3 Ak'bal 6 Zec
Moon is 26 days old.
God 9 rules the night.

It is a spring day; a hot wind blows across the hillside, rustling the new stalks of corn.

Van knows he's not really in the ninth century, knows he is surrounded by concrete and steel walls, that the building he is in hums with 60-cycle, 120-volt electricity. He knows that what he faces is only a screen.

But it seems he smells the river, the rotting, fecund forest beyond cleared land climbing a steep slope, a small farm to his right, the tang of burned vegetation. There are no clouds, only the smoke haze of the burning season. Stumps and large branches still smolder from yesterday's fires. On a hill in the middle distance the city of Xultunich is white and red against the faded blue sky.

He walks along the water's edge, watching it swirl brown and lazy beneath the muddy bank. Perhaps later it would be possible to fall into those waters, to feel their cool tug against his skin. He would emerge, refreshed and wet, yet not wet at all, for it is only typed words and complex vector graphics that build this world for him.

He has left the farm behind, and as yet he has seen no one. Round Stone Water, just beyond the low ridge, is an outlying village of his realm. He goes there today on business to meet his nephew, Reed Altar. As he rounds the hill, Knot-Eye sees Reed Altar standing before his house. Inset into the plastered stone walls on either side of the entrance behind the

Mrs. Yablonsky put a cup in front of Elliot. "Thanks, Mrs. Y." He turned to Wendell. "What kind of things?"

"Well, like. . . ." Wendell stopped, reared back his head, and looked down a moment, then shrugged; his shoulders lifted up into his cascade of long black hair. "Hag into other computers, loog around."

"Hm," Elliot said, sipping. He blew across the black surface, watched the wisps of steam flow away.

"Bangs," the cowboy said softly. "Oil companies are good, lotsa data, innaresting file structures, tricky security, but I like bangs, myself. Great UNIX hack, bangs."

"Banks? I don't care for them," Elliot said. "Stuck with them, I guess, but I don't like 'em."

"Oh, I don't *use* them. Just loog aroud."

"Mmm, I suppose. So you a student? What do you study?" Elliot asked.

"Archaeology. I'b a student of Dr. Weathers, see. His prograbber."

"Wonderful man, Dr. Weathers," Mrs. Yablonsky said.

"That's interesting," Elliot said softly. "Really." He thought for a moment. "Maybe you *could* show me how to use the machines?" Elliot finished his cup and put four dollars on the counter. Mrs. Y swept it up and put a quarter back, but they were gone.

Wendell was eager. Was Elliot a friend, a connection with living flesh? They sat side by side. Elliot began looking on Wendell as a contact, a recruit, even, perhaps as one of his clients, the constituency for whom Saniclor worked its antiseptic magic.

The computer lab hummed with student life. Wendell tapped keys. "This," he said, pointing, "is a prograb that leds us ged onto the Net." He looked over at Elliot. "You dough what the Net is?"

Elliot shook his head, feigning ignorance. Appearance, he often said, is reality.

Wendell didn't notice the twinkle in his eye. "Unlimided combuter det-works, all padged together. All aroud the world, paget switching messages, ibages, video, code and love ledders, fidancial stadements, secrets and sex. Billions of peoble, file servers, phode lines, sadellite and fiber optic and microwaves. Biggest fugging playground in de entire fugging planet, see? De Indernet."

Elliot remembered Dr. Weathers' words: Complete control. "Around the world? Imagine that," he said aloud.

"Here, we loog at Dr. Weathers' projegt, the Xibalbá Gate, see?" The
skeletal serpent jaws opened on the screen. "You want to do this yourself,
you deed a password," Wendell told him. "I can fix that for you, see, sed
up a dubby aggount, give you a handle, and dere you are."

"You mean I could come in here at night and, what you say, log on?"
Elliot cocked his head to one side and squinted.

"Sure." Wendell grinned. "Be a ghosd in de machide."

"Really? That would be very helpful. Yes. A ghost in the machine?"
But he was thinking: That's what I am already.

DEN

Alone in his dark office, Elliot waited. Above and around him the vast
building ticked and hummed, slowing its daily rhythm. Finally, he allowed
the corners of his mouth to rise, and he tapped the side of the key cabinet.
The metal box shifted to the left, revealing a recessed latch. He turned and
pushed, and the cabinet and a narrow section of the wall behind it swung
silently. A black, oblong opening gaped. He stepped into a cool, damp
odor of mildew and rotting concrete.

A room appeared with the touch of a switch as the door swung shut
behind him. It had not taken Elliot long after beginning at Crowley Hall
and studying the building plans to find this empty space. He was certain
only he knew this room was here, knew the sagging old pipes, the broken
concrete footings for long-vanished heating equipment crumbling along
the base of the long wall. Once, huge oil-burning furnaces had crouched
behind his seat in his secret lair, but they were long gone, the building's
heating and cooling chambers moved to a new room all their own at the
other end of the basement.

There were still occasions when Elliot could hear the skitter of rats' feet,
could almost hear the click of their tiny nails on the crumbling masonry.
He'd cock his head and listen, but almost immediately the sound would
stop, as if they heard him listening and paused to *listen back*.

His workbench and sagging mortarboard shelves, the two rusting metal
cabinets, were part of the deception. The bench was solid, the surface spot-
less. The rusted cabinets opened silently, the hinges and locks worked and
oiled. The sagging shelves were meant to sag, to have the tired, abandoned
look of the forgotten and insignificant. If anyone found this room, remote

as that possibility was, they would give it only a cursory glance. This was Elliot's post between the Saniclor and the computer lab.

He leaned over the plank table and directed the narrow light on its flexible stalk onto a notebook dense with lines and columns of crabbed print. He ran the thick pad of his middle finger down the columns and whistled under his breath, a tuneless white noise. No one could hear, but he was quiet just the same.

He put the blue, three-ring binder back in its place on the sagging Masonite shelf above the workbench and took down another with exactly two hundred pages of carefully handwritten print in black ink, no corrections or deletions.

He turned to page 50 and began to read. A ruled pad sat squarely beside the right edge of the binder. Elliot held a mechanical pencil above it, ready for notes. The universe was a messy place, dependent on his input, his knowledge, his design: equations, words, numbers, symbols.

He scratched a note, leaned back, and listened. All was silence overhead. "Hmm, hmm," he murmured. "Hmm, hmm. It wasn't the way it was, there was so much dirt, you see, hm? Father, father, see, he came home every day with that *smell*." Elliot wrinkled his nose and tilted his head, smiling. "Hah, yes, the odor of despair you might say, see. That was Elliot then, and this is Elliot now." He tapped the notebook with the pad of his middle finger. "Here, and now, the seller in the cellar sealed his cell, uhm-hmm. They don't know the energetics of it, do they? They don't listen, so smug in their fog and fear. I'm the strange attractor now, and soon they'll see, hmm, hmm."

Breathing deeply through his nose, he bent over his notes. He wrote words: Internet; Chaos; "the ceaseless motion and incomprehensible bustle of life—Mahler's third symphony." He wrote *ash*, and *orbit*, and *information*. And he wrote *caudate nucleus*, and *medulla*, and *diencephalon*. He wrote equations.

Later he looked up. The vast room, hidden and long forgotten, was silent. The broken pipes, the tang of rust, mildew, and crumbling wet masonry reassured him. He put the notebook away, rose, and stretched, speaking under his breath: "Really."

He checked his watch: 11:47. He put the notebook back on the shelf, patted it gently with his fingertips, and left the room, carefully turning off the light. He climbed the stairs in the now dark and silent building. On the fourth floor, he carefully opened an office door and switched on the light.

The black lettering on the door spelled out "Bryson Jones." He could have stayed, safe in his den, but it amused him to take over an unused faculty office instead.

Elliot started the computer on the rosewood desk. He leaned back in the titanium ergonomic chair and let his eyes drift over the even rows of leather book bindings in the rosewood bookcases. The office resembled an *Architectural Digest* home staged for quick sale. It was by far the most comfortable and elegant office in the building. It also had the advantage of seldom being used.

The screen opened up, and Elliot Blackman, maintenance foreman, entered the digital realm, where he shed his name and occupation and wavered into a new identity: GHOSTMAN came to life.

FIBER

Jag was alone in his room, racing the fiber. He was light, the eye-blink swift push of it, tracing the threads, a million miles of glass spun thin as hair, twined underground, crossroads and junctions, switches and quantum gaps, photon thrust along the pure transparency of it. How fast could he go? He was a ball of light, light as light itself, weightless in the digital domain. Jag was a free bit of information in the run, searching. His name was Catalyst, the quiet one who made things happen, and he was pure electroplasm out of the mundane, free in the Mondo.

He could feel the vast network, the clots of servers and memory, the wild zip of data and talk, text and digits. He started from his house, at number 145. The net spread from here, connecting to the Cavanaugh's next door, to the Miles Standish High School computer lab, to the university where his father taught, to nodes and clusters around the world, to the Pentagon and the CIA, NSA and NRO, Homeland Security, galaxies of corporate intranets, home pages flashing by as he raced the fiber, images, sounds, links woven into links, constantly changing, blinking, swelling, and contracting, forming patterns.

Jag could feel them, the colors rising and falling, the heave and cry of the unimaginably complex, never-sleeping flash and scream of bits around the world, top to bottom, pole to pole, effortless shift from photon to microwave to electron and back to photon, up to satellites and down to dish antennas scattered around the globe, turning abrupt corners, flowing around breaks and back together, endlessly, endlessly.

Others were there. He could sense their electroplasm presence even when they did not speak. His fingers tapped keys. He listened to the chirp and warble of connect, forming new links, new momentary communities. Others were racing the fiber, too, passing him going one way, then the other, zip, zip, flash past, no "Hi," no need. Just the race, the pure, sweet high adrenaline rush of light speed through the fiber. Of others riding the adrenaline, some he knew, some he didn't. Others were looking for the patterns, riding the patterns, feeling out the network as it grew faster than they could race, faster than anything. Warp speed, stars compressed to a tiny sphere of brilliance, the faint afterimage trail of them going, going.

Web sites were like storefronts at the mall. Behind there was a vast complex of tunnels, support facilities, restrooms, warehouses and storage areas, delivery platforms and corridors. Here, in the servers and databases, the ftp sites and intranets, is where Jag could really race the fiber.

So he raced banks, defense contractors, airlines, vast underground economies in Asia, and black-market dealers in Egypt. He raced fiber under the oceans and across deserts, across the Pacific and the Indian, the Gobi, and the Altiplano. He dodged security in a dozen countries, riding the signals bouncing off the geosyncs, shifting from k-band to x-band and back into the fiber. Jag had a way with the fiber: everywhere he saw the patterns—the Mondo was full of patterns, small ones that came together to make larger ones, merging and flowing.

Later he slowed, watched the signs. There were numbers, scrolling lines of code, encryption algorithms, password protection. He ambled around some, jiggered some, tinkered, probed, and took notes.

HFS Corporation was a hundred switches, trunk lines, fiber junctions, and electronic switches from home. HFS Corporation, bland initials that gave no clue to what they stood for, what they did or made or traded or served. Hmm, he said, this looks interesting, and he paused, curious.

Someone was there, text on the bottom of the screen.

Someone said, Hello, I'm Ghostman, who are you?

12 Ik' 0 Sac

Friday, October 21
The Long Count date is 12.19.12.13.2
It has been 1,869,382 days since the Maya Zero Date
The calendar round date is 12 Ik' 0 Sac
Moon is 20 days old
God 1 rules the night

THE VENICE OF THE NORTH

The next morning, Friday, Jag, well into tenth grade, the year of the sophomore, stared through the flawed glass of his classroom window. A series of rapid lines stitched themselves across a high layer of condensed, suspended moisture that indicated a dwindling ozone layer, increasing carbon dioxide levels, and elevated seasonal temperatures. The lines flickered rapidly across the panes of glass. The edges of each rapid streak pulsed with a chromatic aura as it disappeared. The streaks humped up into letters: D, they flickered rapidly. A, they said. He blinked. D. A. It was raining outside.

He was sitting in room seven, row three, seat one of Miles Standish High School Building Four, and there were signs everywhere of changes all around him. He saw it in these horizontal lightning strikes that lit up the insides of the clouds; it was there in the increasing pulse of his statistical processing programs, the slides of certain currencies, the precipitous decline of the amphibian populations, a sharp spike in the price of infant formula, the random encounter last night with someone called Ghostman. Such cataclysmic forebodings made Mr. Sugar's discussion of the Bolshevik Revolution seem strangely irrelevant.

"Mr. Weathers?"

Jag jumped. "Mr. Sugar?"

"We were discussing the cities of Russia, Mr. Weathers. We would all appreciate it if you could join us."

"Yes, Mr. Sugar."

"The city of Dostoyevsky, Mr. Weathers."

Jag closed his eyes and summoned an imaginary Web page. "Sixty-five rivers and canals, 365 bridges," he said. "The word for street is *ulitsa*. St. Petersburg was sometimes called the Venice of the North."

"Very good, Mr. Weathers."

"Will you excuse me, Mr. Sugar, please. I don't feel too good."

Mr. Sugar nodded indulgently, and Jag went into the corridor, closing the door carefully behind him.

He sat on the floor with his back to the wall and waited for it to pass. The jagged lines whispering with strange colors moved across the vinyl tiles and just above the lockers on the other side of the corridor. They were kind of pretty, but they wouldn't stop moving. They were like worms twisting in from the left, only to vanish above the principal's office. DADADADADADADA. . . .

Jag was frightened.

Were they a Sign? On and off. Zero and one. Digital.

He pushed himself up and made his way, one hand touching the wall, to the nurse's office.

When his mother arrived, he had sunk into a frightening silence. She drove at high speed to the university clinic, glancing at him anxiously every few seconds. Jag stared out the window. The skin around his eyes was a peculiar bronze, and his lips seemed slightly blue. It was raining, and the windshield wipers clicked back and forth, back and forth.

She held his hand while they waited. Jag stared into space, breathing, she was certain, too heavily and too slowly. When at last the doctor was free, she nearly carried him into the examining room. Jag kept saying "Don't," but she couldn't help herself. The doctor came in, a blur of white and aftershave, poked around a little, asked Jag to cough, and left the room.

A few minutes later, the nurse came in and laid out an efficient row of equipment. She took Jag's blood pressure and grunted. She thumped his chest and listened through the stethoscope and grunted. She tapped him under the knee and grunted when his foot kicked out.

Finally she picked up an enormous needle. She tied a rubber tube around Jag's slender upper arm, fluffed up a vein, and plunged the needle swiftly into the thin, blue line. Glenna swayed and held the table's edge. The nurse, grunting again, pulled Jag's blood up into the glass tube slowly at first, then with a rush and a fall back, leaving a crimson parabola along the side. She grunted, pressed a ball of alcohol-doped cotton to the place where the needle went into the boy's flesh, and grunted one last time as she pulled out the needle. Then she was gone.

Twenty minutes later, the doctor came in. He told her not to worry, this sort of thing often happened with adolescents. "Just growing pains," he said, patting her shoulder. "He's having a growth spurt, that's all. Don't worry."

FROM AO TO VW: MONOGRAPH

Dear Professor Weathers,

Your lecture on the great migrations into the New World the other day was brilliant. I had no idea the relationship between human beings and the planet on which we all live was so complex! Most people—Charles McGuirk, for example—still think the Native Americans lived in harmony with nature and you have dispelled any illusions I, for one, have left on that score. Charles is still angry about it. Of course, as you discuss in chapter three of your book, the ways in which our species has written on the skin of the planet tells a great deal about our history, and some of the writing left behind has been in the form of piles of mammoth bones.

Do you know that your eyes are a startling clear blue? They seem to see more, and more deeply, than anyone's I've ever met.

Your monograph, "Ideology and Kinship in the Early Postclassic at Altun Ha" was out at the library. Do you think I could borrow a copy from you?

Yours,
Anne Opple

FROM VW TO AO RE: MONOGRAPH

Dear Anne,

We have never been the virtuous creatures we would like to think ourselves. I have been considering the Collapse and what caused it, and certainly much of the responsibility must rest with human error, as they say about other kinds of crashes, airplanes, for instance.

I would be happy to loan you my copy of the monograph, although it is quite a bit written on and messy. I'm afraid I have a bad habit of annotating my own work!

I don't know about my eyes as I seldom see them. They're getting a bit fogged of late. I probably need stronger reading glasses.

Best,
Van Weathers

WHERE VAN WAS

Glenna called as Van was frowning at another email message, this one from Leon Blatskoi. "Jag's all right," she said.

"What do you mean, he's all right?"

"He had some kind of growth spurt. I had to take him to the clinic. But he's all right."

"You had to take him to the clinic for a growth spurt?" Van found himself smiling. "Growth is now a disease?"

She laughed, and he could hear the relief in it. "All right, you think I overreacted? He had some kind of fainting spell at school. Said he saw things crawling on the ceiling. The doctor thinks he didn't get enough blood to his brain or something. I thought I ought to let you know. Don't say anything to him. He's a little embarrassed."

"OK, Glenna. Thanks for the warning." He paused. "He's a good kid."

"Yes. Yes, he's a good kid. We're lucky, Van."

"You're right," he said softly. "We are lucky."

After he hung up, he turned back to the screen, where Leon's message waited.

My friend,
We are excited about your Gate into Xibalbá, Alberto and I. He was here in St. Petersburg only for a few weeks, then went back to Bologna to teach his excellent students. Alberto, at least, has something to do with his time, some of it, anyway. I, my friend, am superfluous, and can merely watch the once glorious Rus collapse into anarchy and despair. This may be what did in the

Maya, my friend, this anarchy and despair. I can see the Maya Mafia working even now, skimming the best cacao beans from the hoards of the kings, cornering the quetzal feather market, extorting protection money from the caravans of porters bringing spondylus shell inland from the coast. The more it changes, the more it stays the same old thing, don't you know. Only now they shoot each other in these new telephone booths the foreign companies have brought to my city.

I have walked around a bit in your city. It is Xultunich, isn't it? But what is it happening there to the west? I don't recall from your field reports that set of impassable hills. Please enlighten me.

Your colleague and friend,
Leon

Van crooked his fingers over the keyboard. It was raining, and outside light was leaching from the day. Thoughts seemed to crowd his mind: Leon's world is truly falling apart. He doesn't know from one hour to the next whether there will be bread, electricity, water. I have confidence these things here will persist. Confidence, or faith. Leon is right, if we do not find out what happened to the great Maya polities, why they fell back into silence, the same will happen to us. He began to type.

Leon,
So good to hear from you. I haven't seen Alberto since the conference in Rome ten years ago now, I think. I will write him about his paper on shamanism and energy use—I could use his numbers for the simulation. What amount of human labor does it take a priest to elevate a pyramid one meter? We know it takes a hell of a lot, anyway, but perhaps I overestimate

Wendell, my programmer, doesn't get enough sleep and he's made a few silly mistakes. At least he tells me they're silly, so the sims don't work quite right sometimes. Please be patient. He promises me it will only be another couple of weeks more to get the kinks out of it. I think it's good, very convincing, especially with the sounds—river, birds, howler monkeys. And the characters behave in a very realistic way. Wendell swears you will never know if a human being is running one of them from another computer somewhere, or whether they are merely doing their canned routines—a kind of artificial intelligence magic.

I would love to welcome you into the sim, but of course that would defeat the purpose, wouldn't it? I can't know when you are there, or who you are;

and you can't know me either. It's a kind of masquerade, like carnival in Venice.

I don't mean to avoid your question about what is happening to the west. Yes, it is Xultunich as accurately as I could make it. I am certain there is something very significant to the west, and I would very much like to find out what it is. But we couldn't secure a permit to dig there, and now there is no funding to dig at all. So I am trying to find out in the simulation, hoping someone who knows something will pass it along, inside the Maya world if not in the real one.

May the Hero Twins protect you.

May they protect us all.

Van.

With a sense of relief Van left his email program and turned to the Xibalbá Gate. The logs told him there were one hundred and thirty-eight real people in the simulation at the moment, some students, some faculty, some foreign scholars. He could take a part or he could see what was going on in other places of the simulated world. He might not know who they were, but there were many old friends in there, and he felt in that moment how very easy it was for him to slip into this other world.

3 Ak'bal 6 Zec

April 10, 837 AD
The Long Count date is 10.0.7.3.3
It has been 1,442,583 days since the Maya Zero Date
The calendar round date is 3 Ak'bal 6 Zec
Moon is 26 days old.
God 9 rules the night.

KNOT-EYE

It is late afternoon and Knot-Eye walks along the road to the west. Afternoon shadow has darkened the white lime surface leading into the forest. This, he thinks, is why the western road is the Black Road, leading as it does finally to darkness and night.

The farmers are still at work in their small fields. The air is still thick with humidity and smoke, but no one approaches him. The road is deserted.

Once he is inside the forest, a silence closes about him. He walks for what seems a long time, and finally he stops. "This is strange," he says aloud.

"What is strange?" a man's voice answers.

"I. . . ." He looks around and at first sees no one. Then the other steps out of the trees.

"Don't be alarmed. I am no one, just a wanderer. You spoke, and I thought it must have been to me."

"I spoke to myself, and said only that it is strange." Knot-Eye looks around and gestures. "There is no one. The road is empty."

"Yet I am here," the man says.

"Yes," Knot-Eye must agree. "You are here." He examines the man closely, but sees nothing familiar about him. "I will tell you that I alone have walked this road today. I would go to Te-Ayiin."

"The Place of the Crocodile?" the man replies. "Yes, Te-Ayiin is not far, and yet too far to go."

"You speak in riddles," Knot-Eye says. "I have never been there, yet I have always lived in Xultunich. Te-Ayiin is close."

The man looks away. "Do not go there."

Knot-Eye waits.

"The mountain is high," the man says.

Knot-Eye says nothing.

"There is no reason to go to Te-Ayiin," the man adds at last. "Te-Ayiin is gone. There is no one. It is why this road is empty now."

"You know this because you have been to Te-Ayiin today?" Knot-Eye asks. The two men stand on the narrow road among huge ceiba trees, and even the monkeys, the macaws, the peccaries, are silent. The air has stopped moving. It is as if the world has ceased to breathe.

"Yes," the man says. The man, if it is a man, so strange is his appearance in the failing light, as if he were not entirely there, stares at Knot-Eye, and the look is not the look of a man. "The Lords do not look on Te-Ayiin with favor. You must turn back."

The King turns without a word and makes his way back down the road toward his city.

XIBALBÁ

It is a dark place, a damp place, and it is filled with fright: the sound of rat claws scuttling on crumbling stone, the slow thick drip of underground water, the still empty places between the roots of trees, and most of all the dark, the suffocating dark.

Into this place a presence forms. It is only a sketch of a human being, a skeletal shape with patches of torn flesh stuck onto it here and there and a round dome skull with clacking teeth. This figure seems to drift through the wall of this narrow chamber and look around. Then it sits with a contented sigh on a bundle, which bursts into sulfurous flame so he jumps up with a loud shriek.

After a moment, he makes something that sounds like laughter, like Hmm, hmm through the nose, and sits again on the flames, which instantly go out.

He sits for a long time, peering up through tangled roots and dark earth and the rotting flesh of animals and humans buried in it. He is going to watch what goes on up there in the Middle World.

XULTUNICH

Its favored place atop a hill in the bend of the river protects it from enemies and gives it water. The acropolis, the steep mountain pyramids with red temples arranged around vast plazas, is the most glorious in this part of the Maya universe. It was here, they say, that the original Wakah Chan, the raised-up sky band of the World Tree, first broke through the blank water of the new world and lifted the arch of heaven overhead. It was here, at the Crossroads, where the first motherfathers of the Maya began the Cycle of Time.

Tikal and Calakmul may have boasted more prowess in war; Palenque, called Bone, may be more intricate; Toniná may have a better view of heaven; and Cloud Hill may now have grown more glorious, but no living city is older or more respected than Xultunich, the Last Stone City, and no ruler is more honored than Lord Knot-Eye, seventeenth of the One Monkey Jaguar Stone dynasty. The first monuments erected in Xultunich bear a carved Long Count date of 8.4.0.0.0, only eighty years after the beginning of the eighth bak'tun, or four-hundred-year cycle, since the beginning of time. This is now more than seven hundred solar years ago.

In the evening, the merchant who calls himself Smoke Wind makes his way slowly into the central plaza. The road loops grandly around the enormous reservoir, a reflecting pool lined with plaster; it climbs between the small twin pyramid-temples dedicated to the water-monster and the sky serpent, the upper and lower anchors of the universe, root and branch of the World Tree.

Smoke Wind has wandered far, and is tired. He has been to the great water to the east to meet the great canoes bearing cloth and shell from farther north; he has been to Altun Ha and Lamanai, to Xunantunich and Caracol. He has wandered south as far as Copan and Quirigua, and now he comes from far to the west, from Toniná and from Yaxchilan on the river. The dust and mud of the trail cover his legs to the knee. His pack, filled with cacao and shell, obsidian and jadeite, seems heavier than it was just this afternoon, not to mention yesterday or the day before. He thinks this is because he has found few welcoming farms along the road. Water was scarce, too, despite the nearness of the river. He has seen several abandoned farms.

"Welcome," someone says, and Smoke Wind raises his head.

The man offers him a gourd of water, and Smoke Wind, although of royal blood, takes it gratefully. Once he adopted the merchant's way and took to wandering among the cities of the world, he became a common man and shared his life with other common men.

When he finishes and hands the gourd back, the man asks, "What of things to the west?" Bringing news is all the payment the wanderers need make for water freely given.

"It is not good to the west. In the mountains some cities are empty. The Lord of Four Water ordered the south plaza blocked by a ball court, and the shadows grow long there. The people hear things in the night. Women die in childbirth. And at Te-Ayiin the priests have burned the lintels. This happened while I was there. They killed the buildings, and now the city is abandoned."

"Te-Ayiin!" the man exclaims. "I have heard Te-Ayiin was a great city."

"So it was, but now only the scorpions and howler monkeys live in the temples. The Lords of Xibalbá live there now, laughing. You can feel them, like a chill and a fever."

"What of the Lord of Te-Ayiin? What of his family?"

Smoke Wind only looks at the cloudless sky, the broad roof comb of the central temple, with its seated figure facing the plaza. The figure looks familiar, and instead of answering, he asks, "Who now is Lord of Xultunich?"

"Knot-Eye, seventeenth of the lineage."

"Ah. So I thought. The ancestor's face up there suggests his descendant." The seated figure is splendid under his multicolored quetzal plume headdress, his jade necklace and pectorals, his intricate deerskin sandals. He holds across his lap the two-headed serpent bar of his office.

"Does it?" The man's surprise brings Smoke Wind's attention back to the plaza floor. "He has been ruler for nearly five years, since he had the roof comb built. That is One Monkey, First Ancestor. Is it so long you have been away?"

Smoke Wind nods. "It has been so long and longer. I have been to the high mountains to the west, beyond the Lands, where the barbarians have their cities."

"Ah." The man looks troubled. "I have heard rumors."

After a silence, Smoke Wind says, "They are true. They have enormous armies, like grains of sand in the river, and weapons that can kill at a distance."

"What? At a distance? How is this possible?"

"They use a stabbing spear and a flat stick of wood. They use the stick to throw the spear."

"But this is dishonorable, to kill at a distance. How could the gods be pleased with this?"

Smoke Wind shrugs. "I do not know; who can explain the gods?"

"Have you heard anything of Waterbird River? We hear things from that way, too, the lowlands to the east."

Smoke Wind looks up again at the roof comb of the temple, where One Monkey watches over the city of his descendants. "I have heard things, but they are only whispers."

A gang of workers walks past, carrying huge baskets of lime to plaster the temple stairs. When they are out of sight, the man asks again, hesitantly, "The Lord of Te-Ayiin?" His voice is a whisper.

"Has played his last ball game," Smoke Wind says. "He was captured and sacrificed. His family has gone down to Xibalbá. His head was made into a ball, so that another city might live."

TE-AYIIN

The Lord of Te-Ayiin looks up. He sees the tangled claws of crocodiles hanging from the ceiling.

The crocodiles are heaven, and he has no choice but to look at them: his head is resting on its back, by itself, separated from his body. Up is the only way he can look.

He hears laughter, far away, and the sound of drums, ta-ta-tumta, ta-ta-tumta. Shrill whistles, pipes, trumpets play the song of sacrifice. He knows it was his heart they tore out, and is content.

He can smell, or taste, the foam on top of the cacao drink, still on his tongue, or in his nose. It is bitter, but good. Ta-ta-tumta, ta-ta-tumta, and the skirling of pipes.

He hears also the faint rustle of paper earplugs, and smells the iron smell of his own blood. Good. All good. All at the same time, the blood, the beat, the smoky torch, and. . . .

. . . The Lord of Te-Ayiin looks up and sees too the form of One Monkey falling through stars, eyes wide open and staring right at him; and beyond One Monkey, old lizard man Itzamná, hunched over, looking down at him. He sees a cranky old lady, Ixchel, the Moon Mother, scolding him. He sees them all at once, and one by one.

He feels cool jade. He feels smoke and resin and fear. He feels Time turn itself right, the Day and the Month, the Cycle, all mesh again, all good, all woven into the royal mat on which the universe can sit.

The Lord of Te-Ayiin, or at least his head or his skull or the sacred ball it has become, would be smiling. He is home again.

EVENING STAR

She is fifteen years old, a princess of the lineage, and a beauty. Her head, beautifully shaped in childhood, slopes at a steep angle, coming to a rounded point far back of her neck. Her nose is steeply curved, and she holds it high, proud of its carefully tended shape. Some slave (she never can remember which is which) prepares her hair for the night in silence, placing on the low bench to her right a series of pins, paper strips, beaded twine, and bangles, skillfully releasing them from the intricate daytime structure.

Evening Star shakes her head with impatience. "Stop it," she says angrily. "You're making a mess of it."

The slave bows and withdraws. Evening Star follows her to the opening and looks out at the courtyard of her family's compound.

A few torches flicker in the night, but not so many that she can't see the broad White Road of heaven. She can even see, over the grove of sacred ceiba trees to the east, the Black Road to Xibalbá cutting across the White Road, a reflection in the sky of the Crossroads of the supernaturals.

Almost directly overhead she recognizes the copulating peccaries, and low to the West her namesake, Venus, the Evening Star.

She avoids looking at the other object up there on the other side of the sky, the baleful one, the intruder. It is bad luck to look. Instead, she watches the slave shuffle in silence around the end of this line of elite sleeping rooms and disappear. Evening Star withdraws, lets the curtain fall.

It is hot, and she opens her wrap to the faintest breeze that makes its way through the *ik'* openings, the T-shaped windows for the wind spirits that ventilate her room. This whisper of air is not enough, and her hair is only half finished. She sighs with exasperation and goes out in search of someone to finish it. If she doesn't, her father, Quetzal Tree, will be angry and won't speak with her for the next *winal* or two. That is always how he punishes her.

She hears a commotion one courtyard over, in the compound of her uncle, and she hastens her steps. There is an argument going on in his council house, and Evening Star loves arguments.

She crouches to one side of the opening, listening to her father, Quetzal Tree, king of Green Mountain, speak. "Our nephew Reed Altar has told us Lord Knot-Eye seeks a wife and an alliance. I must send his messenger back with an answer."

She can almost smell the chilis on the breath of her uncle, Three Sky, as he shouts. "Never! Never will we submit to this alliance with Xultunich! Last Stone is a dying city. Their blood is weak."

There is a long silence, and then she hears her father's low, quiet voice, and is filled with fear. "And what of us, Lord Three Sky? What of Green Mountain? Are we so strong we can say 'No'? Are we so fat with corn and squash we can say 'Never'?"

Three Sky brings his hand down on the mat on which the council sits cross-legged. She can hear the woven fibers break under the blow, hear the cups of frothy cacao jump. But Three Sky says nothing, and she knows from this that there is nothing to say.

After a time, Quetzal Tree continues. "For almost twenty k'atun we grew and prospered. Four hundred years. Except for the unfortunate battle with Lamanai during the dark years of our grandfather's rule, we have had good fortune. Our people have eaten, the gods have protected us, the Tree of our Lineage has grown strong.

"But these are times of ill omen. We are fewer today than we were only a k'atun past. Disease has taken some; others have . . . left. And there is the sign, the God Who Has No Name pulls his loincloth across the eastern sky. We are at a Crossroads. Merchants down from the west bring news of huge armies moving in the highlands. What can we do? We cannot gather armies such as those in the west. And they are coming this way. So the merchants and travelers tell us."

There is silence inside the council house. Evening Star has gathered her wrap under her chin, as if against a chill. Yes, she can see from the corner of her eye the God Who Has No Name in the sky, hanging above the river. She can see the long reflection of his loincloth in the black water. And tomorrow is 4 Kan, a day of ill omen. She shivers, wondering.

"They are far away," Three Sky says at last. "We have heard of these people before, many times. A few have appeared with spear throwers. They have bragged of great armies. Did we run away? No! And there were no great armies."

"There is also the question of Waterbird River," her father says. "Waterbird River, a great city, sent a prince."

"We fed him and sent him back," Three Sky pointed out. "But we can always send for him again."

"Cloud Hill is far away. It is said Cloud Hill grows weak, their lineage is failing. It is said their ancestors are displeased." She can hear Quetzal Tree lean forward and knows he is looking through the open doorway at the plaza a few steps below. He will listen no longer.

Three Sky tries, but his voice has lost its force. "It is said, it is said! Who is this who says it? Who do we believe?"

She smells the pungent aroma of burning copal incense, and the day-keeper, Turtle Claw, already an old man though only a few years older than her father, begins to chant.

She stops listening. She has heard this cycle of chants many times before. Instead, she wonders what an alliance with Xultunich would mean. Xultunich was a long walk on the yellow road south. Would her father be leaving, then, to arrange an alliance?

And what would such an alliance be? Would it be, could it be, a marriage? Evening Star begins to dream.

TREE STONE

In his home a certain distance downriver from Xultunich, amid the gardens of squash and maize, breadfruit and beans, Flint Howler, most favored scribe and carver of Xultunich, is in seclusion.

Flint Howler does not like to be in seclusion, not very much. He yearns for his wife; he yearns for the taste of turkey and squash. But he is in seclusion, and he knows he cannot have these things. In past days, when there were not such baleful signs of ill omen in the night sky, when the gods were closer to men and favored them, before men began to forget about the gods and the proper way to address them, before they made too much noise on the earth, carvers were not unhappy to be in seclusion. Flint Howler knows this. These are days of evil, when spirits grow bold enough to appear in daytime. Only yesterday, a jaguar had carried off Flint Howler's dog. A bad sign.

He sits on a log in his work shed, staring at a slab of limestone. It is the best stone he can find. Lord Knot-Eye has told him he will need it, will need to be ready to carve, and so he is ready.

But he is not happy about this stone. It is soft and coarse, barely adequate for the importance of this ceremony. Because these are bad days, with the God Who Has No Name in the sky and the people saying the gods have turned away, with Maize God and Rain God having gone elsewhere, with the House Corners weak and unable to hold, because of all these reasons and more, this stone is not as good as it should be. Stone in his grandfather's day was better than this, much better. The gods favored Xultunich and its lineage then.

He has been staring at this slab since the sun was high. Now it is late at night and he can barely see it in the firelight. He sighs and goes outside.

He can see Venus following the waxing crescent moon, which is following the sun. They all march according to the way it is written in the books he has carefully stored in the workshop. What is not written is the God Who Has No Name crossing from the other side of the sky. He will go into Xibalbá in the darkest time of the night. Flint Howler knows this because he has been watching for many nights.

He mutters and shakes his head. It is not good. Not good at all. He will carve in wood, in the sacred ceiba log he has brought into the workshop. He will carve a likeness of the God Who Has No Name, and he will offer him in the temple to commemorate the accession of his Lord and uncle, Knot-Eye. He, Flint Howler, had prepared the stucco image of One Monkey, the Lord Ajaw, Ancestor of Xultunich, on the roof comb of this temple. Now, inside, he will place the image he carves of the God Who Has No Name, and they will sacrifice to him, and perhaps the world will right itself, and the God Who Has No Name will go away, will leave the People alone.

It bothers him that he said, even to himself, the word "perhaps." It meant he had some doubts, and a shaman and priest cannot have doubts. He would tell no one that he thought the word "perhaps."

12 Ik' 0 Sac

Friday, October 21
The Long Count date is 12.19.12.13.2
It has been 1,869,382 days since the Maya Zero Date
The calendar round date is 12 Ik' 0 Sac
Moon is 20 days old
God 1 rules the night

DIG

Van rubbed his eyes and looked through his narrow office window.

Was Anne Opple Evening Star? He could check the logs, see if she had been present when he was there, but he did not. It would be a form of cheating.

Van's office, overlooking the South Quad's bare, twisted trees, felt damp, as if a wet autumn vapor rose from the floor. He clasped his hands behind his back. It was hard enough not seeing the sparkle of her nose ring everywhere he looked. She had questions, and he had no answers, so he watched the rain, first of the year, light but steady.

There was a knock at the door, and he turned away from the window. "Come in."

Gordon bounded in, grinning. "I was in there, first time I really got caught up in it. Terrific, Van. Really. Stuff is happening. You can feel it, the tension, the fear, the edges of the culture coming unraveled, really compelling."

"And you were warning me, Gordon. Be careful, you said."

"Ah, well, you should still be careful. I'm impressed, that's all."

Van tipped his head to the side, accepting the compliment.

After a brief moment, Gordon plunged on. "To the west, though, Van. Te-Ayiin. The King of Te-Ayiin. What's going on?"

The archaeologist shrugged. "I wish I knew."

"Right, the permits."

"Yes. It was strange, not to mention disappointing, to lose funding for Xultunich right after I proposed excavating at Te-Ayiin. Xultunich itself spreads out to the west along the road, up to the forest, which of course came closer to the city than it does today. Five seasons of digging there, and everything seemed to be leading toward Te-Ayiin up the slope close to the river. Something happened there. It's in the few hieroglyphic texts we could read, but we don't know what."

"And it's private land."

"Yes. Still, we should have been able to get permits. It's definitely a site, and doesn't seem to be used for anything."

"So who owns it?"

Van shook his head. "Some group with one of those anonymous names. Garcia Holdings Limited. Meaningless. I couldn't find out anything more about them. I doubt they even knew I was trying to get the permits. It was CAPO that cut me off. Of course, now they're funding the simulation, so I guess I can't complain."

"Still, they stopped funding the dig." Gordon sat down in the chair by the trestle table and put his feet up on Van's desk. "Well," he added thoughtfully. "You do have enemies, Van."

"Enemies? What enemies?"

"Simmons, at Southern. He hates you."

"Simmons is a fool."

"He's head of the department. You reviewed his book."

"It was garbage."

"His feelings were hurt. You insulted him, and he's feeling vengeful."

"Jesus, Gordon, whose side are you on? Simmons is an idiot. He calculates limestone densities. He finds correlations between the cycle of Venus and fertility rates in the ninth century. He's a *little* man. He writes *little* articles."

"OK, Rawlings, at Tulane."

Van snorted. "A puppy. He dug up a late Post-Classic outhouse and thought he'd found a Middle Classic palace. His field technique is pathetic."

"He's secretary of the association. He holds a grudge. He's on all the funding committees."

"You're saying I haven't played the politics right. He gives his girlfriend author credit on his articles so he can get in her pants."

Gordon nodded. "It works. He gets in her pants. She gets a resumé. It's the system, Van. Even private funding organizations like CAPO listen to the experts."

"Well, I've put in as much as I know about Te-Ayiin into the project. Maybe we can puzzle out what happened there a thousand years ago."

Gordon put his feet down. "It's good, Van. Really good, but a simulation is not real life."

"Never said it was, Gord, but it's all I've got, at least for now."

"Ha! If Bryson Jones applied for funding they'd give it to him," Gordon said. "He never does research, but he gets a lot of attention, and the administration likes that. You should chase publicity, Van, get on TV. That's the way to get funding these days. Forget research."

"Don't be bitter, Gord. Bryce does the university a lot of good."

"Does he? I wonder what that might be." Without waiting for an answer, Gordon, looking straight at Van, said, "There's more, isn't there?"

Van shifted uncomfortably. "I can't hide anything, can I?" He sat in his desk chair and swiveled to face Gordon. "Got a minute?"

Xultunich had been large, a sort of Pittsburgh, he liked to say. The setting was breathtaking, with the river widening to a broad lagoon constantly stirring with birds and the huge reservoir with the road curving around it. A kind of small alligator called a caiman nosed the banks, and swarms of insects rose with every step.

In spite of the beauty, he'd been worried about everything—the workers, the rains, the stratigraphy, the students. The week before the roof of the bodega, the shed where they stored the ceramics, the fragments of stucco and limestone sculpture, and the burial remains, had started leaking. He'd had to move the lab to an old hotel farther away from the site. Then the flotation tank had ruptured and they'd lost three week's work. Next day, his pollen expert came down with hepatitis.

The day he got the letter rejecting his request for another year, he had walked along the edge of the trench through the main plaza, a subsidiary plaza, and on into the elite residential complex beside the river. The workers, those small dark men with the stolid faces, had gone for the day. He'd learned, after some years of working with them, to read their expressions, but unlike some others his relationship with them was always more formal than friendly. Simmons, at Southern, for example, always seemed to be smiling and waving, spitting out his rapid, heavily accented, fractured Spanish, and they would wave and smile and joke back.

A low wall of broken stone disappeared into the grass. This had been a palace. Slaves carried plates of food, baskets filled with maize, urns of fresh water from the lagoon. He could see through the doorways into the narrow rooms, where the men once sat cross-legged on raised benches against the back wall discussing ceremonies, taxes, the will of the gods, sex, and politics. Later, after dinner, the lord might clap his hands and send for a wife, let the cotton hangings fall across the opening to his room, narrow and obscure after the sun had set. In the dark, they would grope toward one another, generate another prince, perhaps.

Van squatted beside the wall and looked back toward the central plaza, where the ruined temple pyramid, recently cleared, gleamed with the wet of mist rising from the lagoon.

He sat by the river to read the letter. It was polite, of course, but the meaning was clear. This would be his last season at Xultunich. They couldn't continue to fund so unproductive a dig.

There were hundreds of graves filled with long leg bones drawn up in the fetal position, flattened skulls rotten with anemia, a few plain pots and faint traces of feathers and cloth long decayed. The temples had concealed no spectacular jade, no intact sculpture. The monuments erected in the plaza were so worn the writing on them was barely decipherable, revealing an occasional date, a few names, a commemoration of a king's marriage, a lengthy but spotty sequence that referred to Te-Ayiin to the west and of course the tall, eroded stone Glenna called his Weathered Stela. *National Geographic* would never fly in a film crew to tell the world about Van Weathers's incredible finds, a buried treasure of intricately crafted obsidian or painted shells, a huge painted stucco mask façade on a buried temple.

He knew better, of course. This had been a vital center. The people here had lives, loves, passions, hopes, and fears. The north temple had been just under fifty meters high, nearly the size of Pyramid One at Tikal, largest in the Maya area. It had been constructed on a platform the size of a football field twenty meters above the natural level of the land. They had worked for centuries to build so high, to invest so much meaning in the marks they left on the land. And then, in a few years, they were gone.

Working here was like watching disappearing ink, the history of the place fading away before his eyes.

There were no signs of defensive walls, no great caches of spear or arrow points. The images, those faint carvings and stucco friezes, were filled with images of death, but this was utterly normal, even a bit boring. And except for the anemic skulls, there was no remaining evidence of disease or epidemic.

Something was floating toward him in the brown river. When it was close enough, he could see that it was the corpse of an enormous crocodile, one of the biggest he'd ever seen, floating upside down, its swollen belly and four clawed legs jutting up into the humid air.

"Gord, it was coming from the west, the direction of Te-Ayiin, drifting downstream, turning slowly. It bumped into the roots of an overturned tree by the bank and got stuck there, so I turned back to the letter."

The letter concluded that the plantation to the west was private property and the organization could do nothing to facilitate acquiring the requisite permits. They would of course be pleased to entertain other proposals from Professor Weathers should he decide to seek out a more promising site or take his research in a different direction altogether.

"I pushed the letter into my shirt pocket. When I looked up at the river again, the dead crocodile was gone. I'm a rational man, Gord, but for some reason I felt an eerie sensation that raised the hair on the back of my neck, as if this apparition was an omen from another time."

FROM AO TO VW: A DECLARATION

Dear Van Weathers,

It's very kind of you to offer me your copy of the monograph. Believe me, I will take extra special care of it.

I think—no, I don't think, I know—you are the most inspiring professor at this university. I hope you won't be shocked if I tell you that I may be falling in love with you. If you are shocked, please pretend I never said it. I would hate to have anything disrupt the clean flow of knowledge and understanding between us (well, from you to me anyway). It's just that the stream (more of a torrent now, I think) has become the source of life for me. Your wife is a very lucky woman.

I will come by your office to pick up the book. Please forgive me if I've
spoken out of turn.

Love,
Anne

LURKING

Elliot Blackman sat comfortably in Bryson Jones's titanium ergonomic
swivel chair (said to be a gift from the Sultan of Ghoramar) and watched
Jones's computer screen with great attention. A copy of the *Popol Vuh* lay
open beside the monitor.

He felt the small but delicious thrill of danger. Jones wouldn't be coming in, of course, but some unsuspecting student who thought Jones actually taught classes might knock, and it was better to be invisible. The office
was dark except for the computer screen, and the door was locked.

Van Weathers's office was right next door. Weathers was there, working
away, and Elliot had programmed Jones's computer to mirror Weathers.
At this moment, Weathers was checking his email. Elliot had one eye on
the messages, skimming down the subject lines, opening the ones that
looked most interesting. Weathers received messages from all over the
world, Russia, Italy, Korea, and half a dozen other countries. He leaned
forward, pulling up one message after another. In this way, he had made
himself an expert on the archaeologist, his research, his family, his career.
He had changed the lock on Van Weathers's office door. Now he controlled the keys. Because he controlled the keys, he controlled the building.
Information was power. All he had to do was read the signs, the subtle
insinuations of disorder.

He stopped scrolling and leaned back in the chair, which subtly
adjusted to his new position. "Well, well, well," he murmured. "What do
you think of that? He starts out toward Te-Ayiin. He is turned back. This
is what we've been waiting for. What do you think, eh? He won't stop at
that, will he? No, no. He'll be back."

He heard the door open and close. Gordon Flentsch had come to visit.
The two started talking about Te-Ayiin. Elliot heard Van say, "Garcia
Holdings Limited."

So Dr. Weathers is curious about Te-Ayiin, about Garcia Holdings. His boy, Jag, is interested in HFS Corporation, and Weathers's wife, Glenna, is a member of the Friends of the Rainforest. Many threads are weaving together. This job, Elliot thought, is going to provide some real entertainment. He shook his head, grinning as he leafed through the *Popol Vuh*, pausing to read about the Lords of Xibalbá. He read again about the god called One Death. The Hero Twins went down to the underworld and the Lord said, Sacrifice my dog and bring him back to life, and the twins did, and then the Lord said, Kill a person, and they did, and held up the human heart, and then the Lord fooled them and said, Sacrifice yourselves, and the Twins did so. It was a very funny joke.

Of course, in the end, the Twins got the best of the Lords, of One Death and Seven Death. But Van Weathers was not one of the Hero Twins.

Flentsch left, footsteps pattering down the hall. A short while later, there was a sharp knock. "Dr. Weathers! It's Anne!"

This would be the one sending him that mooning adolescent email. Elliot closed his eyes and listened. He could hear Weathers's muffled, "Come in, Anne."

It was as if the Lords of Xibalbá had sent Elliot a message: here is a sweet temptation. In the Trade it was called a honey trap.

ANNE OPPLE

"It's raining!" As if following a divine plan of punctuation, she dropped her book bag on the floor of Van's office with a thud.

"It's the rainy season," Van agreed. "It rains."

She sat with her back to the table that was covered with maps and archaeological debris. He sat opposite, left side toward the computer screen awash in pastel colors that grew and mutated and faded away again. Behind him was the narrow window, with its view of rain. The rain enforced a painful silence.

"You didn't answer my last email," she said.

"No, I . . . will. I will."

"Did they design these windows for archers or something?" she asked.

"You'd think so. It was to seal the building, make it easier to control the climate, I think."

They fell into silence.

"I love the course," she said at last. "The Maya, they're fascinating. Were."

"They're still with us," Van said. "They didn't disappear, that's not what collapse means, but today they're exploited, have been since the Spanish came. My wife. . . ." Van emphasized the word for some reason, then went on in a rush, ". . . is active in Friends of the Rainforest. Trying to help them survive. There are still several million at last count, scattered throughout their traditional area from the Yucatán to Honduras."

She ignored the word *wife*. "Yes, I know. But not the way they were. No cities, not like that."

"Why do you think that is?"

"I'm sorry?"

"Why do you think that is? They aren't building cities like they were? They don't make books, carve monuments, build ball courts."

She shrugged her soft round shoulders. Something leaped in his throat, which he cleared. "I don't know," she said. "They simply disappeared."

"They stopped building cities for a reason," Van suggested.

"It didn't just happen?"

"Nothing just happens," Van assured her. "Everything has a cause."

"Do you think so?" she asked innocently. "Do you really think so, everything has a cause?"

Van didn't answer. He laid his long fingers along the edge of his desk and tapped the tips, one at a time, on the thin band of metal. Did he?

Finally he said, "I'm trying to find out. It's why I built the Gate. People in there make decisions, make history, but it's heading toward the end. The world is already showing signs of strain. Deforestation, conflict, random violence." He gestured at the slow pastel curtains sweeping down across the screen of the computer behind him. "I'm trying to give you an honest answer. I believe everything has a cause, yes. Unfortunately, that's only the beginning. Causes have causes. Anything living, and many things not living, interact with the environment, with other agents, all in motion. The interactions change the environment, which in turn changes them. Every time you step back, look at a larger picture, you see more levels of interaction. So the problem is difficult. We know what happened, but we don't know exactly why."

"They were strange people," Anne said, looking at him so directly he wondered for a moment who she was talking about. "They didn't think like us."

"No," Van agreed. "They didn't think like us, but they were human just the same. They wanted answers, just like us. They suffered and wondered why. They went to . . . extremes to get those answers. In the end, they failed."

She nodded, staring at him. He stirred, forgetting why she had come, what she wanted. She picked up her book bag and stood. Her hands were clasped, hugging her books to her chest. He thought for a moment that her lower lip trembled.

"Why do you think they failed?" she asked. Her voice was almost inaudible.

Van tipped his head to one side. "That's what I'm trying to find out. We have many ideas, many questions. For instance, was the collapse caused by internal or external forces? In his book on the collapse of complex societies, Joseph Tainter lists eleven, including resource exhaustion, invasion, mismanagement, loss of faith, class warfare, some kind of natural catastrophe like drought or earthquake, and so on. We have tried many methods, like systems theory. But Tainter asks an important question: why do some societies under similar stress *not* collapse? What was inherent in the Maya cultural Great Tradition that triggered a reversion to a less complex organizational structure? We still don't know."

In the silence that followed, he shifted in his chair and looked down at his long intertwined fingers.

She interrupted his thoughts. "You promised me your monograph," she said.

"I did? Oh, yes, I did, didn't I?" He pulled it off the shelf. "As I said, it's pretty marked up."

She took it and stuffed it into her bag. "Did they do it to themselves?" she asked softly, as if speaking to herself. Her lips were moist, plump, sweet. She fled the room, leaving the door open.

Van looked at her empty seat for a while. Then he swiveled in his chair and watched the rain. It seemed to be letting up a little.

FROM VW TO AO RE: A DECLARATION

Dear Anne,

You have just left my office and I will answer your last message now, while your presence here is still fresh.

No, I'm not shocked. Sometimes these feelings come with the territory. We cannot of course take any action on them, but I appreciate your confidence in me. It is very gratifying to a man's vanity if nothing else. But you have a fine mind, Anne, and a lively way of expressing yourself, and I know you will do well.

Yours,

Van

FROM AO TO VW: ABOUT LOVE

Dearest Van,

Is that all you can say, that you know I will do well? I am involved in the Maya now, and in their fate. Are we going to go the same way, and if so, what can prevent collapse but sacrifice and love?

You refer to a man's vanity, but you are not a vain man, not at all.

I will take your monograph to bed with me tonight.

I love you,

Anne

HFS

In the darkest hour of a sleepless night, Jag slid into the fiber, following the lure of HFS Corp. Their encryption protocols intrigued him; they were very intricate and difficult. Furthermore, he couldn't figure out what HFS Corporation did, made, sold, or provided. They posted no sales literature, no annual reports, no product lists. HFS Corporation had no Web page, no existence on the Web except this heavily fortified intranet. It was maddening and intriguing. Could it be a secret government agency? A cover for international crime and money laundering? Drug dealers? Stock manipulators?

He contacted others for help. He disliked asking—it was an affront to his pride in skill—but this place was impervious, a smooth surface of digital nonsense, bland numbers and alphanumerics. It represented an anomaly in the great ocean of statistics he was analyzing.

The cursor blinked: Password? and he ran his combination programs, probing at the interface.

The Instant Message window popped open.

That you, Catalyst?

Ghostman?

Yeah. Still trying?

Jag's program was racing through combinations of nine letters and digits, and still the cursor blinked.

You'll never get in that way, Catalyst.

Why not?

Too sophisticated. You could try prime multiples.

Jag tried prime multiples. While the numbers whizzed, he asked: What the hell do these people __do__?

And Ghostman told him: Cleaning solutions, forest products, processed food, pharmaceuticals. . . . Big outfit, very important.

Pretty secret, Jag typed. No Web presence, no advertising.

They don't need to. Other people do that.

Other people?

Sure. Public companies. HFS is a holding company, lots of profits, lots of projects. Big deal. Makers of Saniclor.

What's Saniclor?

Cleaning stuff. Never mind. Any luck?

Naw, no luck. This account's __protected__!!!

Oh, well, Ghostman typed. Wouldn't be any fun if it was easy. Keep trying.

Yeah, I will.

11 Ix 12 Zak

Wednesday, November 2
The Long Count date is 12.19.12.13.14
It has been 1,869,394 days since the Maya Zero Date
The calendar round date is 11 Ix 12 Zak
Moon is 1 day old
God 4 rules the night

FROM AO TO VW: FOLLOW-UP

My Dearest Van,

You didn't answer my last email and I haven't been able to write again these past twelve days, but I watch you in class, the way your hands shape the air when you talk, the flow of ideas, and I wonder that you wrote me what you did, and that I wrote you what I did. Your voice, the voice I hear in the classroom, the voice I hear in memory, and the voice that comes to me from the pages you wrote, binds me ever more tightly to you.

I don't know what to make of this. I fear your disapproval, though you have given no indication of it in class or in our very formal dealings with one another. You have not said I should not love you. Yet I am constrained, even shy, around you. Because of you I have become obsessed with the Maya, with their presence, the story they wrote on the surface of the earth, and what happened to them that they are reduced from such heights to illiteracy and subsistence. I read in your monograph of the ideologies that formed after the Collapse, the Northern Yucatán looking ever more toward the warrior conquerors from the Valley of Mexico, thinking of them as the foreign saviors. You quote the poem by Cavafy, "Waiting for the Barbarians," the line that says, "These people were a kind of solution." Of course you point out that in fact it was no solution, for they were already losing their culture, certainly their glory, the subtle carving, the architecture, the science. What they got was more warfare, and a pervasive cult of death.

Do we have such a cult of death today? What can we do? I believe we must love, and if I have to love you through your work, I will do so.

Anne

TREMORS

Jag said, "There's been an earthquake." He was standing by the refrigerator, arms straight down at his sides. A scrap of paper dangled from his fingers.

"I didn't feel anything." Glenna was making notes. Hmong textiles now from the hill tribes of Thailand and Laos.

He laughed lightly. "Oh, it wasn't here. It was in Costa Rica."

"Ah." She wrote in her lined black-bound notebook: sericulture. The weaving in central Laos was particularly intricate. Then she looked up at him. "In Costa Rica?"

"Ninety-six dead. More than three hundred missing. Five thousand homeless." Jag pushed away from the refrigerator and sat opposite his mother.

"Shouldn't you be at karate practice?"

He shrugged. "It's Wednesday. I don't have practice on Wednesday. I have practice on Thursday. On Wednesday I come home."

"Wednesday." Glenna closed her book. "Yes, of course, it is Wednesday, isn't it?"

"We're talking point 000033 percent of the country's population dead," Jag said, checking his scrap of paper. "And another point 000102 missing. Point 0017 homeless. No doubt these numbers sound small to you, but they are very significant to those affected."

"Honey, there's very little you or I can do just now about an earthquake in Costa Rica." She paused with the art book half closed and looked at him curiously. "Are you all right?"

He looked away, baggy, knee-length shorts, his D. A. T-shirt. "Sure. I'm fine. Just a little tired." The paper joined a collection of others like it in his pocket, statistics of disaster.

Glenna smiled. "Don't worry about Costa Rica, Jag. It's a long way off."

"It could happen here," he insisted. "It has happened here. It will happen here again. There's a Big One coming."

"We're ready," Glenna assured him. "Bottled water in the garage. Extra blankets, portable radio, flashlights, batteries, dried food. Don't worry."

He nodded. "I don't worry," he repeated. "This isn't worry we're talking about. It's statistics. Statistics don't stop."

Jag was right, of course. The statistics don't ever stop; they keep coming no matter what you do. Statistics were like growing pains.

"Can you explain that T-shirt to me," she began, but just then the front door slammed. "That'll be your father." Glenna put *Asian Tribal Textiles* back on the shelf beside the refrigerator and went out to greet her husband. Jag turned on his radio, and a small voice whispered in his ear. "Rainfall is twenty percent below average and reservoirs are at only seventy-six percent," the small voice was saying. "If we have a dry winter, as expected, rationing is a strong possibility again. Marla Delare, a spokesperson for the Water District, said Monday. . . ."

"Well, well, well." Van poked his head around the door jamb. "How's the kid?"

Jag waved.

"Home early, aren't you?"

"It's Wednesday." Jag held up a hand.

"Oh. Wednesday. No karate."

"Yeah. You all right, dad?"

"Sure, sure. Working hard, is all." Van thought his son's skin had a bluish cast to it. Then he realized it was a trick of the light.

Jag changed stations. New trade treaties had altered the world's economic patterns. Imbalances were increasing in some places, decreasing in others. Next week, the flow would reverse, or next month. Currency traders were depressing the value of the peso, the cruzeiro, the quetzal.

He spun the tiny dial again. Van's brown eyes, set in his head still suspended around the door jamb, watched, a furrow of perplexity between his brows. Jag saw the fingers of his father's hand clutching the white-painted wood.

Then Van came all the way into the kitchen, his body appearing suddenly as he straightened, one foot stepping into the room and falling silently onto the tile floor. Van wore soft-sided shoes with rubber soles. They made no noise, but his baggy slacks swished as he walked. He turned a wooden chair around and sat, facing Jag.

"I'm a little worried about you, kiddo," he said thoughtfully.

"Don't worry, dad." Jag took the tiny earphones from his ears and wound up the cable. He put the tiny radio in his pocket. "I'm fine. It's Wednesday."

"Ah, yes. Easy to forget that."

"I got an A on the economics paper. The one about patterns."

"That's wonderful, Jag. I knew you'd do well."

"Did you know there was a group of Maya in Chiapas who protested a scientist studying their medicinal plants a few years ago? They said he was stealing the knowledge and resources to benefit a big pharmaceutical company."

"Is that right? Well, you can't stop people from learning."

"It was in Chiapas."

"Right. They know a lot about traditional healing."

"They seized a dam in Guatemala. They wanted reparations for the massacres, and they got them. The Maya seem to be pretty active these days."

"Yes, Jag, they're still around."

"So, Dad. How is the Maya thing, the simulation?"

Van leaned back and rubbed his eyes. "Up and running," he said. "Almost two months now and getting more real every day. Plenty of people participating. I'd say it's a success."

"That's great, dad. By the way, did you know there was an earthquake?"

"I didn't feel anything."

"You were probably working. Anyway, it was in Costa Rica. Ninety-six dead."

"Statistics are awful," Van agreed.

Glenna stood up. "I'm going to go paint," she said. After a look at her two men, she left the room.

In her absence, the light shifted slightly, like a clock ticking into thick silence.

"All the large mammals were killed off." Jag waved a thin arm. "It was called a Blitzkrieg."

"Thousands of years ago." Van moved Glenna's chair aside. "At the end of the Ice Age."

"Sure. But it never stops, does it, dad? And now an earthquake in Costa Rica."

"Just a tremor, Jag. It's too bad people were killed."

"I guess in light of the big animals ninety-six's not much." Jag let a fleeting smile cross his face and left the kitchen.

Van sighed as he opened the refrigerator. There was milk, and a yellow plastic tub of something that assured him it was so close to butter in taste he would be unable to tell the difference.

He found carrots in the vegetable bin and took out two, which he slowly peeled into the sink. He chewed thoughtfully, staring out at the street.

It curved, first left, then right, down from the cul-de-sac where number 145 ruled. His house. The kitchen window allowed him to look past the small pots of chive and tarragon at the sycamores just turning faintly yellow. The silvery bark was patchy with darker gray and pale tan. A few cars were parked along the curb, the Windsors' Explorer, the Fawcetts' pale blue Volvo station wagon. The lavender and teal dirt bike belonging to the Cavanaugh kid was sprawled on an unmowed lawn drowned in dead leaves.

The phone rang. Van started, then realized Glenna, up in her studio, would get it. He resumed chewing the carrot.

The curved street gleamed where sun shot through scattering clouds and lit the sheen of water on the pavement. The rain had only lasted a few minutes.

Van, chewing, thought of what lay beneath the street: the huge conduits filled with electric, data and television cable, and telephone lines; the enormous round cement tubes of the storm drains and the smaller black sewer lines. He knew these things were there, because he had come out to this faculty subdivision several times while it was under construction, looking for vestiges of the ancient Ohlone culture before they were bulldozed. He took some of his students for a surface survey; they walked transects, eyes on the ground, looking for telltale signs of pottery or arrowheads, the kinds of evidence on the ground suggestive of man's presence buried there. Just beyond the Cavanaughs next door, a student had found a bivalve shell. Since they were far from water, they designed a simple random sample survey and dug a few small test pits. They uncovered a very small midden and five thin layers of charcoal, separated by bands of virgin soil, representing temporary use and abandonment within the past few hundred years.

They turned the dark brown soil and the deeper adobe clay all the way down to bedrock but found no further vestiges of a previous civilization: these particular indigenous peoples had passed lightly over the earth.

He carefully dropped the stub of the first carrot into the disposal unit and began chewing the second, snapping off the sharp tip. He paused, the cone of vegetable caught between his teeth, to examine the bitten end. There were circles there, like the rings of a tree. A young carrot, he thought, just a baby. One ring.

He finished the carrot and took down a glass from the cupboard between the refrigerator and the sink and filled it from a fresh bottle of Evian water. He set the glass next to the dark green plastic pot of tarragon and stared at the empty street. There was no traffic. Yellowing leaves hung motionless. The clouds had passed on, sailed out of sight. The sky beyond the dip in the road was an empty, pale blue.

Suddenly, the glass on the window sill began to tremble, tiny standing ripples forming on the surface.

Van watched it curiously. The glass shivered, danced a millimeter to the left, fell still again. Van waited, but nothing more happened.

It was a tremor, nothing more. Just a tremor in the earth.

AFTERIMAGE

Upstairs, Glenna was mixing paint. The speakerphone hummed. She nodded at the color and said, "Foster? Are you still there?"

"Did you feel it?" Foster asked.

"Feel what?" Glenna had decided *Message, or Messages*, was finished and was at work on a larger piece, a field of rose that seemed to vibrate inside a darker red frame. This painting was warmer than the blue of *Message, or Messages*. Warmer color, warmer content.

"It felt like an earthquake." His voice over the speakerphone was hollow, as if he were in a vast basement or somewhere dusty.

"Don't be silly," Glenna said. "Where are you?"

"In the curators' lounge, by the sofa."

"The sofa? That's nice." Glenna added more titanium white, shook her head, and added some crimson. The color was elusive.

"It felt like a quake. Just for a moment."

"Probably a bus," Glenna said. "Number twenty-seven goes by the museum."

"Maybe," Foster said. "It stopped. I was calling about your sister."

"Mary?"

"Yes, Mary. I mean, does she like me?"

"I don't know, Foster, it's been a couple of weeks since I talked to her. I'm pretty deep into this painting. *Dead Tongues*, I think it is, yes, *Dead Tongues*."

"All right," Foster said. "I thought I'd ask."

"You thought you'd ask. Mm. Do you have any idea what D. A. would mean?"

"D. A.? District Attorney, isn't it?"

"No, it's a T-shirt of Jag's. I just wondered if you knew what it meant."

"No."

After a long silence, Glenna asked, "Do you like the title? *Dead Tongues*. What do you think?"

"I like it," Foster said.

"It's so hard to know," Glenna told him. She finished the large strokes and moved immediately to the left side of the field to begin the smaller, medium ones. Eventually, the brush strokes would disappear, refined out of existence, just the slightest difference in the shade of rose.

"Yes?"

"I mean, I'm not a verbal person. I don't know about titles. But *Dead Tongues*, you see?" She had turned toward the speakerphone.

"Well . . . yes, I like it."

"There you are," she said, bending toward the canvas. "There you are." But she was no longer talking to him.

Foster cleared his throat. "I called to remind you. Don't you have a meeting with the director this afternoon?"

Glenna dropped her brush. "What time is it? Oh, Lord, thanks, Foster, I almost forgot. I'll just make it."

ENTRY

Jag's mother left for the museum in a rush. He watched his father reading on the living room couch, the bottom edge of a monograph on coastal trading in the Yucatán rising and falling on his chest with each breath. After a few minutes, Jag backed from the archway and returned to his room.

HFS called to him. It was the earthquake, the statistics, the numbers. HFS made Saniclor. HFS was a multinational, a conglomerate, big. It might have a presence in Costa Rica, where the earthquake had happened, and in Costa Rica Jag knew of a file server with weak security. He might find some information, especially now after the earthquake, when everyone would be busy.

It wasn't long before he had a listing of Corporations Doing Business in Costa Rica, and in its alphabetical place, organized on a perfect model of Western rationality, was HFS, and under that a descriptive list: Lumber, Fish Canning, Sugar, Light Manufacturing, Tobacco, Energy. Categories and subcategories. Phone numbers. Officers' names. Office locations. Other subsidiaries. And countries: Mexico, Guatemala, Honduras. Cities: Mérida, Antigua, Campeche, San Cristóbal.

In the fiber, all things connect, and once you find the end of one thread it leads inevitably to another. Links appeared everywhere, many with locks and keys, doors difficult to open. But there were other links, other connections, some very old, forgotten, others new, not registered, little connections made by the programmer to debug security and forgotten, back doors into servers and file structures, subroutines dropped from the main programs pointing back to hidden access.

HFS suddenly opened up to Jag Weathers. Through the fiber, the assassin comes in stealth and silence! The assassin is at home in the Mondo, where the fiber ties everything together.

HFS was big, huge, cosmic, so vast the edges blurred into digital distances. Hundreds of billions of dollars. Networks of communications fiber closed to him, utterly proprietary, uncoupled from the global net. Satellites with scramblers and encoders, terabytes of data flowing around the world. Three hundred thousand employees, and almost none of them knew they worked for something called HFS Corporation. They worked for Saniclor, or for Allied Paper, or for Sea Foam or Petromal DF. They were loyal, dedicated (he scrolled through lists of names from six continents, several dozen countries), serious people who owed their lives to their companies.

Jag read secret corporate memos that meant nothing to him, memos about hiring and firing, about investing and dumping, resource allocation and damage control. He found lists of subcontractors, suppliers, government officials on the payroll in thirty national capitals. He found plans for public relations campaigns and countermeasures to attacks on their integrity.

HFS, he discovered, had a number of pollution lawsuits against it. People said it was an exploiter of the impoverished, an oppressor of the weak and susceptible. It controlled a sprawling network of sweatshops in Southeast Asia (where Saniclor was made, among other things) and gigantic assembly plants in northern Mexico. It hid these enterprises behind a complex of front organizations, companies, NGOs, agencies, and religious institutions. Groups they funded had names such as Friends of the Jaguar, the Society for the Protection of the Environment, the Central American Preservation Organization.

He wondered where Ghostman was. Ghostman was someone with whom he could share this sudden wealth.

GANZFELD

At 4:40, Glenna parked the Volvo station wagon and walked three blocks to the Asian Art Museum. The day was overcast with a washed-out fall light and a rising chill. She hurried along the street. A fitful breeze tumbled a Styrofoam cup along the gutter with a low clicking hiss like running water or the whisper of an empty TV channel.

A jogger thumped behind her, padded past with a staccato rhythm, turned slightly to give her a grin before he bore his wispy hair and dripping mustache away.

She nearly collided with two boys in front of a hardware store staring at an elderly man lying in the street. The contents of his broken bag of groceries were scattered across the blacktop. A white, windowless van had stopped, but no one emerged. Glenna, breathing hard, stared thoughtfully at the tableau, the two kids, the van, the old man. She started to move forward, to help, but three men materialized and lifted him to his feet. The man looked dazed, and Glenna wondered whether she should offer to call 911. The jogger had disappeared around the corner.

She looked at the old man's scattered groceries: meat wrapped in white paper, two cereal boxes, packages of yellow and white cheese, a six-pack of beer, cookies, two ears of late summer corn, a jar of pickles, now broken and leaking on the asphalt. The meat package had skidded on the rough surface, exposing a small patch of pale stuff leaking blood. She couldn't tell whether it was chicken or pork.

The white van shifted into gear and gained speed away from the scene, and it, too, was gone.

When her eyes drifted a little out of focus, as they often did lately when she was tired, she saw the abstract pattern of color and shape against the dark road surface, glyphs of meaning, obscure, insistent, and fragile. They said something about the man, his life, who he was with his two ears of corn, his beer. A lonely old man snacking on cookies, drinking as he watched talk shows on television. She felt in that abstract pattern that she knew him.

The three bystanders helped the old man into the hardware store. Since he seemed to be all right, she walked on, lost in thought. The museum was in a park. When she entered the hum and hiss and screech of traffic, all would fade. In the distance was the building, the gray stone, the steps, the glass doors, and across the road the bandstand, the pots of dry flowers and faded shrubs.

She barely saw it. Her feet touched the concrete, lifted, touched again. She thought: white package, with its small smear of flesh showing. The broken jar letting go a fan-shaped arrangement of green, pimpled lozenges. Splashes of yellow and white, pale blue and orange. A diffuse glow seeped around the shapes; it seemed to throb with her beating heart. The whole field of her vision filled with afterimage, the memory of her day, the layered reflections in the glass door to the back of the museum. She pushed through to the other side, where order settled into place, all the messages answered and filed.

EARLY WARNING

Half an hour later, as she was leaving the museum, at the top of the shallow steps, foot poised in its beginning descent to the first step down, thinking about the walk back to her car, she glanced across the road at the esplanade. A movement distracted her, and her foot missed the step. She tilted into an increasingly angular slow motion where time itself sideslipped.

Two figures were sweeping in behind a man walking toward her. The pair bracketed him as she, toppling, split her attention between her fall and the scene across the road.

One figure in a flapping, oversized T-shirt crossed in front, and the man walking toward her stopped. Almost immediately he, too, began to fall, as if paralleling her own tipping orientation to the buildings so that to her he appeared upright and it was the world tilting at an increasingly impossible angle.

The second attacker carried something away in his right hand, dark hair flaring out around his head as he went up the concrete embankment on the other side, and vanished behind the hedge. The first one now bent over the prone body, straightened, and looked directly at her.

It was a moment that came and went. He looked at her and turned away, and she saw his T-shirt displayed two dark, printed letters: D. A.

It was over in a moment. As she tried to regain her balance, she saw gray, featureless fog; the tips of cedar and fir trees; the cornice of the museum building. A hand caught her elbow and pulled her back. She fell heavily the other way, turned toward her rescuer, caught herself against his chest, straightened. "Thanks," she murmured. "Oh, Foster. Thank God, look, down there. Did you see . . . ?" She meant, *D. A., the shirt, Jag.*

"Glad to help," Foster mumbled, letting go of her elbow and touching his bow tie. "Glad. What?" He blinked rapidly.

"Over there, in the esplanade." She pointed at the form sprawled between two sets of concrete benches beside a round planter full of dried weeds.

She couldn't be sure. Not Jag, surely not, despite the shirt.

"He slip?" Foster asked.

"Attacked, two. . . ." Had she imagined the dark letters?

"Come on." Foster sprinted down the shallow steps and across the road. The traffic flowed around him. She followed cautiously, waiting for a break.

Foster intercepted her, turned her around. "Call 911. He's been stabbed. I think he's dead." His bleached face frightened her more than the body sprawled on the gravel behind him.

She turned and fled, hand waving at cars as she crossed the road, up the stairs and into the sudden deep silence of the museum. She stood just inside the door, disoriented. The guard stepped out of the coat room and touched her arm. "Henry!" she cried. "The phone!"

He handed it to her without a word.

Later, she stood at the edge of the esplanade. Foster was seated on one of the benches, his head clasped between his hands, elbows on his knees. She thought he was in shock or something, so she went to him, sat beside him, and put her hand on his shoulder. He didn't move.

When the police arrived, they rolled the man over. His eyes were wide open, staring at the empty gray ganzfeld wash of sky.

CROSSROADS

11 Ix 12 Zak

Wednesday, November 2
The Long Count date is 12.19.12.13.14
It has been 1,869,394 days since the Maya Zero Date
The calendar round date is 11 Ix 12 Zak
Moon is 1 day old
God 4 rules the night

FEDERAL RESERVE

Special Agent Lincoln A. Boytim, on stakeout, thought of himself as right-minded, right of political center (though not too far), usually right in his intuitions and opinions, and most certainly upright. Even as he stood, pretending to fill out deposit slips, at the circular counter between the front door to the bank and the line of tellers' cages, he considered his actions righteous. For over an hour, he'd been writing on the slips and throwing them away, experimenting with various names: Walker Percy, J. D. Salinger, F. Scott Fitzgerald, Imamu Amiri Baraka, Boris Pasternak.

The afternoon had been completely uneventful. Customers entered the bank. Other customers left. Feet fell on the marble floor with various qualities of sound, from soft slaps to hard claps. His ears twitched, testing the footfalls' directions and intentions, their attitudes, hesitations, and fears. If the Adversary's foot falls in the forest, and Linc Boytim is not there to hear, does the Adversary even exist?

Voices, distorted by the traditional high-, hard-ceiling ambiance of banking, echoed. These were transactions, legitimate transactions. Paper moved, money changed place. Hands ruffled through stacks of bills, counting. Fingertips touched from time to time over the stone counters as the worn bills moved. These contacts represented fleeting romance, poetry, the loamy sexual ballet of cash.

Linc Boytim waited for the moment, but it was beginning to look as if the moment was never going to come. He glanced at the clock: almost five. If it didn't happen by five, it wasn't going to happen today. And it was almost five.

It wasn't going to happen. Linc wasn't particularly disappointed. Usually it didn't happen. He hated bank robbery anyway.

His cell phone vibrated against his side. He glanced down, and it was the office, so he answered. A mugging a few blocks away in front of the Asian Art Museum. Not a federal case, just a courtesy to the city, but there were some things we might find interesting. Would he mind going to check it out?

THE LIST

Glenna watched Morton, the man from homicide, squat uncomfortably by a row of manila envelopes beside the chalked outline. The contents of the dead man's pockets were laid out neatly on the envelopes, each of which was labeled as a pocket: Right Trouser, Left Inside Jacket, Shirt.

She thought that because the detective was squatting and the federal guy knew it was important not to introduce subtle hierarchy cues into federal–city relations, he too squatted. She held the federal guy's card in her hand. Special Agent Lincoln Boytim. She thought that Linc Boytim must have learned long ago that too much depended on nonverbal messages to leave them to chance. She wanted to believe that he was sensitive to others. There was something about the way the color was washed out of the scene that reminded her of her own paintings. Messages, she thought, subtle messages everywhere.

Morton was overweight and close to retirement, but there was a deft grace to the way he examined the evidence as he briefed the federal guy.

"We got two witnesses. The woman got a better look. Two perps, one in a T-shirt, the letters D. A. Some kind of advertisement, maybe. Couldn't really tell what the other one was wearing. Looked like they were skating, so they'd be miles away by now. What do you make of this?" Morton asked, taking up from the envelope labeled Left Trouser Pocket a piece of white bond paper creased into quarters. Both men wore Latex gloves. Glenna could see their mouths move when they spoke, could just make out what they were saying.

Linc took the page by the corner and shook it out. "CAPO?" he murmured. "Company? Organization? Italian for chief? Capo di tutti capi? Organized crime?"

Morton shrugged. "A list of names," he said. "Recognize any?"

Four uniformed city police stood nearby, talking quietly in the twilight. "Nope. You?" Linc said, frowning at the list. "Redburn? Walinsky? Van den Driesche? Membership list, contributors, patrons, recruits? Why would he carry it in his pants pocket?"

"Good question." Morton pulled a driver's license from the man's wallet. "Derek Kim. Forty-three years old. Must wear prescription glasses while driving. These would be the glasses." The detective held them up and peered through the lenses. "Mr. Kim was nearsighted." He put the glasses on their envelope (Left Inside Jacket) and sorted through the cards. "OK. Rotary Club, VISA, American Express. He's a member of the Asian Art Museum, so that's where he was headed. His car's probably parked around here somewhere. We'll check. Hello, the Central American Preservation Organization. He was the director. Ever hear of it?"

Linc shrugged. "Some kind of historical group?"

Morton held out the card. "Environmental group, looks like. Check out the background."

Linc shifted a little to catch the failing light. "Rain forest. Some kind of cat?"

"Yeah. Leopard or something."

Glenna leaned her head back and breathed carefully, looking at the sky. The dead man ran the Central American Preservation Organization. They had funded her husband's dig. They were funding his simulation. A coincidence, that's all. It had to be a coincidence.

Linc handed the card back to the detective. "OK, a nongovernmental organization."

Morton stood up and pressed his fists into his kidneys, stretching his back. "Getting dark," he muttered. "Damn, I can't wait to retire."

"There's something else," Linc said, also standing. "How about sharing it? In the interests of interagency cooperation and all that. I'm here to advise, after all."

"Yeah," Morton grinned, pointing to an entry on the list. "What you think?"

Linc frowned. "Interesting," he said. "Why don't I ask?"

Morton lifted his heavy shoulders.

Special Agent Boytim took the paper and came over to Glenna. "Excuse me, Mrs. Weathers."

She looked into his eyes. They were nearly the same blue as her ganzfeld painting. "Yes?"

He showed her the paper. "Isn't this your name?"

BUILDING INSPECTION

Saniclor had already done its antiseptic work. Elliot took from the locked cabinet the Crowley Hall Primus master key, the Key of Keys, and slipped the ring over the middle finger of his right hand. Then he set forth to inspect the offices, the classrooms and lavatories, the utility closets and fire cabinets. He checked the expiration dates of the extinguishers and the soap levels in the bathroom dispensers. He checked the stocks of toilet paper and the shine of the chrome fittings. He checked the electronic panels for the steel fire doors.

He worked his way upward, floor by floor. Only the offices of Professors Flentsch (Anthropology—World Mythologies and Ethnographic Methods, 314) and Wilcox (Philosophy—The Stoics and Epicureans—in 322) were still occupied. He would check them later, when he had finished the others. He hummed softly as he wound his way to the top, opening doors and flipping switches, waiting while the fluorescent lights sputtered. He tested each phone for a dial tone, for message waiting lights (yes, Bryson Jones had messages, seven of them; it was well known that Jones never picked up his messages, so why would anyone bother to leave one?) The lights on the computer surge protectors burned steadily. He examined the surfaces of the desks for gouges or marks, for scraps of paper. Elliot's domain was the night, for in the night he had access and with access came information, and information was power.

He made his way back to the third floor. Wilcox had finally left for the evening. His office was clean, although there was a scrap of paper in the wastebasket with one word written on it: Zeno. It was a paradox: the arrow would never arrive no matter how often you halved the time of its flight; Elliot crumpled the paper and put it in his shirt pocket. Philosophers may worry about paradoxes, but that didn't mean arrows didn't kill people.

He opened the door to Wilcox's office wide enough to see Flentsch locking his. The stubby anthropologist, swinging his arms, made his way to the elevators whistling a terrifically distorted version of the theme from *The High and the Mighty*. He stepped in and pressed the button. The doors closed, and Elliot could hear the whistling grow fainter and fainter.

Elliot checked Flentsch's office. Everything seemed to be in order. Flentsch was a Spartan academic. He had no family pictures, no personal items except a few standard texts on mythology and a frail potted plant.

At the end of his tour, he sat once more at Bryson Jones's rosewood desk. He looked at Jones's computer monitor. He glanced along the books in the dark rosewood bookshelves.

The spines were somber, dark brown and tan and forest green, a serious pebbled material. Titles marched along the shelf. From where he sat near the end he could look down the long row of books, ripples of their spines dwindling away to a vanishing point near the door.

He raised himself in the seat, looked down the next shelf up. A book was indented too far, not aligned. He was certain he replaced books carefully.

He rose and took two steps, now facing the spine: *Mesoamerican Mythology*, a very fat, heavy book. He could barely get his thick fingers between the top of the book and the shelf above, and when he did he pulled too hard and the book tilted out and fell. He caught it near the floor and held it.

That had been close. He might have damaged the book, bent the corner, ripped a page. He sat in the exquisitely comfortable chair and leaned back a little, the thick book in his lap. He began leafing through the pages: Mayan mythology. Xibalbá. The White Road. The Lords of Death.

There was a picture of a bent old man with a big fedora and a swollen belly. He recognized One Death from the *Popol Vuh* (read some time ago and carefully replaced on the third shelf). There were twisted figures, and skull figures, and little rodent gods. Time passed as Elliot turned the heavy paper. Here was the Buenavista Vase again, with the feathered young lord dancing his way out of hell.

He put the book aside and thought, feet up on the desk.

Maybe it was too bad no one had been interested in n-dimensional topologies and chaotic systems in applied mathematics, but it had led Elliot Blackman into this interesting situation.

He turned on Professor Jones's computer and went through a series of menus. He could do it from anywhere, but his favored location was this terminal in the office next to Van Weathers'. GHOSTMAN started skimming messages. It was most interesting, most satisfactory, here in the dark night office, to slip into what that kid Catalyst called The Mondo.

There were two messages for Ghostman. The first was from his employer, Priority Urgent, block red text: The operation was a success, but the patient died. It was signed: Chief of Surgery.

Elliot frowned. Was this his problem?

There were hacker groups, kids who liked to get into computers. They posted information (which was power) on telecommunications companies, bank mainframes, the sprawling private networks that handled computer and voice traffic for the Pentagon, the National Security Agency, NATO. Elliot had learned a lot from them. Oh, yes. The Digital Assassins were legendary hackers of the Internet, freeloaders, pirates, and bootleggers of data. They viewed the world in a very different kind of light. Some of them were street punks, willing to do anything for a fee.

Elliot had recommended them to the Chief of Surgery. And now the Chief was saying the patient had died.

That was too bad, of course, but in the end it could only mean more work for Elliot. They could hardly blame him for any excessive enthusiasm their contractors may have shown. At least they got the evidence back.

The second message was from the kid. Catalyst was digging deep into HFS; he had broken through security. Costa Rica. Damn, this kid was good, really good. You had to admire his persistence, his ingenuity.

Was Catalyst a Digital Assassin?

Things were getting really interesting.

LATE EVENING

Van sat up with a start when the book slid off his chest onto the floor. He grunted and picked it up. He glanced at his watch as he put the book back in the bookcase. It was dark outside.

He heard voices. A car door slammed.

"Funny," he said aloud. He opened the front door to see a car pull away, a gray sedan shiny under the street light. Jag was coming toward him on his roller blades.

"Oh," Van said. "It's you."

"Yeah." Jag stopped by the front door to take off his blades.

"Who was that?"

His son shrugged. "I dunno. Some guy. Wanted to find the student union. He had a map, so I showed him."

"Oh. You been out long?"

The boy shrugged and carried his skates into the house. "Not long. You were asleep."

Van grinned. "Yeah, I think coastal trading patterns got to me. Where's your mom?"

Jag shrugged. "I dunno. She went to the museum for something, but that was hours ago."

"OK. You hungry?"

"Yeah, I could eat."

"Well, then, let's start some dinner. Your mom must've gotten hung up at the museum."

They were boiling water when Glenna got home. "Whoah," Van said when he saw her face. "What happened?"

She came to him and put her head against his chest. He held her, and after a moment she pushed away. "There was some excitement," she said shortly. "What are you making?"

"No, no, you don't slip out so easily. Something happened."

She gave him a look and he understood she didn't want Jag to hear. He shrugged. "We were going to make pot roast. It's what I found in the fridge. And boiled potatoes."

She nodded.

Van thought dinner was a strange affair, a series of tense silences broken by sudden outbursts of rapid conversation.

Finally, the dinner was cleared and Jag went away shaking his head. "Gotta project for Mr. Sugar to do," he said. They heard the door to his room close.

"So?" They were standing in the kitchen. The dishwasher hummed in a series of rising and falling moans.

"So. . . ." Glenna stood tensely beside the sink. "A man named Derek Kim, the director of the Central American Preservation Organization, came to the Asian Art Museum. He was carrying a list of names. My name was on it."

"I've never met him, but he did sign my funding letters."

"He's dead."

"I'm sorry. So is Waxaklahuun Ub'aah K'awiil." The thirteenth king of Copan had been captured and sacrificed by his client state Quirigua.

If Glenna heard his feeble joke, she didn't react. "He was stabbed. I saw it. He was coming toward me and two men came up, and then he fell down and they just disappeared. It's been police and the FBI and answering questions for hours."

Van touched her shoulder, but she gave no sign she felt it. The king had been beheaded, probably after torture. Things didn't seem to have improved since then.

"There's more." She stared out at the dark yard.

Van waited.

"Oh, Van, I don't know. Has Jag been here?"

"Jag? As far as I know. I fell asleep. He went out roller blading for a while, but. . . ."

Her face tightened. "I think they were on roller blades. The killers. And one of them was wearing that T-shirt. D. A."

SURFING

In the computer lab in the basement of Crowley Hall, Wendell watched text scrolling up his screen. "Uh-huh," he said softly. "The cuckoo's back."

The only other student, a girl with stringy hair, looked at him with a curiosity that turned to scorn when he pulled the boots off to reveal his calf-high crimson socks with brown cockroaches stitched in parallel lines up the sides, but he didn't care. She got no response to her look and left soon after.

Wendell had several windows open on his computer screen on top of an overview of the Maya simulation, including several graphic depictions of its social health and logs of participants. In a separate window, he prowled through an alternative computer mythology newsgroup; he often checked in there because it was so weird. People with power fantasies posted their darkest dreams of apocalypse, bringing down the global networks, toppling governments, or directly hacking genetic material, creating new life forms, not always benign. It wasn't really his taste, but Wendell was a graduate student in anthropology and liked to think of it as fieldwork among the truly strange.

And here was the cuckoo, the one called Ghostman. Wendell thought he remembered someone using that name, but he couldn't quite place it. It was a while ago. Someone he met?

Whoever he was he was now contributing an idiosyncratic brand of global conspiracy, this time through cosmic ray manipulation. Was he putting everyone on or did he really believe this stuff?

He posted a message: "To Digital Assassins: Ghostman says check out Xibalbá Gate."

Wendell sniffed. Who was Ghostman? Who were the Digital Assassins? Whoever they were, it looked as if they were going to recognize his work, and that was gratifying. He ran a search and turned up a few references to an informal hackers' group with that name, but nothing of substance. He brought the Gate to the front.

There were 426 people logged on. In the Maya world it was night, and fire was everywhere in the mountains. Burning season still. It was April in the simulation, though here it was November.

It nagged at him. Digital Assassins. It didn't make much sense, but he knew where he could go to find out.

He shut down the computer, put on his boots, and left the lab, pausing only to switch off the lights and lock the door as requested by a prominently displayed sign. It was early for a nocturnal creature such as Wendell, so he drove slowly through downtown. The denizens were out, despite the recent rain and the late chill. All the multicolored hair, vibrant tattoos, chrome and leather, and flesh hanging out on the curbs, the sophisticated cigarettes and terminal depression engaged in petty commerce, the chatter and intricate sexual crosscurrents: Wendell loved it all.

Chips 'N Dips was a cyber cafe near the far end of University. Someone there would be able to brief him about the Digital Assassins.

IN THE DARK

Van and Glenna spoke together in darkness: he, on his left side, right knee overlapping the left, legs slightly flexed, his right hand on her shoulder, turned toward and facing him, inches away, her breath on his chin; she, naked under the light cover of woven Guatemalan cotton, long muscle trains down the length of her upper arms, taut under his palm, eyes for the moment open to the shadow of his form, this man beside her.

He spoke softly against the smooth plain of her forehead. "The Road of Light," and his palm moved along the curve of her shoulder.

She lifted the shoulder up against his hand.

His fingers moved onto her upper arm, squeezed gently the firm flesh there. "They saw the white band of stars across the sky as a road. And the cleft in the Milky Way, that is the Black Road, the road to Xibalbá."

"The road not taken. . . ." Her voice was distinct in the deeper silence of their room. There were no other sounds to break upon them, no traffic, no digging in the dirt for things long buried.

"Their constellations, like ours, all animals. What we call Gemini, the twins, they saw a couple, too."

"A couple."

"Copulating peccaries."

"Pig lust. Nothing to do with us."

"Not true," he said. His fingertips curled into the hard band between her neck and shoulder joint. "As above, so below."

She repeated, "So below." Their bodies, not yet touching, swayed in an intangible breeze.

His hand touched the bend of her elbow, cupped the sharp point of bone, drew her hand to his face so he could kiss her palm. "They believed this world, ours, the current one, was created in 3114 BC, August 13."

"Long time ago," she murmured.

"And it's going to end in just a few years, in December, two days before Christmas. I'll be close to retirement."

She took her hand away, rolled slightly back, leaving her elbow in the bowl of his hand. "Oh, Van, I'm worried."

"I know." He knew she meant Jag, asleep behind his stop sign. "But it just isn't possible. He's not that kind of kid. He wouldn't be involved."

"I know that. But we have to face it, he has the shirt. He wasn't here, at least not for a while. Was he wearing that shirt?"

"I don't think so, but he was wearing a jacket."

"And the car. You said there was a car."

"Glenna, I told you. It was just someone asking directions."

"Yes, but the police might not think so. . . ." She turned that half degree toward him once more. "He doesn't have an alibi."

He moved in the dark, and the mattress sank and rose a little. "He doesn't know he needs one."

"It was the same shirt." She squeezed his arm.

"It's a common shirt," Van said. "Lots of people have it, I'm sure. Now that I think about it, I haven't seen that shirt for a while."

She laughed a little. "I put it in the bottom of the laundry. It's still there, I checked. He never said anything about it."

"Then there's nothing to worry about. He didn't have the shirt."

"He could have found it and put it back," she murmured.

She could feel his shrug, his breath as he spoke. "Let's not make trouble where there isn't any."

"You're right, of course," she sighed.

He let go of her elbow and reached to her belly, strong, firm rounded hill, dimpled navel, the softer dark.

"So below," she laughed, reaching for him in turn. "It will be all right."

There were cycles of time, the circling progressions of Venus and Mars, tighter pulses of the moon, the rapid whirl of days. And there were vast turnings as the galaxies spun.

They meshed and interlocked, these cycles of time. They aligned with one another in a dance of connection and change, reset themselves, and everything was as it was in the beginning. The Great Cycle of the Long Count that began in 3114 BC would come to an end, and in that moment a new cycle would begin, and the world would be created anew.

12 Lamat 6 Keh

Wednesday, November 16
The Long Count date is 12.19.12.14.8
It has been 1,869,408 days since the Maya Zero Date
The calendar round date is 12 Lamat 6 Keh
Moon is 15 days old
God 9 rules the night

FROM VW TO AO RE: FOLLOW-UP

Dear Anne,

I've been really busy the last couple of weeks and haven't had a chance to answer your last message, for which I apologize.

I want you to know that I'm glad I see you in the simulation, even if I cannot know who you really are there.

I don't want to encourage you to be infatuated with me; it would be neither desirable nor appropriate, yet we do seem to have some common interests, and I find that gratifying—more than gratifying. There are only a handful of people in the world interested in my work, and few enough who have the passion you have shown for a subject about which I too have such passion. At the same time you leave a troubling scent in the air.

Perhaps it would be better if we did not see too much of each other outside of class. As you know, there are legal as well as moral difficulties associated with too much contact between faculty and students.

Yours,
Van

GYMNOPAEDIAE

Meaningful sacrifice must not be constrained by time or goal. So it was on a November Wednesday at noon, the exact center of a week, that Glenna

Weathers, tenaciously and without letup, followed the stations of her ordeal.

First was the climbing, stepping always up, reaching for the higher, for the beating of her heart against the ribs and the strain in her thighs and calves, the yearning for more, for the burning of calories and conditioning of the wind.

Next she must strain against the weight, taking it on the soles of her feet, and the balls of her feet, the weight of it increasing by turns, and pushing it away with the muscles in her abdomen and her legs, for the strength of the knees and thighs.

Next she must sit beneath a bar laden with iron, and press upward with the palms of her hands and let the weight down slowly, for her shoulders and her back.

And next she must lift weight in each hand, up and out, to open the chest, and to feel the flesh of her breasts press against the stretched fiber of her garment, for the strength of that round pouch of muscle over the complex interlocked bones of her shoulder.

And next facing the ladder of iron bricks she must pull down for the strength of her upper arm, and the density of its flesh, and its power.

And in between them all she paused to breathe, and to look at herself reflected in the many mirrors of the room, and this is what she saw:

Hair, blonde almost to its roots;

Shoulders, rounded over upper arms, bare below the short sleeve of the dark green tank top, and her breasts still firm, and her stomach and her thighs firm in their tight black covering, to shapely knees and fine calves, her best features she felt, and feet in white athletic shoes, neatly turned, size six;

Her hands, pressed to her firming belly, white fingers a little too long, the fingers of a piano player although she did not play piano, but played some flute when she was a girl, awkwardly, with short breath and spaces between the notes, but with feeling and hope; and the long, narrow backs of the hands joined to the grace of her wrists, still delicate and clean, save where her watch broke the white column of her forearm with its dark and sweat-stained brown leather band;

And with care she examined her face, its oval shape, a bit too round at the cheek and chin, and the eyes, looking widely back, not so sharp as they once were, so the lines she knew were forming, faintly etched just beneath the surface of the skin of her face, were blurred, almost gone, more youthful than if she wore her reading glasses purchased at the discount pharmacy.

It was autumn. There were clouds above the city. The temperature was seventy-one degrees Fahrenheit, winds were light and variable. Jag was innocent. She had no worries.

Trace memory appeared without sound, leaving the faint tang of low tide in her nose: Hawaii, on her honeymoon with Van Weathers, a thousand years ago, it seemed.

INTERVIEW

Special Agent Linc Boytim was waiting in the lobby of the gym, a quirky, boyish grin playing around the corners of his mobile lips. She was still running her towel over her hair and almost passed by him when he called out: "Mrs. Weathers."

She stopped and looked at him, lowering the towel. "Agent . . . Boytim, isn't it?"

"Yes, very good, that's right."

"Ah."

"Can I talk to you a few minutes? A few questions, follow-up, you understand."

"Uh, sure." She looked around helplessly. A troop of middle-aged woman marched through the room to jazzercise.

"We could talk in my car," he suggested. "It's right outside."

"Well, I suppose."

She followed him to his car, a tan sedan, not new, not old, and sat in the passenger seat looking at his profile.

"You're an artist," he said.

"Yes?"

"I talked to Foster, at the Museum, he said you painted. He said you were good. Show opening soon, right after the holiday, he said."

She nodded, wondering where this was going.

He nodded as if she had answered a question. "You told me the Central American Preservation Organization had provided funds for your husband, his archaeology."

"My husband, yes. He's worked in Central America, an archaeologist.

He was excavating at a place called Xultunich. I don't belong to CAPO. I do belong to Friends of the Rainforest. The indigenous people around there need help . . . and the forest, of course. . . ."

"I understand," he said, and it was simply an agreement. "I would like to know why Mr. Kim was carrying that list. Why your name was on it. Could you have been a potential member?"

She shrugged and felt a tension in her shoulders. From the exercise, she thought. "I doubt it. CAPO is a grant-giving, nongovernmental organization, not a membership organization. They support research into the heritage of indigenous cultures. I really don't know why my name was on the list."

Linc nodded. "We're pretty sure he was coming to see you, though. Perhaps he was going to tell you something, or ask something. The killers were probably not after that list. You told us they got something, but we don't know what it was. You said it looked like a piece of paper?" His fingertips were resting on the top of his steering wheel, and she watched them. Light slanted through the windshield and gave them a luminous life as they moved, one, then another, up and down, touching the curve of brown plastic.

"I don't know," she said. "I don't know. That's what it looked like, but it happened so fast. . . ."

"And the boy in the T-shirt," Linc said softly.

She shivered. The light faded, his fingertips slowed, stopped. "What about him?" she said.

"D. A.," he said, looking at her for the first time. "We found out what it means."

"Really? What?"

"Well, if it means nothing to you, I'll have to keep looking." He had turned halfway in his seat to look at her, and she thought for a moment that he wanted to take her hand, to press it to his lips.

"I asked my son about it," she said. "It's a computer group. The shirt is quite common when you know about it. D. A. It's everywhere. People interested in computers, that's all."

He waited in silence, and the moment passed. "Digital Assassins," he said at last.

"Yes, something like that."

"It doesn't sound strange to you? Assassins?"

"They're interested in computer code," she said. "Not killing people."

"OK. Thanks for your time," he said suddenly. He reached across her to open the door.

"No, of course."

"By the way," he said as she started toward the gym entrance.

She turned.

"Where was your son that day?"

"He was at home. My husband was there."

"OK. If you don't mind, I'll be in touch."

She watched him drive away, wondering if it was fear or something else that had moved inside her when she saw his fingers tap the wheel like that.

FROM AO TO VW: AN OBSERVATION ABOUT RHYMES

My Dearest Van,

Have you noticed that our names rhyme, Van and Anne? Perhaps you don't think this is meaningful, but you should. After all, you wrote *Graphic Communication and the Structure of History* and know the significance of such convergence, perhaps not in a metaphysical sense, but certainly on the level of belief. I believe for example that this rhyming means something, suggesting through parallel sounds a powerful directional flow: we are going the same way. So I have entered the Xibalbá Gate and will discover you there (like an unknown land). We would be more completely connected there through the fragile flow of our words to each other.

It may be disappointing for me not to know who you are, although I believe (that word again!) that I will know you when I hear (see?) your words. I'll recognize your voice, your style, and the intonations of your speech even though it's synthesized and you're typing words in a distant place.

I have never seen it, but I have begun to dream of your body, your long arms and lean sides, your secrets. Is this shocking? I want to be honest with you always, to confess my feeling for you, and what happens to me. Perhaps it is my father I dream of (I know that's what they would tell me at the Counseling Center), but that doesn't really seem relevant, does it? After all, you are not my father and yet I dream of you.

Now I am going to really shock you—I seek and find satisfaction with that dream image. It helps me to sleep, and gives me hope that one day this dream will be a reality. Know that I would do anything for you, you have only to ask.

Your devoted,
Anne

I mean anything.

BY THE NEVA

As midnight approached on November 16, St. Petersburg was frozen solid.

Leon Blatskoi, a doctor of philosophy with a complicated mind and a life his friend Van Weathers imagined was simple, sipped tea between puffs on his cigarette. Smoke rose, creasing his narrow, seamed face, twisting across the fluffs of ragged hair in front of his ear, straightened in its climb, hit the high ceiling, flatted in two directions, merged with the layer of cold smoke already up there.

Mara entered the room, carrying a tin of tea. "More?" she asked, holding out the tin.

Leon shrugged and nodded, a curious counterpoint of motions. It seemed as if the cigarette had not moved, although certainly his head had bobbed and his shoulders twitched.

Mara took his cup from him and filled it with hot water from the samovar under the window. The window would have looked out onto the Neva River if the view weren't still blocked by construction. The view had been blocked by construction since Brezhnev.

"I become a new man," he said. His voice was hoarse. The cigarettes, probably.

Mara did not respond. He often spoke like this.

"I have no work, no friends. Alberto is in Italy. America is very far away. I am tired of who I am, Mara."

Still she kept silent, straightening his books, organizing his disordered life.

"Who am I? I am an unemployed armchair archaeologist on a dwindling government pension. Inflation is what, a hundred percent? The world is coming to an end, Mara. Hooligans roam the streets. The stores are either empty, or the prices change by the minute. It is stupid, Mara, to live. So become someone else. Say good-bye to Leon."

She sat in the other chair, the stiff-backed one with the horsehair cushions. She folded her plump hands in her lap and watched him closely. He was often melancholy, but she had never seen him this glum. She didn't think there was a gun in the building, but probably she should take no chances, so she watched him.

He came as close to smiling then as he ever would, though he was not looking at her. Instead he lifted his hand, the one with the cigarette, and waved it toward his desk. The smoke drew zigzags in the thick air. "As long as they don't shut off the electricity, I can use the computer my American friends have given me to become someone else."

Mara said, "Mmn."

"I become an aristocrat, Mara. I have designed a personality for myself, a man of wealth and power. What do you think of that? It is no sacrifice at all, to give up this old body, this old persona."

"Mmn," she said, but he was already tapping the keys and didn't hear.

7 Manik 10 Zec

April 14, 837 AD
The Long Count date is 10.0.7.3.7
It has been 1,442,587 days since the Maya Zero Date
The calendar round date is 7 Manik 10 Zec
Moon is 1 day old
God 4 rules the night

BALCHÉ

One of Reed Altar's wives pours for Knot-Eye, then for her husband. The fermented honey *balché* foams to the brim of the ceremonial cup. Knot-Eye drinks deeply, sighs, and puts the cup down.

"My messenger has returned from Green Mountain," Reed Altar says slowly. He examines the cup. Two elaborately costumed young lords in red and orange dance against an off-white background. The painted glyphs around the rim of the cup commemorate Knot-Eye's accession to the rulership of Xultunich.

They are seated cross-legged in Knot-Eye's informal council chamber. The opening curtain is drawn back, revealing the stars. Because the opening faces east, in the direction of the Red Road, they have to avoid looking at the God Who Has No Name. He has climbed up the roof of heaven since they met last, and his loincloth is unraveled even more, trailing across the White Sky Road.

Reed Altar sets the cup aside. "Very nice," he says.

Knot-Eye waits in silence, as befits the *ajaw* of Xultunich.

Reed Altar continues, "My messenger has told me that Quetzal Tree has agreed to an alliance with Last Stone. His daughter, Evening Star, will be waiting. I will leave in eight days for Green Mountain, and will bring her here."

"That is good. You have done well, Reed Altar."

Reed Altar lowers his handsome head, and the flare of tassel-hair swings forward beside his ear. He is dressed, Knot-Eye realizes, as the young Maize God come to life. A good omen, in ordinary times, but now Knot-Eye is not so certain.

Reed Altar looks up. "I must ask, Uncle."

"Ask."

"You have shown a need for this alliance. The alliance has been agreed. What of the captives, the sacrifice?"

Knot-Eye nods to the woman, who once more pours the foaming drink from the large gourd she has been holding in her lap. Before he drinks, Knot-Eye thinks over his answer. Finally he nods, drinks deeply, and waits politely as Reed Altar also drinks. Then he speaks. "I leave tomorrow. I will have returned by the time you are here with Evening Star. We will bring twenty high-born captives for the ball game. I will sacrifice. Evening Star herself must also bleed. We must speak to the ancestors, we must have the ancestors with us, the ancestors must favor us."

Reed Altar nods. "It has been many k'atun, many rounds of twenty years, since such a great sacrifice was made, if such has ever been made before. This will be a great day for our city."

"And for Green Mountain," Knot-Eye says.

"Yes, for Green Mountain." Reed Altar nods to his wife, and once more she pours into the cups. The two men drink.

"Uncle?"

Knot-Eye is suddenly alert. "Yes."

"It is said. . . ." Reed Altar pauses. "It is said that the city to the west, which is called Te-Ayiin, Place of the Crocodiles, it is said that this city is a place of death."

Knot-Eye frowns. Something is hidden in this question that he cannot see. "It is said that the Lord of Te-Ayiin was sacrificed. He has joined the Lords of Xibalbá."

"It is said," Reed Altar goes on, "that there is something at Te-Ayiin that speaks evil for Xultunich, something that may . . . *interfere* with the wedding, the succession, the lineage."

"Te-Ayiin is abandoned. The lintels are burned. The city is no more," Knot-Eye says gravely. "There is nothing more to speak of this place."

"It is said," Reed Altar persists, "that the Place of Crocodiles holds a secret. That the God Who Has No Name is going there. We would know what that might be. If it threatens Xultunich then it will threaten also Green Mountain."

"You need not be concerned about Te-Ayiin," Knot-Eye says. "Te-Ayiin is no more." He closes the conversation by clapping his hands. Four musicians appear out of the darkness. He nods, and they begin to play.

Turtle drums, deer-hide drums, the clay ocarinas and pipes and the long wooden trumpets skirl and scree. Knot-Eye knows Te-Ayiin is put to one side but is not forgotten.

Tonight, though, Reed Altar's wife dances, stepping high, before the two men, who lean back and watch, cups in hand. Now that the business of the evening is over, they are compelled to drink until they sleep. The gods demand it.

STELA BY STARLIGHT

In flickering light, Flint Howler paints on the smooth limestone surface. He outlines in black the profile of his king, Knot-Eye, holding the two-headed bar of kingship. At Knot-Eye's waist he draws the dangling face of the jester god; at the king's back he hangs a jade skull. Under that, the king will wear the white paper skirt for the perforation ceremony.

Kneeling before him looking up is Evening Star, whom Flint Howler identifies by outlining her name glyphs over her head, though he does not yet know her face. In her hands she holds a group of stingray spines. These she will use for her own sacrifice. Before her knees there is a bowl holding folds of bark paper.

Knot-Eye holds a long torch over her. Around their heads, Flint Howler has already prepared the glyphs to describe this moment in the Long Count and in the calendar round, for the day of the ceremony is set. Flint Howler has written the glyphs for the same day, 4 Ajaw, 8 Kumk'u, when, cycles before, the gods created the People of Maize, the People who live now in the Middle World. The day when a man named Knot-Eye appeared to begin Time itself. So it would begin again, as it had before. There was only a slight adjustment to the calendar needed, for the last such date was only a few months ago. Although the actual date of the event would have a later date, they could create the connection with the Beginning by writing it so.

Flint Howler knows the importance of such statements, the connections through time with the origins. Although he might himself doubt their truth, for he is a man of secret doubts who uses the word "perhaps" when speaking in his own mind, his hand is steady as it traces the intricate, looping lines for the carving he will make, covering the stela from top to bottom with writing and with image.

When he lays down his brush at last he looks up, past the torchlight to the stars, steady in the roof of heaven. The God Who Has No Name wanders freely there, wandering to the west, toward the black road, in the direction of the place called Te-Ayiin, the Place of Crocodiles, the dead city in the hills.

For a moment, Flint Howler wonders about that place. People whisper about it, and now, in his mind, he has made a connection with the God Who Has No Name.

It is as if the world were coming to an end. And this only makes the setting of the wedding date at the beginning of the Cycle of Time that much more important.

The people must believe. This at least he knows to be true.

TRUE

Dreams are true. It is a lesson learned many times during the lifetime of a man, and Knot-Eye must learn it many times, like all who are human and so trapped in the middle world. Knot-Eye, filled with *balché*, asleep, sees the Vision Serpent raise its head, sees One Monkey lean out with empty eyes.

One Monkey speaks words that tumble forth, twist in the air, dark feathers, dry insects, falling.

Knot-Eye looks upward into the face of the founder-father of his lineage, and the older man looks blindly back. Knot-Eye can feel the pulse in both their necks, heart beat and drum beat. That beat will be the pulse of his blood pushing forth.

In the corner of his eye, just inside the shadowed edge of the forest, just under the dark lid of the tomb, just behind the swaying curtain of finger bones and human teeth, he can see his animal *way* caper and leap.

Die, die, die, the *way* shrieks without sound. Its arms are thin and far too long, ending in jaguar paws or crocodile claws, sharp as obsidian blades, sharp as stingray spines. Its mouth is too wide, even for the teeth. And swiftly it comes toward him, opening its jaws. They blot out the world entirely, the jaws of the Vision Serpent, holding the ancestor's face.

12 Lamat 6 Keh

Wednesday, November 16
The Long Count date is 12.19.12.14.8
It has been 1,869,408 days since the Maya Zero Date
The calendar round date is 12 Lamat 6 Keh
Moon is 15 days old
God 9 rules the night

SILENT WEATHER

Van dragged himself out of his dream. His eyes opened to stare at the clock on the nightstand. It was 11:44 p.m. He could see the photograph of himself and Glenna and Jag on their trip to Chichén Itzá when Jag was four or five, a decade ago.

Glenna sat up. "Again?"

Watery street light filtered through the woven blue-and-rose silk curtains into their bedroom, delineating the merest outlines of the carved cedar chest that contained Glenna's Asian fabrics, the dresser.

His breathing slowed. "Gordon."

She put her hand on his arm. "Mm."

"In the mouth of a Vision Serpent."

"Mm." Glenna was sleepy.

"We're going to war."

"Who with?" She was falling back to sleep, and old memories floated up. "The Russians?"

"No. Never mind, I'm just dreaming about the sim, that's all. Go back to sleep." He sat for a time, letting his breathing slow. It had been Gordon's face surrounded by the serpent jaws, the scuttling insect words: "New corn, new moon, new jaguar."

What the hell did that mean? Prophecy, or simply random firings in his neurons?

Gordon was right, the simulation was seductive. It was invading his dreams. As he had invaded the dreams of his student, Anne Opple? As she in turn seemed to be seeping into the nooks and crannies of his life?

He looked at Glenna, falling back into the shallow breath of her sleep, and he was alone in the room. With a sigh, he rose and stood by the window looking across his back lawn. He could just make out the black rectangle of the neighbor's swimming pool. Over centuries, the priests at Chichén Itzá had sacrificed by throwing precious objects, children, and women into the sacred well. But that was far to the north, and well after the rest of the Maya world had lapsed into silence. Cenotes, sacred wells, existed only where the limestone plate of the northern Yucatán had itself collapsed to make a round well in the ground. They collected water, the source of the city's life. If the well went dry, the city died. They sacrificed to maintain their lives. Van shook his head: the Post-Classic Maya of the Yucatán were too different in too many ways.

He dressed quietly in the dark and left the bedroom. As he closed the door carefully behind him, Gordon's face, framed by dripping fangs, began to fade.

Was Gordon a supernatural inside the Xibalbá Gate? He might actually play the part of One Monkey, but that did not give him the right to enter Van's dreams.

On his way to the kitchen, he heard a sound from Jag's room and looked in. His son crouched in his big chair watching television with the sound low. His computer screen flickered beside him.

"Up late?" Van asked at the back of his son's head.

Jag turned and waved. "Oh, dad," he said, turning back.

Oh, dad. "Is it, Oh, hi, dad, or is it, Oh, for God's sake, dad?" Van asked.

"It's Oh, hi, dad," Jag said.

"OK. Don't stay up too late. School night."

"I know. Don't worry." He turned. "Did you know the Maya live in an area covering 126,360 square miles stretching from the Yucatán to Honduras?"

Shaking his head, Van went into the kitchen. He poured French roast beans into the grinder.

The dark beans fragmented in the grinder under a clear plastic lid, curling into the funnel shape of a drain. Anne rhyming her name with his, what had she meant? She found satisfaction with his image, she dreamed of his body. Van Weathers, half a century old, standing by the sink in his suburban kitchen grinding coffee, felt a guilty twinge of lust. He turned his thoughts instead to his son watching a map of the United States, all swift-moving cartoon clouds and animated lightning, taking notes from the Weather Channel with its roll call of highs and lows and no sign of a weather person.

He decided to leave the coffee ground for tomorrow and go out, get some fresh air, breathe away the fragments of haunted dream that still cluttered his memory.

D. A.

Jag waited until he heard his father drive away and swiveled back to his computer. His Mondo mailbox was full of stuff, numbers, seven-digit phones, or ten-digit-long lines, IP addresses, DNS servers, pass codes, PINs, access and encryption and backdoor alphanumerics.

He ricocheted around the fiber for a while, listening to the tones, bleeps, ringing, the shriek and warble of a connection.

Enter your password.

Jag had passwords; he was Catalyst, feline prowler through the silicon forests, predator of the Mondo.

There were layers of protection, of course. There were gates through which he had to pass, gatekeepers he must greet, signs he must give. There were attractions and dangers, but he knew them all.

"Catalyst!" someone typed, and he tapped keys.

"It went down, we're famous, man." It was Mr. Calvert, all suave sophistication who put in the smiley grin :-)

"Yeah," Jag agreed. He was one of the few, the true, the crew.

"So did you hear, they say someone from DA killed a guy, in your city. November second. Asian Art Museum."

"Killed?"

Mr. Calvert answered, "Yeah. Stabbed a guy."

Jag typed a series of signs, swearing on screen.

"Why, man? Just wearing the shirt, that's what they say."

"Never mind," Jag typed. "It's a family thing."

"They think you did it or something?"

"I don't know. I don't think so, but maybe."

"Uh-oh. Did you?"

"Get serious, Calvert. You saw me, you know I wouldn't. Even if I do take karate lessons."

"Well, word is, it was one of us, wearing the shirt."

"So who?"

"I don't know, Catalyst. If I knew that I'd be Chief of Police."

"Yeah," Jag said. "Chief of Police."

He frowned at the television screen. Cartoon clouds sailed over the green heartland like bloated ghosts, and he thought of Ghostman who, like Mr. Calvert and the others, prowled in the Mondo.

Who, he wondered, would Ghostman be in the meat world?

Someone with a knife?

Jag wondered what happened to his Digital Assassin T-shirt and felt a dark tendril of fear.

CHIPS 'N DIPS

Van walked down University Avenue, peering into the faces of the young people. They were varied and unfamiliar, the lean and serene, the plump and devout. Would Jag ever be one of them? Would he dye his hair or shave it, put rings in his eyebrows?

Van found it difficult to imagine their mental life. They seemed to relish pain or the illusion of pain, as if putting wire through their skin proved they were alive.

The Maya had tattooed themselves, and they had certainly pushed sharp things through their earlobes and lips, nasal septum, and tongue; the elite grew up with boards tied to their heads, flattening the skulls into elaborate, back-slanting crests. They were distinguishing themselves from others, marking their bodies with their conceptions of status and the way the universe worked. They were communicating with each other through the pieces of jade they set into their teeth, the way they deformed the heads of their children. They bled themselves to experience ecstasy, altered consciousness to get in touch with the divine, though it was difficult to conceive how the Lords of Xibalbá were in any way divine. Still, why shouldn't this tribe do similar things? They had to mark their transition through adolescence somehow. Their culture offered no clear rituals, so year after year they had to invent their own, each time extending the limits of the acceptable. What would they be doing next year, or at the end of the Maya cycle?

Music—the subsonic thuds of rap, metal, industrial, technodigital—washed over him as he made his way back past the bright fluorescent Mexican taquerias and microbrewery burger joints, the late-night sushi and Thai fast-food outlets, the whole cacophonous global culture-goo of the age. He stood for a moment in front of Chips 'N Dips and on impulse went in.

Green and violet hair dipped, waved, and spiked in front of computer screens scattered around the room, shimmered in the phosphor glow. Complex Web pages rippled with coruscating, high-impact graphics as the generally youthful patrons drank phenalynine, caffeine, and carrot juice from tall glasses and munched on spicy buffalo wings or crisp designer chips of daikon, jicama, yam, or elephant garlic. Every table displayed a terminal and a platter of international yogurt, garlic, curry, cilantro, and pine-nut dip. There was no alcohol, but in the smoking room the atmosphere was dense and obscure.

Van wandered past a gigantic neon depiction of a printed circuit board. He threaded through the archipelago of tables. At those with three or four people, one moved the mouse and clicked while the others offered suggestions in low voices. The groups were hunched toward screens rippling with armed centurions clanking toward them only to evaporate into brilliant orange blossoms as the mouse clicked, leaving behind twisted corpses drenched in digital gore. The cacophony of pixilated explosions, computer-generated music, conversation, whoops, and shrieks was stunning.

He passed a group of aliens from *Star Trek* arguing with three colorful underground superheroes. Two pairs of combatants in virtual-reality goggles bobbed their heads and extended their fingers in response to invisible enemies. He imagined they must be shooting, or perhaps flying over alien landscapes. Gordon should come down here, do some fieldwork.

Wendell swam into view. "Hey, Dr. Weathers. You should look around here. There's people everywhere going into the sim. Awesome, man. Even that student of yours. . . ."

Van started to say "Anne," but Wendell snapped his fingers. "What's his name?" he continued. "Oh, yeah. Charles. That's it, the guy with the ponytail. McGuirk. Even him."

"Yes, Wendell. It's impressive."

The younger man leaned forward. "Just need to say, Dr. W, that you spend an awful lot of time in there. I'm not sure it's good for you."

"Are you warning me, Wendell?"

"Me? No, sir, not warning, not at all." He looked uncomfortable for a moment.

"Listen, Wendell, I've been meaning to ask you something."

"Yeah?"

Van frowned. "Well, about a month ago I was in there and I walked to the west, you know, where we set up the neighboring town, Te-Ayiin, you remember?"

"Sure." Wendell snapped his fingers together with a sharp pop. "I remember."

"Well, one day I was walking that way and someone intercepted me. Now I know we don't really know much about the real land that way, but this is a simulation. How could someone stop me?"

"Stop you? Beats me," Wendell confessed. "Not my doing."

Van stared at his programmer's retreating back for a moment, then continued his slow path through the cyber cafe.

"Hey, hi." She was breathless after running up to him, her even teeth dyed red by the neon trim.

"Ms. Opple!" he exclaimed, uncertain whether to be pleased or horrified.

"Yeah. You come here." It was a statement.

"Well. . . ."

"Me too. It's so sort of medieval retro, you know, like you go with your bad self."

He had no idea what she meant. "It's my first time," he confessed.

"Oh, cool." She deliberately pronounced it with the glottal stop: "k'ul," the Maya word for "sacred." Taking his arm, she led him on a stroll among the tables. In a large back room, another bar offered fruit drinks loaded with spirulina and caffeine. "You still haven't answered my last email. But, hey, you're here, now. I'll buy." She waved her fingers at a bald, heavily earringed man in a female nurse's uniform, who poured two large glasses of a phosphorescent green substance and set them on the bar. She paid and gave one to Van. They walked on, drinks in hand.

At a lighted glass display case filled with what looked like bondage equipment, all black latex and spikes, Ms. Opple murmured something that sounded like "Botron Battle Gear, the latest."

Van Weathers, Ph.D., widely respected dirt archaeologist, father and husband, was out of his depth. To cover his confusion, he took a sip of his drink. After a moment, he surreptitiously placed it on a table.

She guided him to the bookstore area. "I got them to carry your book," she said, pointing. He shook his head in wonder at the University Press edition of *Graphic Communication and the Structure of History*.

"I'm flattered. This doesn't really look like my audience here."

"What?" she shouted. The noise level had gone up.

"I said, I don't think this is really the place for my book."

"Oh." She leaned toward him, looking up into his face. A hard blue neon pulsed like the beat of a vein in her forehead, winking off the polished metal of her nose ring.

He caught himself leaning down and pulled himself back with a start. "My God, look at the time. I've got to go. It's been good to see you, Ms. Opple."

"Call me Anne," she shouted after him, and smacked the palm of her hand on an unused computer. "Damn," she muttered. The bone white jaws of the Xibalbá Gate on the screen jumped under the blow.

ANNE

She sat in front of the terminal, her back to the door, and stared into those skeletal jaws. It was so easy to slip in, and within minutes she had become a wanderer, lost in the texts of a strange, half-known history, staring at a forest scene with animated breezes moving the leaves. Eyes blinked in the darkness.

She sat with her chin sunk into her cupped hands and glared at the phony jungle, and all the noise and gestures of the cafe faded to less than memory. Somewhere in the tangled net behind this screen was the world *he* created. Somewhere in there was the essence, the *genius*, of Sylvanus Weathers.

She was no stranger to the attenuated passion of online sex, the twining of the electroplasm in the digital world.

When she figured out who he was in this world, she would find a better role, a more appropriate persona.

She would find a way to him, if not in the real world then in the other.

FROM VW TO AO RE: AN OBSERVATION ABOUT RHYMES

Dear Anne,

How can I answer? What can I say? I am not a good candidate for romance. I am married, father of a teenage son, with a job and career, a scholar in the dusty archives of the past. Not dashing, not particularly handsome, not rich. My words are for specialists and for you and other students.

You are correct in one thing, though; if you enter the Xibalbá Gate, we will be close in another way, perhaps closer in that way, the way of signs and gestures, of small cultural exchanges embedded in the desperate last days of the Maya.

Warfare is everywhere. Crops are failing. Drought is a constant threat. The cities are already beginning their swift decay. Smoke fills the air. They are desperate times and call for desperate actions.

I see you in class. You are a teacher's dream, a student who really cares. You have an important role in the simulation. We can talk about it.

Van
PS. What will you do for the holiday?

LOOSE ENDS

Chief of Surgery must be very nervous working on a Saturday like this. Elliot could see his client's hand shake in the tone of his short list.

We have two problems:

1. Two weeks. The authorities are involved. Take care of it immediately.
2. You report the subject is looking into Garcia. Do whatever is necessary to prevent this.

If the subject discovers you're involved I assure you the impact will be extremely negative.

"The impact will be negative?" What was this guy, a lawyer or something? The Chief had created this mess, and now he wanted Elliot to clean it up. He was warning Elliot Blackman. Elliot did not like being warned, not even by a client. It cast doubts on his efficiency as a professional.

Consequently, he would simply have to wrap things up sooner rather than later. So he answered: Tying up loose ends. Conclusion within two weeks.

2 Chewen 9 Keh

Saturday, November 19
The Long Count date is 12.19.12.14.11
It has been 1,869,411 days since the Maya Zero Date
The calendar round date is 2 Chewen 9 Keh
Moon is 18 days old
God 3 rules the night

WHAT WE'VE LEARNED SO FAR

Saturday afternoon, Van sprawled across the sofa in Gordon Flentsch's apartment. "We're getting somewhere," he said. He could see the city, and beyond it the slate-gray water of the bay and the two bridges. Traffic was light.

"Are we?" Gordon was seated on a straight-backed chair holding a small African instrument called a *sansa*. He used his thumb to pluck out notes at random intervals on a series of metal tongues.

"Yes. Over six hundred people have actively participated so far. Several thousand have looked in. I've spent almost twenty hours just since Wednesday being . . . well, I won't tell you who I'm being."

"Yeah, don't tell me. And I won't tell you who I am. Don't ask, don't tell." Plink, plink, he played an ascending third.

"People are really interested. The Terminal Classic, just before the end. Within a century, there will only be a few functioning cities left in the northern part of the Maya world. Isolated survivors of a dying civilization. . . ."

Gordon clucked his tongue. "You sound like Bryson Jones doing a television special when you talk like that. 'Dying Civilization!' The Maya stayed around in the north for a long time after the rest of it 'collapsed.' They were civilized right through until the end of the seventeenth century,

Van, when the Spanish finally conquered them, or most of them anyway. They just weren't civilized in a way that we can see."

"Degenerate ceramics, hastily made, badly conceived. No carved monuments. No masonry and plaster cities."

"Plenty of Maya around today, Van, millions, many more than there were during the Classic you're so fond of. Columbus's son Ferdinand described a trading canoe eight feet wide and as large as a galley, covered with palm fronds, with a crew of twenty-five, plus women and children. It carried cacao and brightly colored cotton clothing. Hardly uncivilized. As for your masonry and plaster cities, dumb idea at the time. The tropics, Van. Stone and plaster were dumb ideas. Nice temporary houses, made of wood, thatch roofs. Quick, air conditioned, comfortable, that's the ticket. Perfect for agrarian people adjusted to their environment.

"Bugs. Leaks in rainy weather. Falls down in a high wind."

Plink. "Inexpensive. Fashionable. Easy to move, like a recreational vehicle. They still have it today, farming, complex social structure, the calendar, all that stuff you think is so important for a civilization. It's not all that important, making empires. Better to look at the real Maya today, don't you think?" Plink, plink.

"Hell, no, Gord, that's not the point."

"What is the point?"

"The point is, we're learning something. The field is taking notice. The students are really getting a feel for what it was like to live in that culture. Even Simmons sent me a message. The whole Maya world is under terrible stress in there, Gordon. You can feel it in a way that really has an impact. It's not some intellectual thing, talking about history. When you're part of it, you can feel the tension, the fear, the sense of things falling apart."

Gordon put the instrument aside. "I know, Van. I've been there."

"Oh. Yes, all right, I know. But tell me what you notice. What do you see in there, Gord? How does it feel?"

Gordon walked to the sliding glass doors to his small balcony and looked out. His walls were decorated with New Guinea masks, Polynesian tapa cloth, tribal spears. The tables were covered with small figurines from Alaska and Peru, Anatolia and Burma. "What I see," he spoke softly, his back to Van, "is an absolute interpenetration of the supernatural and the natural. Ghosts are real; dead ancestors are right alongside the living, *inside* the living. The gods, the forces of nature, the entities of disease and decay, night sweats and mortal terror are always looking over your shoulder. It's an ugly place for a twentieth-century rationalist."

Van was nodding. "Good, good, you got it. That's it, it's a spirit-haunted culture. The kings were the mediators, the doorways, the interpreters and supplicants to the supernatural. And, now, too many things are going wrong."

Gordon turned around. "I don't think you understand. It's dangerous, what you're doing." He looked hard at Van Weathers.

Van laughed. "Dangerous? Don't be silly. It's a simulation."

"You can't have it both ways, Van. If it's only simulation, then it's just a game. There's nothing valid in it. It's a novelty, a diverting pastime. At the end of the day, everyone will go home. This is not a profession that takes kindly to games and toys. You'll be left with nothing but wasted time."

Van started to protest, but Gordon held up his hand. "But if it's real, if what happens in there really gives insight into what happened to the Maya, then it will be seductive. Very seductive. It'll make an affair with that student of yours pale to transparency."

"I'm not interested in having an affair with Anne, Gordon."

Gordon laughed and picked up his little piano again. Plink-plink, plink-plink: Oh-yes, you-are.

"I'm not."

"It's dangerous because it could be more interesting than people's real lives. They'll want to stay there. They'll begin to have a stake in it, in what happens." He shook his head. "I don't think I like it, Van. I don't think I like it at all. And then there's that weird place to the west. . . ."

"Te-Ayiin?"

"Yes, Te-Ayiin. I know you programmed it, but can you go there?"

"No."

"Why not?"

"I don't know. There are stories about it, rumors that it's polluted, or haunted, that it's an evil place. Nonsense, of course. But I couldn't get a permit to dig there, and now in the simulation something stops me."

Gordon shrugged. "There you go. Me too. It's too spooky."

"So you won't go back in?"

"Ah!" Gordon plinked a little arpeggio and put the instrument down. "Well, then, you got me, Van. Of course I'll go back in. I've got friends there. Besides, it's fascinating from a myth-making perspective. All those Ph.D. students, that girl Anne, for instance, or that other student of yours, the one I had in the ethnography class last year, McGuirk, all of them, trying to remake a culture they think they know something about. It's bread and butter for an anthropologist, Van, studying academics trying to be part of a different culture. Trying to *create* a different culture. Yep, it's real bread and butter."

"Seductive, you mean."

"Yeah, that's what I mean. Seductive."

ANSWERING MACHINES

Glenna's vast, rose-colored field seemed to expand and contract with each beat of her heart. The edges of the canvas made a smooth transition to shadow. "How long has that been ringing?" she cried, dropping the brush to pick up the phone. "Gotcha!" She was certain she'd beaten the answering machine by a fraction of a second. "Hello."

But the voice that greeted her was the machine's: "Hello, you've reached Glenna and Van. We can't come to the phone, etcetera."

"Hello," she shouted again, over the message. The machine beeped, and she said, "Hello," again.

"Hello."

"Yes? This is Glenna."

"Oh, hello, Mrs. Weathers. This is Special Agent Boytim."

"I know, listen, I'm sorry, I almost missed it, I'm painting, you see."

"No, that's all right."

She frowned. "What's all right?"

"I was going to leave a number. I thought you weren't home."

"No, I was home. Not for long, though. Did you want to talk to me?"

"Yes. We're making some progress on the Kim case."

"That's good, isn't it?"

"Of course it's good. Digital Assassins. Hired to retrieve something and went too far. Otherwise, there's no motive. We know Mr. Kim was coming to talk to you. He told his secretary, although he didn't say why. I was hoping you might know."

"I really don't know. He should really have been talking to my husband. After all, it's his research he was funding."

"Yes, I know that. We've had a look at his computer records, but they were coded. We don't yet know the names, only the numbers. His contacts were all numbers. Do you find that odd?"

"Odd? No, not really. It's the way bureaucrats or accountants think. They give everyone numbers, don't they?"

"I suppose you're right."

"The numbers identify us and conceal our identity at the same time." Glenna was warming to her topic. "Think about it. Social Security numbers, credit card numbers, phone numbers. . . ."

"But. . . ."

"Well, we wouldn't want people to *be* a number, of course, not in real life," Glenna continued. "I think it's OK if they *have* numbers. What would we do without numbers? We'd have to have, I don't know, special nouns or something. Then you'd look in a book for Glenna's noun, you see, and dial the noun on a little keyboard. It would be awkward, trying to reach me."

"What? Oh, I see, you're joking. Sometimes when you work for a bureaucracy you lose your sense of humor. So tell me, what noun would you pick?"

"Do you think we'd get to pick our own noun? What if I wanted an unlisted noun."

"Only nouns that don't exist yet can be unlisted, isn't that so?"

"I see what you mean. It'd be like a dictionary, only the meaning would be someone's name, which is also a kind of noun. Why not just give everyone their name. Dial 'Glenna' to get me."

"Wouldn't work. Too many people with the same name in the world, most likely."

"I'm sure you're right," Glenna said. "Message."

"What?"

"My noun. Message. A painting I did. That would be, let me see, 637–7243." She picked it out on the dial, one number at a time. "Is that shooting I hear?"

"Yes," Linc said slowly. "I'm at the firing range."

"Are you practicing? Shooting, I mean."

"Yes. We have to qualify every few months."

"Good."

Silence again, then "Well, listen," they both said at once, but Linc went on. "What is your message?"

"Well, it's not really, 'Hello, you've reached Glenna and Van. We can't come to the phone, etcetera.' It's more about the ambiguities of communication. Your first name is Lincoln, isn't it?"

"Linc. You can call me Linc. I'm divorced."

"I'm glad to hear that.—I mean of course I'm sorry."

"I know."

"I have to meet my sister and some people in the city in a little over an hour. How long have you been divorced?"

"Is there a relationship?"

"Pardon?"

"Between meeting your sister and my marital status?"

"Questions, questions, but I asked first."

"I'd love to tell you the entire fascinating story some time. But you didn't answer the question. Have you come up with any ideas why Mr. Kim might be coming to see you?"

"No, I really haven't."

"Your son, Jonathan, is a member of the Digital Assassins. Did you know that?"

"My son is fifteen, Mr. Boytim. He does spend a lot of time on the computer, so I don't suppose I'd be surprised if he knew others interested in computers. And that's what the Digital Assassins is, a group of like-minded. . . ."

"Kids, I know. Some of them aren't so benign, though. Some of them are real gutter punks."

"Jag is not a gutter . . . whatever." She almost hung up on him.

"I know that. He's a good kid. Where was he?"

"I told you. Home."

"Ah. OK, it was just a thought. Can you tell me a little about your husband's work?"

"He's an archaeologist. He spent much of his career at a place called Xultunich, in Central America. Now he's building some kind of simulation, to re-create the Maya world, find out what happened to them."

"Anything else?"

Glenna thought. "He tried to get permission to dig at a place nearby. He couldn't get the permits. That's why he's building the simulation. And CAPO of course is funding it."

"I see. That's very helpful, Mrs. Weathers. Thank you. But now, you have a dinner."

"Yes. My husband will be there. And Gordon, of course, and Foster, too. You met Foster. He'll want to talk museum business all night."

"That the dinner tonight?"

"Yes."

"Who's Gordon?"

"Cultural anthropologist. He's always anthropologizing."

"John Wayne says, 'Don't anthropologize, it's a sign o' weakness.'"

"That's good. *She Wore a Yellow Ribbon?*"

"Maybe we could meet some time, more informally. Dinner, maybe? I could tell you all about my fascinating divorce."

"I don't know. I'm married, you know."

"Yes, I know, I know you're married. We'll call it official business. I'd just like to ask a few questions. I'm just assisting Morton, you know, because there are some international repercussions. I'm also looking for a bank robber, guy they call Shakey; he shakes all the time he's holding up the bank, like he has St. Vitus's Dance or something, so they gave him the name Shakey. You don't know Shakey, do you? Of course not. Just an informal dinner, really, if you're free."

"Free?" She tried out the word. It had a strange taste. Was she free? Van was so often away, so distracted these days. Perhaps she was, in fact, free. "Not this Tuesday, though," she heard herself say. "Next Tuesday?"

"Right. This Tuesday's the Tuesday before Thanksgiving. We couldn't possibly meet until we've given thanks."

"Thanksgiving? Oh, God, already. All right, a week from Tuesday, then. By the way, you don't know where I can get a truck, do you?"

"I have a truck."

"You do?"

"Well, it's a van, really. I tinker with cabinet making. On weekends. Why do you need a truck?"

"I have to finish this painting. We start installing my show on Tuesday, and my paintings are rather large, you see."

"Yes, I do see. I will plan to come to your house on Tuesday with my van. We can talk on the way to the museum if you'd rather do that than dinner."

"That's very nice of you. Thanks." She wanted to hang up, or say No, I have to stay home, I have to take care of my family. She wanted to say, No, I'd rather have dinner with you, forget the painting, forget the museum, we can meet for dinner, my husband won't even notice I'm not home. She wanted to ask him where he was right now. Instead she added, "I've got to run. I've got to make Jag some dinner before I leave."

She replaced the receiver and rested her hand on it. *Dead Tongues*, still unfinished, cast a rose glow over the room.

MALL

The vast strip mall unfurled in series—discount stores, lumber and hardware and home improvement warehouses, electronics supermarkets. They were already crowded with early customers in a frenzy of pre-Thanksgiving Christmas shopping. A disordered murmur of spoken transactions rose like early-morning mist from creek bottoms. Thin light seeped between the shops. Elliot Blackman, poised at the edge of this grand panorama of commerce, imagined he could hear the languages of specifications, fractional power increments, and solvent ratios.

Elliot watched the single men, families with small children mounted on their fathers' backs, plump women with narrow eyes squinted against the smoke of their cigarettes, the work of chaos and entropy, the slow heat death of the world.

It is a fact of the universe that complex systems respond to small perturbances of the dynamic. A butterfly can flap its wings over Tokyo and there will be a storm in Texas. . . .

Elliot Blackman would find the place and time for the butterfly. No one had believed in him. Not his father, stern defender of cleanliness, nor his mother wrapped vaguely in flannel. Van Weathers didn't believe in Elliot Blackman, either, but he would. Oh, yes, Van Weathers would come to believe deeply.

He plunged into the largest of the electronics warehouse stores.

FROM AO TO VW: HOPE

Oh, my God, Van Weathers,

you have given me hope. I know you're married, you're my father's age, you have a son. I know all that. It doesn't matter, not really, because your thoughts are in my mind, and your words and ideas. The Xibalbá Gate is a brilliant conception and I know the answer is there. Are we all so desperate now, the world and its people? We need what you know. I need it.

I need you.

You asked about the holiday. Thanksgiving is just another day to me; we don't have such a holiday in Canada. For me it is only another opportunity to be with you in the world, though I suppose you will be with your family.

I've gone through the Gate and looked around. I see where things are, who is important, what is happening. I know who I would like to be.

I will be looking for you. No, I will find you, one way or the other. There is a bond between us now, a connection in the World that will extend into the real one as well. I will know you there as I am coming to know you here. I think of your mouth, how it would taste, and my sight grows dim, I can scarcely breathe, as the poet Sappho says.

I was reading about Lady Ik' Skull, third wife of Itzamnaaj B'alam II at Yaxchilan, who may have been a descendant of Knot-Eye Jaguar. Do you remember, you mentioned Lady K'ab'al Xook the first class? She pulled the cord through her tongue, gave blood for her king? Well, Itzamnaaj B'alam had two other wives, the young Lady Sak B'iyaan, and the third, Lady Ik' Skull. In *Chronicles of the Maya Kings and Queens* it says she was an *ix ajaw* from Calakmul, a princess. Do you see? She came from far away to give the king an heir, Bird Jaguar IV. And she was also called Lady Evening Star!

One way or another, we will make love under the stars, even if they are digital, a simulation as you say, because for me they are real and so will be your presence there.

Anne

SAFETY VALVE

It was a perfect Saturday evening. Jag, alone at fifteen, had the run of town, all the grownups out for dinner, roller blades ready, dark November outside, heavy moisture in the air. He tucked his shirt into his pants, shrugged into a leather jacket, padded knees and elbows, and flowed away into the dusky night, leaving the house behind.

Streets bent, turned, stopped and started, joined one another and flew apart again. Hexagonal red stop signs and triangular merge arrows flashed by. He used the bicycle lanes, back alleys, parking lots, long lean strides that moved across an endless series of urban textures, the rattle of black asphalt, the smoother ripples of white concrete, the irregular rhythms of brick in the downtown mall. Everything was black and white—color drained from the town, white street lights merging with the shop signs along University.

He swooped gracefully to a stop in front of Chips 'N Dips and changed into sneakers, slung the blades over his shoulder, and sauntered in as though he owned the place.

And he did; he was known. "Hey, man," someone said, waving a languid hand and turning to his companion, whispering, "You know who? That's Catalyst, man, one of the best, knows all the numbers, one of the Assassins."

"No shit?"

Jag tapped a girl on the shoulder, and she looked back and up. "Oh," she said, moving to the neighboring chair so Jag could sit at the terminal. He nodded, long hair swinging beside his cheek, flexed his fingers and tapped the keys. "Why you come here?" she asked him.

"Come for the access," he said. "Place's got real broadband, fiber straight in, no wait. At home, just the DSL, you know, half a megabit, too slow."

It was a busy night on the net, though, and despite fiber straight to the keys it was sluggish. Jag didn't mind. When he got impatient, he bailed out of the path he was following and tried another, one few people knew about. He had a rep as the fastest man for access in the entire Mondo, that skinny kid who could slide into his electroplasm and really race the fiber.

Soon he was there: HFS, cursor blinking. A window full of code opened beside the ancient blinking prompt. "Man, those people are in the Dark Ages," the girl exclaimed. "Like a fucking C-prompt, do you believe it!"

Jag didn't answer, scrolling through the code. He highlighted a section and pasted it in after the prompt, and the screen went dark. He sat back and cracked his knuckles, smiling.

"It shut down?" she asked.

He turned a slow head and smiled, tipped his temple toward the screen, barely watching it bloom into kaleidoscopic color, a mandala of critical data, the entire organizational chart for HFS.

She said, "Wow. That's impressive. You're a legend."

He was here to show what he could do. To her, with the plump lips and the nose ring, to the others now gathered behind him.

A man in the crowd behind him said, "I din'no anyone could get into HFS. How?"

"Met a guy; he helped some," Jag admitted modestly, without looking up.

The girl just shook her head. She turned to the speaker, a man with a ponytail. "Really, Charles," she said. She was older, a graduate student from the college likely, but she treated Jag fine, like an equal, like a man. "You met a guy?" she asked, turning back to him. "A guy? Here?"

"Naw, on the net. I run into him a lot. He knows things."

She smiled, and it dazzled him. "How do you know it was a guy?"

Charles shook his head and drifted away.

Jag saw she was teasing. "Don't," he said, grinning. "Just a guess, from the way he talks, what he likes. Likes codes, passwords, numbers. Like a guy, that's all."

"Well, then. I've heard talk of you around here; you're Catalyst. I'm Anne."

"Sure, hi, Anne." He turned awkwardly to shake her hand, which was warm and a little plump in his thin-boned claw with long fingers perfect for stroking code.

Insistence flashed from the screen, someone breaking into the magic meeting. "There he is," Jag said. "Ghostman."

Ghostman asked, Where you at, kid?

Here and there, Catalyst said. Here and there. & how'd you know I'm a kid? but he didn't type the question, only thought it.

Haha. Ghostman sees you got in all the way. Don't want to give away too many secrets, now. Ghostman was chiding Jag.

Naw, don't want that. Jag winked at Anne. Don't want that. It's a safety valve, is all.

The little chat box on the bottom of the screen filled and emptied as they talked, Ghostman and Catalyst, seemingly alone in electronic space far from the world of meat, deep in the endless Mondo.

They were friends, these two, and friends can go on only so long before they have to see a face, know the atom world and its body language, meet face to face, F2F as it were. It was no surprise when Ghostman asked if Catalyst wanted to meet; it would be perfect, a union of like minds, just to shake hands, wouldn't it?

Sure it would, sure it would. Jag thought a minute. How about tonight, ten o'clock, there's a park a few blocks off University.

OK, Ghostman said. See you there.

After all, Jag told the girl Anne before he left the cafe, the bit-world Mondo is so intense, sometimes physical reality is, well, like a perfect safety valve, isn't it?

WATER MUSIC

"It's perfect!" Gordon exclaimed over his first bite of snapper.

"Mongolians." Foster said at the same time, in an effort to propel the dinner conversation forward.

"What?" Mary smiled broadly at Gordon to acknowledge Foster's conversational foray.

"The next exhibit. Mongolians," Foster repeated. "The steppes, vast open spaces, colorful materials, right, Glenna?"

It was almost perfect, Glenna was thinking. They had a table by the window overlooking the water. If she dipped her neck a little, she could see the bridge overhead. The night was black velvet with small lights winking reflection off the water. "Yes, of course," she said. "Mongolians."

"They probably didn't eat much fish," Van suggested.

"The Mongolians?" Foster frowned.

"Lake Baikal," Gordon suggested. "Huge primeval things with enormous jaws, rows and rows of teeth, dredged up from enormous depth?"

"I hear it's polluted," Van said. "Wouldn't recommend the fish."

"Deepest lake in the world, though," Glenna said, turning from the window.

Foster was still struggling. "Really? I didn't know that. What do you think, Mary?"

"What do I think about what?"

"The, uh, the fish." It was almost a question.

"I'm having veal."

"Oh, right."

"Is your show ready?" Mary asked Glenna.

Glenna was thinking: Don't anthropologize. She watched a tourist boat cruise slowly past. It must be cold on the water; after all, it was November. There was no one on deck. One of those dinner cruises. "We set it up Tuesday," she said. "At the Franklin Gallery. It's only a block from the Asian."

Foster started telling Van about the Mongolians exhibit. Van, nodding politely, was thinking about stingray spines and the coming blood sacrifice he would make with Evening Star. Bill Rathje had wondered years before if elites were functional or fungal; that is, did the king manage the well-being of his people or was he a parasite on them, living well at their expense. He wondered if the effort to bring stingray spines up to Xultun-ich was worth the cost. Did he, as king of Xultunich, provide a real service to his people?

Glenna started talking to Mary about Jag. "He had that strange growth spurt," she said. Mary clucked sympathetically. "He tells us the global temperatures are rising at the rate of something like a quarter of a degree a decade or something. I try to tell him that means it'll be a degree or two warmer by the time he leaves the world, and he says it doesn't matter, it's significant anyway. He talks about the ozone hole, but just in numbers, see? Jag's so . . . so *digital!*"

"Numbers," Mary repeated. "Yeah, I've been thinking about numbers, too. It's what we do in real estate."

"Yurts," Foster blurted out.

"What about them?" Van asked.

There was an inexplicable hiatus when everyone else fell silent at the same time.

"Real estate," Foster said. "Round tents, from Mongolia. They're called yurts. We are putting one up in the rotunda, to show how the Mongolians lived."

"Ah," Mary said, putting her hand on his forearm. "That's interesting."

After a few moments, Gordon began to speak. "I've been thinking about a harpsichordist named Wanda Landowska," he said. There was an elusive sense of relief in the way the others sat up, the set of their heads, the glitter of their attention as they watched him. He continued, looking into his wine glass. "She was Polish, of course, and quite famous in the years around World War II. A frail lady with a large, hooked nose, hair done up in elaborate knots at the nape of her neck, and the most amazingly sensitive fingers. She could make the harpsichord, an instrument with no dynamic range whatsoever, sing. She could make it sound soft or loud, expressive or mechanical. She could make Bach soar with this limited instrument. Quite extraordinary. Delicacy of touch, perfect phrasing, an unparalleled sense of legato. No one who knows about such things could believe it, the way she could play. The harpsichord strings are plucked, you see, not hit with a hammer like a piano; difficult to pluck soft or loud."

Gordon didn't seem to notice that everyone had stopped eating. His eyes were nearly closed, looking down the way they were when he tasted the snapper the first time and said, "Perfect." Behind him, the tourist boat passed out of sight, leaving the reflected bridge lights dipping and rising in the swells of its wake.

"There is a recording of her playing the *Goldberg Variations*. One of those scratchy old seventy-eight rpm records, recently digitally remastered on CD, but with the original ambiance. Someone's parlor, it sounds like— wooden floors, parquet, probably a huge Paris flat with a salon, and a very fine harpsichord, one of the extralong instruments built by J. D. Dulcken in Antwerp in the eighteenth century. A superb instrument, and a superb player, brought together in the middle of the war."

Gordon took a sip of his wine, his plump hand holding the crystal glass delicately. He cleaned his lip with his tongue as he set the glass down.

Everyone watched. No one spoke.

"On this recording, just about the beginning of the third variation, you can hear something if you listen very carefully." Gordon looked around the table. "What you can hear, faintly in the distance, is the sound of artillery shells falling and exploding, ten of them at least. She was recording in the middle of an attack, but her concentration was so exquisite she never missed a note."

He looked up into the silence. "More wine, anyone?" he asked, lifting the bottle.

GHOSTMAN

Jag skated from Chips 'N Dips to the meeting place and stopped to watch from the shadows at the street corner.

The man was waiting on a metal bench facing a small concrete circle. At one side was a basketball hoop. The mesh under the basket hung limp at the moment. It was a little before ten, and although University Avenue two blocks away was still at the peak of its nighttime frenzy, the small park was deserted.

It was chilly. From time to time, the man looked at his watch or shifted position on the metal bench, but mostly he sat very still, watching the woven string mesh of the basket.

Jag pushed off and roller bladed gracefully past him left to right, swirled inside the concrete circle under the basket, and looked into his eyes. "Ghostman?" he asked, pushing his hair out of his own eyes.

The man nodded. "Interesting, very interesting. Catalyst's a sharp cookie, up to snuff. Talks like all the kids about the Mondo, the bit world, all that cyberchatter, but I didn't mind. Learn things every day and was curious who he is. He is you, hmm?"

Jag rolled back and forth on his blades. "He is me, yeah. You?"

"Hmm," Elliot answered. He shifted his eyes from the mesh basket to the boy. There was enough light to see general outlines in the disordered patterns of street lamp and shadow, pale skin in patches, the dark line of jaw. Jag's hair hung beside his cheeks as he leaned forward and leaned back, straightening his legs. The rollers moved on the cement path, zzssp, zzssp.

Elliot opened his mouth, closed it again. "*Caudate nucleus*," he said abruptly.

"No—Catalyst." Jag propelled himself into motion, skirted the edge of Elliot's bench, passed swiftly behind him, spun at the opposite end, reached for the pole supporting the basket to swing gracefully around it, and paused once more in front of Elliot. "That's me. I'm Catalyst."

When Elliot moved his head, the diamond pattern of the mesh basket refracted a distant street light in an interesting interference pattern. "No, it's something I've been thinking about," he said. "The neurophysiology of perception. The reprogramming of a certain portion of the hippocampus, you see, with a well-calibrated shock, microwaves, so to speak. . . . Well, well, never mind. The equations are interesting." Elliot stared at the basket again and said nothing.

Jag bent down a moment to adjust the binding on his blades, then made a series of careful circles in place a careful distance away. No doubt about it, Ghostman was *weird*.

Elliot cleared his throat, sending a shard of fear through Jag, but the man only nodded slowly and said, "You're good, kid. You caught on quick to HFS, didn't you?"

Jag tossed his hair away from his eyes and skated around the bench again. "Thanks," he said behind Elliot. "But you told me stuff, gave me the direction to go."

"Yes, I did," Elliot murmured.

Jag executed a pirouette in front of Elliot. "So, Ghostman. You're not a kid."

"No." Elliot squinted. "I'm not a kid. But I like to race the fiber, too, you see. Yeah, it's interesting. And then there's HFS, interesting too, yes? Big corporation, very powerful, very quiet; you'd think they had something to hide, but no, you tramp through their files, it's nothing much, they're just a company. You look familiar. I know you?"

"I don't think so." Jag picked up speed around the post again, left hand holding so his palm squeaked against the metal, back to the bench, quick stop, and he dropped onto the bench at the far end and stretched out his legs, looking at the blades.

Elliot looked over at the boy. "Well, OK, if you say. No real names here, just the handle, right? I'm Ghostman, you're Catalyst."

"Right," Jag said. "No real names." He was up again, sliding back and forth.

Elliot nodded. "OK. Well, I was going to tell you, see, if you think about it the right way, there's the brain, brain stuff."

"Brain stuff?" Jag swirled around and stopped.

"Yeah, brain. Take the *cingulate gyrus*, rhythms in the way station of the limbic system. It's like the Mondo, see, only hardwired right into the brain. It's evolution in action, and what they call exaptation, the use of an evolved system for a new purpose. Humans do it all the time, play the piano with a hand developed for holding branches. . . . Stochastic resonance: a small amount of noise introduced in just the right place can raise the level of a signal above detectable thresholds, bind someone into a permanent state. . . ." He leaned toward Jag and looked intently into his eyes. "Ever want to control somebody else's mind?"

Jag shifted uneasily. "I dunno. Is that what you want? Mind control?"

Elliot reared back. "Me? Oh, no, no, of course not. Not interested at all—it's just an idea. I'm a guy, you know, likes to race. Hacking, that's all, go in here, go out there, poke around. Just looking, that's all. I compare the Mondo to the mind—it's like a game. But you, you look familiar. Shape of your head, Catalyst. Sure you don't want to tell me your real name?"

"I don't think so." Jag spun on the fronts of his blades, hands out at his sides, palms down, a skater in the dangerous dark.

"Ah," Elliot sighed. "Of course not. Wouldn't do, break the code, right Catalyst? Break the ethics. Bad morals, that's what it would be, it would be madness. Never mind. But I look at the complex pattern of the your face, the light and shadow and skin texture, I begin to understand who you are, anyway. Yes, indeed, out of patterned noise comes a signal."

"Whatever." Jag turned in small circles under the mesh. "Why're *you* interested in HFS, anyway? How come you know so much about them?"

"Ah, ah, no. You don't find out who I am, either, not that way. But listen, I have something to tell you—you can help, you know? There's a man, he's doing something good in the Mondo, and he needs, well, some help. So I'm going to arrange it. HFS, they have a lot of money, see. So this man needs a little present, a hint or two. HFS wants to be a charitable organization, you see?"

Jag frowned. Where was this going? "How can *I* help?"

"A little code, that's all. I have it here. You introduce it. The address is there." Ghostman handed him a slip of paper.

"Why don't you do it?"

"No, no, that wouldn't be right. You should be the one. You're a stranger, you see. They won't trace it to you. It's a good thing, you know, helping someone out. You'll do a good deed, Catalyst, doing this. I can't, they might know me at HFS, you see. If I'm known, it wouldn't do, wouldn't do at all."

"So what is it?"

"Routing instructions for an interdepartmental request, that's all. When I see the routing pathway there, I'll introduce a memo, give some direction." He nodded at the slip of paper in Jag's hand. "That'll make it look authentic, all right."

Jag shrugged and pocketed the paper. "Sure, OK."

"You're the best, Catalyst. Best I've seen. Do it soon, though. Tonight. Desperate times, Catalyst. Desperate measures. Gotta help out, right?"

"Right, sure."

Ghostman waved as Jag skated away.

7 Kib 14 Keh

Thursday, November 24
The Long Count date is 12.19.12.14.16
It has been 1,869,416 days since the Maya Zero Date
The calendar round date is 7 Kib 14 Keh
Moon is 23 days old
God 8 rules the night

CELEBRATION

Five days later, Glenna and Mary were in the kitchen preparing the holiday dinner. "Are you excited?" Glenna brushed her hair back with a quick gesture and grinned.

Mary used her spoon to turn over a dissected sweet potato. "Have you ever noticed how these things resemble internal organs?"

"I asked first." Glenna looked through the glass on the front of the oven door. Condensation obscured her view of the turkey, but she could hear quiet boiling. "Time to baste." She opened the door.

Mary laughed. "Am I excited?" She plunged the spoon into the orange flesh and pulled it out. "Almost all the time, but I don't suppose that's what you mean."

Glenna straightened. "Are you? I mean, no, that's not what I mean. But it's interesting, really. I wish I could say the same."

"Probably because you're satisfied."

"I'm afraid these days Van isn't very . . . available."

"Distracted by his Maya thing?" Mary spread the spoonful of sweet potato in the bottom of the Pyrex dish.

"Oh, yes, distracted." Glenna squirted a final blast of drippings over the rounded turkey back and slammed the oven door.

"I suppose you mean am I excited that Foster is here and the answer is yes, I am. He's very sweet. I like him. I like him a lot, Glenna." Mary sprinkled tiny marshmallows on top of the sweet potato. For a moment, the two sisters stood side by side, looking at the orange paste with scattered white oblongs.

"Another layer, right?"

"That's the recipe," Glenna said, frowning at the casserole.

"Can't GET no . . . sa . . . tis . . . FAC . . . tion," Mary sang, stabbing the tablespoon once more into the open yam's orange flesh. "You know, Glenna, you're looking great these days. Working out?"

Glenna bit her lower lip, looking out the window past naked sycamores at the Cavanaughs' silver van. Cavanaugh taught in the business school. The Cavanaughs had no children, and Professor Cavanaugh had written a best-selling how-to book for the terminally middle-aged. Two good reasons not to spend time with the Cavanaughs. She turned back to Mary. "I do feel better. Stronger, more confident."

"It shows." Mary lowered her voice. "And what of the mysterious government man? You're . . . meeting him, mm?" Mary grinned, avoiding eye contact. "An upcoming event, pregnant with possibility. That's an image, isn't it? Pregnant? New beginnings and all that."

Glenna smiled. "I don't think so; he's going to help me move the paintings, and I try to help him solve the mystery. . . ."

"Is he cute? I mean, there aren't that many men left, real ones, anyway."

"You'd like me to introduce you?"

"Mm, no. Foster will do for now." Mary tumbled more marshmallows on top of the second layer of sweet potato. "Oven?"

"Yeah, it'll fit, I think." Glenna pulled down the door and moved the roasting pan to one side. Mary slid the casserole in beside the turkey.

The outside door banged shut behind Jag. "When do we eat?" He was carrying the morning paper. Without waiting for an answer, he asked, "Did you know there are four hundred seventy-three thousand, nine hundred and twelve outstanding arrest warrants in California alone."

"Crime's up," Mary agreed.

"Well, actually, although there were over 14 million offenses reported, violent crime is down a little over one percent," Jag assured her. "But the average age for a violent criminal is also down, so it seems worse. Ten-year-olds commit murder, now. They'll have longer careers, I guess."

"Very funny." Mary raised her glass of wine in a toast to Glenna and sipped, lifting an eyebrow to Jag, whom she sometimes referred to as The Omen.

Glenna squeezed gently on Jag's shoulder. "Don't mind her," she whispered. "She's in love."

"Ho ho." Mary laughed, but for a moment there was a naked longing in her eyes, and Glenna looked away.

"Robbery's up, though," Jag continued. "This guy, for instance." He held up the newspaper to show a composite drawing. A thin, squinting face with lank hair falling over the forehead.

"Oh," Glenna said, looking over Jag's head at the paper, which he had presented to Mary. "Who is it?"

"Bank robber." Jag turned the page so his mother could see. "He shakes, so they call him Shakey."

"I heard. The name makes sense."

"He gives the note to the teller, and he's twitching like crazy," Jag told the two women.

"Maybe it's a ploy," Mary suggested. "He shakes, and they don't notice what he looks like. How many banks has he robbed?"

"Nineteen in the last six months," Jag said.

"Is that high or low?" Mary asked.

"High for an individual."

A dark figure passed outside the kitchen window: Van in his windbreaker. The wind must have come up, because his hair riffled at an angle away from his ear.

Glenna let go of Jag's shoulder to tap on the glass. Van stood at the end of the Cavanaughs' fence, looking across their backyard as if planning where to dig. She tapped again.

This time, he looked around, straight into her eyes. She mouthed for him to come in, then realized he didn't see her. Exasperated, she went through the back door. "Van."

He saw her and smiled. "Hello," he said.

"Is something wrong?" she asked, looking at the kitchen window. She could clearly see Mary talking to Jag.

"Wrong? No, nothing's wrong. The light reflects off the window. I couldn't see you."

"What are you doing out here? It's freezing."

"Is it?"

"Van, come inside. Tell Gordon and Foster dinner's in twenty minutes."

"OK." Van followed her inside.

"Sweet potatoes," Jag was saying as she came back into the kitchen, "are loaded with beta-carotene."

"This is going to be one of those days," Mary said to Glenna.

Van stood at the bay window, looking at the street, deserted now in the middle of a holiday afternoon.

"Whatcha reading, Gord?" Glenna came in and sat beside him.

He lifted *Graphic Communication and the Structure of History.* "Chapter on social cohesion and theater states."

"Put on a show for the people, so they can see how well the king intercedes for them, how he keeps order in the universe," Van muttered.

Gordon frowned at Van's back. "Southeast Asia, Van. The work of Stanley Tambiah."

Van turned. "I was thinking of Arthur Demerest, his essay on Maya cultural evolution in *Ideology and Pre-Columbian Civilizations.* The Maya, like the tropical states in southeast Asia, lasted a long time, but with enormous volatility, and final collapse."

Gordon made a chopping gesture with the blade of his hand. "They were much more ideological in Southeast Asia," he said. "The king enhanced his status and legitimized his power with public ritual. . . ."

". . . like the Maya."

"Yes, like the Maya. But he had to study with holy men, he had to acquire objects that enhanced his prestige. In his effort to bring subsidiary states into his sphere of influence, he had to work hard."

Van sniffed and turned back to the window. "The Maya kings had a weaker hold on others. They had to fight as well. They had to arrange alliances, and take captives, and bleed for their people. A king spent all his time trying to convince the people that he was fit to rule and deserved his high status and privileges. It's why they kept building higher and higher."

Gordon glanced up at Glenna. "It's the chapter called 'Propaganda and Social Cohesion.'"

"Oh, yes," she answered, "Propaganda." After a lengthy silence, she stood up and went to Van by the window. "Are you all right?"

"Oh, sure, fine. Have you ever wondered what your animal was?"

"You mean, like a pet?"

"No. The animal spirit, the one that's yours alone, our connection to the Otherworld. It's called a *way*." He pronounced it like "why." "Nature, we'd call it, with a capital *N*. You're the only one who can see it."

"I don't think. . . ."

"Hey." Mary, leaning against the arch to the dining room, held up one hand. "I hate to interrupt but I heard the timer ding." She went back to the kitchen.

"It's November," he said quietly. "I'm afraid I've been pretty distracted lately. Forgive me. I feel like I've been sacrificing. . . ."

"Your family?" Glenna interrupted.

"No." He looked at her curiously. "Why do you say that?"

"I'm sorry, Van. I didn't mean it the way it sounded."

"I believe I'm working *for* my family," he said thoughtfully. "For you and Jag. I keep telling myself, if I could just solve a piece of the big problem, why some societies don't make it and some do, I'd know more about how a family survives. I'd be able to give more, you see, if I only understood? I just meant I've been sacrificing all my time."

She looked at him for a moment, then touched his cheek. "I hope it's worth it," she said softly. "Come on. It's time to eat."

When the food was on the table, Glenna said, "This is a celebration." She looked at Mary seated next to Foster and noticed that her sister kept touching him, his arm, his collar. "We are celebrating our gratitude for what we have."

"I'll drink to that," Foster said, lifting his wine. Mary smiled at him and lifted her glass.

Gordon nodded. "To gratitude," he said.

"Jag, do you want some wine?" Glenna asked.

"Sure." He moved some food around on his plate. "Almost a hundred million people are born every year," he announced. "The birth rate's up again." He put a bite of sweet potato and marshmallow in his mouth and chewed slowly.

Gordon said, "It'll go down soon. That's a prediction. These things go in cycles."

"We're not watching the football game," Jag continued. "This puts us into a statistically minuscule category. I couldn't find the exact numbers, but certainly a huge percentage of all the people over six years old in America are watching."

"Almost no one I know watches the football game," Gordon said.

"I don't," Mary agreed. "So, Gordon, why didn't you ever marry?"

He shrugged. He was almost as used to Mary's disarming combination of directness and conversational swerves as he was to Glenna's tact. "Never occurred to me," he said. "I traveled, early on. I guess it never seemed like the right person. Or the right time."

"Oh. I see. The right time. I got married at the right time. Wrong person. Or was it the other way around?"

Mary turned to her brother-in-law. "How about you, Van. Did you marry at the right time?"

Van looked at her. "Married? Yes, I am," he said.

Later, over the dishes, Glenna said, "He forgets where he is. He's thinking about his other world." She felt the leaves of the tiny tarragon plant in the window over the sink. "Oh, Mary," she said softly.

Mary touched her arm. "He's preoccupied right now, but he'll come back. Besides," she grinned. "There's that agent, right?"

"Come on, Mary. That's business. He just wants to ask some questions. About Derek Kim. It's just business."

"Mm-hm. OK, Glenna."

"I'm glad about Foster, Mary. You deserve some happiness."

"It's funny," Mary said. "People joke about the holidays, how hard they are. Thanksgiving, giving thanks, all that. It was hard when we were kids, remember? It's still hard. I thought it was supposed to get easier. But it was really hard with Robert . . . oh, never mind, I won't talk about him. Not Robert. He's still sending the alimony checks, but my God he was impossible at holidays."

CONTROL

While Mary, Glenna, and Foster cleaned up, Van and Gordon loitered at the entrance to the living room. "Remember how you said that on the Net you'll have complete control?" Gordon said. He had one foot braced against the side of the archway. It was a way of stretching his back. "You were wrong, Van. You've lost control. It's taking over."

"Do you think so?" Van said absently. He leaned against the wall by Gordon's foot, hands in his pockets. It was Thanksgiving, and he wanted to be here, but he kept seeing dream fragments of a battle, kept hearing the cries of the wounded and smelling hot dust, cut stone, blood.

Across the room, Jag was watching cable news with the sound low, taking notes.

"Forget control, anyway," Gordon continued. "You can't have it, never could. No one can. We fool ourselves, thinking we can even come close. Too many variables."

Van brought himself back with an effort. "We have computers. They're getting better, faster, more sophisticated." His voice was teasing.

"Forget computers. Computers won't help, no matter how many variables they can calculate, all the way back to the beginning of the universe. Bang! Off on the Great Adventure, right? Origin of the Universe." He shook his head, dropping his foot to the floor. "Think about it. You have the incipient collapse of a culture. They're going to give it all up, disperse, forget the rituals, go back to farming. Mostly, they'll stop writing, except for almanacs and magic. No more international trade. No more armies. No more towering temple mountains. Why?"

"Why do you think?"

They could hear CNN reporting the outbreak of hostilities somewhere in the world. The displaced were flowing across borders. The United Nations High Commission for Refugees was overwhelmed. The announcer's voice continued, a low murmur just at the threshold of understanding.

Gordon waved his fingers. "OK, let's say we go back in time. What caused the people of Palenque, say, to leave town? You told me they filled the major temple with stone rubble, like packing it with Styrofoam peanuts, eh, and left. So we ask why? Too many people left and there weren't enough left to keep up with the maintenance. OK, why? Well, perhaps we find there wasn't enough food. Why not? Soil depleted. OK, why? Not enough fallow time for the soil to recover, too many people to feed. OK, why too many people? Because the previous generations had succeeded too well, and the population increased, which in turn meant higher temples, broader plazas, greater public works, huge capital investment, very labor intensive. Pacal's tomb, enormous panels of inscriptions. Why? Because they could?" He waved his fingers again. "No, no, you'll never find it. We can't control what happens. We never could. Go back far enough, find the rainstorm that caused the ripple in the air that sent the hurricane boiling out of the Atlantic to destroy the coastal village of X, which in turn meant the traders had to go farther to unload their boats, which meant that some vital piece of obsidian didn't arrive in time for the ceremony, so the people lost faith, etc., etc. It won't work, see? For want of a nail, the shoe was lost. But in the end, you have to say, 'So? That isn't the cause.'"

Gordon leaned toward Van. "You and Glenna invite me for Thanksgiving every year. Every year, I come because my family's in the East, and I go there for Christmas. We're friends, you and I. Do we even know why we do things?" He leaned back and laughed. "We don't. Listen. . . ."

They could hear shots, shouting, engines. A plane roared, followed by the sounds of explosions. News from somewhere in the world, tinny from the box in the den. They walked to the door. Jag was curled in the leather chair, watching. He had his laptop computer with him and every now and then tapped the keys.

"He collects numbers." Van spoke quietly, but Jag looked up at the sound.

"Hey, dad." His voice came from another world.

"Numbers," Van said, a little louder.

Jag stopped typing. "Sure. I'm keeping track."

"Why?" Gordon asked.

"I'm looking for patterns," Jag said solemnly. He leaned back in the chair. "In the numbers. No one knows how many speakers of Maya languages there are today, but more than five million for sure, speaking around thirty-one related languages. Those are numbers. I'm looking for patterns in them. They're called strange attractors, the patterns. The numbers gather around them, and they tell a story. That's what I'm looking for. The story."

"A chip off the old block," Gordon said, tapping Van's shoulder. "You see, he understands better than you do, old man. There's no point looking for the cause, it won't help even if you find it. The Maya had a complex society. You might get ideas, but you won't get one straight answer."

"Maybe not, but we're close. It's complexity, Gordon. Diminishing returns. They need to increase the level of complexity, make a social change, consolidate an empire. They need to organize, and it's not happening, not yet. But something's going on in there, something important. I feel it. I go in there, and I'm certain the system is alive and growing. Everything's coming together. Can't you feel it?"

Gordon looked at Van for a long moment, then turned away. "It's a trap, Van," he said shortly. "You can't solve the problem so easily." He crossed the room and sat beside Jag to watch the news.

The television flickered, spinning letters, splintered images. Wherever it was, the war was no longer a headline. Now there were aftershocks to the recent earthquake in Costa Rica to worry about.

"Gordon," Van called. "I *need* to get back in there."

LEON

Leon couldn't get online. There was electricity, but the bulb in his high-ceilinged office was pale, a kind of brown dwarf of a light, dimming and brightening unevenly. So this was a typical Friday morning in St. Petersburg. In America they were still celebrating something called Thanksgiving. "Ah, well," he said. "The price of freedom."

The cushion of his antique chair creaked comfortingly, if a bit stiffly, under him. He picked up his battered copy of *Prehistoric Settlement Patterns: Essays in Honor of Gordon R. Willey* and read quietly for an hour, his back to the window to take advantage of the watery sun.

Mara brought in the samovar. "What the hell are you doing?" she asked, setting it down with a thump.

"Reading," Leon said quietly, lifting the book and letting it drop onto his lap. "This book may be more than twenty years old now, but there are still insights to be gained. I was going over my friend Bill Rathje's article on salt and households, and then I reread Richard Leventhal's article on household groups and religion, very enlightening. . . ." He saw the expression on her face and stopped. "Oh, but what's the use, Mara? What else is there to do in St. Petersburg at dawn in November when even the telephones don't work?"

"Ah!" She waved a hand. "What the hell else you do anyway, Leon, but read, tell me that?"

"Sometimes I write papers," he said, a little defensively.

"Ah! Papers, pah!" She drew a cup of tea from the samovar and handed it to him. He pushed aside a stack of American journals to make room on the enormous black table, its ugliness tempered by the intellectual disorder on its surface, the stacks of typescript in Cyrillic and English, the books without covers, the journals.

Mara opened the door. "You need anything, you know."

He nodded, deep in *Prehistoric Settlement Patterns*.

Another hour passed. There was a subtle change in the environment, a shift of some kind. Leon looked up. The bulb in the ceiling was shining steadily, if a little quixotically in the now full morning.

Winter light was out there, a gray, dim northern light. The Neva would flow black past the island to the Gulf of Finland, and Leon wanted to be as far away as possible. Somewhere hot and steamy, where passions could run high. Not like this bloodless criminal place he lived in now.

"Mara!" Leon shouted. "Tea!" He lifted the handset of the telephone, and was rewarded by a deafening dial tone. "Aha."

Mara came in and without speaking drew him another cup as he started the computer and watched the lights flicker on the DSL modem. The gate of Xibalbá appeared on the screen.

Mara set the tea down and withdrew.

Leon was ready. These were troubled times in 837 AD. He was definitely not the ruler. Rulers are constrained by their roles, their positions in the hierarchy; they spend all their time arranging ceremonies, performing sacrifices, putting on a show, just like the tsars. No, he didn't want to be a ruler. Better to be one of the upstarts, someone close to a ruler. It's nice to be an upstart, a troublemaker.

There will be opportunities for an ambitious man . . . or woman.

He clicked on the jaws and watched the cave opening of Xibalbá swing open, and close again, and he entered.

"Now," he said out loud, taking a sip of tea. "Time to kick some butt, huh, as the Americans like to say."

7 Manik 10 Zec

April 14, 837 AD
The Long Count date is 10.0.7.3.7
It has been 1,442,587 days since the Maya Zero Date
The calendar round date is 7 Manik 10 Zec
Moon is 1 day old
God 4 rules the night

DAYKEEPER

Flint Howler, Daykeeper of Xultunich, moving briskly around the small room, pauses a moment to ask, "Why did you agree to this thing, then?"

"Two reasons." Knot-Eye watches in the dim light as the scribe spreads a mat of fresh leaves on the altar. "First, Quetzal Tree would never have agreed to less, not in such times."

"These are bad times, indeed," Flint Howler agrees.

Knot-Eye lowers his chin and looks through the temple opening across the sweep of the central plaza at the city. Already the day comes and beyond the temples men are at work at the edge of the city, building retaining walls for raised fields. They look very small and dark from this height. He speaks almost to himself, barely loud enough for Flint Howler, behind him, to hear. "He believes his daughter is worth at least twenty captives. His fathermother-ancestor would demand so many to set the earth-tree straight in Xultunich. We are a rival city of a different lineage, more powerful than his."

Although it is barely dawn, it is already hot and the air is filled with smoke. Many fires burn on the mountainsides. He can see their dark flame still against the shadow side of the eastern hills.

Flint Howler considers Knot-Eye's words. "There has never been a sacrifice of so many, not in Xultunich, not in Green Mountain. In these times there are too many rival cities."

"Yes, too many cities, and too many people, so we must outdo what has been done before. Waterbird River might get ideas, pushed by Cloud Hill. And then there are the armies from the high mountains to the west, or so we hear. It is the way the Cycles unfold, that the temple mountains grow ever higher and more costly, and the ceremonies longer."

"It is the way of it," Flint Howler agrees. "And the second reason?"

"Quetzal Tree does not believe I can gather twenty captives for sacrifice. He does not believe we can play the ball game and win, either. He believes he can become ruler of Xultunich as well as Green Mountain. He believes the tree will not leave his city, and he is keeping one eye to the east, to Waterbird River. And Reed Altar, although he is my nephew, is also his nephew, and Reed Altar follows his mother's way. So he is working with Quetzal Tree against us; Three Sky and Quetzal Tree are on their way here with Evening Star. They want the sacrifice, but they will also warn Dry Place, just in case Knot-Eye no longer has the ear of his ancestors and the Lords of Xibalbá. Other small cities have defeated larger rivals before."

"You think they would betray us?"

"I believe they are playing on both sides of the ball game, but you are here to tell me if I am right or not." Knot-Eye turns back to the room and gestures at the book on the altar, its fanfolds thick in between beautifully carved and painted wooden covers. "You will read the signs."

"There are things I can tell you without consulting the book," Flint Howler says thoughtfully. "I can tell you that today, 7 Manik 10 Zec, is a day of bad omen. The vulture means betrayal, so to that extent you are right. And then there is the God Who Has No Name."

"The night sky is Xibalbá turned upward." Knot-Eye says thoughtfully. "The God Who Has No Name is a new Xibalbán, a new lord of the Otherworld."

"Or an old one in a new form. We must pay attention. New gods, new dangers." Flint Howler places the spiked ceramic incense burner on the altar and counts out a precise handful of golden lumps of *copal* onto it.

"Then let us get started." Knot-Eye goes to the other end of the altar, now covered with green leaves, and waits with his head bowed.

Flint Howler places a coal on the incense burner. Pungent smoke rises into the small temple space in which they stand. He begins to chant, and the smoke twists upward into the steep pitch of the roof. It coils, lifting itself into the narrowing channel, filling it. Soon, the paintings of the gods and men, the war and sacrifices of Knot-Eye's grandfather, are shrouded, invisible.

Flint Howler's chant calls on the gods, calls on the serpent and the caiman. He dips a branch into a shallow bowl filled with virgin water and shakes it over the altar and the book. Smoke-serpent coils away, slithers through the open doorway into the orange light outside, curling upward from the lintel and over the stucco roof of the temple.

The chanting continues for some time as the room fills. Soon Knot-Eye is giddy, listening to the insistent syllables, in which numbers, and rain-god *chac* names, and the colors black and red, white and yellow, recur. The Old Ones who hold up the sky band of the universe move in and out, carrying their vast indifference to human suffering and hope. One by one, the Lords of Xibalbá, who are the Lords of Death, make a brief appearance, and are named: One Death and Seven Death, Scab Stripper, Blood Gatherer, Pus Bucket, Bone Scepter, and the others. One by one, they are dismissed. The tone of Flint Howler's chanting begins to lose its form, its definition of meaning, turning into what it speaks of. Wind and rain, fear and heat and drought, death by drowning and sickness. The words become fever; they become sweats and pain.

The sun climbs through the yellow smoke, through the orange and brown smoke. The sun climbs, the day turns, the heat grows, and the air thickens.

Day names, month names, the seating of the year, the numbers of the ritual calendar as it goes round, meshing with solar year, bringing days and their attributes together with months and their attributes, until they reach today, 7 Manik 10 Zec. Here Flint Howler stops suddenly, midword, midspeech, midthought, and silence fills the tiny room, fills the steep inverted V of the arch above them, fills the alcoves, drowns the shouts of victor and captive in the paintings, suffocates hope.

Silence, and then: "It is as you have said, Knot-Eye. Betrayal. The winds will fight. It is not clear which one will win. Black is the color, the color of the west, of the sun's death. Serpents come, see, from the eye sockets of death. You can hear them, hear their dry scales scrape over dry bone, hear the soft hiss of their seeking."

"What should we do?" Knot-Eye asks softly.

"There is nothing here to do. The next days are also dark. Hot wind, more smoke, no rain. The Corn God trails his own intestines as he walks;

in this he appears as the God Who Has No Name, dragging his guts behind him across the ocean of pain that is Xibalbá. He dwells now in the Place of Fear. He can see no way to our world. The skeleton gods confer, see. . . ." His finger traces down the columns of day glyphs, the hand-drawn images of the gods, their fleshless jaws clacking as they speak, their narrow finger bones touching skull cheeks in a parody of love.

Knot-Eye knows. "They mean betrayal."

"They whisper to you, seduce you. They make promises they will not keep. They pretend to give as they are taking."

Something has happened to the copal incense, for the smoke has billowed up, thicker than ever, filling even the space between the two men, filling the square opening of the doorway, filling all the spaces of the room. Now Knot-Eye cannot see Flint Howler, and Flint Howler cannot see Knot-Eye.

There are threads of gray and brown, rolling over and through each other. There is the burning sound, copal or the poisonous language of serpents. There is the stench of death, the foul air from the dying body's insides. There is the slime of fever on the forehead, of mildew and decay. There is the acid taste of terror.

"What do you see?" Flint Howler asks, his thick voice coming from no direction at all.

Knot-Eye stares into the swirling mist. "I see the same," he says. "I see the serpents coiling out of the empty eye sockets. I see them crawling through the open mouth, past teeth set with jade and shell. I see the words, written in red, telling of the end of things."

After a moment, he adds, "I do not like what I see."

"Ah," Flint Howler sucks in his breath. "Then we must look elsewhere."

Knot-Eye feels a hand on his arm, leading him away, and they are standing on the platform high above the city, looking down.

It is not their city. It is not Xultunich, Last Stone, Center of the World, Home of the World Tree.

It is a ruin. Smoke from a hundred fires rises straight into a sky full of ash. The plaza is overgrown, the smooth plaster cracked and broken. The temples have fallen, no stone left on another. The colors are drained from the city. Vines and creepers cling to the walls.

There is a faint, persistent sound: weeping.

"This is Te-Ayiin," Knot-Eye says. "The Place of Crocodiles."

Flint Howler's voice is at his ear. "Yes, this is Te-Ayiin. And this is also not the city of Te-Ayiin, which no longer exists, Knot-Eye. Its stone roots sink down into Xibalbá; this is the house of stone and fear, a place of standing water, of mosquitoes and disease, of damp air and foul breath. You see only a part of it, the part that reaches the Middle World, the city of Te-Ayiin."

Knot-Eye turns, but there is no one there. Behind him, the temple glows with an inner light, smoke still twisting over the lintel and rising up the broad mask of the Celestial Bird that covers the towering roof comb. Across the plaza he can see the Great Pyramid, with his own lineage temple on top. His ancestor's idealized image looks out over the city from the roof comb, seated in splendor, larger than life. The colors are bright. People are working in the plaza still. The vision is gone as suddenly as it appeared.

"The other part is the war," Knot-Eye says softly.

"Yes." Flint Howler is beside him. His headdress, entwined with skull and jester gods, bends and sways gracefully as he nods his head. "Even then, the omens are not good. The Muan Bird is rising with night, the K'atun Lord looks away. Both the war and what will follow will require much of you."

"Blood," Knot-Eye agrees, and for the first time the thought fills him with a strange exultation, a fierce joy, thinking of the first cut of the obsidian knife, the first sharp bite of the stingray spine.

"Come," Knot-Eye says. "We will reach Dry Place in late afternoon, when the warriors are tired. We will take captives for the wedding. And when we sacrifice them, I will also give my blood to the gods."

The blood will well up, slowly at first, then more quickly. His blood. And with it will come the vision.

One Monkey, first ancestor, will come.

And will speak.

And will say what to do.

SMOKE WIND

The plasterer named Lime asks, "What do you want me to do?"

"Just tell me where the ruler of Xultunich, the great *ajaw*, has gone."

Smoke Wind, the wandering merchant, is finding it difficult to be patient. The only evidence of this is the way the toe of his sandal taps unevenly on the curb of the plaza. He and Lime are under the shade of a holy ceiba tree. Their voices are almost lost in the shrilling of insects in the dry grass.

Lime puts his finger beside his nose, deep in thought. "You want me to tell you where the ruler of Xultunich has gone?"

Smoke Wind looks at the sky. The sun is almost overhead, a fat orange shape nearly smothered in haze and smoke. "Yes," he says softly. "I do, I want you to tell me."

The man shakes his head, thinking hard. "I do not know."

Smoke Wind opens the bag hanging from his belt and removes a cacao bean. He holds it up before Lime's eyes, turning it in the light.

Lime says, "He left this morning with fifty men."

"I see. This morning. Late this morning?"

"When Xbalanque was halfway to the Tree overhead." Lime points for Smoke Wind. "There." His other palm opens to receive the cacao bean, his fingers close, and the bean is gone.

"Ah."

Lime smiles. He is a slow man, which may mean he is thoughtful or that he is stupid, but either the cacao bean or his questioner's reaction has made him happy.

"And which direction did Knot-Eye go with these fifty men?"

"I do not know."

"You saw them leave?" Smoke Wind holds up another bean.

"Oh, yes."

"Which road did they take out of the city, then?"

"Oh, they took the yellow road to the south. But the road stops at Round Stone Water." Again the bean disappears into his hand.

"Of course. And after Round Stone Water there is no town before Dry Place?"

"That's true," Lime says. "No town before Dry Place. A long walk."

Smoke Wind draws the string on his bag closed and raises his hand in farewell.

Lime watches the merchant walk away, down the yellow road, away from Xultunich, crossroads of the world. He sucks air in between his teeth, then turns back to his plate of fresh plaster and begins to spread it carefully over the place where the merchant had been tapping his foot, smoothing out the damage.

THREE SKY

When Three Sky orders his slaves to walk faster, they look at him without expression but step more briskly along the uneven path through the forest. After all, they know Three Sky, though not the king, is a man of great power, rightly to be feared.

Despite the heat, the small group has made good progress, and their destination is not far, but there is little time to complete this trip before they must return to Green Mountain. It is Three Sky's task to help bring Evening Star down to Xultunich for her wedding. This, he knows, is Knot-Eye's desperate attempt to save his lineage.

The two slaves, captured from Waterbird River in a long-forgotten war, grunt under their loads of food and weapons.

It is a small band, just the three of them walking all the way to Te-Ayiin, the Place of Crocodiles. And back. In just four days.

"Why, Father?" one of the slaves asks. "Why do we go there?"

"We go there because we must."

"But it is a ruined place, a place of stink and death," the slave protests. Three Sky turns quickly. "How do you know this, slave?"

The slave can only shrug under his load and say nothing. Three Sky grunts and walks on. After a few moments, he points, "See, it is just around this hill."

They emerge into a flat place, a place of marsh caught in a cup of hill. The river flows sluggishly from the lagoon, turning away and down toward Xultunich. "It is only a day's walk from here to Last Stone," Three Sky says. "Yet no one comes here."

"We should go, Father," the slave begs.

"Be quiet or you will lose your tongue," Three Sky answers.

The city stretches along the lagoon, which laps against a low hill on the other side. The building walls still stand, but are empty and charred from the fires that burned the lintels and collapsed the roofs. The ground underfoot crackles as they walk along the central road. Several pyramids, grown for centuries, still remain, but their openings are alive only with crows and insects.

What is strange to Three Sky's eye is that there is no writing anywhere; there are no inscriptions, no tree stone stelas telling of accession and marriage, war and conquest, sacrifice and visitation. Yet the place itself seems steeped in meaning. "There is something here," Three Sky says aloud, and the two slaves stir uneasily. He watches their reaction closely. "Something in the air, in the ground. Can you feel it?" he asks, but they do not answer.

"This place is close to Xibalbá," he continues. "The wall between the Two Worlds is thin here." He sniffs the air and smiles. "Yes," he says. "It is close. There is blood, and dark earth, and dry bone. There is death here."

The slaves stare at him.

"Close. Very close. You can touch it. Look across the water. There is a cave that yawns for the water to enter. How deep does it go into the earth, this mouth of Xibalbá? Why would anyone build here?" He walks along the platform of the largest pyramid, poking at the rotting plaster, the badly fitted stone. "Why? There are mosquitoes in the lagoon, and crocodiles everywhere. The soil is poor. One can easily see there is little rainfall. The lagoon water is dark and tainted. Yet people came here, knowing all this. You!" Three Sky points at the older slave.

"Yes, Father?"

"You are from Waterbird River, a great city near the salt water. What do the slaves, the people of your city, say of Te-Ayiin, the Place of Crocodiles? I know you have heard of this place. I see it in your eyes, in the fear there."

"They say this was a place of death before the maize people came. They say the King of Te-Ayiin was a great magician who spoke to the Lords of Xibalbá, who knew the Lords of Xibalbá. They say when he was sacrificed in an ancient war he became one of the Lords himself, and that the place died, and that the people died, too. They say even the crocodiles began to die here. They say that is why the priests burned the lintels and killed the city. They say what you said today, that this is an opening into the Otherworld. They say the people of maize should never have come here, that this is a place left from the time of the mud people, before the People of Maize were made."

Three Sky grunts. "Very well. Let us return to Green Mountain, then."

DRY PLACE

The afternoon sun spreads across the sky, and blood thuds in the skull like the slow beating of a turtle-shell drum. Knot-Eye, Flint Howler, and the warriors walk as in the dream along the edge of the forest. The yellow burns. The hills burn. They have walked many hours, and now as they come over the last ridge before Dry Place, they can see distant temples above the canopy of forest.

"Fire Star, his house," Flint Howler says, pointing. "Dry Place lineage temple. On the left, Fire Shell's father's temple."

They could nearly make out the figures displayed on the roof combs. A third temple mountain, slightly lower, faces away from them. "The third god house?" Knot-Eye asks. "Whose house is it?"

"I don't know," Flint Howler admits. "I was here ten rounds ago, and then it was a small mountain, with a temple for the serpent-footed god." He shrugs. "As you can see, it has grown."

"Then it was for sacrifice, for blood," Knot-Eye muses. "And now it has grown, and become something else."

"So it appears. We won't know until we can see it from the front."

They move on. Dimly, Knot-Eye remembers a dream of this day, but this is nothing like the dream. The fields are different, the day itself is different. This forced march goes on and on through acrid smoke and dry heat. The forest, closing in on them again, muffles their footsteps. Inside their war gear, their padded coats and skull skirts and animal masks, they sweat. Knot-Eye feels the dry heat of anticipation on his tongue.

They walk down the bottom of a flat gully, scramble up the crumbling embankment, and there is a tree stone, carved with the name of the god-patron of Dry Place, a marker for the edge of the city's sacred space. Just beyond the tree stone are raised gardens. Water runs through the channels between fields, a slow, sullen current, dark and thick smelling. The early corn shows only small, tentative leaves, browning in the sun.

"They planted too early," Flint Howler says.

"The swamp is dry," Knot-Eye says. "They are trying for an extra crop."

"They have their own book," Flint Howler points out. "The seventh moon god is a Dry Place patron. Perhaps they have good omens."

"Perhaps." Knot-Eye does not believe it. He smells desperation here. Dry Place is short of food. This means the Dry Place warriors will be hungry. The hunger may make them angry, but it will also make them weak.

They watch the fields, which are empty. A road descends from the city and bends to their right, toward the west, the black road into the darkness of the sun's death. Down this road, the warriors of Dry Place will come when Knot-Eye calls them out.

"We will cross through the fields, there," he says softly, pointing down the channel between two fields. "They won't see us if we stay low. At the edge of the road we'll wait. Then you go in."

Flint Howler looks at the city, the temple mountains rising above the white terraces, the broad plazas dotted with sacred ceiba trees. Only a few people are visible this time of day, crossing the open spaces. Finally, he nods. "I'll approach from here. They'll be watching me. You can move then." He sets off through the fields.

Knot-Eye motions to the warriors, and they move away down the narrow canal. The water barely covers their ankles, but it is the water of the Otherworld, and they don't like it.

They crouch in the muck for a long time before they hear the sound of war trumpets from the city. Knot-Eye lifts his head above the edge of the road.

Coming toward them are the Dry Place warriors, four twenties of them, nearly twice as many as are crouching in the mud behind him. In front, brandishing his stabbing spear, is Fire Shell, Lord *ajaw* of Dry Place.

If ever Knot-Eye needs the protection and help of the gods, his father-mother ancestor One Monkey, and all the Lords of Xibalbá, now is the time. There is no retreat from here. He can only wait, and hope the ritual cleansing this morning is enough to change the flow of fortune in his direction.

AT THE FOREST EDGE

Although he has run all the distance from Xultunich, Smoke Wind knows he is too late when he passes the tree stone that marks the edge of Dry Place sacred space and hears the war trumpets, the howling and thudding of battle. Animal cries, the screams of the wounded, bloodcurdling war shouts, all come raggedly on the faint stirring of the hot afternoon air.

Smoke Wind is a trader and neutral, so it is not for himself that he fears. The tumult comes from the far side of the fields to the north and west of the city, where a road leads into the trees. He can see dust, mingling with the late-afternoon haze and smoke adrift in the thickening forest on the western hills.

He hurries toward the noise of battle. As he approaches, he sees men moving quickly up the road into the trees. He cannot see anyone from Xultunich, only three or four groups running away from the city, as if in pursuit, and his heart falters. Xultunich is an important city for him, a prosperous place on his trade route, and wealthy enough to trade their fine jade carvings for his salt, his feathered ritual objects, his fine ceramics from Lamanai. If Xultunich should fall, he will have a long way to go between cities.

Besides, Knot-Eye, *ajaw* of Xultunich, is his friend.

He has to push down the ditch, through thick green mud dragging at his feet. It is almost painful how slowly the sounds grow louder. The faster he hurries, the more the water swirls up dark clouds of insects and the rank smell of rotting vegetation. He begins to cough as he runs, and the brown air clutches at his throat.

At last, he reaches the end of the ditch where it turns beside the road, but by now the shouting and skirling of trumpets is deep inside the forest. He climbs onto the road, adjusts his traveler's kilt and his flat-carved wooden badge, and begins walking on the road away from the city. Soon enough he will find the battle. Soon enough he will know.

And then he sees the first casualty, twisted half sideways, sprawled off the edge of the road into the ditch. It is a warrior, a young man, perhaps only eighteen or nineteen years. His stomach has been expertly cut open by some hasty warrior's razor-sharp obsidian knife, and his entrails lie strung out along the slope on the far side of the road. Smoke Wind sees the abandoned, short thrusting spear (so effective for jungle fighting) lying by the body, its flint point probably broken off somewhere inside the body, but the sharp chips of obsidian set into the wooden handle are thick with blood already blackened in the sun. The body has been stripped, and the flexible woven-mat shield that did so little to protect him is gone, so there is no way to identify which city he fought for. The merchant can see only that he will never fight again, despite the ragged breath he still draws; then he shudders, and is still.

Darkness is coming. The shouts have faded, distorted by the jungle. The city in the distance is already in shadow. Only the roof comb of the highest temple is in the light, an orange and smoky aura around the towering mask above the ruler's face, hidden in the scales and feathers of his celestial patron.

Toward him, along the road out of the city, comes a man. As he comes closer, Smoke Wind recognizes the *h-men* from Xultunich, the shaman and scribe of the royal house.

Flint Howler stops beside the other man. "What of the battle?" he asks by way of greeting.

Smoke Wind pulls a long face, making his earflares and necklaces jingle. "I don't know, I was too late, but the trumpets and drums went that way." He tips his head toward the forest.

"Yes. They had more warriors than we expected. Fire Shell bragged to me that at the beginning of a dry season some time ago they raided Te-Ayiin and destroyed the city. Fire Shell believes he has grown powerful since we were here last."

"It looks that way, doesn't it?" Smoke Wind is looking at the body sprawled into the ditch. Flies are buzzing around the loops of intestine spilled from its open abdomen. "He, for one, has gone to Xibalbá. What was his city? His body has been stripped, and now he is just a corpse. If this man was from Xultunich, then Knot-Eye may follow him soon enough."

10 Kawak 17 Keh

Sunday, November 27
The Long Count date is 12.19.12.14.19
It has been 1,869,419 days since the Maya Zero Date
The calendar round date is 10 Kawak 17 Keh
Moon is 26 days old
God 2 rules the night

GOBLIN HOUR

The Sunday after Thanksgiving, Jag watched light fade from a troubled autumn sky and darkness come to his street. His mother was painting in her studio, and his father was, well, not home. Jag knew his father's Maya world was growing and he was busy, but Jag was busy, too. He turned to watch statistics flow through his counting programs.

He raced the fiber for a while, but his heart wasn't in it. HFS was there. He had felt a little guilty putting Ghostman's code into the HFS server, but it seemed harmless. The bytes fell into the great stream of data, were swallowed up, and flowed away.

He looked for his code again, but it was long gone, so he rifled through other files at random, bored and uneasy. He circled back from Costa Rica into the HFS Headquarters Information Systems. He was looking for any-thing, a nugget, some random bit of information, codes, or numbers. He scrolled through memos on client-server purchases, graphic translation programs, standards committees. The usual corporate mumbo jumbo—boring, boring, boring.

He scanned the subject fields: Thursday meeting; Draft staff report; Coordination with France, with Thailand, with South Africa.

D. A.

That caught his attention. Probably nothing, a couple of letters, acro-nym for some company project, but why not take a look?

The memo was short and unsigned. "Propose we hire so-called D. A. to reacquire original. Budget $10K."

He checked the recipient and felt a rush of excitement: Robert Hamerslough. Aunt Mary's ex-husband, the lawyer, was named Robert Hamerslough, certainly not a common name, though Jag ran a phone number check to be certain, and found two others in the nation, neither an attorney living in the area. If he was Mary's ex, was it just a coincidence?

His fingers shook a little as he scrolled through directory lists, operating procedures, policy statements. Robert Hamerslough was on the staff of the Public Advocacy Division of HFS. He was in charge of "special projects."

Jag searched backward day by day. What was the "original?" An object? A document?

HFS made Saniclor and lots of other things, but none of them seemed good candidates for an "original." So it was probably a document, perhaps signed, something the company wanted back very badly, so badly they would hire the Digital Assassins, underground hackers of course, but, Jag now knew, not only hackers. There were stories about D. A., its origins in the street, in the uses of electronic subterfuge by sophisticated predators to lure suckers to ATM machines or empty corporate lobbies at night. Dim rumors of violence. Jag hadn't believed them before; the ones he knew were introverts like himself, bit-heads who preferred the Mondo to the wet world of meat IRL. He'd imagined them as thin night dwellers in back bedrooms, young and curious roamers of the fiber. Not killers hired for $10,000. Certainly not in the business of "reacquiring originals."

But according to Mr. Calvert, someone in D. A. had killed Derek Kim in front of the Asian Art Museum. His mother was a witness. She talked to law enforcement from time to time. She'd suspected him, of all people. He hadn't told her much; it wasn't necessary.

The killer had worn a D. A. T-shirt. Jag had owned such a shirt.

Suddenly, it seemed very important that he find out what HFS had hired D. A. to do. His fingers danced over the keys.

There were too many documents, too many messages back and forth, too many things described, noted, forwarded, deleted. Robert's name first appeared ten months before on the new hires list, roughly the time he and Aunt Mary had divorced. Jag knew Uncle Robert had changed jobs and gone to work full time for his client.

At the new job, Uncle Robert prepared a document of some kind. A memo? A letter? A report of some kind?

The document was lost, and now lost must be "reacquired."

He downloaded a copy of the memo and stared at it. It was dated October 19, a Tuesday. Unsigned. Was it sent up the chain of command at HFS to Robert Hamerslough, director of special projects? By someone who had contacts with, or access to, the Digital Assassins, a shadowy underground hacker group, usually, but not always, teenage boys into racing the fiber and stepping softly through the bit world out of curiosity and a burning desire to learn how the Mondo made itself?

Well. There were lots of D. A. members, all over the country. Jag knew many of them by name or reputation. The ones he knew were not the sort to murder. They were mostly kids. Maybe a few girls, but mostly boys. They were just interested in hacking, weren't they? They had ethics, right?

He had to know. His mother was a witness, and though she had said nothing, he could tell she was nervous. She tried to hide it from him, but she was tense. Her name was on the victim's list.

Perhaps she was scared. Perhaps she thought they were after her. Now Jag was worried.

And then he came across his father's name. A year ago, Sylvanus M. Weathers, recipient of several previous grants from the Central American Preservation Organization, was offered funding through CAPO. The memo was explicit that this was specifically *not* to support his excavations at Xultunich but to support Professor Weathers's educational project. This would protect Garcia Holdings.

That was curious.

Garcia Holdings was a wholly owned subsidiary trust of HFS Corporation. It had extensive property holdings in the vicinity of Xultunich, including a plantation called Te-Ayiin. It needed protection.

His father had complained he could not get permits to dig at Te-Ayiin.

Just the other day, Ghostman had asked him to introduce some code into the HFS server to "help someone out."

Ghostman had given him leads to HFS. Ghostman always seemed to be there when he needed a little nudge in this part of the Mondo.

Ghostman had said someone would get some help if Jag entered a few lines of code on the HFS server. And now his father.

He called his father's office, but there was no answer. Not surprising:

Van was always wrapped up in his sim and seldom answered the phone any more. Jag chewed thoughtfully on a fingernail. What had he done? Maybe he'd better pull that code out of there and cover his tracks.

Who the hell was Ghostman?

RECON

Ghostman backed away from the trapezoidal splash of light that glowed through the small, frosted glass pane around the block letters: Professor Sylvanus Weathers.

This late on a Sunday and the professor was still in his office. Did he know what his boy had done? It was a wonderful joke Elliot had prepared for Professor Weathers.

It hadn't been that hard to find the name in the faculty records, now, had it, once Elliot recognized the family resemblance? Oh, yes, the professor's boy Jonathan, racing the fiber, breaking into places he shouldn't. And now he had planted the incriminating code.

Jonathan Weathers, Digital Assassin. Assassin.

Problem Number One solved. Now for Problem Number Two.

Well, there was breaking in and there was breaking out. Elliot was master of the building. And he mustn't forget the Honey Trap, either. That would buy him some time.

The Primus lock was set, so Elliot made his way to the basement.

On the way, he spotted Wendell by the vending machines. "Day of Reckoning," he said aloud.

Wendell considered this. "Reckoning? Payday's the first, Elliot."

The wall clock read 12:14. "Yes," Elliot said slowly. "The first. He'll pay."

Wendell brushed his hair back with a firm hand. "You come in every Sunday?"

Elliot laid his finger beside his nose. "I'd rather not say."

Wendell shrugged. "Whatever."

"I will ask you something," Elliot said.

"Shoot."

Elliot cupped his hands around his mouth and whispered, "Where does he go?"

"Go?"

"The professor." Elliot leaned back, his voice conversational again.

It was such a different tone, Wendell thought Elliot had changed the subject. "What about him?"

"Where does he go?"

Wendell nodded. "Oh, the professor. Yes. Where does he go?" He looked around for a clue to Elliot's meaning. "Home?" he suggested.

Elliot stared at him. "No. I mean in there," he said slowly, aiming his forefinger at the computer lab.

"Ah, the simulation. Xibalbá Gate. I showed you."

"Right, right, you showed me." Elliot, playing the fool, cocked his thumb behind the forefinger, nodding vigorously.

"Yeah, I guess. Come on, I'll show you again. Follow me." He tossed his cup in the waste bin.

Elliot watched him walk away, then did as he was told. He was smiling.

The computer lab was deserted. Most of the monitors were dark; the others sported screen savers from popular television shows.

Wendell tapped keys, moved his mouse. "See." He pointed at the skeletal jaws, the Underworld's gullet, proud of his work.

"Hmm-hmm." Elliot crouched forward, staring intently. "Interesting."

Wendell looked at him, tapped the jaws. The Green Room opened. "You wanted to go in. You asked if you could come in here and enter, remember?"

"Sure, sure, I remember. Been busy," Elliot grunted, leaning into the screen. He was making mental notes while Wendell proudly rambled on. He knew now where to find the Xibalbá Gate's administrative programming; all of Wendell's careful secrets were his.

"So try it," Wendell said expansively. "Go ahead, it's kinda fun. You can be someone, anyone."

"They won't know it's me? They can't know it's me, you know. No, no, they can't."

"They won't know. Only I'll know."

"Not if you leave," Elliot said.

"What?"

"You won't know if you leave."

"Oh, yeah, well, don't you want me to show you how to do it?"

"Oh, sure, sure." Elliot had to keep himself from smiling. Wendell was an unwitting informant, part of the great game.

"I'll help you the first time. Then you can do it yourself, be someone else if you don't want me to know."

"OK," Elliot said, so Wendell made him a slave, carrying rocks from the river to the new temple in a town called Dry Place. There was a battle raging on the other side of the city, and everyone was over there watching it, so there wasn't anyone for Elliot to talk to, which was all right with him. He would have a look around, do a little recon, get the lay of the digital land, pick up some extra intel while playing the fool for Wendell.

He already knew who he was, and it was not a slave carrying rocks from the river, in spite of what Wendell thought.

COLD COMFORT

Leon backed out and looked around.

The samovar steamed quietly against the window, leaving another layer of condensation on the glass. Each layer froze, then cracked and froze again into a crazed mosaic portrait of the construction outside.

He found he was sweating, and held his hand out, palm down. The faintest of tremors was visible in the fingertips. He drew in a deep breath and stared until the tremor went away.

The ruined city lingered, the aftertaste of nausea. Although he had been a scholar all his life, he had plenty of experience with ruined cities, even with war—he remembered well what they showed on television of Afghanistan in the old days. Yet reality had not prepared him for something like this. This was so *graphic*. The Americans were doing amazing things with reality, that a combination of text, image, and sound could be so compelling. Amazing, and disturbing. He would swear he could *smell* the stagnant water, hear the buzz of mosquitoes, and feel the palpable sense of doom about the place.

Settlement patterns. The inevitable flow of history. Curiosity. It was going to kill him.

He went to the door and called, "Mara!"

The electric bulb hanging from the high ceiling burned steadily, its twisted filament almost invisible in the room's bleak winter light. The steam heat was too high, as usual, but for once he was glad. It created a sensory continuity with the unreal world he had just left, its desolation and reek of blood. He stood directly under its pale glow and gazed at his computer screen. The skeletal jaws did not waver. They were nothing but a digital drawing. There was nothing supernatural about them or where they led.

Yet the corners of the room held shadows that had not been there before. The shadows moved when he looked at them, skittered away, flew along the wall to the next corner, stretched *toward* the naked bulb's radiance. He fought the desire to look over his own shoulder, to turn suddenly, try to catch something he could just see out of the corner of his eye.

Finally he opened the door and called for Mara again. This time, she appeared. "What do you want?" she grumbled.

He thought for a moment, head cocked, realized he didn't know why he had called her. The samovar was full and hot, steam still flattening against the frozen panes. He certainly didn't need a sweater in this stifling heat. Finally he said, "Company," and gestured at the fat chair. The horsehair creaked when she sat down and folded her hands in her lap, looking at him.

"We've been married thirty years," he began.

"Thirty-two," she said.

"Ah, has it been so long?"

She didn't reply. Her round dumpling face was in repose.

"Are you content?" he asked.

Her brows knitted. "Yes."

"You don't mind. . . ." He tipped his head toward the computer. "I have been someone else. It isn't easy coming back, I find."

"I understand."

"Ah. But do you care?"

Her look was blank. "Leon, you're tired. You've been working too hard. Take a rest. I'll get you tea." She rose and went to the samovar.

"It makes you uncomfortable, talking like this?" It was not quite a question, and she didn't answer. "I've spent too much time exchanging messages with Americans," he said slowly. "I'm beginning to act like them. Mara, I'm beginning to understand them." It was like a cry torn from him. Mara heard the fear in it.

"I thought it was Indians you were playing." Her voice was soft, almost inaudible. She handed him the cup and sat down.

"Yes, yes, Indians, and Americans, too. It's schizophrenic, really. I am a Russian pretending to be an American pretending to be an Indian in a world that has been gone for a thousand years."

She smiled at him, not without kindness.

"Not so different from being a Russian today, perhaps," he added thoughtfully.

UNREAL CITY

Alberto Bofonchio tapped his screen, where the Mayan city was almost lost in smoke. "Sometimes I think it is not so different in there from our lovely city outside, eh?"

On the other side of the former ballroom of the Palazzo Verbi, now the Centro Accademico Computer di Venezia, Franco La Polla grunted and tugged the underside of his right eye, tapping keys frantically with his left hand. Because he was logged into the University of Padua and didn't want to talk, his message flew back across the room in silence, small bits of semiotic code transmitted visually through fingers, skin, eye position, shoulder set, lifted elbows, tilted heads, eyebrows.

Alberto leaned back in his chair, took a sip of his espresso, and swallowed lustily, waving with his free hand at the implied city outside. He mused aloud, "Dry Place is going under, I have no doubt. Not like Te-Ayiin, not destroyed, but," he snapped his fingers, "no longer important."

Franco looked up and scratched his beard. Venice is still important, he meant. And it is not going under. Reports of Venice subsiding were greatly exaggerated.

Alberto set down his cup and tapped the underside of his chin. A great change is taking place, he was saying by slightly raising his left eyebrow. The American has created a powerful and interesting metaphor that drives us toward a deep understanding of the cultural implications of our own social condition.

I doubt it, Franco signaled back, head tilted to one side and turned very slightly away.

It's true, Alberto insisted, staring straight at Franco while holding his hand out, thumb up, fingers extended, for less than a second. He swept his hand in a semicircle, indicating the city outside the gilded walls of the ballroom. The city of Venice *is* sinking. His head tilted fractionally toward his computer screen. In there, we are learning about the last days of a city. It makes you think.

Franco, now looking steadily at Alberto, lifted his free hand slowly, straight up from his desk, until his arm was extended straight up over his head. He maintained a slightly incredulous, lethargic expression and released a sound like escaping steam. Alberto was, as usual, leaping to totally invalid conclusions; the American was doing what Americans always do, create a lot of technological razzle dazzle with no intellectual depth at all. He, Alberto, shouldn't be so gullible, so credulous, so *utopian* as to believe that anything even potentially significant could possibly come from such juvenile attempts at understanding the world, which, after all, continued as it always had, in its own way, without much, if any, guidance from intellectuals such as themselves. And furthermore, any solutions he, Alberto, thought he had discovered in there would only lead to further, probably more serious, problems.

To which Alberto lifted one shoulder. You're wrong, as usual, blinded by your own conservatism and lack of imagination into living in some vague vision of a past golden age, when in fact the past was nothing but an endless series of failed attempts, each more pathetic than the last. Only by studying such failures can we have any hope of a better future. This is urgent work.

Franco flared his nostrils and nodded fractionally toward Alberto's coffee. You are becoming an American taking what they call a coffee break. You want a coffee, you should go to a cafe. That's why we have them. He pulled his lower lip over his upper, lifted his eyebrows as far as they could go very rapidly, and went back to work, turning a few degrees of his back on the whole pointless discussion. In a world made up almost entirely of signs, the subject of politics was moderately interesting but not important. Soon enough, Alberto would take the train back to Bologna and leave him in peace.

Outside, the city of Venice was struggling to remain above water level.

CODE 459

Elliot logged off and sank back in the chair. It was the middle of the a.m., end of the Thanksgiving holiday; Wendell was long gone, and Elliott was ready to start the two painstaking tasks he needed to prepare for tomorrow.

Before turning off the lights and locking up the computer lab, he paused at the printer to pick up the seven pages of small print he had downloaded from the Digital Assassins archives. Searching the Web could be extraordinarily useful, though it did mean he had a few hours of difficult and dangerous work ahead of him.

He had been working for some time on one project. Mad Brian's Home Explosives Page gave him the list of everything he needed. He had already processed the bleach. (It was called "fractional crystalization.") It took two hours to mix the powdered crystals with Vaseline, wax, and white gasoline, but for a man used to mixing Saniclor this was a trivial, if delicate, procedure. At 4:32 a.m., he carefully placed a small cardboard package tightly clothed in plastic tape beside his workbench in the den and sat down.

He had left his hidden door open so he could see the oblong of light reflected off the mirror over the sink of his narrow, "official" office. He set himself to the task of gently arranging his collection of electronics, small tools, and the downloaded Digital Assassins file. Referring to the printout, he carefully entered a series of numbers on the keypad of a police scanner, put the earphone in his ear, and listened.

It was a quiet night, but occasionally a burst of words followed by a spurt of static came through. It was enough to let him know he was getting what he wanted.

"Two-eleven, 2349 Calabrese, in progress, *snrfft.*"

"Ten-four, *snrfft.*"

He slipped the scanner into his pocket and went into the office, closing the concealed door to the den behind him. He nodded at *his* reflection in the mirror over the sink. He could see the plastic bottles in reverse behind his head: ᴹᵀrolcinaS. He pulled on a pair of thin, black leather gloves and straightened the collar of his black turtleneck.

From the metal cabinet, he took his keys, including the high-security Primus master, and slipped from the office, closing the door silently behind him. Crowley Hall had the deserted glow of emptiness a large building gets when you're the only one there.

He was a shadow within shadows as he made his way up the stairs, round and round, landing after landing, ground, one, two. On the fourth floor, he became Ghostman, slipping into the hallway IRL. The bright glow from Van Weathers's office was gone; it was just another dark door like all the others and opened smoothly to his Primus. When there is no one to watch the watchers, the man with the master key is master of all. His pencil flashlight made a small circle of light that roamed over terra cotta figurines of a woman giving birth and another of a man seated cross-legged, head thrown back in pain. For a moment the light stayed on that face, throwing its shadow against a topographic map of a section of the Peten in the lowlands of Guatemala on the wall behind it. Then it moved on, over mounds of old paper copies of *The Pre-Columbian Art Research Institute Journal*, a tattered announcement for the "V Congreso Centroamericano de Antropología in Nicaragua in 2004," file folders with labels such as "Xultunich Obsidian Hydration Studies" and "Ground Penetrating Radar Research Proposal, Te-Ayiin," bits of broken pottery with fragments of red, black, or cream-colored design. The light danced along the spines of books, picking out the muted brick reds, greens, and tans of their covers.

He saw a copy of *Mesoamerican Mythology*, a book he had been reading in Professor Jones's office not long ago. He pulled it out, flipped through the pages, looking at pictures. Ah, there, the old man hunched over, loose lips, sagging cheeks, a cigar in his mouth: One Death.

He shook the book; nothing fell out, so he put it back. He took a deep breath, drawing it in through his nostrils with a satisfying rushing sound, like the very sound of stealth itself in the darkness.

His earphone twittered. "*Snrfft*, . . . how do you read?"

"Four five nine, *snrfft*."

"Forgot, four five nine?" It was a woman's voice. She sounded very young.

The older man was very patient, very careful. These were trying times, bringing women into law enforcement. Had to be careful. "Burglary in progress," he said.

"Oh, yeah, *snrfft*."

Elliot jumped, then realized they couldn't be talking about him. He had the master key. He had a right to be here. This was his domain.

He took books from the shelves one by one, shaking them and putting them back.

In the *Dresden Codex*, he found another picture of the old man, paunched and grisly, flatulent and grim, One Death leaning down to shake a bony finger at his prisoners, who were the dead. These people, the Maya, they knew what it was all about, they did. They knew One Death well.

He idly flapped the book. A little yellow Post-it note fell out, and Elliot knew this was just his luck at work in the world. He put the book down on the table and bent to retrieve it.

BEHIND THE SCREEN

Although Anne Opple felt her backside tingle as if falling asleep, a nagging itch under her left arm, and an occasional pain shooting up her right wrist as she walked along a trench a meter deep and two meters wide cut into thin soil pale with lime, she kept searching far into the night.

She had not found Van Weathers in the Maya world, not yet, not all week. He was here, she could feel him, thought she could almost smell him, but she could not find him, could not guess who he was.

Today, she was a stooped weaver in the city of Xultunich wandering among a jumble of platforms and pyramids, plaster and stucco sculpture, god-masks and burial chambers, its reluctant history half-hidden still. Yesterday, she had been a cook in the compound of Reed Altar, nephew to the king. The day before, she had been stuck as a slave on a farm upriver from the city. She listened to the talk but said little.

At least she was making social progress.

Tonight, there was a moon (a pale orange oval in the velvet sky sprinkled with white pixels); there were trees (she thought they were a bit generic, all the same, leaves whispering in a complex but repetitive singsong).

The narrow, winding passages between temples and pyramids and the great *sakbe* leading west past the reservoir were mostly empty this time of night, though she did pass small groups standing at the sides of the plazas or seated on the edge of the platforms talking in hushed tones of the war. The central plaza still held the sacred limestone monuments that told the history of the city in finely carved glyphs and images of the kings in war dress, and near them the people speak of the city's warriors, who are far away, the king went with them, there has been no news. They say the king must return with captives for the marriage ceremony. The king must give blood, summon One Monkey, First Ancestor. The King must marry again. Lady Fin has given him no heir and the lineage is dying. Evening Star from

Green Mountain will arrive tomorrow. If the king does not return with captives the city may die. Already the priests are talking about a Termination Ritual.

Overhead the God Who Has No Name trails a pallid light across the dark road.

Eventually, the torches went out, the fires died down. She could pass dark doorways in the eastern residential compounds and hear the sounds of sleep if she listened carefully. Somewhere, a child cried, then stopped. The fields farther to the east were empty, the corn not yet planted. The river made soft sounds in the distance, and frogs croaked in the lagoon beyond the city's edge.

It was no use. She could not find him behind the screen.

TOUR

Most of the Americans dropped out as night swept westward. Three people in New York went off-line at midnight. An hour later, an archaeologist in Chicago departed, followed a few minutes later by two people in St. Louis and one in Denver.

Soon there were no participants in the Xibalbá Gate from the western hemisphere. A retired amateur archaeologist in Shanghai, where it was 8:30 in the evening, entered and wandered toward the ruins of Te-Ayiin. On the road, he encountered, although he did not know it, an anthropologist from Kyoto in the guise of a woodcutter from the western hills and then fell into conversation. It was 9:30 in the evening in Kyoto, and they both recognized that the shrilling of crickets in the simulation was a poignant reminder of their own contexts, although in Shanghai it was closer to the shrilling of cellular phones and emergency vehicles. He never made it to the ruined city.

In St. Petersburg, the power was off again, and Leon, although it was now 3:20 in the afternoon, was taking a walk along the Neva, his muffler wrapped around his thin neck, shoulders hunched against the wind. Debris and trash tumbled in the gutters, for the snow had stopped, frozen solid.

Alberto Bofonchio was forced to leave at noon to catch his train back to Bologna, so with regret he had logged off, given a cheery wave to Franco, who, typing furiously, mumbled something incomprehensible.

Venice in November was foggy and cold, and Alberto, too, hurried along the embankments to the train station, chin down. No gondoliers were singing.

NIGHT TOWN

Van's old Toyota radio was playing the prelude to "Chi mi frena in tal momento" from *Lucia di Lammermoor*, but Van was paying little attention. His success at Dry Place seethed in his head. He had taken captives, more than enough to sacrifice for his wedding to Evening Star.

He drummed his fingertips on the steering wheel. He is walking back along the forest edge, long declining slopes of early corn to his right. His string of captives trudges along, bare feet kicking up dry season dust. Flint Howler walks in silence, almost as if he is worn out from the trip. And the other fellow, the merchant, Smoke Wind, he's there too, walking in and out of the shadows of the almost-invisible demons of death and disease, animal spirit-helpers and ancestral ghosts.

In reality he drives through a warehouse district, and it's November, and beginning once more to rain a little. The streetlights here are far apart, throwing ovals of wan illumination onto the littered street. There are no sidewalks, only down-curving curbs to occasional storm drains. On the drains are painted letters: Do Not Dump, Leads to Bay. He can't see the letters very well, even when they fall under a light, but he knows they are there.

Ahead, two figures are walking along the windowless side of a brick building.

Van passes them, watching in the side mirror.

One is an old man, toothless mouth mumbling with overlapping lips. He is wearing an enormous hat, twisted into intricate and indecipherable shapes. There is something familiar about that hat, and Van slows, watching it in the side mirror. The man notices the car has slowed and increases his pace, forcing the diminutive figure beside him to hop. Van can just hear, over the quiet purr of his engine and the whisper of rain on his windshield still too soft for the wipers, a jingling sound. The shorter figure is a dwarf, wearing a three-tasseled jester's hat. The tassels toss with his skipping steps, ringing the little bells on the ends.

Van's foot was already pressing on the accelerator when the taller figure rapped his knuckles on the door of the sedan. Van was not about to open the door or even unlock it, but he took his foot off the pedal and slowed to a stop. Only then did he realize it was after 3:30 in the morning, he was deep in the deserted warehouse district, and he was alone except for the two derelicts.

When it appeared at his window, Van looked into the man's face. It was ancient, that face, ravaged by some kind of wasting disease. The eyes were deeply sunken into the skull, almost lost to view, and flesh around them looked like the skin of an ancient orange, puckered, shriveled, almost black. The nose hooked out and hung down over the upper lip.

The little jester figure hopped up and down, his trilobed hat flopping. His forehead and eyes would appear over the edge of the window and drop out of sight again. He was grinning, little crinkles of flesh puckered at the sides of eyes that twinkled with malice. Van had never known you could see malice in someone's eyes, but he could in these.

The old man bent over toward the window, and Van could see the hat, with elaborate feather designs, now beaded with moisture. A street lamp a dozen yards behind them threw its left side into inky shadow. The hat was some kind of enormous bird, great wings spread across the window, casting deep shadow.

He recognized the old man: One Death, first Lord of the Otherworld, ruler of Xibalbá. At the same time from the radio, two men launched into a sestet: "What restrains me at this moment?" Edgar and Henry were singing. They know they are enemies, that Henry has betrayed Edgar and Lucia. Both men have their hands on their swords.

In this moment One Death whips out a filthy rag and starts to swipe it across the windshield, smearing a wide path of accumulated dust over Van's field of view.

Little K'awiil, hopping beside the car, raised a filthy hand to knock at the window glass, *tap-tap*, and One Death again swipes across the windshield.

Van pressed on the accelerator and flicked on the wipers at the same time, leaving the two men standing by the brick building. Just as he was going around the corner, he saw their shopping cart, their lean-to of flattened cardboard boxes, two abandoned homeless old men camped in the November streets beside a crumbling brick wall.

FAILURE ANALYSIS

Sleepless, Mary Hamerslough lay in her bed, on her left side, thinking she was an incredibly lucky person. She had found someone. Foster was no dream, no fantasy. He was shy, a little goofy, self-centered, and preoccupied, but he was sweet. And he was attentive.

FINGERTIPS

Glenna snorted in small fits in her sleep. Her sinuses had begun to bother her, a sure sign of stress. Her fingertips twitched on the edge of the champagne-colored flannel sheet.

SERVICE CALL

Elliot leaned back in Van Weathers's chair and held the Post-it up to the light, smiling. With a grunt, he put down the scrap of paper and pulled some small electronic devices and tools from his bag.

His teeth gleamed as he unscrewed the ear piece of Van's office telephone and set to work.

An hour later, the phone was reassembled, the Post-it was back in its book, and Elliot Blackman had cleaned away all trace of his presence, as befit someone code named Ghostman.

DECISION TREE

Van Weathers drove slowly around the crumbling downtown block looking for the two homeless men. They were gone, the street empty, the brick wall blank. The cardboard lean-to and shopping cart were gone.

He grew thoughtful. Could they have simply disappeared?

Finally, he accelerated around the corner and drove back toward the university.

BLOOD

Jag's fingers flap on the satin edge of his blanket, and a coded accounting of body chemicals, of salts and blood, takes shape—levels, concentrations, counts.

He is dreaming down into the cells of his body, where things are beginning to go wrong.

Crimson platters roll and tumble. Their thin centers reveal other things behind them when they surge, reverse, surge again. Tubes go on forever, with a rushing sound, *shoosh, snrfft, shoosh, snrfft,* like surf along the ocean's edge, rolling the gravel up across the sand, letting it roll back down, pungent with the iodine odor of seaweed rotting in the sun. Clouds cling to the horizon like dark tubers.

It is his blood, and Jag is a cunning runner in the blood, a shadow among shadows flowing through damp undergrowth, in silvered moonlight, in barred sun.

His fingers tap on the blanket edge. They spell out an appeal, a hope. They say, follow me. Ghostman blinks and Jag is at a crossroads. Four roads zoom away into the distance as he turns. A white road goes north, a black road west, a yellow road south, a red road east. Which road, here where the roads cross, changing color? Here where the trees grow thick.

Deep in his dream Jag knows he is sick. It isn't exactly the beginning of fever, it is only the subtle mistakes of enzymes, small deficiencies, minuscule mutations, but he knows in a way without words.

It is not growing pains he feels.

What he hears is smooth fur brushing against leaves, against bark, *shoosh, snrfft, shoosh, snrfft.* There are great oily depths beneath his feet, out of sight, and spaces above the trees, huge empty spaces where the spirits grin and leer in the endless wind.

The crisis is coming.

THE NINE LORDS

THE MONDAY AFTER THANKSGIVING

7 Ajaw 3 Xul

April 27, 837 AD
The Long Count date is 10.0.7.4.0
It has been 1,442,600 days since the Maya Zero Date
The calendar round date is 7 Ajaw 3 Xul
Moon is full
God 8 rules the night

ONE DEATH

One Death, Lord of the Otherworld, Ruler of Xibalbá, the House of Fear and Land of the Dead, Great *Ajaw* of Stink City and Blood Creek, scratches at his ribs, all festooned with strips of ragged flesh. Dense brown vapors rise from below him, and he inhales happily. Ah, it is good here, rubbing his palms together with the rasping sound, rattle of bones. It is very good.

The World above, it all comes down from there. What do they do up there? They make love, they eat tamales. They sleep in dreamless dark, breathing in and out.

One Death knows what they do up there. He came from there, from the dirty places. He is a creature of the darkness, One Death is. Better down here in Xibalbá, in the Place of Fear, in the House of Death. He spends too much of his life listening to that nasty breathing in and out. He is cunning, a plotter, a deviser of revenge.

Now he is home where he belongs. Thanks to Wendell's indiscretions, he has slipped into the digital other world without effort, as if he had always been this Lord. Here he is listening to the in and out of breath, and he doesn't know if it is his or if it belongs to someone else.

One Death only knows that he doesn't like it, the breathing. It is too quiet. Too disgustingly *healthy*. He prefers something with a rasp to it, a soft wet gurgle that sends up sharp smells of decay.

Up there they have worries of their own, things that have nothing to do with him or any of his friends, such as Seven Death or Pus Bucket or the others. Up there they bend over their books, all scratched lines and squiggles everywhere. They think it all means something, this reading and writing in books, on white boards, but One Death knows better. All anything means, in the end, is the long slow fall into this very darkness, here where he can catch in his long, misshapen fingers whatever drifts down to him and test it on his tongue. There would be heads and wings and arms and legs. There would be blood, dropping down, seeping into his close earth.

He hears a sound, a squeak, and One Death tilts his head; his hat falls over his ear and he has to lift it back, listening.

Pah. Just bats, quick whisper of wings, back and forth, little Zotz devils.

His tiny office, crowded with paws and skins, skulls and shriveled rodent corpses, bits of paper with the names of those he knew and those he did not yet know but would, encloses him like a flayed human captive skin.

"Come in," he croaks in answer to a scratching at his door. "Ah, Seven Death, what news?"

Seven Death shuffles to a chair and turns away, twitching his scrawny hindquarters over the seat, lowering, dusting, settled at last to rest.

"Nothing good," says Seven Death. "Nothing good."

"Ah," One Death waves his hand. "You always say that."

"True, anyway."

"What this time, then?"

"More noise up there. Fighting, war, disease."

"Sure, sure, that's good. The usual." One Death is beginning to relax. It all means more matter soon falling from the dank ceiling of his office.

"Knot-Eye," Seven Death says slowly.

One Death, struck dumb, finally says, "Hmm?" a bat squeak.

"He's here. I mean, there. Up there." Seven lifts his finger, points at the ceiling, festooned with roots and dank odors.

"Coming?" One Death chokes and tries again. "Coming here?"

"No, no. Alive and well, but planning something big, a sacrifice."

"A game?" One sighs. "Noise and pollution."

Seven nods. "We'll be tricked, again, just like with the Hero Twins. You remember how they tricked us, pretended to kill themselves?"

"They did kill themselves."

"Yes, but they came back to life, One Death."

"All right, all right. This time we will be careful. This time we should cut off his water. Plague, Seven Death. Disease, bone break, fever dream, toothache, pus and blood and bile, stink and stench, rack and rot. This time we should stop him for sure."

"He runs the place, One Death. It's his world, after all."

"Doesn't matter." One Death stands up; he paces the narrow room. "It doesn't matter. His world or not, there are rules. Rules. I will stop him. I will drag him down. Knot-Eye will come to me, Seven Death. He will come to me, and I will have him, and he will beg me for mercy, for life." He punches his fist against the wooden lintel, and the tattered hangings shake. "I'll run him through the Houses, Seven Death. The knives and jaguars howl. Bone-shattering cold, the bats and fear and fire. He won't clever his way out this time. He's no Hero Twin, no magician; he can't change himself to fish or bird, he's a man, and by all the gods I'll drown him in blood, Seven."

"You're ranting again."

"Am not!"

"Are!"

"Am not! Even if he's dead, I'll kill him—thinks he runs it all, thinks he's so great, doesn't pay One Death no mind—I'll take his head and hang it in the Tree! I am One Death, Lord of Xibalbá. No one denies me. No one ignores me. No one lives but I say so."

He sweeps from the room. Seven Death heaves a loathsome sigh and gets up to follow.

11 Ajaw 18 Keh

Monday, November 28
The Long Count date is 12.19.12.15.0
It has been 1,869,420 days since the Maya Zero Date
The calendar round date is 11 Ajaw 18 Keh
Moon is 27 days old
God 3 rules the night

THE NOTE

Glenna woke alone in a cold bed on a cold November dawn. She lay still, watching gray light leak into the room. The dresser slowly took shape.

She stopped washing her face before the bathroom mirror to stare at the pale skin pinched tight around her eyes. Her thin flannel pajamas had bunched up, and she pulled the bottoms down with wet hands, leaving dark prints on the white, flowered material. She thought perhaps she should turn up the heat.

She made herb tea and sat in the kitchen. The small radio squawked about traffic and Christmas shopping and weather (more rain was expected).

She turned the radio off and listened to the silence until it was time for Jag to get up. She walked down the hallway to his room, past the dark pictures. She opened the door and there was Jag, sitting up in his bed, reading.

"Liechtenstein," he announced, looking up, "is slightly smaller than Washington, D.C."

"Yes. It's time to get up."

"OK." He tossed the *World Factbook* onto the foot of the bed and sat on the edge. He was wearing plaid shorts and a T-shirt to sleep in these days. The T-shirt was from Cancún, a place Jag had never been.

His feet were narrow and pale, almost blue. He walked into the bathroom, and Glenna went back to the kitchen.

"What do you want for breakfast?" she asked when he appeared.

He shrugged. "Nothing. I don't care. Whatever. I had a lot of dreams."

She put whole-grain bread in the toaster and rummaged in the refrigerator. "What kind of dreams?"

"Weird. Blood dreams. Things going wrong."

"School," she said. "You're probably worried about school."

"Yeah, maybe, but I'm doing well. Got an A on the economics thing. Where's dad?"

"He must be working. You know how this project preoccupies him. Why?"

"Nothing. Something I found last night is all. I thought he'd be interested. I thought I should tell him about it."

"Something you found?"

"Yeah. You know, hacking around. Just some files, his name. It's kind of a puzzle. I need to talk to him."

"Oh. Well, he'll be home tonight."

When the toast popped up, she spread butter and hummus on it. He ate slowly, looking out the window.

"Like it?" she asked.

"It's good," he told her, still looking outside. "It's fine."

"It's hummus," she said. "Chickpeas."

"I've heard of it."

School was only a few blocks away, but it was raining slightly, so she drove him. And then she drove home. She was thinking that tomorrow she had a date with Lincoln Boytim. Just business, of course. He would bring the van, and she could take *Message, or Messages* and the other big canvasses to the gallery.

She examined *Dead Tongues* for a while, making minor adjustments. Mostly she was pleased; the infinitely small hash of darker rose receded into the background ganzfeld wash, leaving any potential meaning trembling just on the edge of perception. It was, she felt, very much like the Maya glyphs before the code was broken and the meaning burst out, an ancient tongue brought back from the dead.

She decided the painting was finished and began to prepare a new canvas, the clean white blankness of it filled with potentiality. She would, she thought, like to do something ancient, something, perhaps, Etruscan. It was slightly larger than the last canvas, and she obviously would not be able to finish it in time for the show, but she felt it was better to be in the middle of something when she had her first major show than to feel empty of all creativity.

A coppery rust would be the right color for this one: *Etruscan Song.* She began mixing the base color.

She stopped painting a little before eleven, put up her brushes, and went downstairs to wait for the mail. When it arrived, she chatted with the postman for a few minutes. Then she went back to the kitchen, setting the letters and magazines on the counter while she made more tea. Finally, she sorted through the letters.

The one from CAPO gave her a little shock. It seemed like yesterday the president of CAPO had been murdered while she watched helplessly, but it had been weeks. Why would they write him at home and not at the university? And why now? She opened it.

It seemed to be a routine form letter congratulating Dr. Weathers on the opening of his Web-based cultural simulation. The organization was very pleased that its funding had been put to such good purpose, and the early notice the field had taken of it was very gratifying, et cetera. Glenna tossed it on the side table and saw, when the page fell face down, that there was a short note written on the back. "We must talk in person. DK."

She picked it up and examined it. The letter was dated October 31. Two days before Derek Kim had died. Why had it taken so long to arrive? She checked the postmark: last Friday. She imagined Kim was going to send it, decided to visit her, got killed, and some secretary, trying to catch up after the upset of her boss's death, put it in the mail over the holiday.

She dialed Van's office and got voicemail. She hesitated a moment, then hung up. It seemed better to tell him in person. Besides, hadn't Jag said something about wanting to talk to him? Maybe she and Jag could go see him together.

Yes, that would be better. They would go over to the university right after school.

THE CITY OF DOSTOYEVSKY

Leon told Mara, "I can see it coming, and there's nothing to say. Stop—I said stop, don't do it, don't continue with this wedding, this alliance.

Three Sky said it, and no one believed him, and he's the king's brother. So, Mara, I went to that town to the west, to Te-Ayiin. It's strange there, unfinished. Of course I expected that, didn't I? Van has never been there; he couldn't get permits. But he knows something about the place. You can feel it there, the mystery. The whole thing seems wrong, the marriage, the place upriver from Xultunich. Yet I can no longer speak; we are almost there, you see. The ceremonies start today."

He was talkative tonight. She closed her eyes, letting the stream of chatter go on. It was late, and she yearned for bed.

"He knows nothing he will do can change the end—we both know this. He knows the kingships are failing all around him, that Dos Pilas has broken apart, is led by petty kings. Mutal, known later as Tikal, has failed already, ground down by endless war, and Palenque and Toniná have, too. Copan, far to the southeast, will soon fall. So what is Van Weathers trying to do? Damn, Mara, what? We have read all this in the glyphs at Yaxchilan, the fighting and desperation, the final words. The last small temple at Yaxchilan, a 'sleeping house' for the deities, was built just after 800 AD. We learn that K'inich Tatb'u Skull III captured the last ruler of Piedras Negras, and then he is gone from Yaxchilan, leaving only simple houses in the plazas, and there is only silence. Yet Van is trying to change what's happening. He won't learn anything about the collapse, Mara; he's too involved."

Mara yawned and opened her eyes, trying to look interested. "Yes, Leon."

"He wants to marry Evening Star, Mara. Is he not already married? Of course he is, but there is the dynastic succession to consider. It would seem he has no heir by his current wife, by Lady Fin." Leon paced the narrow room, too hot as usual when the heat was working. The dark windowpanes threw back the rippled image of the room.

"Who are you talking about, Leon?"

He stopped beside the samovar. Tea was in short supply this week, and already he had to go to the bathroom again, so instead of drawing another cup, he answered, "Knot-Eye, ruler of Xultunich. He wants to marry Evening Star, and we are on our way there. It is a bad idea. Waterbird River threatens from the southeast, and behind them Cloud Hill can put many twenties of warriors in the field. He's trying to put Green Mountain between Xultunich and his enemies, make it into a buffer state, and that is not good for Green Mountain."

"Oh, I see," Mara said. "Green Mountain will be like Poland or Hungary, eh, back under the Soviet?"

He looked at her sharply, then waved his hand, thinking about what was happening right now outside this building, the ruble gone to hell, thugs on the streets, Chechnya again, the bombings and desperation. "Something like that," he agreed, then muttered again, "Something like that."

THE BATTLE OF POLTAVA

Fifty-five hundred miles away over the top of the world from Leon Blatskoi, in Room Seven at Miles Standish High School, at 11:45 in the morning, Jag Weathers held his chin cupped in his hands and stared at Mr. Sugar, who was about to ask Jag a question about the City of Dostoyevsky. This would be the fourth time in the past week that Mr. Sugar had called on Jag to enlighten his classmates.

"Mr. Weathers," Mr. Sugar said, on schedule.

"Yes, Mr. Sugar?"

"Your father is an archaeologist, I believe?"

"Yes, Mr. Sugar."

"You must have a sense of the past in your blood, Mr. Weathers. What can you tell us of the history of the City of Dostoyevsky, Mr. Weathers?"

Jag thought about the question. He could tell of the climate, of course: the summer temperature averaging between fifty-two and seventy degrees Fahrenheit. Or the geography, mainly swamp and forest poorly suited to development. He could say a visitor should avoid going in March when the snows melt, and November, when they have not yet frozen solid. "It was founded as Sankt Pieter Burkh in 1709, after Peter the Great defeated the Swedes at the battle of Poltava. He wanted a seaport with access to Europe."

"Very good, Mr. Weathers. We are now discussing World War II, however. Perhaps you could tell us a bit about the city during World War II."

"In September of 1941, the nine-hundred-day German siege of the city began. Over six-hundred-and-fifty thousand people died," Jag said. His head felt heavy.

"Thank you, Mr. Weathers." Mr. Sugar's voice was fading. The room filled with a gray haze and the student in front of Jag blurred to a vague outline.

Mr. Sugar began to talk about the end of *Crime and Punishment*, a novel by Fyodor Dostoyevsky. Jag had read *Crime and Punishment*, but he wasn't sure he understood why Mr. Sugar was talking about the messy story of a strange young man who killed a couple of people and then felt so bad about it he got himself caught.

His head tilted to one side, as if his hands would be unable to hold it up, and from this new angle he saw the little shapes up high again, like small, fast-moving creatures darting along the ceiling line. What was Mr. Sugar saying?

Mr. Sugar was saying, "Guilt."

The figures were tiny rodents clinging to the wall up there where tangled roots twisted downward. Their sharp eyes looked at Jag whenever they paused in their ceaseless darting. He could hear the high-pitched chittering they made.

Then they disappeared and the room went very dark.

THE TWO TOWERS

During the day, Alberto Bofonchio could just see from his window the top of the shorter of the two famous towers of the city of Bologna, the Due Torri, the short one leaning into the big one in their little piazza. He had selected his office for this view.

Now he wondered why he had worked so hard to get it. Mostly it was rooftops and orange tile, brick and gray sky out there, and the little lopsided inverted V of the two towers. Not worth all the fuss. At night, he could see nothing at all.

It had been two days since something had startled him and he'd backed out of the simulation.

It was night now in Bologna, just as it had been night there. Frogs, insects, the cough of a jaguar, he could hear them all. Those sounds had come from the speakers beside his monitor.

Two days before, he had built a small altar, broken a clay plate, and used the fragments as a base for burning copal incense. He had offered the usual corn kernels, flowers, a black turkey. He had spoken to the father-

mothers, to First Ancestor, to One Monkey and the Pauahtun, and to the
God Who Has No Name.

Before him the cave mouth yawned, ink-black darkness. For some reason, although it was only an image on his screen, he had been reluctant to
go in. For some reason, he had felt fear.

Was that it, the fear?

It was silly, of course. Alberto Bofonchio was a scientist, not a priest or
a peasant filled with superstition.

He was pretty sure his friend Van Weathers had built this cave to the
west of the city of Xultunich, and that there would be skeletons along the
ledges in there, grinning skulls, painted red. There would be offerings of
pots, of jade and feathers. They would be the reason this was a holy spot,
a doorway into the Otherworld, into Xibalbá. Caves were dangerous places
where priests would bring special kings after they died to help them
through, and where scribes would sometimes paint their dates and name
glyphs. One could feel the damp wind blow up from Xibalbá, and smell
the rank odors of the Lords who lived there. They would be the reason
Alberto was here in the form and persona of Flint Howler, scribe and shaman, artist of Xultunich, cousin to the king, praying over offerings of
maize and *balché* and copal incense.

It couldn't be the skeletons that he feared; they were only glowing dots
on the screen, or would be if he had entered this cave of Ol-ná, called
Middle House. Why should he be afraid of such things? He had seen
plenty of solid bone skeletons in real life.

He shrugged. He shouldn't be afraid. Alberto has spent more than one
night in Etruscan tombs. Alberto Bofonchio was not afraid of the dead.

But something had happened.

Something like a cold wind, a night chill, the damp touch of the grave.

He felt it like a whisper of breeze blowing from the cave mouth, which
was impossible because he was sitting in his office with the electric heater
on, facing a computer screen, listening to the sounds of a jungle at night,
and there were no shapes on the screen but the cave mouth opening, and
the dark outlines of trees, and the stars trailing along the eastern horizon
in a river of white, and the long trail of the comet in the sky overhead.

Something raised the hair on the back of his neck. He felt the cold of it
still on his forearms where the flesh puckered up (his round, soft forearms
lightly haired, and those hairs standing straight away from his skin). He

hugged his arms around himself and stared out the window at the darkness. It had taken him two days to get up the courage to return to his office, to contemplate going back into the simulation. Ridiculous!

The two towers were invisible.

Something had made him throw his head back, made him mash his finger on the button that closed the Xibalbá Gate, leaving those skeletal serpent jaws agape on the screen with the darkness of the cave mouth between them where the "real" cave had been just moments before.

He wanted to tell Leon about this strange feeling, but he thought Leon would never understand. He would think this was mere superstition, this prickling of foreboding. No, Leon would never understand this. Alberto was no longer sure it was real, now that he could look at the glowing coils of his electric heater. Beh! Enough.

This was an important day, getting ready to set the tree stone for Knot-Eye's marriage.

He told himself he'd had to take Sunday off. Yesterday he had gone to a meeting in Ferrara, had dinner with friends. Tonight, he could go back in, no problem.

As he clicked on the jaws, Alberto Bofonchio wondered aloud if the Americans were so good they could program their computers to include the supernatural. Were the Lords of Xibalbá loose in the world?

TWISTED PAIR

At 11:57 in the morning, Elliot Blackman sat at the desk in his lair beneath the classrooms of Crowley Hall. The surface before him held: a computer keyboard, monitor, and mouse; a complex telephone connected to an open metal box crammed with custom electronics; one of his carefully written notebooks open to a late page; a thick text on brain physiology; a half-eaten salami-and-cheese sandwich.

He was watching the clock on the computer screen, humming. He tapped a few keys, clicked. A brain schematic appeared. A column of frequencies and digital parameters joined it. A red line ran from the ear (side view of the head, skull open) to a brain region neatly labeled "Hippocampus." Another red line ran to the "Caudate Nucleus." Complex waveforms radiated from these two regions, creating an interesting and rather pretty interference pattern that shattered into topographic moirés of colored light.

Elliot smiled. These were numbers he liked very much. He tapped more keys and new numbers settled into place. At a certain time at Elliot's convenience, the computer would send a call to an office upstairs. It would send certain radio and microwave frequencies that would create in the wet organic complex of the listening brain those lovely moiré patterns.

Think of it, he wrote in the notebook alongside a table of numbers, as a kind of ball lightning precisely focused. It will create an indescribable experience. Yes, that was the word: indescribable.

He took two lengths of twisted-pair phone wire and carefully connected the box, the computer under the desk, and the telephone. The computer queried the box, captured a dial tone, and reported all systems green and ready to go.

Elliot wrote an email message and sent it off to an anonymous forwarder for resending. Another message went off to the Chief of Surgery telling him to have the HFS IT people check for hacked code on their server over the weekend. They should find the lines he'd given Jag, and from there it should be an easy trace to the kid, tie him to the Digital Assassins.

Then he picked up a package tightly bound with plastic tape, carried it into his office, closed the door, and slid the cabinet back into place with a smile.

A glance at his watch before climbing the stairs to ground level showed it was 12:26 in the afternoon. At a locked closet on the ground floor he paused, deep in thought. Then he opened the door and stepped into a small cavern crammed with emergency earthquake supplies—cartons of blankets, five-gallon jugs of water, flashlights, portable radios, extra batteries, Meals Ready to Eat.

Ninety-seven seconds later, he closed the closet door, leaving behind a gallon jug of Saniclor atop the package, now carefully wired to one of the radios. The dial on the radio displayed a time a few hours in the future: 4:45 p.m.

Elliot was already on his way.

Back in the den he settled into his desk chair with a soft grunt of pleasure, clicked the start button on the screen, and slipped quietly into the simulation beyond the Xibalbá Gate.

One Death was back. This time, he thought, it's personal.

MESSAGE, OR MESSAGES

Anne Opple sat cross-legged in her deep swivel chair in the computer lab, snug, foam-padded, 3D headphones hugging her ears, a tray of tortilla chips and fiery jalapeño dip at hand. It was just after noon, and the room was nearly empty. The glowing white jawbones beckoned, but the message beckoned more. She frowned. Anonymous messages were disturbing, and this one was particularly cryptic.

"Your interests are known. Talk to Knot-Eye, King of Xultunich."

After a moment's hesitation, she sent an Instant Message to Wendell, seated at his own terminal across the room. Who else could it be?

He answered immediately. "Whassup?"

She forwarded the message. "Yours?"

"Hmm, nope. What's it mean?"

"Dunno. Anonymous, though. Can you trace it?"

The screen fell dormant, and she presumed Wendell was puzzling over the problem. The jaws waited. She wanted to go in, find out if the message meant anything, but it was too weird.

Wendell reappeared in the IM box. "Whoever sent this is good. I probably could trace it, but it might take all day and I don't have the time right now. Sorry."

She leaned back and let out her breath. A man at the far end near the door was reading a magazine. He had been reading in that empty carrel since she got here, and was nowhere near a computer when the message arrived, so it couldn't have been him. Besides, he was an older man who looked as if he had come in to get out of the light rain that had been falling from time to time all day. He must have felt her staring at him, because he looked up and smiled distantly before going back to his magazine.

She shook her head. It might as well be a fairy godmother granting her wish. She clicked on the jaws.

VOICEMAIL

Glenna sat at the kitchen table, picking at leftover fruit salad. The letter from Derek Kim was tented in a zigzag beside the dish, the top third tilted away from her, but she could still read the handwritten scrawl on the back. What had Kim wanted to talk about?

She chewed thoughtfully, melon balls and berries, pushed the plate aside, and dialed Van's office number again, the fifth time today. It was afternoon. She got voicemail. Professor Weathers is unavailable or on the phone.

She hated voicemail.

"Van, it's me; your family would like very much to see you today. Jag and I will come by this afternoon after school. Some important matters, so please be in your office. I love you."

He'd been there all night. He had to be there now. Where else would he be?

Tomorrow, she could show this letter to the FBI guy when he came with the van. It probably was nothing important. But she should talk to her husband about it first, get his opinion. It was sent to him, after all. She would wait for Jag to get home, then they would go over to the university, tear Van away from his damn computers. Make a nice dinner. So, go shopping now.

She folded the letter, grabbed the car keys, and headed for the door, leaving her half-eaten fruit salad.

It was raining when she opened the front door, so she stopped to pick up an umbrella. The phone rang. She left the door open to answer it in the kitchen, dropping the letter on the counter to pick up the receiver. Perhaps it was Van.

The nurse at Miles Standish High School told Glenna she had better come. Her son Jonathan had collapsed in English class. The ambulance was on its way.

FILTER

Van's office door was ajar. The computer screen was a searing brilliance of green and white, blue and red, downtown Xultunich, forest and sky.

Wendell sat in the professor's chair, his boots on the worktable, waiting. The city on the screen was alive. He could see people moving around and the half-completed construction atop one of the taller pyramids.

The town was laid out in a haphazard but somehow pleasingly organic way. There were no long, straight lines, no baroque vistas, but a profusion of multileveled platforms, plazas, terraces, with pyramids squat and low, tall and zigzagging into the sky, holding up elaborate roof structures with brightly colored plaster statues. There was purpose, harmony, beauty in the skyline.

But it was all a game, computer graphics, ray tracing and vectors, bits. It was imaginary, and Wendell loved it.

Van appeared in the doorway, rubbing his beard thoughtfully. "Was that Bryce Jones I saw going down the hall?"

Wendell looked up. "Oh, hi, Professor Weathers. Yeah, he actually said hello. But he was on his way out. Said he was late for lunch with the provost."

"Figures," Van nodded thoughtfully. "So, Wendell. I had to get something to eat. How are you?"

"Fine, Dr. Weathers. I'm fine. You know, you oughta check your messages. The light's blinking like crazy."

Van wiped his hand across his face. "Yeah, I suppose so. What do you want, Wendell?"

"Want? Well, I had a couple of items, you know. A couple of . . . things, to say. To you."

"Yes, Wendell."

"I think someone knows who you are in there, that's one thing."

"You think. . . ."

"Actually I don't think, I know. Someone sent Miss Opple a message. Anonymously."

"And told her who I was?"

"I'm guessing, you know, because I don't know what part you have in there, not really, of course, though I could guess, but it looked to me as if this someone wanted her to think you were the king, that they, whoever they are, *knew* that's who you were."

Van stared, and Wendell swung his feet off the table and put those shiny red-and-black boots squarely on the floor. Van pushed into the room and stood beside his chair. "Well," he said.

"Yeah," Wendell agreed. "Well." Van didn't say anything, so Wendell went on. "The other thing is, there's a supernatural, or maybe more than one."

"What are you talking about, Wendell?" Van rubbed his eyes. "What supernatural?"

This was the day before the wedding when he would seal the alliance with Evening Star's city, and maybe Xultunich could hang on for another hundred years. Maybe more, if he had found the right place to apply pressure. Some cities had done that, stayed alive for a while after the end.

"I didn't program them," Wendell said uneasily.

Van felt a cold breeze touch the back of his neck and shook it away. "Are you trying to say that people are going into this world and playing the part of *supernaturals*? Is that what you're saying? People are taking the parts of animal spirits?"

"Yes, sir, but not animal spirits. I think there's at least one Lord of Xibalbá sneaking around. I found some traces on the logs, just hints. I didn't pay any attention at first, but then I started wondering, so I looked over the last few weeks. Whoever it is covers his tracks, but there's definitely someone coming in on a regular basis, but invisible. I didn't program the Green Room to offer anything like this. It's sort of emerged, if you know what I mean. . . . I thought you ought to know. Someone is stalking in there."

"Jesus, Wendell, this is ridiculous. It's a simulation. Don't we have, I don't know, routines or something to keep people from becoming supernaturals?"

"Well, no, but. . . ."

"Then do something about it."

"But. . . ."

"And to hell with people who send insinuating messages, too. They can't do any harm, can they? Damn it, Wendell, stuff is happening in there, history, with us in the middle! Just set up some kind of filter; make sure they're real participants. Can you do that?"

"Well, maybe I can make it so a real human is there to open the door, how about? Like a welcome wagon. And I'll check it out, OK? I'll go write the code now, it won't take long. . . ." He stood and moved around the older man. At the door, he stopped. "Are you sure you're all right? You look tired."

"Fine, Wendell. I'm fine. It's just that we're so close, so very close, the alliance, marriage, the sacrifice . . . you understand. Critical time. Collapse coming, trying to stop it. . . ." Van sat heavily in the chair Wendell had vacated. "Right now, I have to finish up a couple of things in there."

Wendell shrugged. "All right, but you ought to get some sleep, Dr.

Weathers. You really ought to. And you ought to check your voicemail, too."

"I will, Wendell. I will." Van closed the door behind him and heard the satisfying click of the brass Primus lock. He stood for a moment with his hand on the brass knob, then sat down at the computer.

Already he'd forgotten the programmer. The clock read 1:49 p.m.

7 Ajaw 3 Xul

April 27, 837 AD
The Long Count date is 10.0.7.4.0
It has been 1,442,600 days since the Maya Zero Date
The calendar round date is 7 Ajaw 3 Xul
Moon is full
God 8 rules the night

DAYBREAK

As he walks along the edge of the plaza and behind his captives seated cross-legged on the platform edge, Knot-Eye has to look twice to convince himself they are only simulated enemies and not people he has known. He must lean down to sniff their hair. He has to smell their fear and defiance.

Even now, with day full over the jungle and light pushing away the dark world, Van hears Gordon's voice from a vast distance telling him not to think he can have control. Was it only a week ago they talked?

This feels like control, this slow walk down the white-plastered platform before his palace's stone-and-stucco front, decorated with huge earth and sky god-masks, the goggled Venus beast, all the elaborate symbols of his power, his direct connection with the Ancestors and the lineage founder. Gordon's voice fades to silence, and someone calls, "Knot-Eye." He turns.

It is Smoke Wind, the wandering merchant, second cousin to the *ajaw* of Broken Water, a city where the flow of Waterbird River splits before joining the great ocean. He is out of breath. "You have them," he says, admiring the line of captives. "I've never seen so many in one place before."

Knot-Eye stands a little straighter. "Yes. You see there, Fire Shell, ruler of Dry Place."

The naked captives sit, heads bowed, upper arms painfully bound

223

behind them. They are silent, unmoving. Fatigue is written into the slump of their shoulders, hopelessness in the hang of their heads. They stink of defeat.

A warrior walks along the line, slowly spreading blue paint across their backs and cheeks. One turns very slightly away in disdain. The warrior laughs, daubs on the blue, and moves on to the next.

"I have spoken with Flint Howler," Smoke Wind says. "He is carving a tree stone. Your image is on it. You announce this great victory."

Knot-Eye wonders if he detects irony, accusation, disapproval in Smoke Wind's words, but decides he cannot show his doubt, so he lowers his chin. "The wedding is in three days," he says slowly. "Evening Star will seal the alliance with Green Mountain. Green Mountain will be between us and Waterbird River, and so we will be safe from the ambitions of Cloud Hill."

Smoke Wind waits, but Knot-Eye says nothing more, and so Smoke Wind adds softly, "And the armies from the western mountains. I have heard. . . ."

Knot-Eye cuts him off. "I too have heard, but they are far away. No doubt the Place of Reeds is a great city. No doubt they are great warriors, but they would have to come down in vast numbers from the high valley, and they would have to cross the plains to get here. They do not know the jungle. I don't think they will come this way."

"There is talk, too, of death coming down the river from Te-Ayiin. No one goes there. It seems no one *can* go there."

"Do not speak of Te-Ayiin. Te-Ayiin is a dead place. It has been terminated."

Smoke Wind lifts his shoulders. He will not argue with the *ajaw* of Xultunich.

"Besides," Knot-Eye adds after some thought. "Flint Howler is a great *h-men*. He goes to the cave at Ol-ná to talk to the Lords, to burn copal and chant the Four Directions."

"Perhaps that will preserve Xultunich," Smoke Wind says, and again Knot-Eye wonders if there is irony in the words.

The two men step off the platform and walk slowly back along the line of captives. The prisoners' bowed faces are hidden by their long hair. Knot-Eye's warrior has already inserted in several of them the paper earplugs that, along with the blue paint on their defenseless bodies, marks them as captives destined for torture and sacrifice.

They stop before Fire Shell, who looks up insolently into Knot-Eye's face. "Your gods deserted you," Knot-Eye says. "You have no cause for pride."

The skin around Fire Shell's eyes tightens, and he spits into the dirt by Knot-Eye's foot.

"Feed them," Knot-Eye tells the warrior who has been painting them. "They must be healthy for the ceremony. All of them." He speaks loud enough for all to hear. He wants the worm of fear to work through them. They must be broken, or the Lords of Xibalbá will not accept them.

The warrior nods and leaves. The *ajaw* of Xultunich and the merchant climb the steps to the palace. At the yawning entrance, Knot-Eye stops and takes his companion's elbow. "Evening Star arrives soon," he says. "I will be B'olon Tz'acab, One Flower, He of Nine Generations, the Father Ancestor, and the day will be 4 Ajaw 8 Kumk'u, which was the day Little Jaguar Sun turned back, the day of the beginning, the day of solstice."

"I had heard you would do that. Is it wise?"

"To use a day that is not the *actual* day?" Knot-Eye would have laughed had he been Van Weathers. As if anything could be actual in this world. "It is the meaning of the day that is important. The distance number of six-three takes us back to 4 Ajaw 8 Kumk'u, 123 days before the wedding between Lord Knot-Eye and Evening Star of Green Mountain. We will re-create the origin of the world. It has been done before."

Here, outside in full sun, and day over the city of Xultunich, Knot-Eye can see Smoke Wind smile. Indeed it has been done before. "You will be K'awiil, then?" Smoke Wind asks.

Knot-Eye nods. "It is that important. The world depends on it."

THE GOD WHO HAS NO NAME

During the night, the God Who Has No Name asserts himself. Last night, it drifted higher in the night sky and looked down on a small band of travelers stopped at a village in the low hills on the road to Xultunich. The baleful light of the God Who Has No Name threw deep shadows into their eye sockets and beneath their chins. It trails a paper skirt of white light, which at first the people in the city thought were his entrails. Though it appeared less than a *winal* before, nudging just above the eastern horizon at sunset, it swiftly grew bold and strong, washing out the nearby stars.

Evening Star thinks of that smear across the roof of heaven, long vanished now into day, as a sign of her wedding, the light this god will cast across the world. She is more animated than she has been in weeks, more interested and curious, and she was always a curious girl. These days, her namesake is close to the western horizon in the evening, and is separated from the God Who Has No Name by the Road of Light. This she believes is good, just in case those who believe the new god means ill are right. After all, people fear him, not knowing the meaning of "comet," and so they call him by this name. Some think he may be K'awiil, the Serpent-Footed God, or B'olon Tz'acab, the patron of all lineages come back to bless the city of Xultunich.

Others believe he is a messenger from the gods, an expression of their anger, and brings destruction to their city, whatever city it may be.

Van Weathers would know this is the year of Halley's Comet, but Van Weathers is far away, little more than a memory of some future time, so powerful is the pull of Knot-Eye's life. He has spent his day planning his wedding ceremony, an elaborate event to center his power in the universe, to build the people's faith, to stave off the end. And so he has his captives, and his tree stone, and the carved wooden lintels from the workshop of Flint Howler, and the new, small but elegant temple where he will perform before the people with his new wife.

Evening Star knows all this, and so she turns to question her uncle. Three Sky sops up his midday gruel of squash and corn with his tamale and stuffs it into his mouth. He chews noisily and swallows, then leans back against the wall of the village elders' house, for this village belongs to Green Mountain, the last before they move on to Xultunich. She waits a while, then says, "Uncle?"

"Mmm?"

"What will happen today?"

"What am I, *h-men* of Green Mountain? Ask Turtle Claw, he is the seer. Maybe he can tell you what will happen."

Inside the house, Turtle Claw's toothless siesta snores are louder than the howler monkeys in the forest.

"Uncle?" she insists.

"What?"

"Do you still believe this alliance is bad for Green Mountain?"

He sits up. "What makes you think I oppose it?"

"I heard you at council with my father and the *b'acabs*. You said, 'Last Stone is a dying city. Their blood is weak.' That is what you said. I heard you say it."

He looks at her. Yes, there is excitement in her eyes. There is life. "I am not the ruler of Green Mountain, Evening Star. Quetzal Tree, my brother, is ruler, and he has spoken. We go for your wedding." He crosses his arms over his broad chest, and his tattoos jump.

"Will I have to give blood?"

"You ask too many questions," Three Sky says. "Get ready. We still have a way to walk before we get to Xultunich and the ceremonies begin. Soon enough, you will be Knot-Eye's wife."

PASSING THROUGH

One Death is impatient; it is his nature, this irritability, this fret and fuss. He waits at the fleshy jowls of the monster mouth, doorway to the Middle World, and bad gasses rise from him, foul odors, evil thoughts. He is master of pus and fever, of rot and stench, and he doesn't like to be kept waiting.

Even damp earth smells too good. Even swollen bellies, bleeding sores, knotted bone look too good. One Death's pendulous lip, his drooping nose, his crooked ear, all quiver with rage, for the people, those flaccid, fleshy things up above in their decaying bodies and their sinful minds, are making such noise!

He must wait here, it seems, for some hapless human soul to open the door for him, let him flash forth into the awful sun, the dreadful day. One Death prefers the dark and dank, the deep cave with stagnant air, or none.

The monster's mouth is made of stone and does not move, does not breathe, does not greet the first Lord of Xibalbá. "Seven!" he shouts in his cracked voice.

"Yes, One Death, right here." Seven Death, junior Lord, incompetent boobie, nods at his side. He is a dwarf, a midge, an insect buzz beside the grandeur of One Death Himself, but he is all there is today. The others are about their business, spreading disease, unhappiness, fear; and that is good.

"Get this door open, Seven. I want to get up there."

"What?"

"The door! Are you deaf!"

"We have to wait, One Death. You know that. Someone'll be along."

There are sounds like heavy stone balls rolling on hard wood, rising and falling sounds of insects shrilling. Rubbery thuds, and cheers.

"They're playing ball, Seven. You hear them? Oh, how I hate them, always trying to cheat us."

Seven Death nods his head, bobbing it up and down—little flaps on his hat tinkling, little bells on them—misshapen midget, grotesque little monster. He jumps up and down, looking down the monster mouth, deep into the throat, but there is nothing but darkness.

The rolling sound, the thud of feet running, the slap of the ball against the shoulder or the hip. It is a jangly kind of music, tuneless, without rhythm. It has been five thousand years or so since the Hero Twins defeated the Lords of Xibalbá in the ball game underground, but One Death still picks that painful scab, it gives him such pleasure. "This time," he mutters. "This time they will not win. No fooling this time."

"What? What?" Seven Death dances and hops beside him.

"Oh, shut up."

They can hear, over the twittering shouts of the spectators at the ball game, as if it were on a television in a distant room (he cannot say "television" of course, but Seven would understand his meaning), the sound of someone chanting. That's better, he thinks. That's so very much better, some pathetic human mumbling his prayers at the skeletal side of the gate, calling an ancestor or something. Seven Death was right, someone would come along. Someone was singing open the Gate.

One Death leans into the fleshy jaws between the great curving teeth, jaguar or crocodile, and it opens to intolerable light. The light comes from above, through the tangled branches, and the two Lords pass silently through the gate and into a steamy place that is too bright by far.

"Hah hah," One Death cackles. "Fools! They have no idea, they think they're so smart. Total control, they think. Hah! It won't be long, Seven. No, no, it won't be long. Just a little while!"

Seven Death nods his head and jangles the little bells on his jester hat, so faint they can't be heard. He smacks his loose lips, sucks in his breath, and it is just the wind passing through the leaves.

The two float, silent and invisible, right through the praying man kneeling by the opening in the earth, the portal to their world. He is soon to come down to Xibalbá, soon to feed the worms. Old, rotting people! Pah! They mumble their prayers, they ask for things, they demand a better crop, more rain, less burden of work. They demand health!

Fools!

The two reeking, rancid gods walk away from the man mumbling and praying and pass on without a backward glance, through the trees, the chattering monkeys, the raucous macaws. Only the jaguar, pacing the forest floor, pauses, watching with yellow eyes as they flit past, seeking the white road to Xultunich, seeking the ruler of the city, the great *ajaw* of Last Stone.

Ending and Beginning

Monday, November 28
The Long Count date is 12.19.12.15.0
It has been 1,869,420 days since the Maya Zero Date
The calendar round date is 11 Ajaw 18 Keh

April 30, 837 AD
The Long Count date is 10.0.7.4.3
It has been 1,442,603 days since the Maya Zero Date
The calendar round date is 10 Ak'bal 6 Xul

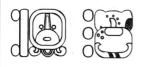

August 13, 3114 BC
The Long Count date is 0.0.0.0.0
It is the Maya Zero Date
The calendar round date is 4 Ajaw 8 Kumk'u

CODE BLUE

The ambulance raced through traffic and intermittent rain. Glenna sat in back cradling her son's head. His skin, leached of almost all color except an extremely pale blue, was clammy against the feather touch of her fingertips. His eyes jerked back and forth under lids translucent as the finest rice paper.

The sirens rose and fell, rose and fell. She swayed back and forth when the ambulance went around corners. The lights on top were flashing, blue and red. Strobes rippled around the top.

She was a mere passenger. She had no control.

"What's wrong with him?" she asked. The paramedic shrugged helplessly, watching the monitors.

How fragile it all was! They were in others' hands. She thought this, that they were always in others' hands. Teachers, policemen, doctors. Strangers.

SIGNAL TO NOISE

A phone rang in an empty house. The answering machine, an independent variable in the long quadratic equation of Van Weathers's life, waited the requisite four rings, then clicked into action. It recited, somewhat mechanically, the programmed message and emitted a tone. The clock stamped the time of the message: 3:45 p.m.

There was the sound of Linc Boytim's throat clearing. Then he spoke, and his words were the signal.

"Uhm, this is Special Agent Boytim."

There was a lengthy silence. Apparently, he was waiting for someone to pick up the telephone. The house contained sounds, of course—the refrigerator, the heating system ticking quietly in its midday relaxation, an occasional snap as wooden joists and studs shrank. This constituted the noise in the system. Perhaps Lincoln Boytim could hear them, but he certainly could not identify what they said.

"Uhm," he continued, forcing more signal through the narrow aperture of the telephone lines. "We've arrested someone. In the Kim killing. I wanted you to know. He confessed. He was hired to secure a document. He secured the document, but didn't know what it was about. He left it where he was instructed. He was a street punk, really, smart but not that smart. He didn't mean to kill. . . ."

There was another long silence, only partially filled by the very faint hum in the communications network, the background sounds of Linc Boytim's office air conditioning in the Federal Building, some distant and unintelligible voices, the Weathers's house.

"I've been doing some research, Mrs. Weathers. I'll tell you about it tomorrow. But you might warn your husband that he's gotten involved, unwittingly I'm sure, with a very large and important global company. It seems that CAPO is a well-funded venture of this company, a kind of public relations gimmick. I'm not sure he will be happy about where his funding comes from. Anyway, like I say, I'll tell you about it tomorrow. And by the way, the D. A. T-shirt, it seems as if there are a lot of them around.

I know your son is a member of the Digital Assassins, but most of them are just nerds, just kids interested in technology." There was another pause. "He was a member, this punk that killed Kim, he had the shirt, but mostly it's just kids, nothing to worry about. OK, see you tomorrow."

The line went dead.

LOCKOUT

Talking to Flint Howler, the two of them at the base of his own accession pyramid in glaring sunlight, felt to the distant Van Weathers like slipping from a dream into wakefulness. He is Knot-Eye.

Flint Howler is standing on the spot facing the steep temple steps where he will set Knot-Eye's marriage stela. "The tree stone grows on the central axis of the temple mountain, in the line between Knot-Eye's father's tomb deep inside and the winter rise of the sun," he says. He is careful to refer to the *ajaw* of Xultunich in the third person, as befits a man already beginning his ritual transformation into a god.

Flint Howler's hands draw the stela in the air, the line down the center of the dark red stairway. He jabs his fingertip toward the core of the artificial mountain towering over them, and Knot-Eye sees his ancestor's red-painted bones bent in prayer, the offerings of pottery and jade and flint carefully arranged around his skull adorned with shell earflares and carved wooden effigies. Almost as if in memory he sees them lay the body to rest and place the cache of precious objects, the food offerings and woven fabrics, so that Knot-Eye's father may join the line of ancestors coming down from First Ancestor, One Monkey.

Already, the limestone slab is waiting at the edge of the terrace, lying face down on wooden rollers. Workmen are wrapping it in cotton and binding it with rope for the planting tomorrow, when they will pull it upright.

"It is already carved?" Knot-Eye asks.

"The rough work is complete," Flint Howler assures him. "I will finish after tomorrow, when it is planted. The people may watch the fine detail take shape over the next months. Meanwhile, we must prepare for the banquet tonight."

"Yes," Knot-Eye agrees. "First wife must be informed. Although she has given Xultunich no heir to carry on the lineage, Lady Fin will have the

place of honor, for she is senior to Evening Star. And the rituals? What of
the rituals, the offerings at Ol-ná?"

A shadow passes across Flint Howler's face. He lowers his head and
moves away, out of earshot of the workmen. Puzzled, Knot-Eye follows.
"Yes?"

"There was . . . something. I prayed to the motherfathers. I spoke the
words of welcome, of reconciliation, of return. I gave maize, blue and yellow, especially yellow, for the yellow K'awiil rules the south sky these days,
and I gave a black turkey. I burned copal, I dropped kernels of maize into
the broken bowl as required. It went well, Knot-Eye."

"What is your hesitation?" the ruler asks, for there is a lengthy silence.

"I felt a presence," Flint Howler says, and his words come very slowly,
as if they have to push through thick jungle to reach the city.

"A . . . presence?" Knot-Eye also hesitates.

"The Lords are loose in the middle world," Flint Howler replies. "That
was the feeling. Later, I went as far into Xibalbá as I could go. It was very
cold."

"Cold." Knot-Eye feels a chill from the words alone. "What is the
meaning?"

"The Otherworld is losing its ties to this one. There is darkness, sudden
wind. The days grow disordered. I felt the cold wind from the far side of
Ol-ná. This cave goes a long way under the earth, and there is a distant
place, and that is at the place called Te-Ayiin, the Place of Crocodiles. Does
not the great *ajaw* know this? Does he not feel the cold reach of death
from up the river?" He changes to direct speech. "Oh, Knot-Eye, we
should fear for the middle world. Without the gods, we too will lose our
way. If the Lords are loose in the Middle World, there will be yet another
ball game. And we have no Hero Twins these days to defeat them and
restore order in the world."

"You are saying it will take much blood."

"I am saying, Lord, that I fear even all the blood there is may not be
enough."

The *ajaw* of Xultunich repeats softly, "Not enough."

There is a single quick shift sideways an inch or two, a moment of suspended silence followed by a sudden whooping, like howler monkeys gone
mad, and a growing hubbub of voices, the sound of feet.

Van looked around. Vaguely, as though through gauze, he saw that the figurine of the woman giving birth had hopped amid the charts and maps on his trestle table. Otherwise, the room, despite its odd sepia tone, was unchanged. Light rain fell outside.

He sat still. An earthquake, no doubt. Didn't Jag say there would be an earthquake, aftershocks or something, from Costa Rica? The voices in the halls quickly died away, leaving the forlorn beeping of the fire alarms.

Was there a fire?

He doubted it. That was an earthquake that set off the alarms, that was all. They would soon stop. He shrugged and returned to the scene before him.

Flint Howler is waiting patiently.

"What did you say?" Knot-Eye asks, and Flint Howler moves as if startled.

"I said, Yes, even if it is not enough, you must give it," he replies. "You must give blood."

"Ah, well, then, I will. I will give blood, as much as may be needed."

Already, so early in his ritual transformation from man to god, the ruler of Xultunich has gained the gift of prophecy.

HIGH-ENERGY INCIDENT

Although it was not large as such things go, just a few ounces of homemade plastic explosives, the event in the Earthquake Emergency Preparedness Closet on the ground floor of Crowley Hall rattled windows with a theatrical bang and flash sufficient to trip the fire alarms. A moment later, an impressive billow of dark gray smoke, shot through with roiling brown threads, flowed out the shattered narrow windows and up the side of the building, which emptied within moments, leaving wailing fire alarms, followed after some interval by silence.

The deputies at the sheriff's substation at the edge of campus ran outside and watched the smoke climb into light rain.

"High-energy incident," the first said.

The second stared. "What?"

"A ten-eighty. Explosion. Where, do you think?"

The second considered it. "Crowley Hall, looks like."

"Where we were going. Let's roll." They drove at high speed, code three, across the campus, lit up and wailing. That was always fun.

By the time they arrived in front of Crowley Hall, the smoke was already blending into the bottom of the cloud layer, and the threads of dirty brown and black were almost vertical. Only a few minutes had passed, and except for the crowd gathering on the lawn it seemed as if it might never have happened. The rain was turning to drizzle.

A side door flew open and a man and woman ran out. The door swung shut.

"Anyone hurt?" the deputy asked.

The man shook his head. "I don't think so. Didn't see anyone inside; I came down the stairs."

"Everybody out?"

He shrugged his plump shoulders. "Couldn't say for sure, but I'd think so. The alarms stopped a minute ago, but everyone must have heard them. There was kind of a rush, but this time of day, between afternoon and evening classes, there aren't that many people inside. Even so, it's a miracle the foyer was deserted when it blew."

"Whatta ya think?" the deputy asked his partner. "Gas leak?"

The other deputy shrugged. "Fire department's problem."

Distant sirens rose and fell and rose, and the campus fire trucks arrived one by one. The smoke was already dwindling, and the firefighters and deputies stood idly watching over the shattered glass of the entry until it was all gone.

"Don't see any more smoke," the deputy said.

The fire chief paced back and forth a couple of times, peering into the lobby, then told the deputy to string out the yellow ribbon just in case. "Probably something simple, but I've never seen smoke that color before, with those weird brown threads in it, like some kinda chemical. Could be toxic, so let's keep folks away. And call the county hazmat people, just in case."

The deputy frowned. "But this building is Liberal Arts and Sciences. Nothing hazardous there."

"Call 'em anyway." The chief disappeared through the empty doorway as the deputies set to work.

The plump man was waiting around. He watched the two cops string ribbon, then said, "You should probably check the faculty offices."

"Who are you?" the deputy asked.

"Flentsch. Anthropology. My floor was empty, but you never know."

"OK, we'll go through the building when the chief says it's OK."

Gordon nodded. His hair was plastered to his forehead and he brushed it away.

The fire chief came out. "Weird," she said. "The stairwell fire doors are locked from the inside, every one of them, and the maintenance department has all the keys in the basement. The elevators are dead. There's no way to get off the ground floor, but there's no sign of other damage."

"Can't you, I dunno, break down the fire doors or something?" the deputy asked.

"They're steel. It'll probably take all night. We'll have to get the building plans over here. Goddamn windows are too narrow to enter. Designed that way for climate control and probably suicide prevention, for all I know. Trouble with modern buildings, they just aren't made for fire services; half the time you can't even open them. Close off this section of the campus and we'll check it out." She walked away.

The deputy grunted.

"You can say that again," his partner said.

ENZYME DEFICIENCY

Jag woke up a little after five. His mother was sitting by the bed, holding his hand, stroking the back of it over and over.

"Hi," he said.

She jumped. "Oh. Oh, my God."

"I feel funny." He lifted his hand and let it drop.

"It's an enzyme deficiency," Glenna said. She lowered her voice, not to disturb the other patients. "Oh, my God. Glucose six phosphatase, they said. It almost killed you. They're running tests."

His smile was thin, scarcely there. "Where's dad?"

She looked away. "I don't know. I've been trying to get him all day. I don't know where he is, but I called the police. They're looking for him. I was going to take you there, after school."

Jag said, "I have to tell him something."

"You had a reaction to hummus. Chickpeas! How would I know that? It's done something to your blood. How *could* I know?"

"It's probably rare."

"Yes," Glenna nodded. "It is, it's rare. You're sensitive to sulfa, we knew that. But the doctors say you're sensitive to chickpeas, too, you had a horrible reaction. My God, how could I know?"

"You couldn't."

"What do you have to tell him?" she asked at the same time, and then after the awkward pause, she nodded.

"Nothing," he said. Then, "It's this company."

A red line of fear tightened around her throat. "What company?" she asked softly.

"HFS," he said. "Big, very low profile. Uncle Robert ran some kind of project. They give money to CAPO, the people who pay for dad's research. I think they're trying to hide something."

"Slow down. HFS funds CAPO?"

"Yeah. It's huge, very diversified. They make Saniclor, toxic stuff. And fish sticks."

"Fish sticks?"

But Jag was tired and only wagged his fingers, patting her hand. The room was a large square, with two sets of beds, the railings with curtains drawn around one. He could see the next bed. The man lying in it was staring up at the ceiling. His eyes didn't seem to blink, but it was hard to tell. It was dim, just some night lights and the oblong through the door-way from the hall. But the man was trembling, just a little. So he was alive, staring at the ceiling. "What's wrong with him?" Jag asked, half asleep.

"I don't know, some kind of nervous disorder. He's been doing that all afternoon. Sometimes he talks."

"What's he say?"

She shrugged. "Can't understand him. It sounds like it's almost words, but not quite. Maybe he's foreign."

Jag closed his eyes. Glenna began stroking the back of his hand, over and over, light brushes with her fingertips, but he was already asleep.

NIGHTFALL

A crowd had gathered behind the yellow tape in front of Crowley Hall. The fire chief used her bullhorn to call for witnesses, anyone who had been in the building at 4:45, the time of the explosion. In a few minutes, sixty-five people were lined up in the rain by the lead fire truck. The chief radioed for a van so she could interview the witnesses in relative comfort.

A few moments later, the television crew arrived and Paula Reed was interviewing her.

By 6 p.m., it was dark. Light rain was intermittent, and the bright lights set up by the fire department reflected the side of the building onto the wet pavement. Three fire trucks stood by on the road, but there was nothing for them to do. The firefighters stood around in their yellow slickers and black hats trading jokes with the team from County Hazardous Materials.

It took time to find the building plans, and more time to bring in a welding team to open the fire doors. By then, the university provost had arrived and was shouting at the men with the torches.

Paula Reed recognized the leonine profile of Bryson Jones in the crowd, dragged him before the camera, and asked him if he had an office in the building. She was looking for the human interest angle on the explosion, but Jones dismissed all the conspiracy theories flying around and assured her the explosion had some completely rational and even mundane cause.

"Yet there is the missing man. His sick son. He works here, too."

"Is someone missing, Paula?" Dr. Jones asked. His voice was resonant, and he looked particularly handsome with the small droplets of water collected on his eyebrows.

"Dr. Sylvanus Weathers has an office in this building," she said, consulting her notes. "His son is sick. Apparently no one can find him, and the boy needs blood—his blood. Apparently he has a rare type. Do you think there's a connection with this explosion?"

"I hadn't heard he was missing, Paula." Jones appeared reluctant to admit there was something he didn't know. "I was in a meeting with the provost."

"I see." Paula signaled the cameraman to stop taping and smiled sweetly. "Frankly, Dr. Jones, until there's something new to say about this explosion, we might as well be discussing this missing-man story. Do you mind if I ask you a few questions about Weathers? On camera? Just general questions."

"Of course I don't mind," Jones gestured generously. "No problem at all, Paula. Always glad to help the press, and his office is, in fact, next to mine."

Paula nodded, and the cameraman slung his camera onto his shoulder and called, "Rolling."

She repeated her question: "Yet there is the missing man. His sick son. He works here, too?"

His answer was lost in a burst of shouting from a firefighter at the entrance, and she had to repeat it for the third time. "Could you tell me about Professor Weathers, Dr. Jones? What kind of a man is he? Why would he disappear? Did he have enemies?"

The interview concluded, and Paula Reed continued with Gordon Flentsch. The rain stopped, started again, stopped.

Finally, the fire chief climbed out of the van. The provost approached. "There doesn't seem to be any fire, and everyone's apparently out of the building. There's no reason to cause more damage to university property by torching the fire doors, Chief."

The fire chief thought it over and decided the provost *might* be right, but it was better to be safe than sorry. "The situation's uncertain—the ground floor's the only one we got access to, and we still don't know the cause of the explosion," she told the provost. "I gotta keep my people here till the County Hazardous Materials unit finishes. We don't know what could happen—could be a gas leak, there could be chemicals. And I'm not through talking to the witnesses."

"What are they saying?" the provost wanted to know, maintaining a careful smile.

"So far everyone thinks the building's empty, but we don't know for sure. There's that missing professor all over the news. He has an office in there." The chief nodded at Paula Reed in her circle of light off to one side, interviewing the plump anthropologist. "If I could find the maintenance guy," she checked a list. "Blackman. He could unlock those damn doors."

"Blackman didn't come out?"

The chief shrugged. "Dunno. No one's seen him. Probably he wasn't here. Is that unusual?"

The provost shook his head. "How the hell do I know?" He was relieved that except for the fire doors his building wasn't going to undergo any further immediate damage, and began fretting about the legal problems. So far, no one was hurt, but there could be someone still inside. He decided he'd better go back to his office, make some phone calls. He saw Jones and waved at him just as he disappeared into the crowd.

The chief went back into the van to finish with her last witness, a plump girl with a nose ring. "So, Ms. Opple, can you tell me where you were exactly in the building?"

The girl's foot was jiggling under the folding table in the back of the van. "In the computer lab, I told you."

"When you left. . . ."

"I was the last one out. I was working and didn't want to leave. I need to get back to it, too, the work, I mean."

"Just a couple more questions," the fire chief assured her. "You're positive you were the last one in there?"

"The lab was empty when I left, and there was no one in the halls. The fire alarms were whooping away. The cafeteria was empty. I didn't see any smoke or fire or anything, no damage. It was weird . . . I almost didn't leave," she added. Her toe kicked the leg of the table, and she jerked it to a halt.

"Good thing you did," the chief assured her. "Did you see anyone else as you were leaving?"

"Only Professor Flentsch. He's in the Anthropology Department. We met at the exit."

"Yes. So you two were the last out of the building?"

"Sure, yeah, the last, I guess."

The deputy sheriff stuck his head into the van. "We tried calling all the faculty offices in the building. No answer," he said.

"Thanks. Well, Ms. Opple, I guess you can go."

When the door closed behind her, the chief looked at the deputy. "If everyone got out," she muttered, "who locked all the fire doors?"

HOSTAGE

Elliot Blackman, a.k.a. GHOSTMAN, has switched off all the telephones but one, disabled the elevators, and locked the fire doors at the ground floor stairwell landings.

Elliot Blackman controls Crowley Hall, but he knows it is only a matter of time before the authorities realize they have a Hostage Situation on their hands.

Now Ghostman is not Ghostman; nor is he Elliot Blackman. Now, seated in Bryson Jones's office, his name is One Death.

Van Weathers is isolated; he simply doesn't know it yet.

The day has passed and Van Weathers is finishing a banquet in 837 AD under warm, star-filled skies. Halley's Comet washes the red-and-white painted pyramids in ghostly radiance. It is nearly as bright as the pine torches and campfires that burn around the city of Xultunich, but the darkness of deep jungle presses in on all sides, making the city into an oasis of light and motion, of music and talk.

This is a festive night in celebration of the impending marriage of Knot-Eye, ruler of Xultunich, to Evening Star, princess of the polity of Green Mountain. Everyone speaks of this night and the coming day. The Ancestor will come to rededicate the city. The great *ajaw* will summon One Monkey from the mouth of the Vision Serpent coiling up from the doorway to Xibalbá, from the burnt offering, from the smoke of copal incense and the burnt blood of his hallowed body.

Many are drunk already. The sacred *balché* flows into the cups, foaming over the edges and onto the hands and laps of the elite of Xultunich. If they see sullen looks, resentment, and thin-lipped anger in the faces of those pouring the drinks, they pay no heed. Though the peasants are always resentful, always angry, always sullen, they know their place in the order of the universe. They know what they have to do, and this night they do it. They pour the *balché*; they prepare and carry the food. They pour and stir the sacred cacao in the ritual cups, those formed and painted and dedicated by the best potters and painters in Xultunich, those brought from as far away as Waterbird River or even Cloud Hill. There are plates from Place of Reeds in the highlands to the west, and shell dishes from the coast at Broken Water. The king is beautiful; his jade pectorals and bracelets, his shell-and-bone necklace, jingle when he moves. The tall crest of his feather headdress nods and sways as he speaks.

Beside Knot-Eye, Lady Fin sits in silence, speaking only when directly addressed. As afternoon wears on into night, and the night itself wears on, she sits calmly amid the revelry, head lowered. The king imagines she regrets not giving him an heir.

Evening Star is young, only a little older than Van's son in the Real World. Yet she seems animated, almost manic, as she talks with her uncle, Three Sky, and with Turtle Claw, the *h-men* of Green Mountain, almost as if someone is in there, giving her life. She keeps glancing over at him from under her elaborate headdress, and her eyes burn. He grows a little uncomfortable and drinks too much *balché*.

Van has paid no attention to the passage of time (in fact, time in the simulation is not the same as time in the Real World). This evening is too important, too pivotal.

He is no longer studying why the Maya civilization collapsed.

He is trying to save it.

He is no longer a scientist, not even a participant–observer. He is only a participant.

MISSING

The pudgy anthropologist hurried away from the scene of the explosion through the light drizzle, head down, lost in thought. Until the interview, he hadn't known Van was missing.

Van could be anywhere, that was true, but he was more likely to be in some places than in others.

"I warned him," Gordon said aloud. "Damn it, I warned him."

"What?" A boy with ice blue hair was staring at him.

"Oh, sorry. Nothing."

"Did you hear about Crowley Hall? What's happening? I heard the police were there."

"There was a small explosion, but I think it's pretty much over," Gordon said. "They're just cleaning up. Everyone got out."

"Not terrorists, then? OK, thanks." The boy walked away in the opposite direction, all curiosity gone.

"At least they say everyone got out," Gordon murmured. The boy had vanished into the darkness and mist between street lights.

He'd have to drive home. It was the only place he could think of that had an adequate Internet connection.

Wherever Van was, he had to be inside the simulation.

WAITING GAME

Anne Opple ran from the campus and nearly collided with Wendell in front of Chips 'N Dips.

"Hey, hi," he said.

"Did you hear?" she was gasping for breath.

"Hear what?"

"Crowley Hall. It's closed indefinitely, the explosion."

"Wow, you kidding? It's closed?"

"Yeah." She was eager to go.

"Do they know what it was? Terrorists or something?"

"Nothing like that," she said in a rush. "But it pisses me off, cause I was in there, in the simulation, see, it was fantastic! I mean, there's going to be a banquet, big celebration. I want to be there. I've got to get back in."

"You'll never get on in there," he said, waving at the mob inside the cafe. "Rains like this they all come out."

"It's not raining now," she said, looking up.

"Yeah, but it was. Anyway, good luck."

"Shit, I'll have to go home."

He snapped his fingertips, watching her walk away and thinking she had nice soft contours, maybe he should get to know her, but she was gone, headed back to the graduate student housing complex. So he found a student in the Computer Science Department to play 3D chess with, and soon he was totally absorbed.

Halfway back up University, Anne passed a television display in the window of an electronics store showing a picture of Van Weathers.

He was missing. His son was sick and needed his blood.

She should tell him. Shouldn't she?

How? Even if the message was right and Van Weathers was Knot-Eye, she could hardly come up and say, "Your son needs your blood. Go to the hospital."

It took her almost twenty minutes to make her way back to her apartment, alternately running and walking. She pounded up the two flights of stairs and barely had time to sit down before her fingers were dancing over the keys.

The banquet was still going on. The robust sims were sitting around, drinking and talking. She slipped easily back into the role of Evening Star, the New Wife, whose head slopes nicely back and who carries a lovely jade inset in the side of her nose.

The conversation flows among the people sitting cross-legged on the woven mat in front of the principal ruler's residence. Lady Fin, the first wife, listens carefully. So does the new wife-to-be. She has her eyes on the ruler of Xultunich, on Knot-Eye, as she listens to the others talk.

She should tell him about his son. She should tell him about the explosion, the television cameras, the fire doors. Where was he? Is he even in the simulation?

She can't tell him, not right away, not yet. She has to listen first, to grow into her role. Otherwise, she will make a mistake and lose her chance to be with him.

She has to know that he is here, in the simulation. It would do her no good to tell a piece of software to go to the hospital.

So she listens attentively as they speak of politics, and of sacrifice.

PRIMUS

It is late in the evening when Van admits the banquet he is attending is only simulated and that real hunger has crept up on him. With reluctance, he leaves the computer, allowing his simulation to run without him.

He stands by his chair for a moment, looking down at the screen, where Xultunich winks and glows in torchlight. He can hear the faint music, the skirling of ocarinas and wooden trumpets, the thump of tortoise shell and deer-hide drums and wooden clackers, an eerie reconstruction of ancient, lost music.

"Oh," he says aloud. "What time is it?"

His watch tells him it is 12:44. After midnight.

With a shiver, he goes to the door and takes hold of the knob. It does not move. He squeezes hard and twists, but nothing happens.

He grunts, looking at the handle. At first, he sees nothing wrong, and then he thinks something is a little out of place, and finally, he realizes the keyhole is on the *inside* of his office. He says, "Odd," as he fishes out his keys. Someone must have turned the lock around by mistake. He can see the word PRIMUS. High security, Elliot told him. The best. Unpickable, unbreakable. Case-hardened steel inside, couldn't be drilled out.

Van's door key fits but refuses to turn. He shakes the door, pulling on the knob, but the door is solid and the lock doesn't even wiggle. He tries to peer through the small glass pane, but the glass is frosted; there are no lights in the hall and it is pure black. His world stops at this door.

For the first time, a faint tendril of anxiety threads up from his abdomen. He shrugs and picks up the office telephone. All he has to do is call the maintenance guy, what's his name? Blackman. Have him open the door.

The phone produces a faint hum, but no dial tone. He tries a few numbers, but nothing happens. He dials the code for his voice mail. Nothing happens. He listens to the empty silence, a low, fluctuating noise that seems to almost form words.

As he puts the receiver down, he looks out the window at the courtyard. It is as black as the hallway, no light anywhere. He might as well be looking out at dense jungle.

The overhead lights in his office don't work; neither does his desk lamp. Only his monitor illuminates the room, casting soft pastel light across the edge of his desk. There is power to the computer and the network. He could exit Xibalbá Gate and send someone an email message, except that it's 12:44 a.m., the middle of the night! The trouble with electronic mail is that people have to make an effort to pick it up. No one picks up electronic mail at this hour. He'll have to wait.

He looks for his email program anyway, but it has disappeared. He cannot leave the Xibalbá Gate.

Driving alongside a warehouse a couple of weeks ago, Van saw an old man with a pendulous nose and elaborate hat. The man tried to wipe his windshield, even though it was raining, and the man's companion was a dwarf. The image of that man with his greasy rag smearing the dirt around on his windshield suddenly imposed itself on the dark window.

"Strange," Van said. "Memory starting to spook me." He spins his chair around and sees his copy of *Dresden Codex* lying open on the work table. Had he left it out last time he opened it? When was the last time?

He'd kept his new password in there, on a yellow Post-it. There is no Post-it now, and the book is open. He pulls it into the light of the screen.

One Death glared at him under the brim of his elaborate hat. His eyes glittered on either side of a pendulous nose. He was accompanied by a dwarf, hopping up to the height of his car window, the misshapen head rising into view, bearing tiny malicious eyes glittering in misty light cast by the street lamps.

He sits down at the computer.

THE CITY SLEEPS

Knot-Eye tries to imagine himself somewhere else: in a world of wonders, where he can speak his mind. Where if he had trouble, he could speak of it. He tries to imagine a place where people can talk instantly with one another over great distances, where you don't have to walk everywhere you go, where no spirits haunt the night or dim the daylight with terror.

He finds he can scarcely imagine such a place. There was a window at his right side, but its black rectangle was a mirror that reflected only the ghost of a frightened face back at him. It is better at the banquet, even though the spirits of jungle and animal and ancestors send searing streaks through the darkness, or wail over the scree and tiddle of music. At least there are people here, some of them friends. He simply has no way of knowing which ones.

The banquet has died down. One by one, or in twos and threes, the revelers stagger off or fall asleep, slumped against a smooth plaster wall.

He can hear shrill sounds from the jungle, insects and frogs. The God Who Has No Name slides across to the west, the black land, toward Xibalbá, the Place of Fright.

He cannot sleep, though, so he goes in search of someone else awake in this ancient city. He wanders the terraces and platforms, through the narrow alleys between temple pyramids, along the river's edge. When he walks past the craft quarter, broken shells crunch underfoot. When he steps onto the steep, narrow stairs to his father's temple, he can feel the soft texture of the plaster under his sandals, and hear the soft, calm creak of leather as he climbs up, one step after another, zigzagging in a series of diagonals to the top.

Once there, he seats himself on the edge of the highest platform and stares at the faint outlines of other temples. Their dark sides and flat surfaces are visible under the light of stars and the enormous comet that seems to dominate the sky even this late as it sidles away from the roof of heaven toward the darkness beneath the earth. He avoids looking at the God Who Has No Name.

Even here the fear comes to him. He jumps at every small sound. Even at this great distance he thinks he can see the eyes of the great jaguar shining from beneath the trees. His *way*, his animal companion, is out there. They are connected, he and it, by invisible ties, strands of spirit that fade backward into time, and forward also into time, until the two ends meet somewhere beyond where he is now.

This is a night, even though it is spring, when the dead would come around. This is the hour when they come, wanting, wanting. They have lost life, and so they regret. They were diseased in life, and so they are sick in death. If they died violently, they move swiftly, with perfect violence, here, now, in the darkest hour. It almost seems as if sitting here on the edge of the pyramid in the deep of night and keeping very still and silent he can see them just at the edge of vision rushing madly back and forth in a rage. It is almost as if the hair on the back of his neck is answering to a nonexistent breeze, and the chill he feels is the presence of something unseen.

He leans forward, looking down into the plaza. Did something move down there? Is someone standing in the center of the open space looking up at him, judging him? Is it One Death down there, intangible but real, calling to him? One Death would cackle with glee. He would wheeze and cough, laughing so hard the awful smells would fly away from him, and others nearby would turn away, hands over their noses and mouths. Someone had warned him of supernaturals here, but he cannot remember who it was.

For a moment, he sees the flash of starlight on white bone, skull or shoulder.

For a moment, he hears a faint whisper, the dry crackle of laughter.

The Lords are abroad this time of night; they are loose in his city; they are coming for him.

ONE PLUS ONE

Evening Star knows she can be Blood-Moon Princess when she comes to the king. One of the first fathers can spit in her palm, and she will bear a child, she will bear twins, she will bear the Hero Twins. This is how it is done in the first days before the beginning of this Time. This is how it was done then; this is how it is done.

Knot-Eye is sitting on the top of the highest pyramid, his feet over the edge on the top step. She looks at him from the plaza far below. He is sitting on the edge, and she goes to him. So she begins to climb the steep staircase. The white paper hangings in her hair sway with the night breeze. They nod with her steps as she climbs crabwise, sideways, left foot up the high riser, then the right foot up, moving slantways across the staircase to the edge, then turning, right foot up, left up, back, zigzagging across and up until she stands beside the king staring down at the plaza as if he has seen a ghost. His nose cuts a curve of darkness against the star-splashed sky, against the God Who Has No Name. His nose is like the smooth obsidian blade her uncle carries sometimes, and her heart leaps in her breast and she knows now that this is the time for her to lead him into her so that she may give him an heir.

She sits beside him, and he lifts his head. His eyes are dazed, dark pools of doubt in his dark face. She reaches up with her hand to touch his cheek, to trail the electric tip of her fingernail down the line of his jaw to the edge of his lip, to the corner, to the plump center of his lower lip. She touches his lip and gently pries open his mouth, and then she leans forward and kisses his lips, and a current passes between them, deep and swirling like the deep swell of the river that flows past both their towns.

She can feel him stir, can feel her presence moving him, and knows that he may be a king but he is also a man. She is not one to care about politics, nor the future of the city, but only for this man to whom she is given, and for the reaction she sees in him.

He is a great leader, ruler of his city, yet there is something about him of sadness, some deep regret or lost hope. It is to this that she is reaching when she touches the cotton skirt and feels the muscles of his thigh through the cloth. She finds he is looking at her, burning her with his eyes, and she feels like shifting her body away from that heat because she is young and somewhat uncertain.

Instead, she turns toward him, kneeling on the soft plaster at the edge, and puts her hands on his shoulder, turns him to face her.

"I am Evening Star," she tells him. "I will give you an heir."

"Yes." His tone is noncommittal, but certainly in his eyes she sees something else. And she feels under her hand what that is. He will be a reluctant lover, but there is no longer doubt that a lover he will be.

"Tonight," she says. "Now."

"Tonight," he answers. "The wedding is not tonight, nor tomorrow."

"The wedding *is* tonight. The wedding is when we say, and we must say it now. The God Who Has No Name is above us. The city needs an heir, and I am here to serve."

"I have a wife," he says, and for a moment Evening Star is Anne Opple and feels a sharp pain, like guilt.

"Pfu! Lady Fin is barren," she says. "You must have an heir. And I love you."

He had not expected this. Absently, he thought that Van Weathers (who was he?) did not anticipate love in this world.

She pushes him gently back onto the warm plaster floor before the temple of his ancestors. She opens his skirt, sits astride him, sinks onto him, and they fall into rhythm together, and their cries together rise into the night air above the temple to nest in the vaults of the roof of heaven, which is also Xibalbá turned upside down, and yet is also the place from which the Hero Twins are watching.

Later, in the earliest hint of dawn, she takes his manhood in her hand and examines it closely. "Today," she says, "this will be pierced?"

"Yes," he replies. "This day it is written. I will give blood."

In that moment, Anne remembers about his son and can find no way to tell him directly, so she says, "Yes, you must give blood. It is urgent that you give blood."

If he understood her real meaning, he gave no sign.

CLINICAL DIAGNOSIS

"The boy needs the transfusion, Mrs. Weathers." The doctor clasped his hands together on his beige desk blotter as if forcing them to stay still.

Glenna stood, too agitated to remain seated across the desk from him. She looked out the window at a November morning growing bright outside. They had watched all night, but Jag slept the sleep of the dead. "Well, give him one, for Christ sake!" She turned away from the green gardens, the trees outside. Her lips trembled.

The doctor, seated behind his desk, looked down at a sheet of paper. "We would, of course, but the problem remains."

"There must be a way to find the right kind. This is the best hospital in the state!"

"As I explained last night, your son has a rare type. In this instance it has to be a near-perfect match."

"Take mine!" Glenna felt as though she was walking uphill through some thick liquid.

He shook his head. "Mrs. Weathers, please." He lifted the sheet of paper. "All the records are in the computer—yours, your husband's, your son's. We've been running searches since we admitted him, but the only

match so far is the boy's father. That won't change. We're doing everything we can, but it is essential we find your husband."

Glenna sank back into the visitor's chair. "I know, I'm sorry. The police
are looking for him. How much time do we have."

"Not much. Jonathan's blood has hemolyzed. He can't make enough
cells fast enough so he's weakening."

"How much time?" she whispered.

He came around the desk to put his hand on her shoulder. "Find your
husband, Mrs. Weathers. As soon as possible. We might have ten, maybe
twelve, hours, best case. If Jonathan doesn't get some whole blood by this
evening. . . ."

"They found his car in faculty parking, but they think his building's
empty. He must be in there, though. Something must have happened to
him."

"They'll find him," the doctor said softly, squeezing her shoulder.
"Don't worry, I'm sure there's a simple explanation. As you say, he must
be there. And of course we'll keep the computers searching, too, but he
would be by far the best donor."

She went back to Jag's room. He was still sleeping soundly (she preferred to think that than the word "coma"). In the next bed, the thin man
trembled continuously, shaking the covers. His eyes were open, and when
she entered they turned toward her, flickered once, and returned to the
ceiling. Although she had been there all night and most of the previous
afternoon, he didn't seem to recognize her.

There was a phone by Jag's bed. More than once, she had lifted the
receiver only to put it down again and creep out to use the pay phone at
the end of the hall. It seemed too desperate to make the call before that
palsied stranger.

This time she grabbed the phone and dialed, and to hell with the
trembling stranger in the next bed. As usual, though, it rang without
answer. She didn't even get Van's voice mail.

She looked at the clock on the far wall, over the empty bed. Eight-fif-
teen in the morning. She dialed Mary.

Her sister picked up before the second ring. "Yeah?"

"Mary, it's me. I'm going nuts, can you come?"

"What? Glenna?"

"University Hospital, it's Jag."

"My God, Glenna, what is it? Does this have anything to do with the explosion at the university yesterday?"

"Yes, no, it's Jag, he's had a, he's collapsed, he's sleeping now, but they only give him twelve hours. Mary, please, you've got to come. I can't find Van, and he's the only one who can give a transfusion, and that's what Jag needs, Mary. Jag needs Van's blood."

"Slow down, Glenna. Tell me what I can do."

"OK, OK. Could you stop by the house, get him some things. I just didn't think of it, but he's going to be here . . . unless they can't find the right blood. Oh, God."

"I'm on my way, Glenna. What room?"

Glenna told her and put the phone down. It would be all right. Mary was coming. That's what sisters were for, to be there. "Oh, Jag," Glenna wailed softly, taking his thin hand between hers. "Oh, Jag."

Her son's eyes fluttered. She leaned over him as if he were trying to say something with those delicate small tremors of flesh, as if he were signaling to her in a secret code she could have understood if only she had the key.

DESCENTS

By dawn, the central plaza is filled with people, for it is the day of Knot-Eye's wedding ceremony.

They have walked from Green Mountain, from all the villages of Last Stone, even from as far away as Broken Water down on the coast by the great ocean. Everyone from Round Stone Water is here to view the captives from Dry Place tied naked in the sun near the sweat houses, paper earflares dangling along their blue-painted cheeks and shoulders. The former ruler of Dry Place, Fire Shell, stares back defiantly, his lip curled in disdain. It is a gratifying sight, for he will make a worthy sacrifice to the First Ancestor. Others, a younger brother of Waxaklahuun Ub'aah K'awiil, ruler of Saal (known in the future as Naranjo) is coming, and even K'inich Toob'il Yoaat himself, the great king of Caracol, who had set up the 7 Ajaw altar at the baktun ending not long ago in 10.0.0.0.0. Already so many kingdoms had fallen: Toniná, and B'aakal, which would one day be called Palenque, to the northwest, and even mighty Tikal itself. Now people said that Yoaat's kingdom had in turn fallen on hard times. Perhaps he hopes for something from Knot-eye himself.

Smoke Wind, too, is here. This event will give the wandering merchant currency, stories of the great ceremony binding the lineage of Green Mountain with that of Last Stone, Xultunich, stories he might tell to the elite of other places. In another world, he is here to see if he can understand who his friend Van Weathers might be. He is here to warn him.

For now, though, he sits in silence near an ancient tree stone that proclaims the prior period ending and watches closely. He has left behind his pack of trade goods, quetzal feathers from the coast and some small wooden carvings from Caracol, and carries only the carefully wrapped gifts for the ruler: one slender, fine, green obsidian blade from the southern highlands of what will become Guatemala and a cacao cup from the fertile bottom lands to the south of the former city of Te-Ayiin. The cup is signed by the artist and holds around the rim the standard announcement with the name of the cup's first owner, who was the Lord of Te-Ayiin.

The morning breaks clear and warm, a huge orange sun swelling up from the green fringe of the eastern forest, from the Red Road. The cisterns in the High Plaza are full and ready. Fires burn everywhere, and copal incense smoke rises into the windless air, bearing with it from the pens a cacophony of captive animals, the bellow of caiman, the cries of macaw and *mot-mot*, the gabble of the black turkeys destined for the Lords of Xibalbá, even the low growl of a rare captured jaguar.

As the sun breaks free of the forest, the howler monkeys set up a tremendous din, shrieking joy or rage at the day, shaking the treetops with their running and leaping. First Ancestor One Monkey would be pleased; the howlers know this is his special day. One Monkey will come back to renew the world. He will do so because Knot-Eye will give of himself for the re-creation of the world, the replanting of the World Tree, and the raising of the roof of heaven from the four corners. He will set the three hearth stones. He will make the proper offering.

A skirling of wooden trumpets and pounding of turtle-shell drums come from the central precinct of the temple complex, twisting in intricate rhythms around the rising smoke. Then the procession appears at the top and begins its laborious descent of the steep staircase carved with the hieroglyphic story of Knot-Eye's glorious grandfather's defeat of a city now long forgotten, its own emblem hieroglyph carefully chipped away, erasing its memory from the world.

The priests wear enormous green-and-red feather headdresses that dip and sway above their white turbans. Their woven tunics bear patterns unique to the Xultunich polity, appearing intermittently through their elaborate ornaments of shell, jade, wood, cotton, paper, and stone.

The descent will take time, and so the hawkers of tamales and water, of small paper or animal offerings, of charms and prophecy stones, small containers of *balché* and chili, even a rare cacao bean they might give to propitiate the gods, move among the crowd, shouting their wares.

The festive air is dense with anticipation, however, for great and terrible things will happen this day.

On the stairway, the dwarves, their own comical animal or jester hats on the backs or tops of their heads, tumble and leap around the skirts of the solemn priests. The musicians gather at the edge of the top platform as they play, sending their music out over the crowd gathered below.

As yet there has been no sign of the *ajaw* of Xultunich. Some in the crowd have noticed this and spoken of it, but of course it is early as yet. Meanwhile, the spectators anticipate others: Three Sky, uncle of the bride; Quetzal Tree, the bride's father and *ajaw* of Green Mountain; Flint Howler, daykeeper of Xultunich, who will preside over the tree-stone dedication, setting it before the tomb of Knot-Eye's father; Turtle Claw, *h-men* of Green Mountain; Reed Altar, *b'acab* of Round Stone Water. It is fitting that all these important guests appear before their own ruler.

And here is the first, Three Sky, now at the temple opening far above the plaza, known by the great balloon headdress he wears, emblem of the Green Mountain elite. He stands quietly at the top of the pyramid as the procession of priests continues its descent, winding back and forth, pausing briefly at each of the nine terraced landings before continuing down. There are three twenties of priests. When the last of them has left the top platform, Three Sky waits a few moments to create a space between himself and the end of the procession, then he too begins his slow, solitary descent.

Now the sun has lifted high enough to throw some light into the central plaza. The dwarves at the bottom are capering and dancing around the ranks of priests drawn into an enormous square before the low platform in the middle. The dwarfs tumble and somersault, frog-hop one another, run in circles, and do comic turns that keep the audience laughing, while the priests stand absolutely still and unsmiling, for theirs is the serious business of the day.

When Three Sky reaches the middle platform, Quetzal Tree, accompanied by Reed Altar, appears on the highest platform, as if rising from the center of the pyramid itself. Another group of musicians gathers in the central alley of the ball court alongside the main temple group and begins to play answering volleys to the group on top. The music flies back and forth, up and down, in scales and shrieks and flutters, in taps and beats, diddles and thumps. The high melody of the ocarinas is supported by the breathy wheeze of the wooden trumpets. The mood is festive and lively, in anticipation of the afternoon's solemn events.

Quetzal Tree and Reed Altar begin their descent. By now, the sun throws long yellow lines between the temple buildings and through the lattice of the roof combs, and it is full day. The noise from the plaza grows louder, the sounds of hawkers shouting above the music coming from two places, one answering the other. The dwarfs and dancers in the central plaza tumble and spin, and now five tall figures, fantastical animals in impossible colors, come skipping and leaping on high stilts, looming over the nodding plumes and fluttering paper streamers of the priests' headdresses.

"It is almost time for the *ajaw* to manifest." Flint Howler, scribe and artist for Xultunich, has sidled up to the wandering merchant Smoke Wind, who nods agreement. Flint Howler looks at the other man for a time, then shrugs and pushes through the crowd, closer to the foot of the hieroglyphic stair, where he reads the names of ancestors, their accession to the rulership, their ceremonies, marriages, and great conquests. He reads of ball games performed in cycles before. One in particular, on the fourth step, catches his attention, for here is described something very close to what will happen later today, when the captives of Dry Place will play the story of the Hero Twins and be sacrificed.

As Three Sky steps onto the plaza to stop beside Flint Howler, Evening Star, attended by her twenty of maidens, appears and begins her descent, step by slow step. She wears the cotton *huipil* woven in the patterns of Green Mountain, and the jade pectorals and bead necklace of her rank.

Flint Howler nods to Three Sky and returns to reading the hieroglyphs of the stair, although he has certainly read them many times before. Only when he hears a collective indrawn breath from the crowd does he look up at Evening Star moving right to left across the upper terrace.

He sees it is her elaborate headdress that has stirred the people. As expected, it includes the elements of her name, but even from this oblique angle he can see the Venus sign, the outcurved nose on the half-skull Tlaloc image missing the lower jaw. The diadem is softened by maize images on the sides, but the people know the subtle language of costume, and this is almost an affront. The Venus signs imply, though they do not directly assert, warfare events.

Is this an insult to Knot-Eye by the people of Green Mountain? Does it imply Green Mountain resents agreeing to this alliance and marriage under pressure from Xultunich?

"She suggests that although the alliance is forced, it may yet be fruitful," Flint Howler muses, speaking to Evening Star's uncle Three Sky, standing nearby.

Three Sky nods. "It may be so. She wants this marriage." He says no more. Flint Howler knows that he means that he and perhaps even the *ajaw* of Green Mountain have reservations about the alliance.

When Evening Star reaches the central terrace, Three Sky says, "Is it not time for the first wife of Knot-Eye to appear, to follow Evening Star down to the plaza?"

Flint Howler looks up, shading his eyes against the sun glare. "Yes," he says, pointing, and there is Lady Fin with her own attendants, appearing to float to the top of the stair. Her *huipil*, inset with polished obsidian and pyrite mirrors that reflect the sun as she moves, is more glorious than Evening Star's. All eyes are on her as she begins her own descent a half a pyramid height above Evening Star, the dazzling flame of her figure shimmering with each step.

"Where did she find that gown?" Flint Howler asks, puzzled. It is not fitting for Lady Fin to outshine the new bride. Yet she does, and it is time for the visitors to draw breath between their teeth in disapproval. An insult to Green Mountain!

The visitors grumble and buzz among themselves; people say that it is time for the *ajaw* of Xultunich to appear.

Soon, everyone in the plaza is looking up, waiting, and a hush falls over the city when the music stops.

LANDINGS

Elliot Blackman had been working all night, dipping periodically out of the simulation to respond to the Chief of Surgery, who kept interrupting him with a seemingly endless series of anxious messages. The Chief of Surgery was losing control. First it was a question about his plan to frame Jag. "What the hell did you mean by that message about hacked code? Our security people couldn't find a trace. Another one of your stupid schemes?"

This meant the kid had covered his tracks. Well, he shouldn't be surprised. The kid was good.

Then the messages started to turn querulous:

"What the hell is going on there?"

"I never should have asked your advice."

"Your people went too far, and now the Feds are sniffing around."

"God damn it, Ghostman, our servers are getting hit all the time with queries about Garcia. Something's gotten out."

At first, Elliot tried being polite. "Suspend all queries," he suggested once. "This is a delicate time. The subject will cease to be a problem as soon as I find out what he knows. It won't be long. I've made some adjustments to the simulation. All the problems are close to resolution, but you are breaking my concentration."

It consumed precious time to decipher the messages from the Chief and encrypt his replies, time he could ill afford. Van Weathers still didn't know how trapped he was. Too bad the kid had fooled him, but never mind. At least the girl had kept Van busy much of the night, as Elliot had hoped—the Honey Trap had worked perfectly. Now the ceremonies were beginning and that would keep him busy, too, but not forever. He'd want to eat or relieve himself, sooner rather than later. Already, Van had been in the simulation all night and on into the morning. It was almost time for the final phase, and these messages kept interrupting Elliot's surveillance.

His request kept the Chief quiet for a little over an hour. Then the messages began again. Finally Elliot sent a last message. "All will be settled within an hour. Please leave me alone until then. I'll be in touch."

He leaned back in Jones's titanium chair and frowned at the ceiling. What did Van Weathers know?

He had held his knowledge very close, Elliot thought. It looked as if

Van knew there was a physical connection between the cave at Ol-ná and the lagoon at Te-Ayiin, he had known about that, which meant he must have explored the cave, at least far enough to know they connected.

He knew the city had no writing in it, though he couldn't guess the reason. He knew Te-Ayiin was a place of death, but he could not know why.

So perhaps Elliot knew enough to move into the final phase. Yes, the secrets of Te-Ayiin were safe enough.

It only remained to remove Van for good. He called up the software controller for his little box in the basement. It was time to find out what he could do to the caudate nucleus.

FIRST BLOOD

Van's head, cradled on the surface of his desk, lifted slowly into morning light, but the dream still clung to him.

He was standing knee deep in virgin water. The surface shimmered in all directions to a vague and undefined horizon blurred by mist or smoke.

Groaning sounds, creaking, the sway of tree limbs rubbing one another, the sharp cries of prey caught in strong jaws come from somewhere beneath his feet, which he cannot see through the shimmer of sourceless light off the surface of the water.

He turns slowly, making a full circle, but the water in all directions sends sharp lances of light into his eyes, blinding him. The sounds repeat unevenly, at odd intervals, staccato snaps, low rumbles, and the creaking. A long time seems to pass before he sees a darkness undulating on the water far away, coming closer.

He recognizes the Vision Serpent. It moves at a leisurely pace, rippling with dark semicircles above the golden surface of the water, head high. Small, bright eyes look at him. A body length away, it stops, and the jaws open.

Gordon Flentsch looks at him from the open mouth with blind, milky eyes, and then the flesh dissolves off Gordon's face, leaving a bleached skull with long, grinning teeth. A hand moves alongside the skull and jabs a short stabbing spear toward Van's face.

Distantly, he hears the telephone ring. What is that sound? The skirling of trumpets? The ocarina?

His hand reaches out and lifts the object to his ear. Absently, as if in another world, he says, "Hello?"

The software that runs this universe hears the word, matches sound patterns, jumps to a subroutine.

The device in the basement of Crowley Hall switches on.

Current flows into the object in his hand, a sliver of silicon implanted in the receiver takes on a new quantum configuration, there is a sudden coruscation of radiant energy into Van Weathers's ear.

He feels a stab of pain, and

a clap of thunder out of a cloudless night sky shakes the ledge on which he sits, red fire bright as day streaks toward him and leaves a searing pain at the side of his head and the base of his skull. He tips from the edge of the pyramid into the inky void and somersaults onto his back. His arms and knees float up with the wind of his falling passage; the long topknot of his hair blows up and forward over his brow.

He falls for an endless time, hearing only a distant tinkling, like small bells on the tips of the jester's hat or shattered pieces of obsidian glass tumbling down with him into the yawning skeletal jaws of Xibalbá. He opens his mouth to scream and

blinked. From the top of the central temple pyramid, the screen revealed the vast plaza filled with people looking up at him. They were not moving. He could hear only silence at first. Then, slowly, came the crackle of distant fires and the subtle hushing of thousands of people breathing as one.

He put his hand to the pain in his ear and brought it away. What appeared to be half-congealed blood marked his palm, and he recognized the shape, the irregular glyph of blood sacrifice with its trail of droplets like a chain of pearls. He looked around instinctively for a mirror, and saw nothing but night, and he was no longer certain who he was.

Cold air blew, bringing moisture. Thick fog pressed through the window.

The building around him was absolutely silent. Only the faint crackle of fires and breathing from his computer's speakers reminded him that sound was real. He looked at his palm again and blinked. There was no glyph, only a random splotch of shadow.

The faces in the plaza stare up at him, at *him*, expectantly. They are waiting for him to move. They can't see him from down there, for he is inside the temple, in the darkness by the altar stone, looking out into the sunlit world.

His attendants stand by, waiting for him to speak.

Then he feels the cold like November fog seeping into the sunlit world.

He can see Flint Howler standing at the base of the pyramid, looking up like the others. He wears his *h-men* cloak, his headband, and his knotted scarf. "The Lords are loose in the middle world," he'd said just a few days before. "I went as far into Xibalbá as I could go. It was very cold."

It is this cold he feels. A presence. He looks around the small temple space. The altar is spread with ferns to catch the blood. The plates with their folded papers are ready, and the incense burners. Aside from the three attendants, though, the temple is empty.

He grows suddenly dizzy and puts his hand to his ear. The touch sears him with a pain like trumpets screeching, like the smell of humiliation and defeat.

"Help!" he tries to shout, wincing. His voice is curiously muffled. He stops, breathing heavily, head lowered.

He takes a deep breath.

There has to be a way out.

He looks at the window into another world, one he has already lost, a world of machines, files, databases, university servers.

He remembers these words as if from a dream.

Someone had locked him out of that world. Or in this one. Why?

He has no answer. He has only one avenue to other people, through the Xibalbá Gate.

He reaches for the keyboard and mouse, his only road back to the Middle World.

XBALANQUE AND HUNAHPU

Oh, the Hero Twins can barely contain their mirth! They hold their sides, gasping for air, long wheezy breath drawn in, huff huff huff laughter let out.

Sacrifice! Sacrifice! Sacrifice! they cry. Do it to yourselves!

Hunahpu holds a stone ax high in the air, long flint blade knapped sharp. The wooden handle is smooth in his grip, and his catfish barbels flap in the air as he laughs, waving his ax.

And Xbalanque? He lowers his head. Chop it off, chop it off! he cries, wheezing with laughter. Lop off my head, Hunahpu! That'll fool them good!

Fireflies flicker everywhere, blinking. And the dogs howl. Are they laughing, too, at the sacrifice?

Xbalanque waves his jaguar paws. Huff huff huff, he laughs, cut off my head, brother! The people of the Fourth World are making too much noise! Silly, silly people. The Lords of Xibalbá, *they* make too much noise, running around, stinking up the world. Cut off my head! The Fourth World is almost finished anyway, heh? So chop it off, let it roll. We'll fool them all, fool the Lords of Xibalbá, fool the Lords of Death, fool the people, too!

Oh, they are laughing hard. Hunahpu swings his ax, and away rolls his twin brother's head, laughing.

A SITUATION

It had been one of those mornings.

Hell, it had been one of those nights. Linc had called Mrs. Weathers to tell her about the investigation so far. He had begun a number of queries through the research people and then spent the evening in a quiet neighborhood bar drinking Manhattans and reading a crime novel. When he asked the bartender to turn on the television, he was told it was broken.

He'd overslept and was almost late for the squad meeting. The Western region had improved a little on arrest rates in the past month, but the conviction rate remained lower than the national average. The pending caseload had increased again, and greater effort was needed to bring it back down. They had helped solve the Kim murder case and had the gratitude of the city police homicide division.

While the special agent in charge gave his usual pep talk, Linc thought about Raymond Delcotto, twenty-one years old, a street punk. His arrest for the murder of Derek Kim satisfied Lincoln Boytim, but there was something puzzling about it also.

Research had turned up the fact that CAPO was a public relations front for HFS Corporation. HFS was one of those huge global companies no one has ever heard of. And here was a little item from the file search Linc found intriguing: HFS, it seemed, had hired the Digital Assassins to recover a document.

Why did HFS want it? What was it? How was this all related to the lovely Glenna Weathers?

After the meeting, he sat in his tiny windowless inside office and read memos. No need to requalify at the firing range, so he could toss that one. Next week there would be a one-day course in lock picking. Slots at several upcoming training sessions at Quantico were still available. He put aside for later an application for a course on the latest in behavioral sciences and flipped through the usual flurry of theories, pleas for brainstorming or tips, regulations regarding informants, requests for foreign-language specialists, and personal classifieds. Maybe he could find something that would help him catch the bank robber known as Shakey, though that was a very low priority for Special Agent Linc Boytim.

He found nothing. Tuesday morning, November 29, 9:47 hours. The statistics fluctuated. Nationwide, violent crime decreased slightly in November, but white-collar crime was up. Abductions were up. Random terrorism and sabotage were up. There was another train derailment, seventeen bomb threats, 715 cases of arson. Mugging and other street crimes were increasing in neighborhoods previously low, down in other neighborhoods previously high. It was difficult to keep up.

He leaned back in his chair, clasped his hands behind his neck, and stretched with his eyes closed. There must be something she hadn't told him, something he should know, some piece of the puzzle that would come to light, perhaps later today, when they took her paintings to the gallery.

Why hadn't she called back? He'd left the message yesterday. You'd think she'd be pleased they had caught someone.

Still, his statistics were looking better; he wasn't quite ready to admit that he had another reason for wanting to spend time with Glenna Weathers. It was just business. He picked up the phone to confirm their dinner date, just in case.

He had barely finished leaving another message when he got the call from the agent in charge. "You took the hostage negotiation class, right?"

"Sure, three years ago. Why?"

"It's the situation at the university," the agent in charge said.

"What situation?"

"Possible hostage. You're the only one available right now."

"Possible?"

"My office. I'll brief you."

Two people were missing. One was a professor, Sylvanus Weathers. The other was the maintenance foreman for Crowley Hall, Elliot Blackman. Didn't Linc ever watch the news? They were looking for Weathers all over the place. Now the police believed he might be a hostage in the building. And then there was this problem with the boy. It had been all over the news. . . .

Linc felt as if a sudden gap had appeared in his life. Where had he been?

The agent in charge stood beside the American flag in his office. "Since the name Weathers was on that list, there might be some connection. I wondered, if you don't have anything else to do right now, perhaps you would be good enough to check it out?"

Linc ignored the irony in his supervisor's voice. "Of course. I'm on my way."

Linc called Glenna again on his cell phone while he drove to the university.

ETRUSCAN SONG

Mary stopped at Glenna's house. She threw some clothes and toiletries into one of Glenna's overnight cases for Jag and went into the kitchen. She cleared away the dirty dishes left on the counter and tidied up.

That was when she saw the letter from CAPO.

She let out a slow breath. They funded Van's research, and the man who was killed, Kim, was it? was president of CAPO.

She couldn't explain why, but she picked up the letter and started out. Glenna's paintings were propped against the wall beside the studio entrance at the top of the stairs. The studio was cold and empty, and with the lights out was a bleak, November gray that matched her mood. Mary climbed the stairs to look at them, ready to go to the gallery.

Among other recent paintings, *Dead Tongues* and *Message, or Messages,* were propped against the wall. The faded rose of *Dead Tongues* overlapped and concealed most of the strange electric blue of the other.

She saw a new painting entitled *Etruscan Song* (the name was painted in large transparent letters behind the growing ganzfeld wash of color) propped under the skylight. The still-transparent wash was an even verdigris of tarnished copper, a color borrowed from a small spouted oil lamp she'd seen once in the Etruscan museum in Florence. Drawn in pencil and nearly invisible in the wash were small hints of the Etruscan alphabet, half-formed words. Glenna had apparently started the painting recently.

Mary knew Etruscan writing had never been deciphered; it was, like all Glenna's paintings, pregnant with the promise of meaning.

The studio phone rang suddenly, and Mary noticed the answering machine light blinking rapidly. She snatched the receiver, hoping it was Glenna calling to say never mind, Jag was going to be fine. "Hello, Glenna?"

"No, this is Special Agent Linc Boytim, FBI."

"Who?"

"Boytim. Linc. I was calling Mrs. Weathers. I left a message. . . ."

"You left a message? Oh, I see. That must be what I'm looking at."

"Excuse me?"

"The answering machine. Never mind. What can I do for you, Mr. Boytim?"

"And you are . . . ?"

"I'm sorry. Mary, Glenna's sister. There's been some kind of accident or something. I was picking up some things for Jag."

"Her son?"

"He's in the hospital. I'm just taking this stuff for Jag. Did you want something with Glenna?"

"We had a . . . an appointment. To bring her paintings up to the gallery. I have a van and volunteered."

"Oh, you're the mysterious government man."

"Excuse me."

"Never mind."

"What do you know about CAPO?" Mary asked suddenly.

"CAPO? I don't. . . ."

"There's a letter for Van here from CAPO. On the back is a note: 'We must talk in person. DK.' Do you think it's important? I mean, DK must be Derek Kim, the man who was killed."

"Yes, it might be important," Linc said. "Hang on to the letter. CAPO is owned by a company called HFS. Do you know it?"

"HFS? I don't think so. Is it important?"

"Do you know where your former husband works?"

"Actually, I don't. The only contact I have with him is through his alimony checks, and they're personal. I heard he went to a large corporation, but I never was that curious, you know."

"OK, don't worry; take the letter with you to the hospital. I'm on my way to the university."

"Why, has something happened to Van?"

"I'm sorry. You should go to your sister. I'll try to catch up with you there, when we have this situation under control." He hung up.

She stared at the phone, puzzled. Then she put it down.

Etruscan Song trembled when she slammed the front door.

ADMINISTRATION

Elliot Blackman stands at the edge of town watching the darkness drain away.

When he moves, One Death walks through the crowd in his funny walk, a kind of shagging twitch of pelvic bone and iliac crest, as though to knock aside those meaty mortals who unconsciously move aside, although he is invisible.

There is music, just for a moment, and then the music stops, so suddenly he thinks it is because of him. But they cannot see One Death! Does he give off a smell, the dank rotten-earth smell of Xibalbá, the intestinal gases of decay? Or does his passage make a cold breeze they can feel?

It doesn't matter. He moves through the crowd as easily as he could move down the stairs and into his own little den in Crowley Hall until he reaches the foot of the great hieroglyphic staircase where the nobles wait.

Here are Three Sky, the visitor from Green Mountain, and the scribe of Xultunich called Flint Howler. And up there (he cranes his head back like everyone else) is the great *ajaw* of Xultunich, looking down.

He has the piece of paper on which is written the word KAAHHUB.

He knows very well who that really is up there. That is Van Weathers, neurophysiologically locked into his little world for good, now.

Elliot has three windows open on the computer in Jones's office, one for the simulation, one for his telephone device, and one for the simulation overview with the list of who has logged in. He thought perhaps he could have hacked all this on his own, but befriending Wendell had saved him a lot of time and effort, after all. There, he sees, is Leon Blatskoi, of St. Petersburg, and Alberto Bofonchio of Bologna. There are others from various universities, and several from this one here, including some he knows. Professor Flentsch is a wandering merchant, and if he is not mistaken, that is the wandering merchant Smoke Wind over there. If he were a human in this middle world, he could talk to Professor Flentsch, and the professor would have no idea he was a mere maintenance foreman in the building.

It doesn't matter. Elliot is invisible.

And there, just as he'd hoped, standing on the lowest landing in a glorious gown, is Van Weathers's enamored graduate student Anne Opple, providing some extra incentive for the professor to spend time in the simulation. She did such a good job during the night, and she is still here.

It is delightful that no one can warn the professor. Those wonderful lexical filters Wendell designed prevent any anachronisms. Nearby, there he is, Elliot's good friend Wendell. Now he has to laugh, for Wendell has chosen a persona close to his own—he is there as Seven Death, one of the underworld Lords; and like Elliot, he is invisible.

That is interesting because Wendell was so recently surprised there was a supernatural in this world; only yesterday, he installed that annoying requirement that someone real open the portal to let him in. Today, it seems he wanted to try it out himself. . . .

Finally, yes, Knot-Eye is active. Well, he was out of it for a while, wasn't he, sprawled at his desk next door? Elliot congratulates himself. The moiré patterns flashed and flowed through Van Weathers's brain and drove his hippocampus into overdrive. Now he should be in the simulation for good, trapped by a lovely interference pattern between the caudate nucleus and the hippocampus. Van Weathers will confabulate inside the Xibalbá Gate. Whatever he knows about Garcia Holdings will stay in the simulated world.

It is like ball lightning thrown at his enemy. One Death laughs and claps his hands in glee. It is so sweet, a lovely, lovely trick!

Knot-Eye has nowhere else to go except back to the city by the river, just in time for his wedding day.

And, Elliot thinks, his sacrifice.

OFFERING

The attendant holding the elaborate caiman-snouted headdress of wood and plaster asks, "Are you ready, Lord?"

The cool darkness of the inner temple is a relief from the glaring sun outside. Knot-Eye bows his head, and the attendant sets the enormous apparatus on it. Light flashes from the myriad inset mirrors. The long snout of the beast protrudes over his forehead, its spiral eye sits above his ear, and higher still is the face of the jester, the skull, feather and flower, and the faces of gods. The entire structure rises like fire from the ruler's head in a spray of red and green feathers. He spreads his arms and one by one the attendant takes from the altar and places on him the feather back-rack, the jeweled pendants, neckband, the pectorals and waistband of skulls and godheads. When Knot-Eye steps into the sandals, the attendant ties up the three knotted straps of blood sacrifice.

The *ajaw* is transformed. He is now the embodiment of the ancestor, the spirit of Time itself. He has become the nexus for the flowing together of past and future, an assertion of the cyclical nature of the cosmos.

He is desperate to speak, to tell, but the lexical filters would block any attempt to reveal what is happening. And there was the tone in Evening Star's voice. Was she trying to warn him, to tell him something? He puts his hand to his neck as he looks down onto the vast plaza. All the open faces stare back at him, so many he cannot see the white-plastered paving, only the faces, the woven texture of their clothing, a mottled pattern of brown and red. Is it awe he sees there, a transport of spirit? Or clever programming?

Somewhere in that crowd are real people, friends, colleagues in the Middle World.

Knot-Eye feels a strong threat of real danger.

A drumbeat begins. He turns and reveals himself, pauses and begins his descent. Unlike the others, he must step straight down the narrow, steep risers. No slow serpentine undulation back and forth for the great *ajaw* of Xultunich possessed by the spirit of First Ancestor One Monkey.

The attendant remains hidden in the shadows of the temple atop the temple mountain. The steps are dark red, Maya red, the color of dried blood. *His hand holding the mouse seems to be the same color.*

With each beat of the drum, he steps down. The backrack catches on the riser, the deerskin sandals slip. The long-snouted headdress, although light, is unbalanced, and he must hold his head carefully. With the growing pain in his ear, the beat of the drum becomes the hollow boom of his blood.

At each terrace, he pauses. Conch shells shriek from the top and from the ball court beside the pyramid.

At the middle terrace, the fifth, he raises his arms, and a sigh like wind moves across the crowded plaza, for his arms are great feathered wings, connecting him—caiman reptile of the watery underworld and serpent of the dry earth—with the celestial bird. Now he becomes the intermediary and nexus of the natural and supernatural worlds, the point where time and space come together.

A voice speaks out of empty, stunned air. "You will die."

He dare not look around, dare not move his head, but he is certain there was no one there as he was descending.

"Who are you?" he asks, voice low.

"One Death."

"Ah." He draws his breath in a hiss.

So the Lords *are* programmed into the Middle World.

"Why is One Death here?" he asks.

"One Death is here because the *ajaw* has grown proud and arrogant. The Lords want revenge."

"Knot-Eye speaks for the ancestors, and the Lords were defeated long ago. You have no power here."

"Oh, but you are wrong, Knot-Eye. I know who you are. I know where you are. It is I, One Death, who demands your blood and will have it."

A thick fog hides a once-familiar world.

"I am ruler of Xultunich, seventeenth descendant of First Ancestor. Today, I will sacrifice Fire Shell, ruler of Dry Place. That is blood enough for the sagging belly of One Death, least of the paltry Lords of Xibalbá."

There is no reply, and Knot-Eye begins the descent of the next tier.

Ripples like heat rise above the outspread wings of the flaming serpent. Sharp lights fly away from his headdress faster than the eye can follow, leaving a streak of afterimage. A low, thrumming sound increases underneath the solemn drumbeat.

An avenue of attendants forms between the bottom of the hieroglyphic stairway and the dance platform in the center of the great plaza, bright with feathers. Smoke from copal incense grows thicker in air shimmering with power.

Knot-Eye reaches the bottom, steps onto the white platform, walks down the alley formed of attendants past the visitors from Green Mountain, past Smoke Wind and Flint Howler and Three Sky, past Turtle Claw and Reed Altar. He pauses before Evening Star and dips his headdress so the feathers and paper streamers nod and ripple. He starts to reach for her as he did not long ago, but behind him he feels the force of events. They are no longer under his control. He looks at her with a yearning matched only in her expression, and her hand rises, she reaches to touch his face.

"You have a son," she says. "You must give blood."

He starts to answer, to ask what she means, but the attendants fall in procession behind him, and he is driven on. At the base of the dance platform, the captives wait. He seizes the hair of Fire Shell and drags him up the short flight of stairs to the top of the dance platform above the heads of the crowd in the plaza, high enough to be seen from the far edges, from the sweat lodge and the ball court. People sit on the walls, the pyramid steps, the viewing stands.

Despite the pain, Fire Shell straightens defiantly when they reach the top. Knot-Eye forces him down and stands beside the kneeling captive, holding his hair for a long moment. Then he releases the hair contemptuously and steps to the center of the platform.

The remaining captives, upper arms bound behind them, are dragged halfway up the square platform, five on each of its four sides. They face outward at the now utterly silent audience. The priests flow in single procession around them, holding the knives and axes of sacrifice.

The ceremony has its precise demands, and not even the ruler of Xultunich can break the pattern now set in motion. He cannot speak, not yet, for he is no longer a man and not quite a god, and now, just before noon, it is time in spite of all fear to give offering.

CROWLEY HALL

Linc Boytim flipped open his identification for the fire chief.

"What's the Bureau doing here?"

"Helping out," Linc muttered, looking around. "I'm a hostage negotiator." The yellow tape was still in place. Light drizzle had driven most of the spectators away, leaving only a few standing around under umbrellas. The chief's red car and one small truck were all that remained of the emergency vehicles. There was no sign of a police presence. It was all extraordinarily anticlimactic.

"Do we need a hostage negotiator?" the fire chief asked, more puzzled than annoyed.

"Two missing persons. It's a possible hostage situation, and the sheriff asked for a negotiator, just in case."

"OK, but listen up," the chief said. "I was here mosta the night. Then I went home, got some sleep, came back. No evidence of terrorists or anything like that. No demands, anyway. All that time, nothing's happened."

"What about the fire doors?" Linc squinted into the foyer. He could just make out hissing sounds from deep in the building.

"We got a welding team in there. It's taking a long time, but they're almost through. Locks probably tripped accidentally in the explosion."

"Any theories about cause?"

"The explosion? Nope. Pranksters, most likely. Kids wanting to get out of class. No gas leak we can find. Doesn't look deliberate, like terrorists or anything. Burned up something looks like cleaning solution. Hazmat checked some gas samples. Said it looked like something called Saniclor, what the maintenance people here use for cleaning, so it was probably just kids, or a accident, is all."

Linc nodded. "But the fire doors were locked from the inside?"

The fire chief took off her hat and combed her fingers through her hair. "Yeah, it's a puzzle. But they're triggered electronically, with a mechanical backup. Could've been a short or something."

"Did you check Weathers's office? Look in the window or something?"

"Yeah. During the night one of my people climbed up. All he could see was the wall. Looked like it was lit by a computer screen. He could make out a little section of a trestle table covered with stuff, but not much else. No sign of a person. It's possible someone's there, but he didn't respond when my guy banged on the window."

Linc muttered, "Hmph," and walked away. The shattered glass doorway was covered with plywood. The foyer was empty. He crossed the tape,
listening to the hiss of acetylene down the hall. The guard station showed
signs of hasty abandonment. He could see an underground comic book
with a picture of a humanoid resembling a heap of rubble punching
through the wall of a high-tech installation. Linc flipped through a few
pages, then wandered over to watch the welding crew.

"Any sign of people inside?" he asked.

One of the welders looked up and shook his head. The huge welding
mask concealed his personality, even his gender. Linc assumed it was a
man, then wondered at the assumption. Times had changed.

He went back outside and a plump man approached him. "The fire
chief said you're investigating?"

Linc nodded.

"Well, *I* think there's someone inside."

"And you are?"

"Flentsch. Anthropology. I think Van Weathers might still be inside."

"What makes you think so?" Linc had his notebook out. He already
had pages covered with his nearly illegible scrawl.

"I've been worried about him—he's been spending a lot of time lately
in his office."

"What do you mean, a lot of time?" Linc scribbled Gordon's name.

"He's been working on a simulation, computers, you know? It's kind
of, well, addictive, I'd say. Hard to stay away. I've been in it all night and
I'm convinced Van is there, too. There's something about one of the characters. . . . Anyway, he usually logs on to the simulation from his office.
Fast Internet connection, good computer, convenient. There's no answer
at his house. . . ."

"I know," Linc replied. "But the power is off in at least part of the
building. We won't know anything until they cut through the fire doors."

"Well, we have to find him," Gordon said glumly. "There's no real
there in the simulation. I mean, it's all online, in the computer. There're
usually other people participating, but it's hard to tell. The simulation is
remarkably realistic, but it's just not real. He's somewhere."

"OK, I'm not sure I understand what the hell you're talking about, but
there's not much we can do about it, now. Can you get back into the simulation with him, see if he's still there, ask him where he is?"

"The system is designed to keep you from knowing, but as I said, I'm pretty sure I know who he is. I can borrow an office in one of the other buildings on campus. I'll go online and give it a try."

"OK, do it," Linc said. "You try to find him through the computer. As soon as they get through the fire doors, we'll check inside. If he's there, we'll get him to his son. If he's somewhere else, you'd better find out where that somewhere else is." He took down Van's office number, gave Gordon his card, and went back to watch the welders finish cutting through the fire door.

RITES OF TIME

So it is that the sacrifice of the minor captives goes well, they die in silence one by one in solemn ritual, bound with lowered head, and it is soon finished. Under the sun overhead, blood glistens on the steps of the dance platform and lends its coppery scent to the hot air. The priests stand in their ranks, holding in one hand the executioner's ax and in the other the captive heads for the people to see. Already the bodies are gone, and the flow of people turns toward the ball court, with much jostling and pushing for advantageous views. The ball game replays the Hero Twins contest with the Lords, and thus opens a door to the other worlds, allowing the ancestor-spirit to speak through it to the city of Xultunich on this great occasion.

Of all the captives taken in battle, only Fire Shell remains alive. His manner changes, and he grows somber and subdued, knowing what is to come. He stumbles a little behind the great *ajaw* of Xultunich.

Knot-Eye stands in the center of the court between the two sloping walls and looks up at the assembled nobles. "Long ago," he says, as he must, "the Hero Twins played ball with the Lords of Xibalbá for their brothers' sakes. Today the game is played again." He stretches out his arms, and the great wings of the celestial serpent bird spread in the sun. Lances of light flash off the feathers. "Today is many days," he says. "It is 10 Ak'bal 6 Xul. It is also 4 Ajaw 8 Kumk'u."

Before him, Fire Shell kneels, head bowed, in the broad shadow cast by those great wings. They lift the captive ruler to his feet and bind a paper yoke around his waist. His paper earflares flutter by his blue-painted cheeks as he endures this preparation.

When they are finished, they push him down again and turn to Knot-Eye. First, they remove his regalia, the great headdress, the flared backrack, the wings and pendants and heavy belt with its shrunken heads. Then they dress him before the audience in the ritual yoke and heavy padding, for it is deemed appropriate that the great *ajaw* of Xultunich must emerge triumphant from this game as he has from the battle that came before. This is no ordinary game: the first in rank among the sacrifices has given his head as the ball with which Fire Shell and Knot-Eye must play.

The alley between opposing slanted walls is clean and white but for the red and blue circular markers at each end, and for the brick-red rings set in the center of each wall the height of a standing man.

Silence gathers into the heat shimmering over the ball court.

Flint Howler holds aloft the ball which is the head of Fire Shell's second. He looks at Knot-Eye curiously. The ruler nods, and Flint Howler shakes as if awakened and throws the head into the air. It spins, long black hair spiraling as it flies. It falls, and Fire Shell leans forward with a grin at Knot-Eye and uses his shoulder to send it flying toward the ring. The crowd hisses indrawn breath as the skull hits the rim and bounces back. Knot-Eye pivots, dropping to one knee, and throws his hip into its path, sending it toward the opposite ring.

The silence as the head sails through the ring is absolute, and then the noise of their triumph rises like a roar from the plaza.

Fire Shell is given the honor of a swift death.

Knot-Eye sheds the yoke and padding and, wearing only a loin cloth of plain white, walks slowly back to the base of the hieroglyphic stair, for now the most important and private part of the sacrifice begins.

Now Knot-Eye himself must give of his substance to answer the ancestor who will come.

When he reaches the bottom step, Lady Fin approaches from the opposite side. She looks at him fiercely.

Together, they turn and climb the steep central stairway, followed by Quetzal Tree, his daughter Evening Star, and Turtle Claw, the daykeeper of Green Mountain. Their progress is slow.

As he climbs past the center terrace, the voice speaks again out of the air only to Knot-Eye. "You will never bring them back," the voice says. And an echo whispers, "Bring them back. . . ."

"I know who you are," Knot-Eye speaks without breaking his steady climb. "One Death." The pause does not say whether he is naming the voice or addressing it, but the voice does not respond.

On the summit, Knot-Eye turns for the last time to the thousands gathered in the plaza. He is surrounded by robed attendants and the participants in the ritual to come, the wives, the allies, the shamans and scribes. One by one, they disappear into the ancestor's temple, winding their way through the zigzag of narrow rooms and out the back. They descend a short flight of steps to the small eastern plaza, which is surrounded by the council house, the rain and corn temples, and the elite private residences.

Only the announcer remains in view at the top of the ancestor temple to relay the happenings in the small courtyard behind him to the vast crowd far below.

The procession moves across the open space to the central platform, raised a meter above the plaza floor. At each corner sits a stone caiman, facing outward. The steps of the surrounding buildings fill with nobles, cadet branch members of the lineage, and those of Quetzal Tree's attendants of sufficient rank. Soon the steep stairs around the plaza are painted in with the green and red, yellow and blue of high-ritual clothing.

Knot-Eye, followed by Lady Fin, Evening Star, Quetzal Tree, Three Sky, Flint Howler, and Turtle Claw, ascends the platform. An attendant hands Lady Fin the bloodletting bowl with its folded scraps of bark paper, and she kneels before Knot-Eye, who seats himself on a rush bundle set atop a woven mat, his official throne.

The drum begins softly atop the rain temple, *tock tock tock*, and then there is a rush and a roar, and water pours from a series of drains around the plaza, flooding it until only the caiman heads and the central platform rise above the surface. Now the watery underworld is manifest in the middle world.

Evening Star takes from an attendant a cloth bundle and slowly unwraps it. On the beat of the drum, she removes two obsidian lancets and hands them to Lady Fin, who places them on a square of cloth spread on the ground before her. Evening Star lifts the precious stingray spine once to the temple of the rain god on her right and once to the corn god on her left. Then she hands it to Lady Fin.

"You have a son," Evening Star says to the king. "He needs you. Now."

Knot-Eye looks at her. What is she saying? How could she know so soon she was bearing a son?

The pressure of the ritual pushes him on. He spreads his knees and moves his loincloth aside. Lady Fin hands him the spine, and he pierces his penis with a sudden, fierce stab. Blood flows; Lady Fin catches the drops on the bark paper.

Still staring at him, she takes one of the obsidian lancets and slowly slices across the end of her tongue. Her blood falls to join with his, for she is a direct descendant of First Ancestor, too.

Evening Star takes an obsidian blade and, as befits her virgin status before wedding the *ajaw* of Xultunich, slices the skin behind her elbow with one swift stroke.

Blood flows from the three of them for a long time. Knot-Eye grows weak with blood loss, and still he keeps the precious liquid flowing, until all the folds of bark paper are wet crimson.

Turtle Claw steps forward and ignites the paper with a coal from his incense burner, and a long coil of white-and-gray smoke twists into the air. Knot-Eye and Lady Fin lean back to watch it climb. It is a serpent uncoiling, and as it looms over their heads it opens great jaws wide, and wider still, exposing the white inner mouth. The huge curved fangs move back, and from the mouth the tongue, dark red, darts twice, then swells, and First Ancestor appears, first his head, then his torso. He holds a battle spear and wears a Venus war headband.

Knot-Eye starts, a sharp stab of fear through him, for the face is a familiar one. He has seen it in a dream, the face of a friend who once described the music of a harpsichord flowing out as explosions rocked the city. Yet Knot-Eye cannot speak of this, for in this world there are neither bombs nor harpsichords, only the steadily increasing beat of drums and a shrill wailing of trumpets. The vision blots out the Sun's face as it tips toward the black road of the west.

Evening Star stands deep in trance with her feet apart and her arms akimbo. Drops of blood fall from her fingertips, endless pearls in a string. She sways back and forth, growing weaker.

Flint Howler steps forward and helps Knot-Eye to his feet. The great *ajaw* can no longer hear the announcer atop the Ancestor pyramid shouting his commentary of the events behind him, the flooding of the world, the four caiman gods, the letting of blood, and the appearance of the Vision Serpent. He can hear only the beat of his heart in his own ears, louder and louder. He does not feel as the attendants wrap the white paper skirt around his waist. He does not notice as they remove the block of rushes on which he was sitting, leaving a clear space for him in the center of the central platform in the very center of the earth, where he will dance, spinning drops of blood onto the inside of the paper skirt to prove to the people assembled there that he has made the offering and been rewarded by the vision. He does not notice Lady Fin, now holding the bloody sting-ray spine upright as he begins to spin.

When he has finished and the inside of his skirt is dark with blood, he will prophesy, and Knot-Eye knows that only in his prophecy does Van Weathers, trapped so far in the future, have a single small chance of bearing witness to events in another world sometimes thought of as the real one, where the three great cycles of Time flow together.

LINC'S WATCH

One of the firefighters gave Linc a sandwich. He chewed on it absently. It was already almost 3:30 in the afternoon, and time seemed to stand still. Nothing had happened. Classes were canceled. Except for the welding crew, the building was deserted. Van Weathers and the maintenance guy were still missing.

By noon, the fire chief had returned to the station, taking her trucks with her. She said she had to type her report.

Linc finished the sandwich and wandered around the lobby. He paused at the vending machine to buy a grape-cranberry drink. It was warm and a little sour. He tossed it into the trash and went back to the torch crew. The line of cut metal extended up one side, across the top, and almost to the bottom again.

"Aren't these things supposed to open automatically in case of trouble?" he shouted over the hiss of the torch. "You'd think you wouldn't want people trapped inside, in case of earthquake or something."

"Yeah," the figure hunched by the door shouted back. It was not an informative answer.

He cut the last inch and snapped off the torch to sudden silence broken only by the ticking of the cooling door edge. The welder turned his head in its enormous mask and nodded at the man standing beside him, who reached out and pushed on the door. It toppled slowly inward, gathered momentum, and landed with a terrific crash and a cloud of white dust that swirled around inside the darkened stairwell.

"What the hell's that?" the welder said, pushing his mask up.

"What?" His associate leaned into the opening.

"That! That thing!"

Linc, standing behind the men, had to move to get a view.

Inside the cavern beyond the still-hot door, something swirled in the darkness, lit by the red edges that were rapidly fading to black. It moved and swayed.

"Looks like a goddam snake."

"Big fucker," the welder said, backing out of Linc's way.

It must have been a meter in diameter, its huge coils trailing away into darkness. The head, lifted up the stairwell, was turned away, but as they watched, it turned to face them, small red eyes glinting.

It opened its mouth. Long fangs curved inward at first, but as the jaws opened wider their tips swung out until they were pointing at the three men in the open doorway, the jaws now open an impossible 180 degrees.

A face formed inside the mouth, extruded toward them as the jaws yawned, edges blurring, dissipating, the sharp-edged serpent dissolving, drifting apart, only smoke from the welding torches thinning away, twisting up the stairwell and gone, leaving the dim outline of the first flight of stairs themselves.

The welder shook his head, taking the heavy mask off entirely to reveal a wide face with a bristling gray mustache. He rubbed his eyes and squinted into the darkness, then turned to Linc. "Did you see that?"

Linc thought for a moment, then shook his head. "No," he said. "We imagined it."

"All of us?" The welder's partner had his doubts.

Linc nodded. "Yeah, all of us. Trick of the light. Looked a little like a snake for a minute there, coiling down the stair, but it was just the smoke."

"Yeah," the welder said. "I guess. Just the smoke, huh?"

"Yeah," Linc said, stepping through the doorway. "Smoke."

CALENDAR ROUND

Smoke—burning forest, tamale fires, the hearths of Xultunich—rises from the distant hills, from the plaza below. Smoke from incense burners and altars around the flooded courtyard fills the air with the sweet smell of copal. It winds around the viewing platforms, among the cloaks and jewelry of the nobles, and clings to the woven cotton *huipil* and skirts of the commoners.

Far above, in the courtyard, on the central platform above the watery world, above the dank regions of Xibalbá, above the water lilies and carp, the caiman and tortoise, the ruler of Xultunich, Knot-Eye, the great *ajaw* of the Maya world, has finished his dance. The inside of his white paper skirt is spattered with the blood of sacrifice. He feels the pain, and yet he feels also the elation, for he has become god, a lord of the thirteen spheres overhead. He is a star, a companion of the baleful God Who Has No Name, and now he must speak what he sees, standing above and outside the cycles of Time.

He lifts his arms, streaked with blood. He raises his chin, and blood speckles his cheeks with the jaguar spots of Xbalanque, of Little Jaguar Sun. He stands with legs spread, and the blood of his sacrifice falls onto the dance platform, onto the speaking platform, each drop a kernel of life-giving maize, each drop a jade bead, each drop a pellet of copal, a pearl of rain, each drop giving life to the dying city.

"It is a day," he says, his voice echoing from the four sides, the four sloped stairs, the four temples.

"The day is 11 Ajaw 18 Keh," he says, and stands silent, watching the crowd, looking for understanding. They are puzzled, those daykeepers among them, for this day he has named, 11 Ajaw 18 Keh, is not today, is not soon; it is long past or far in the future.

After a moment, he speaks again: "It is 4 Ajaw 8 Kumk'u." He is definite. "But it is also in my time 11 Ajaw 18 Keh. It is the twelfth bak'tun. The Cycle is almost finished."

Flint Howler is puzzled, and he whispers to Lady Fin, "That'll be," and he counts on his fingers, his toes, "over seven thousand k'in, seven thousand days, before that date comes in the twelfth bak'tun, the end of the Cycle."

"He is prophesying," Lady Fin answers vaguely.

The king continues. "We believe this day it is 4 Ajaw 8 Kumk'u, the day this world began ten bak'tun ago. It says on the tree stone we plant this day that this date is the same date, for on this day the world begins again. So we have spoken.

"But it is not this day. Nor is it 10 Ak'bal 6 Xul. No, it is *11 Ajaw 18 Keh*, and the great *ajaw* is dying!" Knot-Eye's voice is thunder, his eye flashes light, he is streaked with blood, with precious red jade. "In a dark place, in a small place, the *ajaw* is caught."

Those seated on the steps around the small court stir. Yellow smoke is reflected on the waters; black smoke is in the sky. Red smoke and white smoke roll together, bringing in the four directions with their dreams. The ruler is dying, so he says, on this day.

Knot-Eye looks to the left at Evening Star, who stares back at him, her eyes shining. She says firmly, "The *ajaw* has a son. An heir. But now the lineage is in danger!"

One Death, standing waist deep in the water below the dance platform, says, "What the hell are they talking about?"

And Seven Death, standing behind him, snaps his finger bones. "He's prophesying, One Death. That's what he's supposed to do."

"I don't like it!" One Death wipes at the liquid dripping from his pendulous nose and sniffs. "He's trying to tell them something."

Seven Death, bent low, looks up into One Death's red-rimmed eyes. "What do you mean?"

"He's trying to get away! I won't have it!"

Seven Death cocks his head, puzzled. "Get away?"

"I don't know what he's doing, but I'm going to stop it." One Death slogs away through the water without a backward glance. He passes through the stone caiman at the corner, on through the people, the stair, the stone wall, and is gone.

Seven Death shrugs at the funny lord and turns his attention back to Knot-Eye.

"I see a great city," Knot-Eye is saying. "The plazas and alleys of the city are empty. Forest grows through the plaster, dust and death are everywhere. Insects and birds live there, the scorpion and centipede scurry in the walls." He turns a quarter turn to the right, one heel raised, his arms bent at the elbows, hands holding up the smoke sky. He stops and says, "There are cycles of time. Some are small, the *k'in* cycle of day, the *tun* cycle of the ritual year, the *haab* cycle of the sun. There are the twenties of years, and the twenties of twenties, stretching back to the Beginning of this Turn, stretching ahead to its End. There are the turns of warfare, of Venus and Evening Star. Now it is the time of the God Who Has No

Name. That time will come again; sixteen times will the God Who Has No Name return."

A surprised murmur erupts from one or two of the people in the crowd, then silence again.

He turns another quarter, facing now the House of Bacabs, the Council House, with its woven mat relief along the cornice. "The world, filled with people, the Great Land filled, the Middle World thick with people. And the forests are cut, and the animals are gone, and the sky is dark with smoke, and the great cities are empty. The sun is bright in the heaven, too bright, but the world tree is old, is dying, for the end of the Cycle of Time comes near, there is decay in its heart and death in its limbs, city struggles against city."

Again, he makes the quarter turn, now facing the Maize House, where Evening Star now sits with her people, Three Sky and Quetzal Tree, Turtle Claw and the others. "I see temple mountains that reach the sky, and great knowledge of time, and knowledge of the heavens, but the world, like the *ajaw*, is dying. The Lords of Xibalbá will triumph without our offering, our sacrifice. The Lords of Xibalbá will spread their pestilence, their disease, their fever and jaundice, their stink and death. The *ajaw* is dying without our help. Without the blood of the king, the lineage will die.

"It is as the place to the west, the Place of Crocodiles, of Te-Ayiin, a place of pestilence and death, a place where the Lords have ruled. People have died there, the crocodiles have died. The temples have been stripped of their words. Who has done this to the world? The same ones who would kill the *ajaw* of Xultunich in this distant place."

Again he waits, looking from one face to another for some flicker of recognition, some understanding. He repeats, "It is 11 Ajaw 18 Keh, near the end of the twelfth bak'tun." To make certain that those here understand him, that this day in the *tenth* bak'tun, this year in the ninth century of the western calendar is not the day of which he speaks, he repeats: "I speak of the *twelfth* bak'tun."

He looks from the platform across the flat water to where the indistinct outlines of the high temples are reflected through haze. There he sees Three Sky standing. Three Sky looks back at him a moment, then turns and climbs swiftly up the stairs, threading among the seated nobles. Evening Star nods; she has understood. Three Sky, too, has understood.

At an angle to the left, Flint Howler also stands and pushes his way up the stairs and out of the plaza.

Seeing this, Knot-Eye lowers his arms and bows his head.

VIGIL

Mary stood in the doorway of Jag's room at the hospital, chin tucked down into the soft silk folds of her scarf, and saw only the boy, sound asleep, and the man in the next bed staring at the ceiling. The man had a tremor of some kind, and his covers vibrated with a tiny, rapid rhythm. There was no sign of Glenna.

Mary stepped into the room and put down her bundle by the door. She stood beside Jag's bed for a few minutes, her hands on the cool metal railing, and watched a faint pulse in his temple repeat its uneven rhythm *ta-tum ta-tum*, slowly, too slowly.

"What is it, Jag?" she asked aloud.

The man in the next bed jerked his eyes back and forth, but said nothing. His fingers twitched at his sides under the sheet.

Glenna returned an hour later. Mary had been sitting in an uncomfortable metal chair by the door. She reached up her hand, took her sister's, and held it.

Glenna shook her head. "No answer," she said, and it may have meant the doctors had no answer to Jag's condition, or there were no answers to the unspoken questions in Mary's face. "Home, office, nothing." She sat in the other chair, and the two women remained side by side, watching the sleeping boy slip away from them to another world.

REACH OUT

Leon Blatskoi looked up from his aging computer. "It is not 11 Ajaw 18 Keh," he said aloud, though there was no one else in the room. He lit a cigarette, leaned back in his chair, and pointed at the screen, holding the cigarette between his third and fourth fingers. "In there it is 10 Ak'bal 6 Xul, in the tenth bak'tun, what we would call the ninth century after Christ. Yet Knot-Eye was not speaking of this day in the Maya world, in the simulation. Why would he speak of a day in the twelfth bak'tun, today, if not to tell us something, to warn us? But warn us of what?"

He drew deeply on his cigarette, an imported American brand now popular in Russia, and said out loud, "Knot-Eye must be Van Weathers. And the twelfth baktun is a thousand years in the Maya future," he mused.

In fact, and now he tapped keys on his ancient computer, it is exactly 426,817 days, approximately 1,169 years, after the Maya date.

The numbers meant nothing. The Maya date meant nothing except it was near the end of the Cycle in Maya time, and the end was still several years away and couldn't be significant.

The windows were dark. It was after midnight in St. Petersburg, and snowing again, small hard flakes on the city of white nights, of fog and swamp and depression. Yet Leon Blatskoi felt strangely elated. Here was a mystery unlike any his scholarship had offered him before. This had nothing to do with settlement patterns, agrarian development, the energetics of building cities in the jungle.

Van had spoken of Te-Ayiin as well, a place of death, a poisoned place. Te-Ayiin was the place Van wanted to dig but could not get permits.

Who was Knot-Eye, then?

Who but Leon's friend Van Weathers, creator of the Xibalbá Gate, speaking across the world and across eleven hundred years to him, to Leon Blatskoi in St. Petersburg.

He was telling them that he knew something about Te-Ayiin, and that he was in desperate trouble. That he was dying.

Leon crushed out his cigarette and picked up the telephone.

COLLAPSE

The world suddenly shifted with a peculiar wrenching twist, as if the crystal screen itself had exploded and frozen in midblast.

It had been an eventful day. Anne Opple had fled her graduate student apartment as soon as the cafe opened in the morning, anxious to be around other people, and then plunged back into the simulation without talking to anyone. She had spent hours at the blood-letting ceremonies in the simulation and was exhausted, and then suddenly the world stopped.

She shook her head, trying to clear her vision. It didn't help. "What the hell happened?" she said.

Wendell, seated at the next computer, answered immediately, as if he had been waiting for her question. "Weird," he said. "I don't know." The figures on the screen were locked in place, their outlines blurred as if they had been captured in motion.

She knew Van Weathers was Knot-Eye and that he had understood her message. Now it was imperative to find him, but where was he in the real world? "Come on, you're the computer geek here. What happened?"

"Froze, looks like. I mean, you can see the king, right?"

"*Ajaw*," she said absently. "A ruler."

"Yeah," Wendell said. "He stopped. He's not moving."

"What do you mean, froze? It can't freeze up. I assisted his sacrifice. He's about to marry Evening Star. It can't freeze now!" *My God, we made love on top of the pyramid under the light of the God Who Has No Name!*

"Yeah, you're right, it sure as hell shouldn't."

"You're being sarcastic." She tapped the screen of terminal nine at Chips 'N Dips with a crimson fingernail. "That's Dr. Weathers, and he's in trouble."

"I know, damn it. It's impossible, really, it shouldn't freeze like that. Did you notice two people, well, three, maybe, got up and left?"

"You were in there? Who were you?"

"You couldn't see me. I was Seven Death, a kind of goblin. Someone was playing a supernatural. I thought I could find out who this way."

"Who? A supernatural?"

They could barely hear each other over the din at Chips 'N Dips. Someone was laser-blasting Botrons in full battle armor, which shattered. It sounded like someone smashing cheap crockery in an empty warehouse.

"Excuse me," a voice said behind them.

Anne turned. "Professor Flentsch!"

"Hm, yes. You were in my Intro Myth course, weren't you? One of Van Weathers's students?"

She bobbed her head. "Communications and Texts," she said.

"Have you seen him?"

"Seen him?"

Gordon patted her shoulder. "No, of course not. He's missing, you see. I'm pretty sure he's in the sim."

Wendell cleared his throat. "He was. It froze."

Gordon's eyebrows danced up and down. "Froze? Can it do that?"

Wendell shrugged, tossing his hair. "Did."

Gordon leaned down to look at Anne's screen. "Doesn't look frozen to me."

She and Wendell looked. The small flooded court was in chaotic motion, a swirl of color slowly draining away as the people faded one by one or in small clusters. Knot-Eye stood alone on the central platform, head bowed, immobile as the stairs emptied.

"No," Wendell murmured. "It doesn't, does it?"

"More like panic," Ms. Opple said. "Milling around."

"The Collapse," Gordon whispered. "We're watching the Collapse of the Classic Maya in fast forward."

The water that flooded the plaza grew murky and dark, splotches appeared and bloomed, the plaster on the stairs cracked and fell away.

"Did you program that?" Anne asked.

"No, I sure didn't. It was supposed to happen on its own, and a whole hell of a lot more slowly than this. Of course, time is more flexible in the simulation than the real world, but still, something's gone very wrong with the software. . . ."

"I don't think this is going to be very helpful," Gordon said. The screen had grown dark, as if dense jungle had grown up over the buildings, shrouding them in darkness in which small lights seemed to wink and dart.

"Freaking weird," Wendell drummed his fingertips on the edge of the table. "Like somebody's messing with it."

"The Lords of Xibalbá," she said.

"What?" Gordon, leaning down between the two of them, stared at the darkening screen.

"The Lords of Xibalbá," she said. "Supernaturals. Van, I mean Knot-Eye, said they were going to win. Chaos, darkness, despair. Death. Yeah, it's Collapse."

NODES

Linc was standing in the dark stairwell, waiting for the smoke to clear, when his cell phone buzzed. He checked the signal strength and moved back into the lobby. The welders were still coiling hoses, so he moved to the far side by the vending machine, flipped the phone open, and barked into it. The shift supervisor asked him where he was.

"Lobby of Crowley Hall. They finally cut through the fire door. I'm about to go upstairs, see if I can find anyone."

"We've had some weird calls. And some results on your requests."

"Shoot."

"First, we got a call from some guy in Italy."

"Great. Glad to hear it." Linc's sandwich was beginning to turn sour in his stomach. He kept seeing an enormous snake cracking its jaws open impossibly far.

"Bofonchio, Alberto, University of Bologna. *He* got a phone call from St. Petersburg."

"Florida?"

"You a comedian? Russia. Blatskoi, Leon, independent scholar. The Russian guy tried to call us directly, but his long distance lines didn't work and he couldn't get through, so he called Italy instead. You believe that, can't get through to the U.S. of A., greatest telephone system in the world, but he can call Italy where they go on strike all the time, even when things are working, and things don't work half the time, but he has no trouble at all? From *Russia*, you understand, where nothing *ever* works, right? Go figure. Anyway, Blatskoi and Bofonchio talked it over and decided that this Weathers, Sylvanus, is in some kind of trouble."

"What kind of trouble?" Linc asked.

"Look, I don't get it all, but it sounded like they believed he was in danger. Seems he used the calendar—I didn't get all this. Bofonchio thinks he's trapped in his office; don't ask me how he thinks this, but we gotta check it out, so get on it."

"I was going to," Linc said. "I can go up now that the doors are open."

"What about the other guy, Blackman, Elliot?"

"No word." Linc was looking at the vending machine. The orange-apple supply was exhausted. "What about my requests to Savannah ITC?"

"Information Technology Center report says HFS Corporation, through Garcia Holdings, owns an old plantation near where Weathers was doing his excavations. Place called Te-Ayiin. The place has a very bad reputation, and no one wants to go there. Seems about ten years ago a whole village on the property died."

"What? Why?"

"The government down there prepared a report. We had it translated, and looking it over I'd have to say it's a little vague. Small village, forty-seven people, died. They apparently dropped dead over about four days, some trying to hike out. It's pretty remote, and nobody made it. Wasn't discovered for a couple of weeks, so the bodies were pretty well decomposed. The health people wanted to quarantine the place, but it's an archaeological site, so a government team went in, looked the place over. They took a local archaeologist with them, just to be sure. All dressed up in those bunny suits they use for biological hazard. The report says the archaeological site itself is small and of virtually no interest. In light of the poisoning or whatever it was, they denied permits to dig there. That's all, and no one's been there since."

"Interesting," Linc said. "Very interesting. What about the other item?"

"Yeah." Linc could hear the shift supervisor tapping his computer keys. "Savannah ITC did a lot of digging, Linc. This man was an officer of HFS named Robert Hamerslough. He was in charge of special projects. He hired our friend, the one the city police picked up for the Kim murder."

"And?"

"What and?"

"There's something else, isn't there?"

"Can't fool you, can I, Linc? It also appears Hamerslough hired a sort of consultant code-named Ghostman. Ghostman, it seems, is none other than the maintenance guy down there, Blackman."

"Jesus." Linc turned back to the stairwell. "Look, do me a favor. Have someone do an art search, see if there was a sudden rush on Mayan artifacts on the black market ten years ago, stolen or looted stuff. I know looters go in and cut up stone monuments, rob graves for pottery; there's a big market for stolen art, and those people made things out of jade, for instance."

"Sounds like you have an idea."

"Yeah. HFS is involved in some messy stuff."

"You think they're interested in art?"

"Just a hypothesis; Weathers's wife told me he thought the place nearby was important, but you say the report denies it. There's a lot of money in looted art. I'd appreciate it if you could check."

"I'll get right on it. Now go find Weathers, Linc. The Italian was certain he was in trouble. Someone set off that bomb. I'd say the current suspect is Elliot Blackman. I'd call it a hostage situation."

"So would I," Linc said.

"And I'm told the kid doesn't have much time left. You should hurry."
"I'm on my way." He snapped his phone shut. The phone's digital time read 5:17. Linc stared at the gaping opening at the fire door lying flat inside. The smoke had finally thinned.

BLACK ROAD WEST

Elliot One Death, deep in his root-twisted darkness, breathed in and out, in and out. He could hear the great iron gate fall in the eastern stairwell, the great Red Road open now to the meddlesome creatures of the middle world, and so he melted back into Elliot Blackman, ghost of Crowley Hall. He left his glowing screen, and went west on the Black Road to the next office. He let out short hiccoughs of silent laughter.

In his hand, he carried an antique Colt revolver and a pocket full of slick lead bullets. Ghostman wasn't sure why he carried this heavy modern item, but he thought just maybe it was time he went ahead and finished what he had begun.

OL-NÁ

Linc Boytim followed the dodging, gyrating white circle from his penlight, up the flight to the landing, up the next flight, zigzagging back and forth as he climbed, only to be checked at the fourth floor, the fire door locked tight, keeping him to the core of the stairwell.

He'd assumed it would unlock from the inside, but it did not. The small circle of light in the darkness revealed strange shapes, distorted tubes and pipes, edges tilted at crazy angles, writhing shapes at the edges of his seeing, the surface textures not of plaster wall and steel door, but of stone etched by water and time. He shook his head, squeezed his eyes shut, opened them again, and once more saw walls and the outline of a door that wavered indistinctly, lost definition. He moved his torch to new shapes, shining metal, empty space beyond the reach of light, sharp angles where surfaces came together, wavered ripples of distortion darkening to muddy browns.

He shouted down the stairwell for the welding team. "Tell those deputies to come up, too."

The welder with the mustache said, "Give us light," and set to work on the metal bar, cutting around the lock. Harsh blue flickered over uneven walls and ceiling that seemed to seethe with moisture, with rivulets of condensation running down, to expand and contract as if the building itself were alive and breathing.

"Dark as a cave," the second man observed over the acetylene hiss, holding the knob of the gas cylinder in a tense hand. The deputies stirred uneasily, hands on their weapons.

Linc Boytim touched the reassuring texture of his own pistol grip.

LOST AND FOUND

Elliot Blackman's swift steps carried him to a door, where he paused, breathing slowly through his nose. He could smell the fear inside. It was good. The small meshed glass oblong in the door glowed a pale gray.

He looked thoughtfully at the door handle. It seemed so long ago he'd reversed it so the push button of the locking mechanism faced out, but it was only yesterday while Van Weathers was out getting something to eat. He took a chance Van wouldn't notice, and he hadn't. Or course, he had not anticipated Wendell dropping by, but he hadn't noticed the door knob, either, so it was all right.

He touched the knob with his fingertip and the button popped out, unlocking the door.

Elliot was reaching for the knob, ready to turn, his fingers curved already to the shape of an extended claw, when a voice from the room said calmly, "One Death."

Elliot's hand stopped, hovered over the brass knob.

This was his secret identity, his other self. One Death, his dark half, his invisible half, the fetid, rotting corpse he carried around, the black wing, the running sore, the pus pool and blood stench, the voice that whispered in his ear *You are flesh, you are blood, you are the dark angel.* Yet the man in there knew who he was.

"Yes," he answered.

"Come in, One Death."

He opened the door.

Van Weathers was seated by his desk. Dark shadows had settled onto his cheek and neck, yet he sat calmly before the glowing screen, hands resting on the keyboard.

Elliot heard metallic, rhythmic sounds from the far end of the corridor, the hissing of the great serpent uncoiling, and for a moment the ruler of Xultunich gazed down from the high roof comb of the temple of the ancestors.

Elliot stepped into the presence of the great *ajaw*. "I've come," he said.

The ruler nodded slowly. "And I am here." After a moment, the seated man lifted a hand from the keyboard and pointed to the other chair. "Sit," he commanded.

Elliot sat. The two men looked at one another.

Knot-Eye said, "You think that I don't see you."

Elliot stared.

"I do see you," he continued. "Is this what you want of me?"

"I don't. . . ."

"The Lords of Xibalbá," Knot-Eye mused. "They are always with us. You are One Death, perhaps, but you're a fraud. You could not exist without the Middle World, without human beings, without all the mother-fathers and their children." He shakes his head. "The world, the Middle World, is ending. We cannot change that. And soon the Cycle too will end, and the Fifth World will be born. You see, there is always another."

"You are too noisy," One Death said. "You make fuss and stink, you break things." Elliot wondered why he was talking like this. He was here to do something, but he couldn't remember quite what it was. There was something heavy in his pocket. He touched it with his hand. It was cold and greasy. What was he going to do? Well, it would come to him.

The other said, "We feed you, you and Pus River and Broken Wing, all of you, all the Nine Lords. What time is it?"

The sudden question surprised One Death, who could only stare.

"Dates," Knot-Eye said softly. "What time is it? When are we? There is so much darkness, you see. We must try to save the world, knowing the world cannot be saved. No, that isn't right. *We* cannot save the world. The rituals are more elaborate, more powerful, yet the world goes on. Drought, famine, war, plague." He slumped in his chair.

More than five minutes passed. Suddenly, he straightened. "All right," he said firmly. "I'll play."

"What?" One Death was suspicious, his head cocked to one side so his broad-brimmed hat flopped over.

"I'll play," Knot-Eye announced. "You and I, One Death. Whose head shall we use?"

One Death nodded. "I understand you."

The place was vast and dark and empty. A sky without stars spanned over them. The field was dusty. The light had a violet tinge and was very dim, as if it fell on the last days of the world.

The ball court was long, the walls were high, the goals impossible, three times the height of a man. One Death could change his shape, could stretch himself high, could shrink himself small. Knot-Eye, being human, was a prisoner of his shape, but he stood proudly, waiting.

The open ends of the court filled with figures, shades of the dead gathering silently to watch. A moon was there, not full, not new, and it was orange in the sky, and there was the white trail of the God Who Has No Name.

Knot-Eye wore only the yoke and padding of the ball player. One Death looked ridiculous with his floppy hat, his pendulous lip, his paunch, his stark ribs and bow legs, and he smelled awful, made rumbling noises, gurgling noises, bleating and farting noises, and there was nothing funny about it.

The moon began to spin and roll in the empty, bleak heaven, and then it curved out and down, arched down over the ball court, fell spinning onto the field, bounced once high, higher than the walls, and fell, bounced less high, bounced once more, spinning, twirling, turning in the air; Knot-Eye leaned in with his hip to catch the ball on its final trajectory, its last fall against the yoke he wore around his waist and hips, to stop the fall and hit it through the goal, to defeat the Lord of Xibalbá once more. In that moment he saw that the ball was not a ball, never was a ball; no, it was, he saw, a head.

Van thrust out against his hip, his padded yoke; the head struck it and flew away, turning the other way.

It was smiling, this head, this recognizable boy head that had once belonged, or would one day in another time belong, to a boy named Jonathan Weathers.

THE END OF THE WORLD

Linc Boytim stands in the doorway, looking at the two immobile men shrouded in vague shadow inside the narrow office. They do not appear to notice his presence.

"Excuse me," he says.

The closer one, the one with his back half turned to him, turns slowly. "Yes?" he asks politely.

Linc says, "Dr. Weathers."

The man nods his head toward the other, the one sitting before a frozen computer screen. "Him," he says.

"What's wrong with him?"

Elliot shakes his head. "Don't know," he answers slowly.

"You're Elliot Blackman?" Linc asks. Behind him, the deputies have gathered, looking past his shoulder into the gloom. Van Weathers stares into the bright screen. His eyes are wide and unblinking.

Elliot nods. "Yes. He's just sitting there."

People are talking down the hall. There are footsteps, thuds.

"Did you lock the fire doors?"

"Automatic," Elliot mutters. "Trapped."

Linc can't tell if he is talking about himself or someone else. "I've been told this simulation thing is very powerful. Compelling. Some people do get trapped in them, psychologically."

Elliot nods. "I suppose."

"You were just waiting to be rescued?" Linc persists.

Elliot stares at him. Finally, he nods.

"Why didn't you use the phone?" Linc steps into the room and points at the receiver lying on the desk.

"Doesn't work," Elliot says shortly. He puts his hand in his pocket and Linc stiffens. Then he removes his hand from the pocket and scratches his nose.

"OK." Linc pretends to think for a few moments, starts to speak, thinks better of it, and asks suddenly, "You know HFS Corporation, Mr. Blackman?"

Elliot cocks his head to one side slyly. "Sure. They make Saniclor. What we use to clean."

Linc nods thoughtfully. He had noticed the heavy object in the man's pocket. "Right, right, clean," he says. Elliot seems confused, but he is armed and Linc thinks it best to treat him gently. "Any ideas why HFS would fund the Central American Preservation Organization?"

Elliot looks up and shakes his head. "Clean up?"

Two paramedics and the deputy appear at the door. Linc gestures for them to wait, purses his lips and frowns. He starts thinking out loud.

"Mm-hm. HFS funds an environmental group called CAPO, but HFS isn't very environmental, now, is it? Do you think they store toxic waste down there at Te-Ayiin, Mr. Blackman? We do know, of course, that the company hired a Digital Assassin to steal a piece of paper from a man named Derek Kim. You ever hear of Derek Kim, Mr. Blackman?"

"Kim? Might be Korean."

Linc spreads his hands, palm down. "How about Robert Hamerslough?"

Elliot suddenly laughs, a strange, short bark. "Oh. That'd be the Chief of Surgery, I bet."

"Really." Linc lifts a quizzical eyebrow.

"Yeah," Elliot says, smiling at the joke. "The operation was a success, but the patient died. Sense of humor. Chief of Surgery."

"I see. You worked for the Chief of Surgery, didn't you? And the patient would be Derek Kim, president of CAPO?"

Elliot displays an engaging grin. "Could be."

"What did the Chief of Surgery want to get back from Derek Kim?"

"Oh," Elliot says. "I wouldn't know about that."

Two paramedics signal from the door with a stretcher. Linc says, "Well, Mr. Blackman, these folks would like to come in and take Dr. Weathers to the hospital. You don't mind if they do that, do you?"

Elliot frowns. "I don't know. It seems to me Dr. Weathers was not supposed to come back."

"He's pretty sick, Mr. Blackman. You wouldn't want to stop him from getting medical attention, would you? Come on, let's you and I just step out into the hallway and let the medics do their work."

Elliot stands up. "OK." He is suddenly docile and cooperative. "I'm One Death, you see. The world in there is the real one, isn't it?" He points for a moment at the computer screen, then shrugs helplessly, giving a little laugh.

Linc leads him outside, and the paramedics soon have Van Weathers on the stretcher. Elliot frowns thoughtfully, watching them carry the professor down the hall toward the stairs. Van's eyes are wide open, but he sees nothing.

Elliot pauses at the door to look back. He says, "He was the king, but I took care of him. He couldn't defeat the Lords, not in the end."

"The Lords? What Lords are those, Mr. Blackman?"

Elliot starts and looks at Linc as if he hadn't seen him before. "Who did you say you were?"

Linc grins. "Oh, sorry. Lincoln Boytim. FBI. The deputy here will have to put you under arrest, I'm afraid."

"What for?" Elliot seems to want to put his hand in his pocket, but there are too many people around.

"Oh, I don't know." Linc gestures to the deputy, who deftly handcuffs Elliot's hands behind his back. "The deputy here could start with unlawful possession and use of explosives, and attempted murder for the explosion. I bet you made the explosive yourself, didn't you? You're not the sort to go out and buy something so obvious. And then there's conspiracy to commit mayhem or murder for brokering the Digital Assassins contract. Accessory, perhaps. When they figure out what happened to Dr. Weathers, the deputy will probably be able to think of some more things."

"What about my rights? You didn't read me my rights." Elliot had gone from confusion through defiance to complaint.

"We just had a little conversation, you and I, Mr. Blackman, that's all. It's not really my job to read you your rights. I have no jurisdiction, after all. But the deputy here, he does have jurisdiction, and he will read you your rights, I'm sure."

Elliot lowers his chin, as if he has fallen deep into thought.

Linc says to the deputy, "You might want to check his pockets."

The deputy nods, removes Elliot's revolver, and reads him his rights in a monotone. Ghostman, hands behind his back, stumbles a little as the deputy leads him away.

BLOOD RELATIONS

The streetlights throw a sodium glare across Linc's windshield as he follows the ambulance to a stop in the parking area by the entrance to the emergency room. The attendants pull out the stretcher and hurry inside. He follows.

On the third floor of the south wing, the gurney rolls smoothly over polished yellow tile along a hallway wide and white as a road.

As they approach Intensive Care, a gurney propelled by a slender, tattooed youth in green hospital scrubs emerges from a room and rattles down the hall past them, going the other way. The patient on the gurney stares at the ceiling lights flickering overhead, his body vibrating the white sheet tucked under his chin. Lincoln Boytim glances casually at the patient, and a thought passes through his mind that a bank robber nicknamed Shakey had a tremor like that.

Then the thought is gone forever, and they hurry on into the room.

Glenna, pale under fluorescent light, stands and reaches for him. The skin around her eyes is tight. "Thank God," she murmurs, putting her head against Linc's shoulder for a moment, then jerking away. "I'll tell the nurse."

Linc leans down and watches Jag Weathers's eyes dart back and forth under parchment lids.

A medical team rushes in, followed by Glenna and Mary. Van is moved onto the newly emptied bed next to his son.

A nurse swabs the inside of his elbow as orderlies assemble tubes and needles. The monitors over the head of the boy's bed bleep endlessly.

The doctor enters briskly, leans over Van a moment, pats him on the knee, and steps back. Glenna takes Van's hand. Mary and Linc stand by the door, watching.

"Good," the doctor says. "He got here in time."

A moment later, the blood begins to flow through clear plastic tubing, from father to son.

AFTERMATH

People in different places are facing screens.

Chips 'N Dips is nearly deserted in late afternoon, in one place on a round world, at a particular time.

The calendar flies round, meshes, locks. The great roof comb with the image of the seated ruler slumps. The colored plaster falls away in large pieces; the stone armatures that hold the face, the chest decorations, the hands, tumble down the carved hieroglyphic stair.

Gordon and Wendell and Anne Opple stare, the screen's glow shining off the ring in the girl's nose, the programmer's high cheekbones, the anthropologist's glasses. They are in different places, at different times. Nothing moves on the screen.

Wendell is annoyed. He worked hard, and this has happened, anyway: there is something very wrong with his code.

Gordon shrugs his round shoulders and snaps off the monitor. There is little point in continuing. He thinks of Wanda Landowska playing, enraptured, oblivious to the bombs falling on Paris. There is a ruined world. There is always a ruined world, somewhere.

The girl draws in her breath, dismayed at the rapid passage of time, the loss. She has looked everywhere, but the world is unmoving. Stiff grass grows in the plaza. The birds are silent.

Shadows gather in the courtyard. Lilies grow on the water, bloom, and die. Vines tighten around the caiman heads, probe the cracked plaster on the stair, pry apart the limestone blocks of the high, narrow arches in the temple itself. The altar falls; the roof comb slumps, tilts forward, and topples in huge fragments that scrape the lip of the hieroglyphic steps.

Some time in the past, a few people crouched in these ruins. They burned their fires when they could find something to burn, in the courtyards, on the floors. Finally, they decided to kill the city, and so they burned the lintels of the buildings, and the stones fell, and the people went away.

The calendar turns again, years flying by as the city subsides into earth and silence.

In the jungle on a mountain slope, the macaws shriek as they dart among the dark branches. Rain falls, fades. Clouds slide away, and the sun shines, raising mist from the forest.

Beneath the tree roots, stone dreams in an unknown tongue, the carved symbols speaking the names of men and deeds. Two slumping walls of green face one another, twisted with root and branch. Beneath the dirt is a round stone, and on the stone is the image of a man in a high feather headdress and jade jewelry. His face is stern, his eyes heavy and lidded.

A howler monkey pauses above the stone and stares into the far distance. After a moment, it scampers into the trees again, and behind it, just out of earshot, comes the soft slither of a vast serpent moving across dead leaves and fallen branches.

Beneath the earth, the round marker stone dreams and the narrow profile of the ancient ruler of Xultunich lies mute in the darkness.

LOOSE ENDS

It must have been an hour later. Glenna and Linc Boytim might be having a long-delayed dinner. Or perhaps it was a week, or some other indefinite time after it was all over. The two of them might be at a restaurant by the water, or one near a small grove of trees, or, more likely, they would be in the hospital cafeteria. Glenna was probably eating spaghetti, which reminded her fleetingly of dark blood flowing through plastic tubing. She lowered her fork.

"How's your work?" she would ask to make conversation.

"Oh, you know. Some things get finished, others don't. I was after a bank robber, but he stopped robbing banks and the case remains unsolved. These things happen."

"Yes," Glenna answered vaguely. "I guess they do. Like some of my paintings. They just don't ever quite get finished."

"But your show. Your show is finished?"

"Yes. A great success. *Message, or Messages, Dead Tongues, Etruscan Song* even, all sold, or will be. A great success."

He would look at her for a long time, his fork halfway to his mouth. Then he decided something and put the fork down beside his plate. He leaned toward her. "Van was trying to get through," he said slowly. "We got a call, very roundabout, from Russia through Italy. Your husband was trying to tell them something was wrong. It was the dates, they were all mixed up; he was in that simulation talking about today, our time, but he had to do it in Maya numbers. I don't understand it, but it was true."

Glenna said, "They say he had some kind of seizure; he's stuck there somehow."

Linc said, "The Russian, Leon Blatskoi, knew the dates were wrong, that Van was in trouble; he was speaking about today's date. He said things about the heir, the lineage, he had to give blood. So your husband *knew*. At first, we thought maybe it was the explosion, the fire doors, that maybe he was trapped in his office. The phones were wacky, too, so he couldn't call. That's what we thought at first.

"Then it was clear Elliot Blackman had trapped him. Robert Hamerslough had hired Elliot to watch your husband."

"Robert, yes," Glenna said. "Poor Mary. No more alimony."

Linc grinned. "We don't know, of course, not until the trial. But I'd say Mr. Hamerslough is going away for a while."

"At least she has Foster."

"Yes, Foster. You told me about him, and the others. Before you went out to dinner."

There is a slight indefiniteness to the night, to the place itself, as if it is a little out of focus. As if it is suffused with a softer light than usual.

"We'll find out what happened to him, won't we?" Glenna asked.

"They said it was a seizure. You said he was obsessed with the simulation. Now it seems the simulation took him. I'm sorry." He looked down; he might pick up his fork again and begin eating.

"Thank you," she murmured. "You're kind."

"His office door, the lock, that was Blackman."

"Yes, they told me. He installed it backwards."

Linc looked down at his plate. "Strange. Blackman really wanted to trap him. I think he was planning to kill him, but it all fell apart." He paused. "Your son?"

"He's going to be all right. It was a bad crisis, but it's over. He got Van's blood in time. He'll have to stay away from chickpeas."

Linc shook his head. "Chickpeas!" He might lay his own fork down again about now, announcing that he was finished eating. He might consider reaching across the table and taking Glenna's hand, which is lying beside her plate, very relaxed, the delicate fingers slightly curled.

It is possible also that he would do nothing but look at her hand, and her curled fingers, and simply strongly feel the need to reach for her. It is equally possible he would not. Everything is so indefinite, so uncertain, so unpredictable. Van Weathers was still in the hospital, had not spoken. Catatonic, they said. Withdrawal from reality. Stress, breakdown. There were signs.

"Te-Ayiin," he continued instead. "Garcia Holdings owned the place. Someone looted the archaeological site years ago. There are rumors, of course, but no proof. The name is well known. He happens also to be on the board of HFS. And then there was a mass poisoning. HFS was storing waste in the cave at Te-Ayiin. It got into the water. Kim found the proof. He was going to talk to your husband about it, tell him where the funding came from, that someone at HFS was dealing in stolen art, everything the Central American Preservation Organization was supposed to prevent. Then he thought of coming to you, of getting the museum to help.

"But they killed him, took his proof. They've probably destroyed it by now. Kim died for it. I think your husband suspected and was trying to find out. I think he hoped the simulation would somehow flush out the truth about Te-Ayiin, the toxic waste, the looting, all of it. Maybe those involved would enter the simulation to try to find out what he knew; maybe they'd make a mistake and he'd find out who it was and what they had done. I think he knew they would pursue him, and he was willing to take the risk, make the sacrifice, to get the truth."

Glenna is gazing in admiration at Special Agent Lincoln A. Boytim when an orderly makes his way through the room to her table.

"Excuse me. Mrs. Weathers?"

"Yes?"

"Your husband, ma'am."

Glenna starts to rise up. "What is it?"

"He's awake, ma'am. He's asking for you. He wanted me to say something to you. He said you'd understand."

"What . . . ?"

"He was real insistent that I get it right, word for word. He wanted me to say, 'The Lords are out.'" The orderly paused. "'They're here now. All Xibalbá is going to break loose.'"

A cold shiver ran down Glenna's spine. At the far end of the hall, a very short man wearing a strange, three-tasseled jester's hat was pushing a laundry cart toward her. He looked right into her eyes and started a peculiar caper, a hopping dance that tilted his head back and forth. He pushed the cart in short, erratic jerks, and as he did she could hear the tinkling of small bells.

Selected Bibliography

Abrams, Elliot M. *How the Maya Built Their World: Energetics and Ancient Architecture.* Austin: University of Texas Press, 1994.

Aveni, Anthony F., ed. *The Sky in Mayan Literature.* New York: Oxford University Press, 1995.

Balick, Michael. *Rainforest Remedies: 100 Healing Herbs of Belize.* 2nd enlarged edition. Twin Lakes, WI: Lotus, 1995.

Benson, Elizabeth P. *Maya Iconography.* Princeton, NJ: Princeton University Press, 1988.

———. *The Maya World.* New York: Thomas Y. Crowell, 1967.

Carrasco, David. *Religions of Mesoamerica: Cosmovision and Ceremonial Centers.* San Francisco: HarperSanFrancisco, 1990.

Chase, Arlen F., and Diane Z. *Mesoamerican Elites: An Archaeological Assessment.* Norman: University of Oklahoma Press, 1994.

Coe, Michael. *Art of the Maya Scribe.* New York: Harry N Abrams, 1998.

———. *The Maya.* 4th ed. New York: Thames and Hudson, 1987.

———. *Breaking the Maya Code.* New York: Norton, 1992.

Coe, Sophie D. *America's First Cuisines.* Austin: University of Texas Press, 1994.

Culbert, T. Patrick, ed. *Classic Maya Political History: Hieroglyphic and Archaeological Evidence.* Cambridge: Cambridge University Press, 1991.

Demarest, Arthur A., Prudence M. Rice, and Don S. Rice, eds. *The Terminal Classic in the Maya Lowlands: Collapse,Transition.* Boulder: University Press of Colorado, 2003.

Freidel, David, Linda Schele, and Joy Parker. *Maya Cosmos: Three Thousand Years on the Shaman's Path.* New York: HarperCollins. 1993.

Hammond, Norman. *Ancient Maya Civilization.* New Brunswick, NJ: Rutgers University Press, 1982.

Harrison, Peter D. *The Lords of Tikal: Rulers of an Ancient Maya City.* London: Thames & Hudson, 2000.

Houston, S. D. *Maya Glyphs*. Berkeley: University of California Press, 1989.

Leon-Portilla, Miguel. *Pre-Columbian Literatures of Mexico*. Norman: University of Oklahoma Press, 1969.

———. *Time and Reality in the Thought of the Maya*. Norman: University of Oklahoma Press, 1990.

Marcus, Joyce. *Mesoamerican Writing Systems: Propaganda, Myth, and History in Four Ancient Civilizations*. Princeton, NJ: Princeton University Press, 1992.

Markman, Roberta H., and Peter T. Markman. *The Flayed God: The Mythology of Mesoamerica: Sacred Texts and Images from Pre-Columbian Mexico and Central America*. San Francisco: HarperSanFrancisco, 1992.

Martin, Simon, and Nicolai Grube. *Chronicle of the Maya Kings and Queens: Deciphering the Dynasties of the Ancient Maya*. London: Thames & Hudson, 2000.

McAnany, Patricia A. *Living with the Ancestors: Kinship and Kingship in Ancient Maya Society*. Austin: University of Texas Press, 1995.

Miller, Mary, and Karl Taube. *An Illustrated Dictionary of the Gods and Symbols of Ancient Mexico and the Maya*. New York: Norton, 1997.

Miller, Mary Ellen. *Maya Art and Architecture (World of Art)*. London: Thames & Hudson, 1999.

———. *The Gods and Symbols of Ancient Mexico and the Maya: An Illustrated Dictionary of Mesoamerican Religion*. New York: Norton, 1993.

Montgomery, John. *Dictionary of Maya Hieroglyphs*. New York: Hippocrene, 2002.

———. *How to Read Maya Hieroglyphs*. New York: Hippocrene, 2002.

Nelson, Ralph, trans. *Popol Vuh: The Great Mythological Book of the Ancient Maya*. Boston: Houghton Mifflin, 1976.

Nicholson, Irene. *Mexican and Central American Mythology*. New rev. ed. New York: Bedrick, 1967.

Pearce, Kenneth. *The View from the Top of the Temple: Ancient Maya Civilization and Modern Maya Culture*. Albuquerque: University of New Mexico Press, 1983.

Proskouriakoff, Tatiana. *Album of Maya Architecture*. Norman: University of Oklahoma Press, 1977.

———. *Maya History*. Austin: University of Texas Press, 1993.

Reed, Nelson. *Caste War of Yucatan*. Stanford, CA: Stanford University Press, 1964.

Reents-Budet, Dorie. *Painting the Maya Universe: Royal Ceramics of the Classic Period*. Durham, NC: Duke University Press, 1994.

Sabloff, Jeremy A. *Cities of Ancient Mexico: Reconstructing a Lost World*. New York: Norton, 1989.

———. *The New Archaeology and the Ancient Maya*. New York: Scientific American Library, 1994.

Scarborough, Vernon L. *The Mesoamerican Ballgame*. Tucson: University of Arizona Press, 1991.

Schele, Linda, and David Freidel. *A Forest of Kings: The Untold Story of the Ancient Maya*. New York: William Morrow, 1990.

Schele, Linda, and Mary Ellen Miller. *Blood of Kings: Dynasty and Ritual in Maya Art*. New York: Norton, 1986.

Schele, Linda. *Maya Glyphs: The Verbs*. Austin: University of Texas Press, 1982.

Schele, Linda, and Peter Mathews. *The Code of Kings: The Language of Seven Sacred Maya Temples and Tombs*. New York: Scribner's, 1998.

Sharer, Robert. *Ancient Maya*. 5th edition. Stanford, CA: Stanford University Press, 1994.

———. *Daily Life in Maya Civilization*. Westport, CT: Greenwood, 1996.

Stephens, John L. *Incidents of Travel in Central America, Chiapas, and Yucatán*. 2 vols. New York: Dover, 1969.

Tainter, Joseph. *The Collapse of Complex Societies*. Cambridge: Cambridge University Press, 1990.

Tate, Carolyn E. *Yaxchilan: The Design of a Maya Ceremonial City*. Austin: University of Texas Press, 1992.

Taube, Karl. *Aztec and Maya Myths*. Austin: University of Texas Press, 1993.

Tedlock, Dennis, trans. *Popol Vuh: The Definitive Edition of the Mayan Book of the Dawn of Life and the Glories of Gods and Kings*. Revised and expanded. New York: Touchstone, 1996.

Webster, David. *The Fall of the Ancient Maya: Solving the Mystery of the Maya Collapse*. London: Thames & Hudson, 2002.

Whittington, Stephen L. *Bones of the Maya: Studies of Ancient Skeletons*. Washington, DC: Smithsonian Institution Press, 1997.

Willey, Gordon Randolph. *Essays in Maya Archaeology*. Albuquerque: University of New Mexico Press, 1987.

Witlock, Ralph. *Everyday Life of the Maya*. New York: Dorset, 1976.

Yoffee, Norman. *The Collapse of Ancient States and Civilizations*. Tucson: University of Arizona Press, 1988.

Vogt, Evon Z., and Richard Leventhal. *Prehistoric Settlement Patterns: Essays in Honor of Gordon R. Willey*. Cambridge, MA: University of New Mexico Press and Peabody Museum of Archaeology and Ethnology, Harvard University, 1983.